NOT BLACK AND WHITE

From the Very Windy City to
1600 Pennsylvania Avenue

A Novel by

G. A. Beller

G. ANTON
Publisher

Chicago

Cover design: Vivian Craig
Cover Images: Chicago Storm © Bradford Cavanaugh;
White House/Public Domain

Library of Congress Cataloging-in-Publication Data has been applied for.

ISBN 978-0-9966766-0-9 Hardcover
ISBN 978-0-9966799-1-6 Paperback
ISBN 978-0-9966799-2-3 ebook

AUTHOR'S NOTE

I'm a political junkie. The idea for this book came out of the constant media reminders of political shenanigans—national, state, and local—as well as the nonstop negative campaigning filling the airwaves, our voice mails, and our mailboxes. This constant flow fuels my desire to write.

I was intrigued when a relatively obscure local politician raised his standing to the national stage almost overnight and was instantly embraced by the voters to become our first African-American president. I, too, was captivated by his charm and charisma as I enthusiastically cast my vote.

Living in Chicago, surrounded by a history of political corruption and incompetence in our state politics, my curiosity prompted me to research this specific era of rampant criminal behavior—a time when it appeared things couldn't get worse. As our convicted politicians and their cronies were being released from prison, I decided to utilize articles that appeared in the press and on the internet to create a fictionalized accounting of the characters and events, and I depict through my imagination how things might have played out.

ACKNOWLEDGMENTS

I wish to thank and acknowledge Vivian Craig, a coworker for the past six years, who sat with me for extended hours at a time and proved to be a valuable collaborator. Her skills, patience, and good humor provided encouragement throughout the writing of this story.

Two of my very close friends critiqued and challenged the way many of the storylines were depicted. They offered countless hours of constructive comments, greatly enhancing the storytelling. To them I offer my sincere thanks, and hope one day I can return, in kind, their generous contributions.

I am fortunate to have a family member who has spent his entire career in the book publishing business. I thank him for providing advice and guidance throughout this, my first attempt at being an author.

I'd also like to thank the team who provided the professional editing of this book. They were exceptional. They offered valuable comments and suggestions, many of which were incorporated into the final copy.

From the Memoirs of Mars Gregory:

So, HERE I AM. The last man standing. The only one left to tell the tale. My name is Marston Gregory—Mars. Everyone else is either dead, in prison, or untouchable. Frankly, I never thought I'd be alive to tell you this story.

I grew up in Chicago, where you quickly learn how the game is played. Political corruption is nothing shocking. You get used to seeing our elected officials frog-walked in front of the cameras. It's a 50/50 shot that someone you voted for will eventually be indicted. It's the Chicago way, right?

But it's hard to fathom that this story began as the result of one specific traffic accident.

Looking back on it now, it reminds me of dominoes, how once the first one is tipped, the last one will eventually fall, no matter how long or how complex the chain happens to be. It's physics. And it can't be stopped no matter what you do or how hard you try.

———————————

It was 1994.

Bill Clinton was president.

Richard Nixon died.

Justin Bieber was born.

Forrest Gump told us, "Life is like a box of chocolates."

And O. J. Simpson, in the white Bronco, led police on an exceedingly strange low-speed chase down the 405.

But it's another memory that snaps me back to that time in full color and reminds me of exactly where I was and what I was doing.

I mean, who remembers traffic accidents?

Almost 41,000 traffic-related deaths occurred on the nation's highways and byways during that year, but one accident that killed six young children did more to change the course of history than any other.

It ended the careers of two governors and elected a president of the United States.

Chapter 1

THE RADIO SQUAWKED OUT an unusually frantic call to all state police in the area of Waterston, Illinois. Joe Connor was the first officer to arrive at the scene. Joe was new to the force, only six months on the job, and this was his cherry-popper, his first serious car wreck. He'd never heard such a level of concern and panic in the voice of the dispatcher. Joe's heart was pounding in his chest; adrenaline pulsed through his veins as he drove closer to the scene.

He snaked his way past the last stopped vehicle and pulled as close to the crash as he dared. The entire area was shrouded in a gray, eerie fog. Joe quickly scanned the scene and followed the smoke to a blazing van.

Joe saw a short, Hispanic-looking man jump into the cab of a large eighteen-wheeler and drive off. Oddly, several people in cars parked nearby pulled out onto the road and took off in pursuit.

Officer Connor remembered his training: always attend to the injured first. He stopped his squad car and jumped out. The smell of gasoline was overpowering, but there was something else, too. The air was laced ever so slightly with another odor—an odor that until that moment was unfamiliar to Joe, but one that he would never forget. It was the sweet, sickening scent of burning flesh.

There were several people around the crash site: civilians attempting to comfort a man and a woman who looked to be the surviving victims. The woman was hysterical, sobbing uncontrollably, desperately trying to get back to the burning van. Bystanders held on to her as she flailed and struggled in an effort to head back toward the flames. It's always easy to spot a panicking, distraught mother attempting to get to her kids. The man stood in shock, tears pouring from his eyes. Someone put a blanket over his shoulders.

"Holy shit," Joe breathed out in a slow whisper to no one. He could feel his blood rushing past his ears as his senses heightened.

He grabbed his shoulder mic and called it in, "Car 110 on Highway 47 at Route 14."

The dispatcher shot back, "Car 110, what's the status?"

"Car 110. I need paramedic support and fire support, together with further police backup. There is a significant fire. A van is fully engulfed in flames. There are no other units on the scene."

"110, additional units are approaching your position. It was reported from other drivers and witnesses that a vehicle involved in the accident left the scene. Do you see a semitruck on 47 heading north, fleeing the scene?"

"110. I did. He is now proceeding northbound on 47, some distance from my position."

Two more squads arrived from the west. The lead vehicle was driven by Joe's sergeant, Robert Lewis. Lewis jumped out of his car and took charge. He immediately began barking out orders to the other officers. Joe could see Lewis talking into his vest microphone and looking directly at him. He was attempting to communicate something. Joe gave him a quizzical look. Lewis pointed to his microphone, then at Joe. It was only then that Joe heard the dispatcher's voice coming from the small radio receiver attached to his shoulder. He'd been so focused on the chaos of the scene that he had not heard the call.

"110 . . . 110 . . . respond, please."

"This is 110," he quickly spoke into the mic.

"110, pursue the truck you identified."

"110. 10-4. Will do."

Joe nodded to his sergeant, jumped into his squad car, and maneuvered through the smoke and around the burning wreckage. The second he was clear, he punched the accelerator. He flew northbound on 47, lights flashing and siren blaring. Joe was determined to catch up to that truck. This was his first high-speed chase.

It ended within minutes. He could see a large semitruck pulled over to the side of the road. Two other motorists' cars were blocking the truck's path, both parked in such a way that it was clear they had somehow forced the truck to stop.

A man was standing outside the truck's driver's-side door, screaming up at the occupant, pointing and shaking his fist.

Joe exited his car and approached the man.

"Sir, I need you to back away from this truck, right now!"

"This motherfucker caused that accident back there, and then he just took off!" The man was red with anger, breathing heavily, screaming at the top of his lungs.

"Sir, I will talk to the driver. I need you to back away—" Joe didn't get to finish his statement.

"He was all over the road, driving like a fucking idiot! He almost drove into me!"

"I understand, sir. Back away from the truck. I need you to go sit in your car."

Joe unsnapped the restraining strap on his holster. He rested his right hand on the Glock 22 on his belt and raised his left hand to the radio on his vest.

"110. Requesting backup approximately four to five miles north of the accident scene on Route 47 . . . at the intersection of Harvard Street and 47. Send backup."

Joe turned back to the man and looked him square in the eyes.

"Sir, get to your car right now!" Joe mustered all the authority he could.

The citizen eyed Joe's right hand. He got the message, finally. He started to walk backward as Joe walked toward the truck. Joe pulled out his weapon and pointed it at the passenger door, holding it with both hands.

"You, in the truck, let me see your hands!"

Two small, brown, wrinkled hands appeared in the window. They were shaking, trembling.

A weak voice came from inside the cab. "No shoot me, please. Please, no shoot." The voice had an unmistakable Hispanic accent so thick that his words were barely intelligible. "I come out. You no shoot?" It was half a question, half a tentative statement.

Joe could hear that the driver of the truck was surrendering. However, he was trained to remain suspicious and cautious.

"I'm going to open the door of your truck. Do not move your hands, sir! Keep your hands where I can see them! Do you understand?"

"Si," the driver squeaked out. "I no move. You no shoot?"

Joe reached up and opened the passenger door, revealing a frightened little man seated behind the wheel of the big rig. The man's tan, weathered cheeks were streaked with tears. He was at least fifty years old, and couldn't have weighed more than 130 pounds soaking wet. He wore tattered jeans and a faded flannel shirt, and trembled so badly that he was almost convulsing. Abject fear filled his eyes.

Joe felt much less threatened. This guy wasn't going to hurt anybody, but Joe continued to follow procedure. He kept his sidearm trained on the diminutive truck driver.

"Slowly, get down out of the truck, no fast moves. Keep your hands where I can see them!"

When the little man reached the ground, he bent over and sobbed uncontrollably. He held his hands above his head, which put them horizontal to the ground as he was bent over nearly in half. He kept them outstretched and limp. He continued to mumble and sob in broken English. "No shoot me. No shoot. Please, no shoot me . . ."

Joe cuffed him, sat him down on the ground, and propped him against the giant front wheel of the truck. The little man hung his head next to a bright red scrape that discolored the white front fender of the big rig.

"Do you have a driver's license? Your commercial driver's license, where is it?"

"Pocket . . . in pocket." The little man was trying to point with his nose at his shirt pocket. "I have license in pocket."

Joe reached into the pocket and pulled out a State of Illinois commercial driver's license bearing the name Juan Espinoza. Juan was fifty-three years of age and lived in Cicero, Illinois. The license had been issued just two weeks prior.

"Do you know what happened back there, Juan? You've been involved in a terrible crash."

Juan just shook his head from side to side, still sobbing.

Joe crouched in front of Juan. He was face-to-face with him.

"Mr. Espinoza? What happened, sir?"

Juan Espinoza, utterly confused and terrified, looked at Joe and cried out, "I never drive truck like this before. It too big."

Joe was stunned. "What are you talking about? You have a commercial driver's license?" Joe held the license in front of Juan's face. "That's you, right? That's your picture. They test you on trucks like this. You have to qualify on an eighteen-wheeler to get this. Is this license a fake, or something?" The license was inches from Juan's face.

"No . . . no . . . no fake. It belong to me. I give the man a thousand dollar. My sister buy the tickets, she buy the tickets." Juan was nodding his head in the affirmative, forcing a smile. He seemed sincere, maybe even proud. "My sister buy all the tickets," he repeated, flashing brown broken teeth.

Joe was completely baffled. "Your sister bought the tickets? She bought what tickets?"

Just then, a second squad arrived—Joe's requested backup. Tim Moran, one of Joe's fellow cadets, came walking up. "I'm your backup. What can I do?"

Joe stood to talk to Tim. They huddled together. "I don't understand what he's trying to tell me. He keeps saying something about tickets. I gotta get him to the sergeant." Joe paused, looking at the door of the truck. On it was the name of the company Juan worked for. "Moran, call Ajax Transport and tell them to come and get their truck out of here. Their driver is under arrest. Wait! Just tell them about their driver. Have the truck towed. It's evidence in a traffic accident resulting in a fatality."

"*Six* fatalities," Tim emphasized.

"What?" Joe looked at Tim with stunned horror. Tim just nodded and looked at the ground. "All of them kids," he said, shaking his head.

As he guided Juan's head into the back seat of his car, Joe recited, "Mr. Espinoza, you are under arrest." Joe slammed the door. He continued speaking in a monotone. "You have the right to remain silent. Anything you say can and will be used against you in a court of law . . ." While he continued, he got behind the wheel. Tim could still hear Joe reciting Juan's constitutional rights as Joe's car pulled away, spitting gravel behind it.

———————

When Officer Joe Connor returned to the crash scene, it was worse than anything he could ever have imagined.

Five black body bags were lined up in a row on the asphalt. All five bags were zipped up tight, each holding a body too small to fill its length. A sixth bag was unzipped and laid open as two uniformed paramedics wearing plastic gloves and surgical masks gently laid blackened remains into it.

Joe stopped his car and watched in horror as the two medics zipped up the last bag. He couldn't take his eyes away.

Juan Espinoza snapped Joe back to the present.

"Open door! Open! Sick!" Juan was convulsing in the back seat, his olive-skinned face white as chalk. All of the blood had drained from his features. Beads of sweat popped on his forehead. Joe jumped from the front seat and opened the rear door just in the nick of time. Juan bolted from the car, wretching uncontrollably, splashing what seemed to be everything that he had ever eaten in his life at Joe's feet.

Juan hung his head, crumpled on the ground next to Joe's squad car, sobbing, broken, wracked with guilt. He had children of his own.

Joe actually felt badly for this little shell of a man. He was obviously in great pain. His life was over. He sat Juan upright in the car and closed the door. He looked out over the scene. He saw the guy he was looking for. "Sergeant Lewis," Joe called, approaching his boss.

Lewis, whose crew-cut head sat on his shoulders as if he had no neck at all, stood taut in his starched white uniform shirt bearing a shiny gold star as he oversaw the final cleanup of the accident scene. The body bags were loaded into a coroner's black van and the wreckage was set precariously onto the back of a flatbed tow truck. The tow operator began lashing it down.

"Hey, Sarge, I've got the suspect in my car."

"You got him? Great work, Connor. We'll be able to tie up all the loose ends on this clusterfuck."

"He's not making any sense. Could you talk to the guy . . . see what you think?"

"Sure, let's go talk to the son of a bitch."

Espinoza sat in the squad car looking up at Sergeant Lewis and Officer Connor. Connor held Juan's commercial driver's license in his hand.

"Mr. Espinoza, where did you get this license?" Joe spoke gently to the broken man. "Tell the sergeant what you told me before. You said you never drove an eighteen-wheeler. Tell the sergeant why."

Juan looked up at his interrogators. He was the picture of sincerity—no shifty-eyed con, as was so often the case. This guy was telling the truth.

"I give the man a thousand dollar. In envelope, like they tell me. My sister buy the tickets."

"Juan, were you in an alley, a bar? Did you buy this on the street? Who took your picture?" This license had not been created by some back-alley hack. Whoever had made it was an expert.

"No, no, no . . . at the DMV . . . the DMV. My sister buy the tickets."

Sergeant Lewis was incredulous. He demanded, "Are you saying you got this at one of the Department of Motor Vehicle offices of the secretary of state? Which office? Where?"

"Joliet. I go to Joliet."

"And, you gave a man an envelope? Was he wearing a uniform?"

"*Si*. In his office."

Connor looked at his sergeant. Lewis shook his head in disbelief.

"Juan, who told you to go to Joliet? How did you know about this?" Lewis asked.

"Everybody . . . my cousin, my friend, his friend . . . everybody know. We buy the tickets."

The sergeant was suddenly beet red. Joe feared that the guy was going to stroke out. "What tickets are you talking about?"

"In my pocket, back," Espinoza said, tilting his head to indicate his back pocket.

Joe reached behind the prisoner and pulled a wad of tickets from his back pocket. Joe was a political novice, but even he could tell they were tickets to a political fundraising event:

Friends of Edward G. Parker
Secretary of State
June 25, 1994
The Palmer House Hotel
Chicago, Illinois
5:00 to 7:00 p.m.
Donation: $100

Lewis and Connor looked at each other, realizing at the same time that commercial truck drivers' licenses were being given to unqualified drivers who bought tickets to a political fundraiser for the secretary of state. How many more were out there? How many more idiots like this guy were barreling down the highways in huge rigs without knowing how to drive one?

"Thank you, Mr. Espinoza. We have no more questions at this time," Joe said.

As the officers walked away, Sergeant Lewis was talking fast. "You put every bit of this in your report, Joe. You put all of this right in your report. I'll sign off on it. Put it all in there. 'The suspect indicated to me that he offered a bribe to someone in a uniform at the Joliet office of the Illinois secretary of state and it was accepted. No test was ever taken.' You use those words, Joe. Make it perfectly clear."

Joe was lightheaded. He wasn't sure how to act. Should he smile? This was a good thing for him, a feather in his cap, right? But, it wasn't a good thing. It was a crime, dammit, and it had led to a nightmarish tragedy. He grimaced a smile at his boss.

"Good work, Connor," Lewis said, as he patted Joe on the back.

Neither Joe nor his sergeant had any idea the first domino had just tipped.

From the Memoirs of Mars Gregory:

YOU'VE HEARD OF A chick magnet? Well, I'm a crook magnet.

It really didn't start out that way. I was a nice Jewish boy from the North Shore suburbs of Chicago, following the well-worn path with my friends and classmates, the words of our mothers echoing in our psyches: *Do well in school, then you'll go on to college. Maybe you'll go on to medical school or law school. Then you'll make something of yourself.*

So that's what I did. I studied. I kept my nose to the grindstone, got the good grades, and didn't stray from the path. I was accepted to Harvard, Yale, and Brown. I chose Northwestern University in Evanston, Illinois, a suburb just north of the city, rather than going back east, because Northwestern had the prettiest girls. I continued on at Northwestern for law school.

As a law student in my early twenties, I did pretty well with the girls. I was average height, five foot ten, dark brown hair, better than average looks, although more rugged than a pretty boy, and I kept myself in good shape. I worked out at least two or three times during the week and jogged on weekends. It was very important to me to make a good first impression. This is a trait I've carried through my entire life.

After graduating with honors, I waltzed into a coveted position at one of Chicago's most prestigious law firms and began my life as a young LaSalle Street lawyer. All was as it should be. Everything was right with the world.

However, the practice of law and I didn't quite hit it off. Oh, it was a great job, as jobs go, and I wasn't digging ditches, for Chrissakes! I learned a great deal about tax law. But I saw my life in stages. All I had to do was look at the partners and the junior partners at the firm. It was all mapped out for me. Work eighty- or ninety-hour weeks for a few years and they make you a junior partner. Then, the hours stay the same, but instead of putting those hours in at the office, you do the cocktail parties and the luncheon circuit. You spend those hours hobnobbing. You cultivate the firm's clientele, acquire some of your own, become a rainmaker, and then enjoy summers in Lake Forest or Winnetka at the club, lots of golf, winters on Marco Island or in Palm Springs, with lots more golf.

I played the game, moved along in the firm, kept working nights and weekends, impressing the senior partners and the clients.

In 1978, when I was twenty-five, I met Rochelle, a nice Jewish girl, herself the daughter of a prominent lawyer at another firm in Chicago. Rochelle was very pretty and very thin, with a great, small, tight ass. I was a sucker for a small tight ass. She was more interested in sex than most of the other Jewish girls I dated. In less than a year, I figured it was time to come home to a warm body in my bed after those long hours at the office. Her family connections were excellent, so we married. Rochelle gave me enough sex to produce a couple of kids, and the relatives were really pleased.

But, there seemed to be no challenge to my life, no thrill. It seemed like my whole future was already etched in stone.

THE FIRST CRACK IN that stone occurred one day when one of the partners stuck his head in my office.

"Mars, I'm supposed to have lunch with a client, but I'm under the gun on another deal. Can you cover for me?"

I sat up straight. This was a test; I knew it. They were going to see how I would handle a client one-on-one.

"Sure, Neil, what do I need to know?"

"His name is Carlton Fleming. He's a black guy who runs a little travel business. I've helped him with his corporate formation, nothing too complicated. He wanted to talk about raising some money, bringing in a partner, but he'll own 51 percent, so it'll qualify as a Minority Business Enterprise. That makes him eligible for all kinds of government and charity business. Usual bullshit rip-off, but he makes a lot of money off that angle."

I went to lunch with Neil's client. Looking back, I think now that my concerns about the future were destined to collide with this lunch meeting. Carlton was tall and slim, with dazzling white teeth and handsome features. He looked like he was chiseled out of a block of ebony.

He just couldn't say enough about his travel business and its perks.

"The travel is the best part, Mars. I was in Rome last month, Berlin the month before. I have to go and check out the places where I will be sending these kids, right?"

Carlton provided travel services for not-for-profit organizations like schools and church groups. He seemed very enthusiastic and sincere.

"When your kid comes home and tells you their whole class is going to Europe and then begs you for several thousand dollars to pay for it, I get a piece of that money."

Neil had told me that as Carlton's lawyer he saw his accounting books, and Carlton was making a fortune.

"So, you get to travel to all of these places?" I asked.

"It's basically my job to be on permanent vacation. I have to preview potential hotels, restaurants, and tour companies. They're all vying for my business, in competition for it, so they treat me like a fucking king . . . all the best.

"I take a different woman with me every single time I go. Imagine being in the club, Mars, and instead of asking a cute little mama if she'd like to see your etchings, or some shit like that, you can ask her if she'd like to go to Paris or Rome for a week! No one gets laid more than I do, man . . . no one. It's a great gig, my man, a great gig."

That was an interesting image. I could see how it might be a fantastic life.

It turned out that Carlton was seriously looking for a partner who would own 49 percent of the company. "That way," he said with a smile, "we qualify as a black-owned business, and a lot of these charity groups bend over backward to do business with us."

"This sounds pretty interesting." Then, I couldn't help but ask, "What if the partner was me?"

He looked surprised, but quickly recovered. "Sure," he said, "with your legal and tax background, we could make a great team."

"Allow me a few days to confirm, and we'll work out the details," I suggested. Carlton agreed.

That night at dinner I shared my decision with Rochelle. Rochelle didn't like it one bit. "You're leaving the law firm? Are you nuts? What are we going to do for money?"

It was our first major fight, but I put my foot down, showed her who was boss.

Within a few weeks, Carlton and I were shaking hands and celebrating our newly formed partnership. It was 1982, and I was twenty-nine years old. I put the day-to-day practice of law in my rearview mirror and began my life as a businessman and entrepreneur.

SOON I WAS SEEING the world—France, Italy, Greece, Ireland, Israel. And I was seeing it all first-class. Carlton and I were living the high life, traveling the world like millionaires, with stunning beauties on our arms in every port. It was a young man's wet dream.

In the '80s, credit cards and credit card statements were still relatively new. People didn't check them as well as they do today. Carlton had been charging a $10 annual membership fee to each of our clients. In an effort to make even more money, Carlton charged an additional $10 membership fee to each and every one of our thousands of clients a second time. Yes, they paid their membership fee once, and then he charged them all again.

My first business partnership ended when I discovered this little scheme and walked away from the business. A couple of years later, the authorities caught up with good old Carlton, and he eventually went to jail.

I thought I would never hear the end of "I told you so" from Rochelle.

I was officially done with partners. I swore to myself that I would never take another one. I looked for a business I could run on my own, partners be damned.

If only I had kept that promise to myself.

A GOOD FRIEND FROM law school invited me for drinks to catch up. During our second round, he told me about one of his clients who was looking to sell his business, a company that produced ice for restaurants, bars, banquet halls, schools, and hospitals.

The business model intrigued me. Every single location where people buy cold drinks, there must be ice. I started thinking: people take for granted the clear little cubes of ice clinking in their glasses, or the crushed ice cooling their favorite soft drink or tropical cocktail at restaurants and bars all over the country. They don't realize it, but part of the purchase price of that cold drink pays for the ice—frozen *water*.

In the early days of *Saturday Night Live*, the Not Ready for Primetime Players did a skit that was a spoof on selling water. Evian water, supposedly derived from a secret, special spring in deepest, darkest France, was being sold to the American public. For the first time in all recorded history, Americans were buying water in a bottle. I never forgot that skit. What could be better than selling water? The punch line was delivered by someone wearing a beret, maybe Belushi, acting French and speaking in a condescending French accent, who said, "Zee Americans . . . zay weel buy anysing!"

Within weeks, I was able to obtain financing, and along with my savings I bought the company and went into the business of selling frozen water. Just like I'd planned, I was in business without a partner. Although Rochelle was nervous, she realized I was determined, and offered virtually no resistance.

My instincts proved right. Frozen water made my first million dollars, and put me in a position to meet and become friends with Saidah "Sam" Alsheriti.

———————

ONE BEAUTIFUL SUMMER DAY in 1985, as I was taking advantage of Chicago's gorgeous lakefront, jogging along the shores of Lake Michigan, I stopped for a Coke at one of the concession stands on North Avenue Beach. I peered into the concession booth, and I realized that the booth did not have its own refrigeration. Everything that needed to be chilled was being chilled by ice, which was quickly melting in the hot summer sun and running in a tiny little stream right back to the lake, where it came from in the first place. The perfect customer for ice!

I made it my business to find out who operated the concessions along the beaches, and I was told by my sources that I should talk to a man named Sam Alsheriti. I called him.

"Mr. Alsheriti, my name is Marston Gregory—my friends call me Mars—and I understand that you have the contracts for all of the concession stands along Lake Michigan."

He spoke with a thick accent. I wasn't sure of the origin—somewhere in the Middle East, I thought. He was warm and congenial, but he sounded suspicious of my motives.

"I only have the concessions on the north side of the city. Why do you ask?"

"Well, sir, I want to sell you ice. I will beat any price that you are now paying."

For some reason, he sounded relieved. His demeanor immediately changed to a much more comfortable tone.

"I don't know how you can say that, my friend. I have a supplier who gives me a very good price."

I had a pretty stock answer for that response. "Well, Mr. Alsheriti, it's frozen water, water I derive from the city water supply. All I have to do is freeze it and deliver it. I will beat any price that you are now paying."

I heard an interested chuckle on the other end of the line. "I want to meet you, my friend. And, by the way, call me Sam."

After a series of meetings and a few lunches, we both concluded we could expand our respective businesses. Sam's dream was to have restaurants all over the city. I was building a successful ice business, which would be making a lot more money with this newfound relationship with Sam.

We were off to a great start.

Chapter 2

SOMETIMES THAT FIRST DOMINO takes a long time to fall.

Officer Joe Connor filed his report right away. Juan Espinosa was summarily convicted of six counts of involuntary manslaughter, but Sergeant Lewis and Joe Connor knew that Juan wasn't solely responsible. They waited for the crooks at the DMV to get their due, for Secretary of State Ed Parker's office to be exposed. They waited weeks, then months; three years went by, and nothing. Then one day—a day that just so happened to be the day that one Sergeant Lewis retired after thirty-five years on the force—a copy of Officer Connor's 1994 report made its way to the inbox of a *Chicago Tribune* reporter.

Suddenly the world knew all about the accident that had killed six young children, including the statement that the driver of the semitruck who caused the crash had received his commercial driver's license through bribery. Reporters with tape recorders and press passes descended upon Springfield. They camped outside the office of the secretary of state like sharks off Amity Island; they smelled blood in the water.

A scheme to issue commercial driver's licenses for bribes was big news. However, it would be an unbelievable story if the secretary of state, a man who was not shy about letting people know that he had ambitions higher than his present office, was somehow personally involved in the scandal. If he knew about this, it was one thing. If he'd profited from it in any way, well, that would be an entirely different animal. It would be a news story on which a young reporter could make a career.

Inside the secretary's office, it was a war room. Edward G. Parker, the secretary of state, was planning to make a run for the governor's office. This accident could be a death-blow to his coming campaign, especially if it was discovered that Parker himself was part of the scheme. Even in Illinois, it's tough to run an effective campaign for the office of governor from a prison cell.

Parker was a caricature of the old-time, cigar-chomping, glad-handing politician: a short, rotund, baritone-barking, ruddy-faced Irishman, just over sixty, who had a charming way about him in a crowd, and a tough, decisive, no-nonsense manner in the back room.

He'd come up through the ranks of the Republican Party in the state of Illinois, having first held minor offices on the city council of his hometown and on various county boards. He served as an officer in the US Army, and he married his high school sweetheart, Lillian. He had a squeaky-clean record as a businessman, having inherited a small chain of local pharmacies from his father. What could be more all-American? As a politician, he was a good soldier in the organization, rising through proper channels, making the right friends, waiting his turn. And for a couple of years now, he'd been looking realistically at the governor's office.

But a statewide race would be very expensive, and Parker needed to fill his war chest. So, like any wide-awake, ruthless politician, he'd been relentlessly using his current office to raise money for his dreams of higher office.

One way to raise money was to pressure employees who were under his control. They were expected to do whatever they had to do to sell tickets to fundraisers or otherwise obtain donations for their office holder. There was even a sliding scale: the more an employee earned, the higher his expected contributions. And the office holder would simply look the other way when it came to this low-level corruption within his office. A little bribe here and a little payoff there couldn't hurt anyone, right? This sort of thing had been going on since time began. The boss, if he looked the other way of course, would get a taste of the resulting payoff, and that cash would go directly into his campaign coffers. That's how a war chest was built.

Some of Parker's people, under pressure to cough up money for the boss's campaign, had cooked up a scheme.

The requirements to get a commercial driver's license were tough. There was a challenging written test, and a road test during which a uniformed officer from the secretary of state's office accompanied the candidate to determine if the driver was qualified. Many applicants failed. This presented a rich opportunity: the failing applicants would be only too happy to pay money to be given a passing grade. It was just a matter of coming up with the proper price. Not only was there an initial bribe paid to the officer giving the test for procurement of a commercial driver's license; the person obtaining the illegal license was also required to buy tickets to fundraisers for Ed Parker. It was a perfect plan. Money was pouring into the campaign like a casino.

Parker, of course, knew that his people were being asked to sell tickets to his fundraising events. But he had studiously avoided the details of just how that was being done. "I don't want to know," he would often say to his top aides. "That's your problem. Just make sure they keep the money coming in."

But now this seemingly harmless scam had burst into the public's awareness. Someone who'd obtained a commercial driver's license by bribing one of Parker's underlings had caused a catastrophic accident that not only killed six innocent children, but burned them to a crisp. It was a media nightmare.

———————————

PARKER AND SEVERAL OF his top advisors huddled together in a conference room in the secretary of state's office to discuss how to handle this potentially disastrous situation. This had "big trouble" written all over it, and Parker's team was in full crisis-management mode. They were pulling out all the stops. The men's sleeves were rolled up and ties loosened. Styrofoam coffee cups, fast-food wrappers, and overflowing ashtrays littered the long mahogany conference table.

Parker had his characteristic cigar clenched between his teeth. He was wheezing and screaming into the phone, waving a copy of Officer Connor's police report in the air.

"This asshole killed a bunch of kids up in Waterston, the son of a bitch. Why couldn't he have been drunk at the time? Then we wouldn't be dealing with this business of him being able to *buy* a goddamned commercial driver's license from *my* goddamned office! Am I exposed on this shit?" He paused to stab the cigar into a nearby ashtray. "I wanna know, Johnny, and I wanna know quick!"

Parker was on the phone with Johnny Jarzik, one of the best political operatives in the state. Jarzik had no political affiliation whatsoever, not even a political leaning. He wasn't a registered voter. He didn't seem to have an ideological bone in his body. He was just a hired gun, a mechanic, a fixer available to the highest bidder, whose job it was to put out fires, to make unpleasant problems go away. He was particularly adept at heading off the problems that were touchy by their very nature—problems that needed special attention, the kind of problems that could not be handled through conventional methods.

"This is big trouble, Ed," Jarzik was saying. "It's going to take an extraordinary effort to contain this mess."

Parker ran his hand through the thick mop of silver hair atop his head. "What can we do, John? That damn report identifies the Joliet office. The Feds are going to get to the guys who did this. They're going to sing like canaries."

Jarzik paused for a few moments. "Ed, you've studied a lot of Chicago history, isn't that right?"

Parker had a puzzled look on his face. "Yeah, sure, but what—?"

Jarzik cut in, "You remember how they eventually got the Great Chicago Fire under control?"

"Yeah, sure," Parker said tentatively, not sure where this was going. "They tore down houses in the path of the fire, creating a firebreak, so the flames couldn't keep spreading. But what's that got to do—?"

Jarzik snapped, "You've got to create a firebreak, Ed. The path upward has to stop short of you!"

Parker was silent, thinking.

"Who's the biggest sucker you got working for you, Ed? That's the house you have to tear down."

There was another long pause, as Parker's eye fell upon young Skylar Stillwell, one of his bright-eyed and bushy-tailed aides.

"I think I got it, Johnny," Parker grunted. "Do what you can to get the media off this story. Let me work on your idea." He set the phone back on its cradle.

"Well, boss?" Skylar asked innocently. "What does he recommend?"

Skylar Stillwell's path in life had been apparent before his birth. His parents had devoted their careers to the Republican Party of Illinois, providing leadership as high-level strategists. Sky was handing out campaign literature at shopping malls by the time he could walk. He was a political animal from the moment of conception. He really had no choice in the matter. Politics was in his blood.

It was no surprise to anyone that it was Skylar Stillwell who had risen through the ranks to become the man who'd helped run Ed Parker's successful campaign for secretary of state. He may have looked bookish, he might have seemed to be a twerp with his soft voice and reedy frame, but at twenty-eight, he already showed signs of being a political mastermind.

"So, what did he say?" Skylar asked again.

Parker paused to consider his answer.

"Ah, fuck, what's he gonna say, Sky? He says he's on it and everything is going to be fine. That's what the guy is paid to say, right?"

Everyone in the room nodded their assent.

"Hey, guys, can I have the room?"

Parker pointed directly at Stillwell.

"You stay, Sky."

After everyone filed out, Parker looked at Skylar Stillwell with conviction, cigar smoke circling his reddened face. "Sky, I want you to personally see to it that those guys in Joliet are hung out to dry. I want to make a public spectacle of them, serve them up on a platter. I want to throw them so far under the bus that they are forever unrecognizable."

Stillwell was grimacing.

"I want the press to focus on two or three people in the Joliet office as the source of all of the bribes, all the corruption. They acted on their own, they are being dealt with in the harshest way possible, they are losing their jobs, hung from the highest yardarm. Then, through back channels—very back channels, people who you absolutely trust—do whatever you have to do to make sure they will forever keep their mouths shut. We are not going to abandon them, not at all. You make sure they know that once this all blows over, once I'm governor, they will be taken care of."

Skylar interjected, "We have to be very careful on that score, Ed. Very, very careful."

Parker pressed him. "You have to make it clear to everyone you talk to: Ed Parker never knew anything about what these guys were doing. Ed Parker had nothing to do with it, it was all a scheme down at the local office level, blah, blah, blah."

Skylar hadn't slept for a couple of days, since the news of the crash had broken, and he sported stubble. He rubbed his jaw, pondering the implications of all this.

"Sky," Ed said, hunching over the conference table to whisper in a conspiratorial tone, "you know as well as I do that we have a wide-open path to the governor's office. I've got a straight shot at it. It's the big enchilada, Sky. The governor controls everything in this state. Everything. You can be the guy who puts me there, and I won't forget. You'll be the second most powerful guy in the state before you're thirty."

Skylar's bright blue eyes widened. He saw clearly the path to power Parker was dangling.

"But this thing must be contained, or I could go down, Sky," Parker grunted. "We all could go down. If that happens, you'll be back in DuPage County, writing out legal descriptions for the recorder of deeds."

Skylar shuddered. He made up his mind. "I got it, Ed. I'll get this thing under control. Don't worry about a thing."

From the Memoirs of Mars Gregory:

SAIDAH "SAM" ALSHERITI WAS born in a small town just outside of Damascus, Syria, in 1955, to a prominent Syrian family.

After graduating from college in Syria, Sam moved to Chicago to continue his education and earned a degree in civil engineering in the late 1970s. He joined an engineering firm designing roads for the state transportation department, and made less than $22,000 his first year.

Being an engineer, drawing a weekly paycheck, was not the reason Sam had come to the United States. He possessed incredible charm and charisma, with limitless potential and a willingness to do anything to succeed. Absolutely anything.

Sam saw an opportunity to buy vacant lots in lower-income neighborhoods and develop and rent single-family residences. He began investing in fast-food restaurants as well. Within a short time, Sam met a prominent African-American business leader who asked him to support the mayoral candidacy of Chicago's first black mayor. Not long after, Sam and the business leader he'd befriended won a food concession contract for the Lake Michigan beaches and many South Side parks. They opened the restaurants under the city's minority set-aside program. Sam was making a name for himself, and he was just getting started.

My ice business was a beneficiary of Sam's success.

As Sam and I did more and more business with each other, we continued to spend more time together. We were both driven by ambition, and over time we began discussing what we wanted to do next.

Sam expressed to me that his dream was to have restaurants of all types all over the city. I told Sam I really wanted to build things, to do real estate development. The more we met, the more we thought forming a partnership made sense.

In 1988, Sam and I formed Sammar, LLC as equal partners. Within a short time, money started to pour in from every direction. Our horizons were infinite.

At least, that's what I believed. Rochelle, however, let me know in no uncertain terms that she didn't like Sam.

Chapter 3

Sam Alsheriti considered it a priority to make a great first impression. He was of the opinion that expensive clothes and impeccable grooming signified success. Though primarily bald, Sam brought in a barber once a week to give his remaining dark hair a close trim, and his favorite manicurist was on call at all times. His olive skin had a nice even tan, and he was always clean-shaven; he even stored an electric razor in his desk to keep his thick five o'clock shadow under control. At five feet eight inches, Sam was roughly twenty pounds overweight, but his Armani suits were tailored to detract from his thickening waistline.

As a little boy, Sam heard the "streets paved with gold" stories about America, and he was determined to grab his share. Thirty years later, he actually had gold-plated faucets installed in the master bathroom of his mansion, along with a huge mosaic *A* made of solid gold pieces as the centerpiece of his bathroom floor. Every time he took a piss, he stood on tiny pieces of solid gold.

Sam believed there are three forces that drive men's souls: power, money, and sex.

In his own case, the number one motivator was power. He was helplessly and hopelessly addicted to it. He loved to walk into the best restaurants in town, without a reservation, with a party of six businessmen, and immediately be seated at the premier table by the window. He couldn't get enough of people tripping over themselves to fulfill his every whim.

Some people use money to make their lives more comfortable; Sam used money as a tool. He purchased a sprawling 10,000-square-foot mansion on Chicago's suburban North Shore even though he couldn't afford to furnish it. He and his family lived in a couple of rooms in their huge house like tenants, never taking advantage of the comforts that type of home could provide.

No, the mansion was never a source of comfort for his family, merely a tool to attain more power. Everyone knew that the Middle Eastern billionaires Sam palled around with, and the politicians he had in his pocket, and the big-ticket contributors he invited to his soirees, wouldn't give him the time of day if they thought he was a mere millionaire. After all, who *wasn't* a millionaire? If Sam entertained, or had one of his famous political fundraisers, he would rent furniture appropriate for that particular function and return it immediately following the event.

"All the world's a stage, right?" At least that's what Sam thought.

While the rest of this planet's one-percenters were jetting around the globe, busily using their great wealth to enhance their own personal comfort, Sam was obsessed with making it *look* like he belonged among them. Regardless of the lack of furnishings and the austere, Spartan lifestyle lived within, when you approached the front door of the Alsheriti residence, first you were engulfed in the beautiful landscaping—easily one of the most meticulously crafted, tastefully designed yards on the block, maybe in the whole town. It was the kind of landscape you couldn't help but notice, even if you were simply driving by.

Then, said door was answered by a uniformed Arab man, Sam's answer to a butler. The man was from Saudi Arabia, not England, and worked for peanuts and a roof over his head, but nevertheless, the door was answered and you were announced and immediately offered a tray of olives. Meals were prepared by a live-in cook and the endless dusting and cleaning of the primarily empty house was attended to by a live-in maid. It wasn't that Sam wouldn't spend money; it's just that he would only spend it on amenities that made him look wealthy. Rich people always have live-in help. It was a requirement, in Sam's mind. Plus, their homes must be showcases that make others jealous as they drive by. That is how things are, he believed, so that was what Sam had.

Sam Alsheriti was a bit of an anomaly, a singular man, not one who fit well in any particular mold or stereotype, nearly impossible to categorize or to explain.

The deal, the game, the manipulation, the political advantage—these were his only goals and aspirations, his only motivations, his true loves, and he went after them with a single-minded sense of purpose very few men could muster.

NONE OF THIS IS to say that Sam did not value money. During the early days of his career, Sam ingratiated himself to the heavyweight champion of the world—"the Champ." They became close friends. The Champ actually gave Sam a beautiful diamond-encrusted watch that had been presented to the Champ by a Saudi prince during one of his many trips to the Middle East. The Champ never wore a fancy watch. He always wore an old Timex to remind him of his roots. So, he gave this fancy, expensive watch to Sam.

In an incredible show of affection and trust, the Champ invited Sam to accompany him to a dinner at the Reagan White House. The Champ was the single most famous person in the world, and President Reagan wanted the Champion of the World at a dinner party being held in honor of Mikhail Gorbachev, the enlightened leader and general secretary of the Communist Party of the Soviet Union. Sam told his friend and new business partner, Mars Gregory, about the Champ's invitation.

"That's fantastic, Sam," Mars said enviously. "You'll be an observer to world history. What an amazing opportunity!"

"I am not going," Sam said flatly. "I have already told the Champ I will not attend." He shrugged off the entire matter as if it was a trip to the corner grocery store.

"Why on earth wouldn't you go?" Mars was baffled. "This is history. This meeting could lead to the end of the Cold War, a truly historic summit! Why are you begging off?"

Sam's answer was simple. He delivered it in his characteristic monotone with his thick Middle Eastern accent. "All people, Mars, they want to make money. I, too, want to make money. This trip to Washington, DC, it will not make me any money."

And, so it was with Sam Alsheriti.

———————

SAM'S WORK IN THE engineering firm allowed him to make his very first personal contacts in the world of politics, beginning in the late 1970s. The firm contracted work for the city, so Sam met politicians and political underlings.

And if sucking up to political types without looking like you were sucking up to them was an Olympic sport, Sam Alsheriti would take the gold medal every time. No one could do it better.

Very quickly, Sam formulated a plan for his future endeavors: he would put himself in the company of politicians and sap the power from them.

Sam wined and dined aldermen and ward bosses. He schmoozed their assistants and underlings. He bought tables at fundraisers, and slapped every back and shook every hand in sight. He calculated with amazing precision which city workers could help him and which ones could not. Those who could not help him were dismissed out of hand.

Sam made friends. He learned quickly how "the City that Works" actually worked. He began looking to diversify. He wanted more restaurants, and he would get them over time. However, regardless of the field of business he explored, he was particularly adept at identifying a political advantage that could be turned into a business opportunity.

He rose from nowhere to being considered by the political class to be "the man"—the one to host a fundraiser or bend a rule when one needed to be bent. He had the connections to get it done.

Sam became the consummate political operator.

Sam Alsheriti might have become a great man. He had a gift, a true talent that others envied. He was a master at the art of persuasion. That gift, combined with just a smidgen of conscience, could have brought Sam greatness. Unfortunately, he never did have a conscience, and his gift instead became his undoing.

From the Memoirs of Mars Gregory:

SAM AND I WERE kicking ass and taking names. Our little business had made us both millions. I was the CEO and president of what had become one of the higher-profile real estate development firms in the entire city. I had seventy people under me, all of us working toward a single goal: to change the face of one of the greatest cities in the world, to make it a more beautiful and a more pleasant place to live.

We were building low-income housing and primarily using public tax dollars to do it. I was an expert at using tax incentive programs set up by the federal government to encourage rehabilitation of blighted areas of the inner cities. Chicago had plenty of those.

We concentrated on the South Side of the city, and we were making progress. We felt we were doing our part to improve the quality of life in those otherwise forgotten areas. It didn't hurt that we were raking in the cash as well. Our market-income properties were written up in the *New York Times* as examples to other big cities—examples of how inner-city life could far out-class the snore that the suburbs had become, with their strip malls and their endless rows of ticky-tacky track homes.

We were moving in the right direction; however, we were managing thousands of residential units all over the South Side, so we felt we needed a liaison between ourselves and the members of the community, the church groups, and the civic leaders in the neighborhoods—a person who could understand our business and what we were trying to do, what our overall goals were. We needed someone who could communicate our vision better than we could.

That's how I happened to meet the future president of the United States.

———————

I FIRST READ ABOUT Malik Alawi in *Newsweek*. This kid was a rising star making quite a name for himself. It was a very flattering article about how this young man had quietly and quickly attained the coveted position of editor-in-chief of the law review at his prestigious Ivy League university. This might not have been notable had he not been the first African-American to do so in the nearly 200 years of storied history at that fine institution—an institution, mind you, that has graduated several past presidents, hundreds upon hundreds of captains of industry, and thousands of the finest attorneys-at-law to ever haunt the hallowed halls or grace the courtrooms of stately courthouses all across this great land. Alawi had risen to the top of this distinguished heap with such dignified grace and aplomb that it was almost scary. Even his peers agreed. This guy deserved the attention. He was special.

I decided to fly him in for an interview. We were revitalizing the city, and we deserved a rising star.

———————

I WAS A LITTLE late for our lunch appointment, as usual, and as I quick-stepped it across Walton Street and approached the grand entrance of the Drake, I had a good feeling. It was early spring of 1991 on Chicago's Magnificent Mile.

Spring may just be the best season in the city of Chicago. Everybody has his or her own favorite, but I like spring. The snow and cold of winter becomes a fast-fading memory as the temperature warms, and city crews fill the planters and small patches of grass that peek out from the endless concrete with splashes of tulips and daffodils to add color to the otherwise drab cityscape. The short trees that line Michigan Avenue begin to bud, creating a green haze on their once frozen branches. The air smells fresh and clean in spite of the buses and the cabs and the endless traffic. Somehow, all that hubbub matters less in the spring. Plus, summer is just around the corner.

As I entered the elegant dining room of the Club International in Chicago's historic Drake Hotel—a room that had hosted kings and queens, movie stars and corporate giants for nearly sixty years—I saw him. He rose to greet me as I was led to our table near the expansive window overlooking Lake Shore Drive and Oak Street Beach.

The view was breathtaking, one of our city's best. Malik was framed in it, his tall, lanky frame sporting a gray pinstriped Brooks Brothers suit, a blinding white shirt, and a bold deep burgundy tie. He looked like he belonged there.

"Sorry I'm late," I murmured, holding out my hand. "Traffic in this city is insane . . ." My words trailed off. "I'm Marston Gregory. Call me Mars, everybody does. And you're the famous Malik Alawi."

His grip was strong and confident, his smile warm and charming.

"No, no, don't think twice about it," he said, as he sat back in his chair. "I just got here. Thanks for inviting me. Thanks for this opportunity."

That was diplomatic, I thought. This guy didn't really need opportunities, did he? He had made his own. His résumé was plastered across the pages of *Newsweek* magazine, for chrissakes.

"Good. Shall we order? You want a drink first?" I said with a smile, as I settled into my seat. I liked him right away.

"I AM THE SMARTEST son of a bitch I know."

I'll never forget those words as long as I live. A pretty bold statement, when you think about it, especially when you consider it was a first person assessment. And this was in a job interview. He wasn't alone looking at his own reflection in a men's room mirror, about to return to battle, attempting to bolster his confidence and pump himself up. He said those words to me while he kept my gaze, quietly smiling, looking me square in the eyes.

That is a level of confidence few men or women possess. Thing is, he wasn't kidding. This wasn't some guy trying to be cute. It wasn't the crass braggadocio of a person who would justify putting his name in lights on a building. He offered this extraordinary self-assessment as a quiet, measured statement of fact, and he was dead serious.

WE TALKED FOR THREE hours. We didn't miss many subjects. He liked sports and the law, but he could talk about any topic that came up. He was a relative newlywed, married less than two years, just feeling his way. He had been to Chicago before. He did short stints summer-clerking for a couple of the big law firms in town.

However, this was the first time he was considering making our fair city his permanent home. He thanked me several times for flying him in, but he didn't trip over himself doing it. He just snuck it in from time to time so you heard it, but didn't get sick of hearing it.

I told him we needed someone who could bridge the gap between ourselves and the African-American community on the South Side. I explained how we built many projects in those neighborhoods and we needed someone who better understood the residents' needs, someone who could bond with their community and church leaders and convince them that we were sincere in our efforts to try to help. He seemed to fully grasp this concept, and I liked that. He understood that we needed a black face, but we were not looking for a token black face.

But, by far, the topic that was most discussed: politics.

He was a political science major as an undergrad, and it seemed to be his true passion. He didn't come right out and say this, but I could sense it. He was a liberal, that was clear, and he didn't have any qualms about having anyone know it.

At one point, with all the politics in the air, I just came out and asked. "You know, Malik, my partner, whom you'll meet, is very connected politically. You might say that he's one of the most politically well-connected men in this city who's not already in office, nor has any interest in holding office. Sam knows everyone. As you get your footing here, you might consider running. You would make a great mayor. I could see you as mayor. And we could raise a lot of money. We've done it before. This is a doable thing! Would you ever consider anything like that?"

He just smiled. He wasn't condescending or dismissive, but he was clear and direct, like maybe he had given this some prior thought. "If I decide to run for any office," he said, "I would be more interested in a national setting.

You know . . . Washington."

That made me smile. Our little newbie law school grad was not fucking around. He had his sights set high.

We finished our coffee and I signed the tab. We walked out together. Standing in front of the Drake Hotel, we said our good-byes. I promised to get back to him shortly. We were not his only interview. I knew that. If we were going to woo him, we'd have to move quickly. However, I never make an offer during the very first interview. It seems too needy. I touched on some of the specifics of the job during our conversation, but this was more of a get-to-know-you kind of meeting.

If someone had told me right then and there that this young man would be taking the oath for the highest office in the land in less than twenty years, I might have said, "I could see that."

———————————

I PLANNED TO CALL Malik within the week to extend an offer. However, I received a phone call from him only a few days after our meeting at the Drake.

"I'm sorry, Mars," he said with real concern in his voice. "I really appreciate your interest in me, but I've decided to take a position with Monica Wicklund's firm. You know them, right? Wicklund, Brice and Jackson? Monica said she knows you."

I knew Monica Wicklund well. Her law firm had represented us on several deals. She was a real mover and shaker in the African-American community on the South Side, in and around Hyde Park. Frankly, they were like family over at her firm. We were all part of a larger force that was trying to rehab the South Side neighborhoods of the city. We had already completed several deals together and were planning many more. In a way, Malik would still be part of the team.

"Of course I know Monica," I answered with enthusiasm. "We work together all the time! They're lucky to get you, Malik. You're an impressive guy. If you have to go somewhere besides our company, you picked the right place. You'll be a perfect fit over there with Monica and her people. You'll love working with them, and they will love working with you. Congratulations, honestly."

"Yeah, they have a spot for me that'll allow me to do a great deal of organizing in the community, which is a passion of mine, as you know. Plus, I'll be able to use this damn law degree that I worked so hard for and actually do some legal work, go into court, all that. You understand, I'm sure."

"I don't know how much Monica has told you about her practice, but we'll be seeing each other all the time. In fact, you have to meet my partner."

"Just name the time and place."

A COUPLE MONTHS LATER, after Malik had graduated, I called him and talked him into taking a break from studying for the bar exam, commiserating with him about my own struggles with getting ready to take that all-important test. I arranged to meet Malik at Sam's favorite restaurant, Gene & Georgetti, not far from our office on Milwaukee Avenue. Gene & Georgetti has been a Chicago staple since 1941, with the best steaks in the city and a reputation for hosting politicians, Hollywood celebrities, and VIPs from around the world. It's been rumored that back in the day G&G had a secret room where the occasional big-stakes poker game was played. In a city like Chicago, rumors become legends, and soon everyone swears it to be fact.

Truth is Gene & Georgetti has been the site of some of the biggest business and political deals ever to be made in Illinois.

We sat in our regular booth. Sam was having his favorite—chopped salad with sliced steak on top, drenched in ranch dressing.

Malik brought along a young woman I knew well, Janet Andersen. Janet was part of a growing, upwardly mobile group of young African-American intellectuals who hung around Hyde Park and the University of Chicago. They were all incredibly bright, and they were busily trying to revitalize the area surrounding the university campus, together with the greater South Side of the city. They were also making a few bucks for themselves in the process. It was a win-win situation.

I'd met Janet a few years before when she worked for the Department of Planning and Development. I started telling the story of our first meeting.

"The first time I saw your friend, Janet, she was buried in mountains of paperwork. Her desk was covered with applications . . ."

She completed my sentence. "Mars saved my butt that day, I'll tell you. I don't know if I have ever thanked you, Mars. Mars walked in, making an application for some special tax status for a low-end housing development he was working on. He has an understanding of the ins and outs of tax law. He helped me get a handle on some of those crazy new regulations. Like I said, Mars, thank you. You really helped me out."

It was clear to me that Malik had done his homework. He knew we'd worked with Janet in the past, and he knew we welcomed future projects with her. That's why he invited her. He was already working the room, making connections for himself and setting up connections for others. It was brilliant. He had been in town less than two weeks and he was already pocketing favors, on which he would one day be able to collect. This was no dummy.

Sam, however, was just smacking his lips once again. He saw a very young, very smooth operator with clear political ambitions. In a world where favors reigned supreme, Sam was the master. He would do favor after favor, raising money, making political connections, making friends, and never asking for anything in return. He was simply banking uncollected-upon good deeds, political chits.

He perceived Malik would be hard to control. Yes, Malik was extremely smart and very savvy. But so was Sam. Where most politicians needed little coaxing to become one of Sam's pawns, Malik would take a little extra finesse. This was not a problem, though, not for Sam. He simply sat smoking his cigar, blowing blue clouds into the air, just plotting, but smiling . . . always smiling.

Chapter 4

AMONG CERTAIN CIRCLES, A word-association game with the prompt "corrupt Illinois politics" will invariably elicit a response of "Chicago Democratic Machine." And fair enough: the Chicago Democratic Machine is indeed fabled for its endless scams, scandals, fraud, and payoffs. In his book, *Boss*, Mike Royko describes the reign of Richard J. Daley as mayor of Chicago; it's a veritable manual of municipal corruption and political patronage.

However, a true political insider to the game of Chicago and Illinois politics would give a different answer, the true answer: most of the Chicago version of corruption has always been penny-ante in scope when compared with the statewide corruption that exists.

While the Democrats in Chicago were busy over the years lining their greedy little pockets with assorted minor kickbacks for zoning changes, bribes to building inspectors, payoffs to cops for looking the other way on various street crimes, etc., the Republicans in and around Chicago and downstate were quietly raking in the really big money.

The true political insider would respond with the other half of the story, the really big half: the Republican Combine.

Illinois is a major agricultural state. In farming parlance, a "combine" is an enormous piece of agricultural machinery that picks the corn, separates it from the husk and the cob, and then spits a seemingly endless stream of clean corn kernels into huge waiting semitrucks.

The Republican politicians had built their own combine over decades, a combine to harvest money—the mother's milk of staying in office.

There are key parts to the building of the Republican Combine.

First, Republicans systematically created a series of regulatory oversight agencies, all under the banner of "good government." *Republicans are the good government party, the uncorrupted party, the family values party! They aren't like the dirty rotten Democrats.* Republicans came up with "good government" reasons for each of their proposed agencies, committees, and boards.

Want to build a new hospital or nursing home? You need a permit from the Illinois Health Facilities Board. What could be more necessary? Have you ever seen a hospital in Mexico City or Calcutta? We need oversight here in our fair state to insure the highest of standards. This is, after all, the United States of America, not some third-world, backward country!

Perhaps you have a magnificent real estate development deal in which the state pension fund should invest. You need approval from the State Pension Board.

Want to sell something—anything at all—to the state government? You need to make it through the State Purchasing Commission.

Nearly anything you can imagine that has to do with financial or business dealings with the government of the State of Illinois must be approved, overseen or accepted by some kind of board or commission. Eventually, the State's bureaucracy came to encompass literally hundreds upon hundreds of such organizations. It took years for the Republicans to build this perfect system.

There's a board to regulate weights and measures, a board to regulate plumbing licenses, a board to regulate real estate brokers. There's even a board that you must see if you want to cut hair. And, to get approval through any of these boards and commissions, you have to hire the right lawyers, the right consultants, the right contractors. You have to deal with the right people during every phase of every project.

This, of course, was the second key to the forging of the Republican Combine: how did one become one of the *right people* to deal with? How did a person or company or firm get to be counted among the Republican elite? Well, that was easy. All one would have to do was contribute money to the right Republican candidates, over a period of many years. Depending on how significant your business was, the more you needed to contribute to be noticed. But, once noticed, you were in.

Why was it so important to make these political contributions over a number of years? Simple answer: contributions made over a period of many years could not be traced directly back to a particular deal struck or favor done on behalf of the contributor. This makes perfect sense, after all. The Republicans weren't like the dirty-rotten-no-good Democrats who practiced patronage and pay-to-play. They were Republicans, the family values folks.

All of those donations, all of those political contributions that were necessary if you wanted to be counted among the *right people*, enabled the Republicans to keep electing Republican governors every four years. Between

1968 and 2002, the Republicans held the Illinois governor's office for thirty of thirty-four years.

Why was the governor's office so critical? Because the governor appoints the members of all of those boards and commissions who have a death-grip on the power to approve all of that state business being done by the right lawyers, the right consultants, and the right contractors . . . the right people.

Some of the political insiders and the political beat reporters around the statehouse dubbed this very well-crafted and very deliberate phenomenon "Pinstripe Patronage."

THE MASTERMIND OF THE Republican Combine was Vince Perino, a Springfield businessman who started out as a modest city council member, and then in 1970, got himself appointed by the Republican governor to be secretary of the Illinois Department of Transportation, known as IDOT. For Vince, running IDOT was like going to school. He quickly learned about how all kinds of scams had been run in the past: the lucrative intricacies of bid rigging, supplying substandard materials while charging full price, and finder's fees paid to consultants who arranged for the awarding of various contracts. But Vince wasn't your ordinary, run-of-the-mill political hack. Vince had a genius for manipulating the Combine while staying out of the limelight. Very soon, he became the top Republican fundraiser in the state, the man no Illinois Republican could even think about getting elected without.

Despite his enormous power, Vince was a very small man, almost frail-looking. He proudly sported a full head of long graying hair, parted on the side, impeccably groomed. He was mild-mannered, soft-spoken, and almost humble in his interactions with powerful people. Because he was such a smooth talker, "Butter wouldn't melt in his mouth," they said of Vince, who was all the while taking the money he raised for them. And once in office, they all paid homage to Vince by letting him tell them who should be appointed to all those boards and commissions, granting him massive amounts of power over virtually every facet of daily life in the state of Illinois.

To work his magic, Vince needed operatives: guys who could be counted upon to do what Vince wanted them to do once they were appointed to office. And with so much regulatory apparatus out there, Vince needed lots of operatives.

Marvin Rosenthal was born into the lap of luxury, scion of a well-to-do family of Jewish merchants who lived on the North Shore. He glided through a prestigious East Coast college, picked up an MBA at the University of Chicago, and went to work as an executive at a small health insurance company owned by one of his father's cronies. Marvin had a real talent for the health insurance business. He figured out that if you charge premiums and then pay for and provide as little actual coverage as possible, you can make a lot of money. Marvin's company did just that.

Realizing what a lucrative business he had stumbled into, Marvin proceeded to buy the company's controlling ownership interest, and succeeded in building it into one of the largest private health insurers operating in the state of Illinois.

In the course of growing the business, he came to realize the government of the state itself was one of the largest potential customers, because it provided health coverage to its thousands of employees—prison guards, state troopers, state university professors, road crew workers, tax collectors, etc.

Marvin wanted to land the state's business, which was put out for bids every four years. However, what Marvin didn't know was that the bidding wasn't done on the basis of price alone. There was a fancy, rather arbitrary selection process in which a number of relevant factors were considered, such as customer satisfaction, the scope of coverage, and other similarly vague terms, all of which were code for the one true criterion: reliable contributor.

Like a naïve babe in the woods, Marvin worked overtime for weeks assembling his company's bid. He compiled numerous letters of recommendation, labored for hours on a pricing schedule, and printed a pretty brochure with glossy color pictures.

In spite of his tireless efforts, the state awarded the contract to someone else.

Marvin wasn't simply disappointed; he was pissed. He'd worked hard on his elaborate bid, and he knew it was a good one. He contacted his state senator and asked for a meeting. When he told the state senator what had happened, the senator laughed at him.

"You need to talk to Vince Perino," the senator said.

"Who's that?" Marvin asked.

The senator looked at Marvin like he was an idiot. "Here's Vince's number. Call him and introduce yourself. Tell him I suggested you call."

VINCE PERINO WAS CAUTIOUS in such introductory meetings. There was always a chance the person he was meeting with might be working for the Feds. He was very self-deprecating, always understating his own influence. He merely made "suggestions."

But there was something Vince liked about Marvin. After years of experience in recruiting operatives, Vince had developed a sixth sense about who
he could trust and who he should avoid. With Marvin, he recognized the
type immediately. Marvin was a guy who wanted to do business, and would
do whatever he needed to do to get that business. Vince suggested that the
next time the contract was up for renewal, Marvin might want to engage a
certain consulting firm to help with the application.

He also suggested Marvin might make use of the intervening four years
before the next contract was due to improve his relationships throughout
state government, possibly starting with his own state senator, who had so
kindly arranged their introduction. By this point in his life, Marvin perceived
himself as a shrewd businessman. He made inquiries while getting the drift
of how things really worked in Springfield, and he wanted to be on the inside.

Marvin Rosenthal became one of the most dependable and consistent
contributors to various Republican campaigns. Whenever Vince was trying
to assemble a war chest for a particular candidate, Marvin was always there,
ready to help. Such donations were made by Marvin personally, in his own
name, and as a result he was becoming quite well-known—and quite well-
liked—in Republican circles.

When the state's health insurance contract was up for renewal four years
later, Marvin didn't just hire the consultant recommended by Vince. He hired
the law firm recommended by Vince, headed by a former Republican senator;
the lobbyist recommended by Vince, headed by a former Republican official;
the public relations firm recommended by Vince, headed by the state senator
who'd introduced Marvin to Vince; and the marketing firm recommended by
Vince, headed by a charming fellow who happened to be a member of one of
the various state boards, appointed on Vince's recommendation.

Marvin's firm was awarded the contract. But there was a twist.

The state decided the contract was too big to be awarded to just one firm. So they gave Marvin's firm half the business, covering certain state agencies, and gave the other half to someone else.

Marvin called Vince, fit to be tied.

"What the fuck happened here?" he screamed into the receiver.

Vince, ever cautious, refused to talk about it on the phone, and told Marvin to meet him at Tarantino's, Vince's favorite Italian restaurant in Springfield.

At the restaurant, Marvin's tirade continued.

"Why did you split the fucking contract like that? What happened here?" Marvin demanded to know.

"Stay calm, stay calm," Vince said soothingly. "The other guys had a lot of friends too."

"That's bullshit! I did everything you ever asked me to do. I threw a shitpile of money at your guys . . . a lot of motherfuckin' money, Vince!" Rosenthal was furious.

"So did they." Vince smiled. "And calm down, or I'm outta here," he warned.

A light bulb went on in Marvin's brain. He began to understand what it meant to truly have power. He took a deep breath and let it out slowly. He would wait.

"I appreciate everything you've done for me. I'm going to show you in the years to come that no one is a better friend to you than me," Marvin acquiesced.

"That would be great," Vince said knowingly. "We have lots of tough challenges ahead." Four years later, the State decided having two providers for health insurance was too complicated. They merged the two contracts back into a single source award. Marvin's firm was awarded all the business.

AND TWO YEARS LATER, Marvin sold his little insurance company for fifty million dollars.

"Congratulations," Vince said to Marvin over dinner at Tarantino's. "What're you going to do with yourself, now that you're really rich?"

Marvin had his answer ready. "I'm only forty-seven years old. I can't just play golf every day for the rest of my life. I want to stay active. I'd like to get involved in the state government, which I can do now because I no longer do business with the state."

Vince studied his friend for a moment. "You realize, right, that elective politics are probably out of the question for you?"

Marvin joked, "Who ever heard of a Jew running as a Republican?"

They both laughed.

"No," Marvin said. "I'd like to serve on a board or two."

Cautious as always, Vince started out slowly with Marvin, bringing him right to the edge of the inner circle.

He began by suggesting to the governor that he appoint Marvin to the Health Facilities Planning Board. With a stroke of the pen, Marvin Rosenthal suddenly was involved in whether or not a hospital would be built or whether any existing hospital would be allowed to expand, in the entire state of Illinois.

Marvin quickly distinguished himself as the best operative Vince had ever recruited. He was absolutely dependable, giving the nod to whomever Vince wanted approved for a permit.

After a couple of years, Vince was convinced Marvin was totally reliable. Recognizing the talent in his middle-aged protégé, he decided to promote him to the big bonanza, the ultimate mother lode.

From the Memoirs of Mars Gregory:

SAM AND I WERE having lunch one afternoon when he turned to me and said with a smile, "I learned a new American word. You Americans, you have a word for everything, you know that? Gloss-a-phobia," he said very slowly and very deliberately, with his heavy Arab accent, trying desperately to pronounce the word correctly. Then he laughed. He butchered the pronunciation. "Glossophobia," he said again.

"Yeah, what's that?" I asked, surprised by Sam's knowledge.

"It is the medical term for the fear of public speaking. If you search your soul, ask others, or read books, you will find that among people's most common and greatest fears is the fear of standing up in front of a group of people and speaking out loud. Most people cannot even think about doing it without sweating. Jerry Seinfeld once quipped that at a funeral most people would rather be the corpse than have to give the eulogy." Sam started laughing. I guess he liked his own joke . . . or Jerry's.

"What truly fascinates me is the simple fact that most politicians are not that bright. They discover early on in life that it is easier to stand up in front of the class and talk about nothing than it is to be a member of the class that has to do all the real work.

"If a person overcomes the fear of public speaking," he continued, "if he or she is willing to stand up on a stage and talk out loud, then he or she can become a politician. That's it! The ability to speak in public is the one and only singular qualification.

"You do not have to be good-looking; just look at Strom Thurmond or Ted Stevens. You do not have to be distinguished; look at Barney Frank or Charlie Rangel. You do not have to be charismatic; there are people like Richard Shelby or Jeff Sessions in the Senate. How does anyone stay awake when they start talking? You do not have to be handsome—there are many examples, right, Mars? Hell, Mitch McConnell looks like a damn turtle. You do not have to be funny; Al Gore looks like a wax statue. You do not even have to be interesting when you talk. And, you sure as hell do not have to be smart. That is not a qualification by any stretch of the imagination. This is why politicians sometimes do incredibly stupid things. All they really know how to do . . . is talk. They can't fix a car, or pound a nail, or do a dance. They just talk. They cannot write a book, or bake a cake, or drive a truck. All they can do—their only recognizable skill on this planet—is that they can *talk*."

It seemed to me like Sam had given this some thought.

"When all you can do is talk," he continued, "and you know that about yourself, deep in your soul, you are very insecure. That is why so much effort is spent on making politicians *feel* important. They are all lavished with big offices, a doting, obsequious staff, first-class travel, all the best. As a result, these silly creatures think they actually are important, and, if they are important, well then, they simply must be smart. What a misguided perception that is."

"So, what's your point?" I asked him. "That's no surprise. Everybody knows many, or most, politicians are not very smart."

"Politicians have power, Mars, and through them I can get power for myself."

———————————

THE NEXT MORNING I stopped by Sam's house on my way downtown with some papers for him to sign. Sam was sitting in the shade on the patio of his mansion next to the pool. He was reading the morning *Tribune* over orange juice and toast, dressed in a silk robe the color of butter and sporting fine leather slippers. His young son was paddling around in the water, and I had to be alert to avoid getting splashed. Sam's wife, Eloise, was stretched out on a chaise lounge on the other side of the pool, taking in the sun. She was a pleasant woman, reasonably attractive, and with a nice body, even after a couple of kids. Eloise waved to me as I sat down beside Sam.

"Mars, this is incredible," Sam said, scanning an article on page three. He had a look on his face that I had seen before, and I could just hear the wheels turning. Sam read aloud:

FEDS SAY BRIBERY CAUSED FIERY DEATHS OF SIX CHILDREN
A 1994 traffic accident that killed six children in one family may have been the result of corruption in the Department of Motor Vehicles. During questioning, the driver of the semitruck that hit the family's car, causing it to explode in flames, reportedly admitted to having given money in exchange for an Illinois commercial driver's license without having to take a qualifying test.

On Saturday, April 30, 1994, Henry and Ruth Winters were traveling from Waterston to Chicago for a Cubs game. Their family van, carrying their six children, who ranged from age six months to 12 years, was traveling as part of a caravan with other members of the Third Evangelical Church of Waterston. The group had been given tickets to a game at Wrigley Field by another member of the congregation.

According to Henry Winters, the family had been driving northbound on Highway 47 for about five minutes when Henry noticed in his rearview mirror a huge eighteen-wheeler barreling up behind him, whose driver seemed to be either drunk or having trouble handling the rig. It was weaving across the center line of the two-lane blacktop, erratic and unpredictable. Several times Henry saw the truck veer onto the shoulder, only to jerk back onto the road, gravel flying.

Suddenly, the giant truck accelerated, and though Henry tried to get out of its path, the truck careened again, smacking up against the van with the force of a locomotive.

Ruth and Henry managed to get out of the van, falling onto the roadway, and somehow dodged the oncoming traffic. However, the tremendous impact of the collision had ignited the van's gas tank, and before they could reach even one of their children, the van was a raging inferno. Paralyzed with terror, Henry and Ruth could only stand and watch, listening to the heart-wrenching screams of their children, as all six were burned alive.

The investigation of the crash and the alleged bribery is ongoing. According to an unnamed source close to the investigation, as yet unconfirmed and unverified reports indicate that the corruption may go much higher in the secretary of state's office.

Sam slowly and distinctly reread the last line: "... unverified reports indicate that the corruption may go much higher in the secretary of state's office."

"Pretty incredible," I nodded. "But, what's this got to do with us, Sam?"

Sam's eyes narrowed to thin slits. "Ed Parker is planning a run for governor."

I had heard this, of course. The incumbent Republican governor had just been released from the hospital after suffering a mild heart attack. "So?" I asked.

Sam gave that wry smile of his. "There is opportunity here, Mars. Opportunity."

Chapter 5

TARANTINO'S WASN'T USUALLY OPEN for breakfast, but for Vince Perino, they made an exception. Vince had a small investment with the owner, and knew his partner would tell him if the Feds ever showed up to install any bugs in the restaurant. Today, Vince was having breakfast with the secretary of state, Ed Parker.

"So, how is the governor's health?" Parker asked Vince genially. The sitting governor had a year left in his term.

"Well, it was a scare, but nothing serious. They put in a stent, seems to be working. He's going to be okay."

Parker frowned. "Oh, that's great."

Vince smiled at him knowingly. "Unfortunately, the doctors told him he needs to get the stress out of his life. The job of governor is killing him. The first lady put her foot down. He's not running for reelection."

Parker relaxed. "Well, then, I am." And then he caught himself. "Assuming, of course, you're going to be with me."

Vince spread some jam on his English muffin. "You're the man for the job, Mr. Secretary. But I'm very concerned about this thing in Joliet."

Parker's jowly face screwed into anger. "That's such bull. Those guys in the driver's license station were nuts, doing that shit, selling those licenses. But I didn't know a thing about it. They'll never pin anything on me."

Vince chewed his muffin slowly and swallowed. He took a sip of coffee, scrunched up his nose, and added some cream. "Now that the *Tribune* has run this exposé, the Feds are going to be all over this, Ed. You need serious damage control."

Parker nodded. "I know, I know. I've got it under control. I've got a fire-break in the chain of command. It'll never hit my level."

"I may be able to give you a little help," Vince said quietly.

Parker sat bolt upright in his chair. "Yeah? How?"

"Our guy running for the Senate, this John McKenzie fellow, looks like he'll win. The Democrats are putting up another idiot," Vince said, stroking his chin thoughtfully.

Parker looked concerned. "He may be a rogue, this McKenzie. The only reason he's leading in the polls is that he's a multimillionaire, and is spending a lot of his own money. He's going to be trouble, mark my words. But what's that got to do with me?"

Vince gave him a knowing look. "We may get a Republican president in three years. The other senator from Illinois is a Democrat. So when McKenzie is in, he gets to recommend who the president will appoint as the US attorney in Chicago."

Parker shot a worried look at Vince. "Is Gallagher leaving?" This was alarming, as Dan Gallagher, the present US attorney in Chicago, had been slow-rolling the driver's license investigation—that's why so little had happened over the last three years.

"Not anytime soon," Vince said reassuringly, seeing Parker's obvious fear. "But I suspect he'll leave to go make some real money in private practice in a couple of years."

Parker looked unconvinced. "I don't know, Vince . . ." His voice trailed off. "This guy is going to be hard to manage."

"Now, Mr. Secretary, let's not focus on the negative. Let's talk about what we need to do get you elected governor."

Parker brightened. "Yeah, let's talk about that."

Vince sat back in his chair while the waitress poured more coffee for both of them. When she was comfortably out of earshot, he said, "I have a candidate to head your campaign finance committee."

Parker was busy trying to wedge out bites of grapefruit without squirting the juice on his suit. He knew that Vince himself never let his name be listed on any campaign committee, let alone a high visibility post like chairman of the campaign's finance committee. "Okay, who's that?"

"Marvin Rosenthal," Vince answered.

Parker scowled again as the grapefruit juice hit his tie. "That fat little Jew?" Parker tilted his chin down and looked at Vince over the top of his glasses.

"He's okay," Vince said reassuringly. "We can depend on him."

"Are you sure?" Parker asked, sopping up juice.

"I'm certain." Vince waited a moment until he was sure Parker was giving him his undivided attention. It was time to take the big plunge. "And, after the campaign, when you're the governor, he'd be perfect as our guy on the Teachers' Pension Board."

Parker put his fork down, hunched forward to whisper.

"You told me that the Teachers' Pension Board is where all the big money comes from; now tell me how."

"Yes," Vince replied, also hunching over his scrambled eggs. "There are tens of thousands of teachers in Illinois. Every day they show up at work, and the state makes a contribution to their pension fund. It's a colossal bucket of money, billions of dollars, and it gets bigger every single day. That money has to be invested. The Fund makes allocations of money to various investment managers. Every investment manager in the country comes in asking for money. But unless they hire one of our guys as their application consultant, they don't get an award. Our guy gets a finder's fee every time the Fund makes an award. He gets to keep half, and he gives half to whomever I tell them to donate to."

The wannabe governor nodded. "How big is this finder's fee?"

Vince smiled. "It's one percent. So on a Fund investment of $50 million, say, the fee is $500,000. Half of that comes our way for the campaign."

Parker's famous bushy eyebrows arched again. "That's really big."

"That's why we have to have someone absolutely dependable on that board. He's got to make sure that the only people who get the nod for an investment allocation are our friends."

Parker nodded. "You sure you trust this guy?"

"Yes, I'm very confident in him," Vince said.

"Okay, he's the guy," Parker said with a nod. "One other thing . . . do you know an Arab guy in Chicago named Sam Alsheriti?"

Vince nodded. "He's got some kind of a park concession contract in Chicago. Wants to be a player. What about him?"

Parker pushed his plate away, finished with his food now. "He contacted us. He thinks he can help us raise money for the campaign. I thought maybe you could use him."

Vince Perino did not hesitate, not even for a minute. "No way, Ed. Not a guy like that. He's bad news, doesn't have the subtlety we need, especially with all the scrutiny you're going to be under. Leave this to me. We'll have plenty of money for the campaign."

From the Memoirs of Mars Gregory:

SAM AND I WERE finally beginning to hedge our bets a bit by moving into the business of building higher-end projects. After months of maneuvering, posturing, negotiating, and outright bullshitting, we were in position to grab the holy grail of Chicago real estate: 64 acres of prime property, with nearly a mile of frontage on the Chicago River, just south of the Loop itself, and totally vacant.

The site was extraordinary for its sheer size, and also for the fact that the property was in single ownership. It was formerly a giant railroad yard, back when railroads mattered and Chicago, as Carl Sandburg described it, was "hog butcher to the world." The site had been sold years earlier to a prominent Chicago family who thought they had the inside track to build a casino on the land. However, a casino in Chicago was such a potential gold mine for so many politicians that they were unable to agree upon how to carve up the pie among themselves. And so legislation to allow gambling in Chicago was debated every year, but never passed. The property just sat there, fallow, racking up hundreds of thousands of dollars in insurance costs and real estate taxes, year after year. Eventually, the affluent Chicago family tired of carrying the cost of this major land holding, and offered it for sale.

The asking price was $24 million—way beyond anything we had ever done before. Our plan was to place the property under contract, and then figure out how to get the money. This required a lot of fast talking on our part about all our contacts, money sources, etc.

One day I said to Sam, "We're getting really close to telling lies, Sam. We don't have the money."

Sam looked at me mischievously. "We're not lying, Mars," he said, giving me that charming smile of his. "We're bluffing!"

We put together a master plan, carving the 64 acres into over two dozen individual development parcels. For several of the parcels, we were contemplating condominium and townhouse units, numbering in the hundreds. It would take twenty years or more to fully build out, costing billions of dollars. We were working with Phil Angelino, a high-profile and well-connected real estate attorney in town, who was also very capable of raising money from investors. Phil was portly and could be overbearingly opinionated, but he was a brilliant lawyer and knew everybody in the business. As he put it to me early on, "Mars, this project is a veritable cornucopia of work for all of us for the rest of our careers!"

We were really cranking on this deal, burning the midnight oil, and I was having visions of grandeur . . . and then the phone rang. It was Phil Angelino.

"I'm afraid I have bad news," Phil said. I could hear the disappointment in his voice.

"Uh-oh," I said, steeling myself. "What's happened?"

There was a long pause. I could tell Phil was trying to pick his words. Finally he said simply, "I just got off the phone with the attorney for the sellers of the 64 acres. Somebody else has made a bid, and they will provide proof that they have all the money to buy the property, sitting in the bank. The attorney said if we can't do that, we're out."

I was stunned. "Well, there's no way we can match that."

I was totally crestfallen. The real estate business can be a bitch.

———————————

I WALKED DOWN TO Sam's office to break the bad news.

I was surprised to see Malik Alawi sitting there, puffing away on a cigarette.

"Malik, how are you?" I said, taking a seat as far away from the wisping cigarette smoke as I could. I hated to get that foul smoke smell on my clothes, and I was wearing a brand new suit.

Malik flashed that warm, toothy grin of his. "Great, Mars, great."

Sam was sitting back in his big leather swivel chair. He folded his hands in his lap. I knew this pose. It meant he was wheeling and dealing.

"Mars," he said softly, "Malik wants to run for the state senate."

This was intriguing.

"Really?" I said, trying to get the gears in my head to run as fast as the ones in Sam's head were already spinning. I knew Malik was living in the Hyde Park neighborhood, home to the University of Chicago, one of the world's great academic institutions, where he had lined up a job teaching constitutional law after finding out that working as a community organizer wasn't going to pay his bills. "That's very exciting. You live in Hyde Park, right?"

Malik nodded.

"The incumbent senator down there is . . . Molly Brannigan? Isn't she going to be tough to beat?"

Sam gave me that knowing look of his. I knew something big was coming.

"I've been telling Molly Brannigan she ought to run for governor. We're going to help her get the Democratic nomination," he said with certainty. "That will open up her seat. Malik is going to be a candidate. He's perfect for it. He's on the faculty of the university, and obviously is becoming a well-known member of the community."

I pondered this for a minute. The word "community" in Chicago parlance means "black people." I could see this was a helluva move. Sam was right. Malik had one foot in each of the two major voting blocs in the district.

"Wow," was all I could say. "This is fantastic."

"We're going to help him," Sam said with certainty. "He's going to win."

Malik flashed that big grin again. "Thanks, Sam. With you on board, we can't lose!"

We exchanged small talk for a few minutes more, discussing some of the campaign logistics, all of which Sam was going to coordinate. "You just concentrate on not saying anything foolish," Sam said to Malik. "We'll take care of the rest."

"I know you're really busy, Sam," Malik said cautiously. "Should we get an organizer to help us?" He was talking about hiring a paid campaign professional, someone who toiled daily in the political arenas and knew all the details of how to circulate petitions to get on the ballot, how to form a legal campaign committee and file all the disclosure forms, and so on.

Sam did not hesitate. "You are absolutely right, Malik. I have the perfect person for the job."

I tilted my head slightly, waiting for the punch line.

"His name is Johnny Jarzik," Sam said. "He's the best in the business."

AFTER MALIK LEFT, BEAMING with joy that his campaign was going to be well funded and well managed, I turned to Sam and told him the bad news about the 64 acres. He seemed non-plussed. "Don't worry, Mars," he said airily. "That deal might fall through. We might get another bite at the apple."

I was a little miffed at how easily he was willing to write off all the work we had put into the now failed effort on the 64 acres, so I asked, "Do you really have time to take on Malik's campaign? I thought you were trying to get more active in the Parker campaign for governor."

It was rare to see Sam get angry, but fire exploded from his eyes.

"They don't want me," Sam said, nearly spitting it out. "They don't want an Arab involved in their campaign."

Now, I was surprised that any politician would ever pass on taking money from a willing donor, but as I thought about it, it made sense. Parker was saddled with the nagging problem of the license-selling scandal, and so they were probably being squeaky-clean in staffing the Finance Committee for the campaign.

"Wow, that's an outrage," was all I could say, feebly. "Is that why you're going to support Molly Brannigan for governor?"

Sam gave me a look that bordered on contempt. "Molly Brannigan is an egghead," he snarled. "She can't possibly win against Ed Parker. It's just a convenient way to move her out of the way for Malik."

"Wow," I said again, realizing I was repeating myself. "So you're pissed at Parker, but you're going to get a patsy to run against him?"

Sam was not the kind of guy to admit he was out of the game. "What goes around comes around," he said with conviction.

Chapter 6

THE TRAGIC NATURE OF the accident in Waterston had drawn a tremendous amount of negative press due to the obvious ties to the secretary of state's office, but the investigation into the way in which the truck driver had obtained his commercial driver's license had stalled. Although a few employees at the satellite Joliet office had been fired, and there seemed to be a bit of a shake-up at lower levels within the office, the actual investigation of corruption at higher levels had been going nowhere.

Dan Gallagher, the current US attorney for the Northern District of Illinois, had been recommended to the president by Vince Perino at a time when there'd been no Republican senator from Illinois to make the appointment. Although he had kept the investigation alive, indicting and convicting a few of the small-fry driver's license officials along the way, Gallagher hadn't made the investigation of Parker a priority. However, that wasn't the only reason for the delay. Parker had made certain he was well insulated from the corruption. The illegal campaign contributions were made through an elaborate scheme of selling tickets to fundraisers, sometimes involving the relatives or friends of the person receiving a commercial driver's license, and was therefore hard to unravel. It would take a sitting US attorney who was much more determined in his efforts to lead the investigation if the details of this plot were ever to be uncovered. There were journalists who would ask the occasional embarrassing question of Gallagher at press conferences, but, in general, Ed Parker had been spared any true scrutiny regarding the incident. Any actual connection of Parker to the corrupt activity had, so far, not been established.

Parker officially announced that he was running for the office of governor of the State of Illinois, and launched a very credible, very well-funded campaign. As far as anyone knew, he had been a competent secretary of state. He could point to colorful, elaborate charts and graphs as he traveled the campaign trail, which clearly set forth the conclusion that his heroic efforts against drunk drivers had been successful and all traffic deaths were down statewide. The tough laws he'd proposed and continued to support were working.

Molly Brannigan was increasingly looking to be the likely Democratic nominee for governor, leading a feeble group of contenders. Inexplicably, she was raising more money than any of the other mopes who were trying for the Democratic nomination. Clearly, somebody behind the scenes was significantly helping her campaign.

The primary election came and went. Parker and Molly Brannigan were nominated by their respective parties, and Malik easily won his primary against a pie-in-the-sky professor who had tossed his hat in the ring. Johnny Jarzik had actually engineered the primary challenge by getting a professor pal of his to run, as a way of getting Malik's organization launched and giving it a modest battle test—a tune-up if you will, for the coming general election.

EIGHT MONTHS LATER, IN November, 1998, Edward G. Parker was elected governor of the State of Illinois, with 56 percent of the votes. In politics, anything over 55 percent is a landslide.

John McKenzie, propelled by a heavy television advertising campaign largely funded with his own personal fortune, won the US Senate seat, polling 52 percent against a lackluster Democratic opponent.

Malik won his state senate seat with 80 percent.

The next morning, Mars congratulated Sam on Malik's victory.

Sam gave Mars that sly look of his. "Now," he said, "Malik really owes us."

Chapter 7

MARS SAT IN HIS office doing some paperwork. There was a knock at the door. It was Sam, looking very satisfied, with Malik in tow behind him.

"Malik!" Mars said, getting up from the desk. "Congratulations, Mr. Senator!"

Malik grinned broadly, and shook Mars's hand. "I owe it all to you guys," Malik said. He almost sounded sincere.

They chatted a few minutes about the upcoming inauguration and other happenings in Springfield, and talked about Malik's family. Malik had married a woman he'd met while working as a summer law clerk at a big Chicago law firm, and they now had two young daughters. He took out his wallet and showed them photos of his beautiful little girls.

"That's what we wanted to talk to you about, Mars," Sam said. He said it in that silky manner of his, the one that always signaled trouble.

Mars sat back down, and motioned for them to take seats in the comfortable chairs facing his desk.

"Malik, my friend, what can I do to help you?" Mars asked.

Sam pulled a folded sheet of paper from his coat pocket and put it on the table. It was a page torn from the Multiple Listing Service, a database of various properties for sale. It showed a lovely Victorian mansion, on a nice street in Hyde Park, with a large vacant lot adjacent to it. The asking price was $1.6 million. A lot of money, even for Hyde Park.

"Vicki loves this property. She's all over Malik to buy it," Sam said.

Malik gave a sad, hang-dog look. "It's out of our price range."

"Isn't she working as an associate at Corrigan & Sanders? I should think she'd be making plenty! And you'll be getting a salary as a state senator," Mars said.

Sam shook his head. "Vicki wasn't happy practicing law," he explained. "She's leaving to take a job in the community relations department at the University of Chicago Hospital. It's a substantial pay cut."

Mars pondered this for a moment. Vicki Alawi was giving up a job at a prominent law firm to take a cut and work in community relations at a not-for-profit organization?

"Between her salary, their savings, and what Malik will be earning, they can afford to pay about one million," Sam said. "The asking price is $1.6 million for both the house and the big vacant lot. Additionally, the seller is insisting on both parcels closing at the same time. We must figure out how to bridge the gap."

Mars knew instantly where Sam was going with this. "Let me guess," he said, picking up a pen and a yellow pad. "Sammar will buy the house and the adjoining lot, keep the lot, and sell the house to Malik and his wife for one million?"

Malik nodded his head, but Sam was looking conspiratorial. "That's too risky for Malik," he said in a hushed tone.

Mars drew a box on the pad to symbolize the whole property, and then a smaller box inside to represent the house. "Now," he said, thinking out loud, "the trick to this whole thing is to find a friendly appraiser to agree that the house is worth only $1 million, and have him appraise the vacant lot for $600,000." He then drew a dashed line, dividing the house and the adjoining lot.

Malik tugged on his ear. "Vicki really wants a larger yard for the kids."

Mars noted, with some annoyance, that Malik's wife had just crossed over into the "high-maintenance" category. But Mars was the world's leading expert at managing a high-maintenance wife, so he couldn't say much about Vicki.

"Okay," he said, drawing a second dotted line, giving the house a bigger side yard. "Can we get her to go for something like this?"

Malik nodded in agreement. But Sam questioned, "Mars, how can the vacant lot be worth $600,000 if the house itself is worth only $1 million?"

They all sat thinking about that problem for a few seconds. Then Malik piped up, "Hey, the lot is on the corner; it's got a street on both sides. Can't we say that's what makes it really valuable?"

Mars broke into a big grin. "Of course we can, Malik. That's exactly what we'll say."

But Sam was still wary, "Are you sure we can get an appraiser to give us the right numbers so this all looks legitimate?"

Mars laughed. "It is legitimate, Sam, and yes, I know just the appraiser who will come up with the right allocation."

Sam stuck his hand out, and all three shook on it.

"Who's going to be the straw man for this thing?" Mars asked Sam. "We need somebody reliable, who'll sign all the papers and do whatever we need him to do."

Once again, Sam did not hesitate. "His name is Orenthal Mitchell. He works as the special assistant to the president of the Cook County Board. Well-connected, and a good friend."

"Okay, fine," Mars said, writing the name on the pad. "Are you sure he's reliable?"

Malik and Sam looked at each other and laughed.

"Absolutely," Sam said with conviction. "One hundred percent reliable!"

After Malik left their office, Mars told Sam he didn't want Sammar on any of Malik's home purchase filings. It was a paper trail he wanted to avoid.

Sam said, "Mars, you worry too much. You arrange for the appraisal, and I will handle the details."

Sam was gathering his future political favors. He made certain Malik's home purchase transaction was completed just as Malik and Vicki wished.

Chapter 8

IN HIS VERY FIRST official act as governor of the State of Illinois, Ed Parker, as directed by Vince Perino, had named Marvin Rosenthal to the board of the Illinois Teachers' Pension Fund.

At his first meeting, Marvin voted to approve an allocation of $100 million to a money management firm from Los Angeles recommended by a designated investment consulting firm, which, of course, had been identified by Perino. As was the case with all such awards, there was full disclosure of a legal payment of a million-dollar finder's fee to the investment consulting firm. Marvin had been fully briefed by Vince on how the whole thing worked. Marvin felt satisfied and smug. He had made it inside the Combine, and now he was one of the primary cogs in the machinery.

After several months on the job, however, Marvin became unhappy with a key feature of the operation, and decided to broach the subject with Vince.

"There's something I don't understand," he said to Vince one day as they were playing golf at the Springfield Country Club. Vince loved to talk serious business while playing golf, as it was virtually impossible to bug a golf course.

"What's that?" Vince asked, sizing up a putt.

"You let these damn consultants keep half the finder's fee. That's huge. Those fuckers are getting rich off of this gravy train, *our* gravy train."

Vince pulled his putter back from the ball and gazed at Marvin.

"Well, congratulations, it only took you what, three months, to wake up to it."

Marvin was confused. "Wake up to what?"

Vince started laughing. "Did you really think all this time that I've been letting them keep half of the finder's fee?"

Marvin began to wobble on the putting green. "What are you saying?"

Vince stroked the putt, draining it square to the middle of the cup.

"Nice shot," Marvin muttered.

"The consultant splits the finder's fee with a real estate firm that I control. I've been expecting you to ask me for a share ever since you got on the damn board."

Marvin was in shock. "Shit, Vince. You mean all this time I could have been getting a piece?"

Vince fished the ball out of the cup. "In this world, we would say, you deserve a taste."

Marvin started laughing. "A taste? I think I should get a slice!"

Vince climbed back into the golf cart. "A slice is what you hit off the tee. We'll start you off with a taste. If things go well, we can consider moving you up. But you have to be careful. Have your lawyer write up a contract between you and the finder . . . call it 'for consulting services,' or something like that . . . so if anybody ever starts sniffing around, there's a cover story for why the payments were made."

Once he felt like he was really on the inside, Marvin worked harder than ever to please Vince, raising unprecedented sums for the Combine and the Republican Party.

Both of them were rolling in the dough. Life was good.

———————————

THE NEW REPUBLICAN SENATOR, John McKenzie, didn't look like your typical US congressman. He was slightly over six feet tall, with a slender build, pale complexion, and receding hairline, and always wore off-the-rack suits, despite his wealth. He looked more like a tenured college professor than a professional politician.

McKenzie became a major thorn in Vince's side.

He had quickly established himself as a total maverick, refusing to toe the line on a series of important Republican initiatives, and even worse, taking several positions that infuriated important big donors. These well-connected money men complained vigorously to Vince. After all, he was the de facto head of the Illinois Republican Party.

Initially, Vince put them off, assuring them that McKenzie was just posturing, trying to impress the media, but that deep down, he would be a dependable, solid Republican, defender of the rich and powerful.

And then, after a year in office, just as the party was gearing up to face a tough presidential election the following year, McKenzie announced he was going to oppose a banking reform bill, a proposal that would significantly loosen the long-standing regulations on the activities of commercial banks. The bill was very popular among bankers and bank stockholders, because it would open up all kinds of new opportunities to use bank deposits (which of course are insured by the federal government) to speculate in exotic investments such as derivatives and complicated trading instruments. Even better, the bill was going to loosen the regulation of home mortgage lending, in an effort to expand home ownership to millions of lower-income Americans. Who wouldn't go for that?

Well, John McKenzie wouldn't. He predicted that the banks would make lousy investments, lose the depositors' money, and the banks would have to be bailed out by the federal government, because, after all, if they didn't, there would be a run on the banks. Remember Jimmy Stewart in *It's a Wonderful Life*?

Within hours of McKenzie's announcement, Vince was inundated by calls from angry bankers across the state, all of whom had been loyal contributors over the years, providing much of the oil that had greased the gears of the Republican Combine. Vince quickly realized he had to do something. He called McKenzie's office and asked for a meeting. Incredibly, McKenzie stalled in setting a date, and wanted to know what the meeting was going to cover. Vince was astounded. *Nobody* treated Vince Perino like that. After a couple rounds of calls, a meeting was eventually scheduled, to be held in McKenzie's Chicago senate office.

Vince prepared carefully for this meeting. He realized he had to be cautious. This guy was a complete wild card, having gotten himself elected mostly with his own money. He was beholden to no one. Vince rationalized that McKenzie certainly would want his help the next time around, in 2004.

The setting wasn't what you might expect for a US senator's office. It turns out the fancy offices are in Washington; back home, the senators get government-issue space and furnishings in a relatively nondescript federal office building. Most politicians would use their discretionary spending funds to upgrade their furniture, but not John McKenzie. He wasn't like most. The more understated his office, the more it represented his unassuming style.

The meeting started badly. McKenzie walked into a conference room adjacent to his main office accompanied by a young staffer, whom he introduced as his assistant on the banking bill. Once again, Vince was astounded.

"Uh, Senator," he said after the initial greeting pleasantries were exchanged, "I was expecting that we would meet privately."

McKenzie shrugged. "I like to have a staff person with me when I take constituent meetings."

This was an insult. Vince was no mere "constituent"—he was the head of the fucking Combine. But he was also a consummate pro, and he kept his wits.

"Senator, this is a very sensitive matter involving the Party's relationship with some of our most important friends. If you won't meet privately with me, then I don't feel comfortable in continuing."

McKenzie of course had met Vince a number of times. He knew all about Vince, knew all about the Combine, and frankly, didn't relate to or support Vince's type of politics. It's why he had used his own money to run. He genuinely believed he was above all the trivial back scratching and influence peddling that goes on every day in Washington. He pondered the situation for a moment. Here was a chance to toss this fixer out, to send a signal to the whole party establishment that John McKenzie was his own guy.

But he paused.

This was Vince Perino, the most powerful Republican in the state, more powerful in fact than that glad-hander who was in the governor's office, Ed Parker. If he totally pissed Perino off, McKenzie realized he might not get anything done during his senate term, and that was a sobering thought.

"Okay, Vince, I understand." The senator turned to the aide, a scrawny fellow with a button-down collar and tortoiseshell glasses. "Bob, give us a few minutes, would you?"

Vince smiled apologetically at the kid as he was leaving, "I'm really sorry, Bob. No offense intended; I just need a few minutes privately with the senator." This was part of the Perino persona—he was always polite to everyone, even to nobodies he'd just tossed out of the room.

Alone with the senator at last, Perino started off smooth, as always.

"Senator, I want you to know, we're all very impressed with the way you've begun your term," he said, easing into the conversation. "You're really making a name for yourself."

McKenzie tilted his head, as if to acknowledge this phony praise. "Well, thank you, Vince, I'm trying to do what's best for the people of Illinois."

"Absolutely." Vince nodded. "That's what it's all about. That's why I wanted to see you. We're very concerned that you're, uh . . . not fully seeing the big picture on this banking bill."

The hairs on the back of McKenzie's neck began to rise. "Oh, I think I see the big picture very clearly," he scoffed. "This bill is a license for the banks to gamble with depositors' money, which is insured by the taxpayers."

Vince was expecting this answer; it was the same statement the senator had made at the press conference announcing his opposition to the bill. "I understand your view, Senator, and frankly, I think there's a lot of truth to what you're saying. But the fact is, most of our friends in the business very much want this bill to pass. And you have to admit, it would definitely open up the American Dream of home ownership to millions of people who never before could even think of buying a house."

McKenzie shook his head. "That's crazy, Vince. Most of those folks have no business trying to buy a house. They'll never be able to afford the payments."

Vince smiled sympathetically, but said, "Now, Senator, that's not the kind of talk that will get us minority and working-class votes in the next presidential election. We need to be the Party of the Big Tent; we need to broaden our appeal to lots of new voters."

McKenzie was amused by this cynical approach. He knew damn well that neither Vince nor any of his banker buddies gave a crap for minorities or working-class people—that was just a smokescreen to cover up what was really going on with the bill.

"I'm sorry, Vince, I just don't see it. I can't be supporting this bill."

For the first time, Vince let the Senator see a flash of ruthlessness in his eyes. "Senator, I have to be candid with you. If you work against us on this, it will be very hurtful to our friends. I may not be able to get them to forgive you."

A heavy silence hung in the room for several long moments.

"What are you telling me?" McKenzie said. "Don't give me all that bullshit posturing."

Vince did not flinch. "I'm trying to help you, Senator. You know me pretty well—I really hate it when we have vigorous battles in a primary. I much prefer that we spend our money in the general elections, where we're facing the other guys."

McKenzie's eyes narrowed to a hard focus. "You're telling me that if I buck you on this, you'll run somebody against me in the primary next time?"

Vince put up his hands in protest. In his most ingratiating voice, he said, "I would never make a threat like that, Senator. I'm just telling you that if you make all the bankers and their shareholders in this state line up against you, they'll find somebody very good to challenge you. And they'll put up a lot of money for whoever that is. Not even I may be able to help you overcome something like that."

McKenzie took in a deep breath, and let it out slowly. "Vince, I appreciate your insight. If I have to be a one-term senator, so be it."

Despite all his efforts to convince himself that the outcome would be different, in his heart, Vince had known that this was the way it would likely play out.

"Thanks for your time, Senator. We wish you all the best." He did not bother to shake hands before he left the office. It was the ultimate kiss of death.

———————————

On the way back to Springfield, Vince called the governor's office. He was, of course, put through to Parker immediately.

"So how did it go?" Parker asked in his gravelly voice, not even bothering with an exchange of greetings.

"About how we expected," Vince said. "We aren't going to get any help out of that asshole."

"Didn't I tell you that?" Parker grunted.

"Yes, you did," Vince said glumly.

The banking bill passed despite John McKenzie's opposition.

The Republicans took the White House in the 2000 election, and a governor from the South took over the Oval Office.

Shortly after the inauguration, in early 2001, Dan Gallagher announced he was leaving the US attorney's office to take a job in private law practice.

The ball was now in John McKenzie's court.

From the Memoirs of Mars Gregory:

I HAD JUST FINISHED a meeting with the accountants who were working on the tax return for Sammar. We had so many properties and so many things going on, preparation of the tax return had become a horrible, time-consuming ordeal every year. I was in a grumpy mood because of it.

Sam came in and sat down in my office. He was wearing what looked to be a new suit.

"Nice suit," I said, sarcastically. Frankly, I was annoyed because Sam took no part in helping with the tax return, or anything else involving the actual work of running Sammar, for that matter.

Sam gave me a sheepish look, and patted his ever-broadening belly. "Had to move up a size," he said. "I really need to go on a diet."

I was tempted to make a crack about too many steak salads, but thought better of it.

Sam gave me a very self-satisfied look. Usually this meant something interesting was about to emerge. This time, it was a blockbuster.

"The 64 acres," he said with a smug tone, "are back on the market."

I couldn't believe what I was hearing. Over three years had passed since we had been knocked out of the running by a buyer who supposedly had all the money they needed to buy the property.

"What happened?" was all I could muster.

Sam looked up, seemed to be counting the bulbs in the light fixture. "Oh, the other buyer had the money, no problem. But they couldn't get the City to rezone the property. Turns out, they didn't have the clout."

I immediately knew where this was going. "And I suppose you think we do?"

He gave me a knowing look. "I believe our friends in politics will help us."

Sam had become a master of the understatement.

Sam pushed the phone on my desk toward me. "Call Phil Angelino," he said simply. "We need him now."

———————————

We may have had the clout, but we were illiquid and definitely hurting for cash.

With the failure of the prior buyer staring them in the face, the sellers weren't able to raise the price from the $24 million they'd been talking about back in 1997. We thought that was pretty sweet. The way Phil structured the deal, we were going to have a contract to purchase the property, which gave us eighteen months to get zoning approval from the City, and then we would be obligated to close the transaction within nine months. But there was one big problem. The sellers were insisting we make a substantial deposit: ten percent of the purchase price, or $2.4 million, to prove we were serious. And we didn't have $2.4 million cold cash just sitting around.

We had to assemble a group of investors to help with the deposit. Working with Phil and some of his investor clients, we cobbled together about $2 million. But we were still about $400,000 short.

"Sam, I just got a call from Phil. He's having difficulty lining up the additional $400,000 for the deposit."

Sam waved me off dismissively. "That'll be no problem," he said. "That's chump change. I'll get someone."

And so I decided to quit worrying about it.

———————————

BUT SAM COULDN'T GET it done. Maybe he had tapped so many of his people for political contributions, maybe they weren't interested in real estate—whatever the reason, we couldn't come up with the cash.

By late summer of 2001, we had faked and stalled all we could, but we were still short $400,000. The sellers gave an ultimatum: put up the full $2.4 million by the end of August, or they would sell the property to someone else. And the sellers were adamant: if Sammar put up the deposit but failed to close, the entire deposit would be forfeited to the sellers. This was big-time risky.

I was petrified. We had spent countless hours on the potential purchase, not to mention hundreds of thousands of dollars on legal fees, planning fees, and environmental assessments. If the property wasn't put under contract, all of that investment would evaporate.

I was more than a little pissed at Sam.

Sam, meanwhile, was spending most of his time maneuvering politically. There was another election for governor coming up in 2002, and lots of potential contenders were calling on Sam to see if they could enlist his support. Sam was spending more time picking a horse than he was getting us an investor for the 64 acres.

"We're in deep shit," was all I could say. "I don't know what we're going to do."

Sam gave me a quizzical look. "Mars, aren't you trustee of your mother's estate?"

This was true. My mother was still alive, but she had been slipping deeper into dementia every day, and the family had been forced to put her into a home. Thanks to a life insurance policy that had paid off when my dad died, I controlled over a million dollars in my mother's investment account.

"I can't make my mother an investor in this deal. She doesn't even know what day of the week it is," I responded to Sam, angrily.

Sam gave me a look, the kind that said, *What kind of idiot are you?*

"You don't have to make her an investor," he said, like he was talking to kid in kindergarten. "I agree. It would not be an appropriate investment. Just borrow the money from her estate. Make out a promissory note to her, sign it, and put it in the file. When we find more investors, we'll repay the note. What's the problem?"

This one really set me back. "Jeez, Sam, I don't know. I'm a lawyer, for chrissakes. That's borderline, at best."

"Mars, we're out of time. We're up against the wall. We're going to lose our asses if we don't get this contract signed," Sam said again, giving me a frustrated look. He clearly had no qualms about it.

I went back down the hall to my office, closed the door, and sat at my desk staring out the window. I didn't want to do it, but we were in a hell of a jam. I started rationalizing. The $400K was only a portion of my mother's funds. She had plenty of other cash to keep paying her bills until we were able to find additional investors. My brother and I were the only beneficiaries of her estate if she died, so in effect I was only taking an advance on my own inheritance.

In the end, I went along with Sam's suggestion, arranging for the bank holding my mother's money to issue me a check for $400,000. On the check was written, "Loan to Mars." I wrote up a formal promissory note, evidencing the loan to myself, and signed it. Hell, I even provided for the payment of interest at the prime rate plus two percent, which was a typical rate charged by a third-party lender.

A few days later, Sammar was able to make the deposit, and the property was under contract. And about two months after that, Phil Angelino came through with two additional investors: $200,000 from one and another $250,000 from the other. Sammar repaid the $400,000 to my mother's account, plus interest, and the remainder went toward paying the costs of the South Side development.

Problem solved!

Chapter 9

IT WAS A GIVEN that Senator John McKenzie would have the opportunity to appoint Dan Gallagher's replacement for the US attorney seat, and he wanted to make certain his choice would have the most impact. Though there were many good things that Gallagher had accomplished, McKenzie knew that Gallagher had strong political ties to the Combine. McKenzie was angry that Gallagher hadn't made it a priority to investigate the Parker involvement in the Waterston accident back in 1994. He was convinced that there was a cover-up and that the party leaders had shielded Parker from connection to the incident.

McKenzie buzzed his assistant, Kate, and asked her to find the *Chicago Tribune* article from 1997.

"Which article, sir?" Katherine Craig had been Senator McKenzie's administrative assistant for more than four years and had reached the point, like all really good AAs, of being able to anticipate her boss's thoughts almost before he had them. She was good, but she wasn't an actual mind reader.

John chuckled to himself as he realized he asked an impossible task. "It's the article that appeared right before the Parker campaign for governor. The one about the traffic accident where all the kids died."

"Oh my God, I remember that," Kate replied. "What a horribly sad situation."

She found the article later that day, and as he read once again about the horrific crash, he realized he was not totally without recourse against the sons of bitches who were forcing him out. If he played it right, he could leave a legacy from which the scoundrels in his own party would not soon recover.

THE NEXT MORNING, JOHN called Kate into his office. "Kate, please get me that list of young lawyers, the list of candidates for US attorney. I want to see who the fat cats have in mind for the job."

"Sir, I hate to remind you of this, but I think the president makes all appointments of United States attorneys," Kate said, tongue in cheek. She knew if her boss wanted a particular man or woman to be appointed US attorney for the Northern District of Illinois, he could get it done. It was a matter of senatorial privilege to pick the US attorney for a senator's home state. McKenzie intended to exercise that privilege.

"I know, I know, but you know how I am once I set my mind to something. I'm pretty sure I can see to it that the person I choose gets appointed, aren't you?"

"I'm quite sure of it, sir," she responded dutifully, giggling. "I know you'll pick the right person."

Kate felt badly for her boss. She knew he would be forced out of office at the end of his term, and she thought that was a true shame. She knew how dedicated he was and knew he was a good man with worthy intentions. It would serve those others right if her boss recommended someone for US attorney who would go after some, or all, of that entire crowd—maybe clean up some of the mess that had taken over Chicago and Springfield.

"I'll get right on it, sir," Kate added.

John removed his glasses and tossed them onto his desk, gazing out the window. He was formulating a plan.

———

SENATOR JOHN MCKENZIE SAT at his desk looking over the list of candidates for the US attorney. The list was unsurprising and uninspiring. It was filled with politically active young Republican lawyers, all of whom the senator had met at one fundraiser or another, each hand-picked by the political bosses. They were men, and a couple of women, who would "go along to get along," as the old saying goes.

McKenzie couldn't forget how the Parker investigation had been mishandled. He just couldn't let it go. He was deeply troubled by the image in his mind's eye of the burning van, the hysterical mother. He was in a unique position to do something, and do something he would. This was the original reason why he'd come to Washington, after all.

As John bounced from one name to another on the list of lawyers before him, he realized he needed a fresh face. *Someone who is not involved in Chicago or Illinois politics in any way. Someone from somewhere else. Someone who is not on this list,* he thought. *Someone who has never heard of Vince Perino.*

He picked up the phone, punched a button. "Kate, come see me."

She bustled into his roomy office. "Sir?" she asked, ever efficient.

"I need a list of prosecutors from other states who are making names for themselves. I need up-and-comers who show promise and who are not politically connected to this or any other particular administration."

Having anticipated such a request, Kate was quick to respond. "I was recently reading about a young prosecutor in Boston who's been receiving a lot of ink, getting some recognition as a do-gooder, a straight shooter," she said. "I remember him specifically because he has your name: Franklin McKenzie. I believe he might be just what the doctor ordered."

"Boston, huh? I don't know. Boston is no different from Chicago when it comes to politics, is it?"

Kate knew her boss well, and she knew what he was looking for. "No, no. This guy is different. You should at least check him out, sir. I don't think you'll regret it."

"Okay," John agreed. "Would you please put together a file with everything you can find about him? A full-scale, detailed, research report. I want everything. I want to know about his parents, his grammar school, his high school, college, law school. Everything."

Kate had already done much of the research concerning this man. She believed him to be a perfect fit. It appeared he had the balls he'd need to shake up the entire political landscape of Chicago and the State of Illinois.

John McKenzie spent several days reading through everything Kate had found on Franklin McKenzie, and he decided she was right. He thanked her profusely for alerting him to this candidate from Boston. In John's mind, he was perfect. This fellow Irishman had laid waste to corruption and gang crime in his home city with prosecution after prosecution. He bucked the established powers and simply did his job as a prosecutor. Just as a kicker, the sweetest of sweeteners, his last name would be a constant reminder to the good ol' boys back in Illinois who were putting John out of office. Long after he was gone, they would remember exactly who it was that had royally fucked up their lives.

FRANKLIN MCKENZIE WALKED INTO Senator John McKenzie's office with an air of subdued inner confidence. He was of medium height, reasonably trim, with his dark brown hair thinning slightly. He exuded the attitude of a bulldog, which impressed John immediately.

"How was your flight?" John asked, as he motioned to Kate to bring in coffee. "How do you take your coffee, Frank? I hope you don't mind me calling you Frank?"

"No, of course. Please do, Senator."

Frank looked at Kate and whispered, "Cream and sugar, please." Then he turned toward John and said politely, "The flight was fine, no complaints. Thanks for asking. And thanks for considering me for this position, Senator McKenzie."

The senator motioned for Frank to sit in a huge wingback chair right in front of his desk.

"First things first. Please call me John." He continued, "Your reputation precedes you. You really tore those gangs a new one back there in your town, and I bet that alderman . . . what was his name?"

"Fiochhi?"

"Yes, Fiochhi. I bet the former Alderman Fiochhi won't soon forget you. How many years did he get?"

"Twelve," Frank answered humbly.

"Frank, look, I'm not going to be a senator much longer, so let's just cut to the chase. Are you willing to move your family to Chicago?"

This question completely surprised Frank McKenzie. He'd expected a lot of questions about his background, his experience, his ethics. "Well, sir . . . John . . . my wife and I haven't discussed it. I just got the inquiry from your staff the other day, and I really didn't know if this was a serious opportunity."

The senator eyed his candidate. "It's serious, Frank. What I want to know is this: will you go after the corruption in Chicago—and Springfield—like you did in Boston?"

There was a slight pause while Frank collected his thoughts. He looked around at the richly paneled walls and all the photos of important people hanging here and there. There were a number of presidents pictured with John, both past and present. Everybody was smiling. And Frank was being offered his dream job, a chance to make history as a prosecutor.

He sat forward in his chair.

"John, I'm a prosecutor. That's my thing. My calling, so to speak. I hate politicians who think that their shit doesn't stink. I despise them. I have no problem with honest politicians. I respect public servants. The people who dedicate their lives to public service deserve all the respect that can be given to them. However, there are way too many men and women who see public office as a way to make a score for themselves and their friends. I can't accept that. It makes me crazy."

The senator nodded. He liked what he was hearing from this determined young man, who seemed almost like a choirboy in his earnestness, but with just enough edge that John felt confident that Frank wouldn't let anything— or anyone—get in his way.

"So, Senator McKenzie—uh, John . . . my answer to your question is this: you bet your ass I'll go after those sons of bitches. If there's a public servant, a politician out there who is thinking of violating the public trust by committing a crime on my watch, he better think twice."

John looked long and hard at Frank McKenzie, paused, and asked a question both men would long remember.

"How would you like to go after a sitting governor who might well be responsible for the deaths of six little children?"

Franklin McKenzie looked at Senator John McKenzie with an expression of cold hard steel. "For that," he said quietly, "I'll move my wife and kids to Chicago."

WHEN FRANK RETURNED TO Boston later that afternoon, he was feeling guilty that he had accepted the position in Chicago without discussing it with his wife, Mary Margaret.

After dinner, with their two children put to bed, Frank and Maggie were finishing the last of their bottle of wine. Frank took a deep breath and turned to his wife.

"I want to tell you about my meeting today with Senator McKenzie."

"Yeah, sorry we didn't have a chance to talk about it before. So how'd it go?"

"Well, the senator seems like a good man. He wants someone to take over as US attorney in Illinois. The political corruption is rampant, and he's offered me the job."

Mary Margaret turned toward Frank and said, "I have no doubt he's chosen the right man."

"Thanks for that, Maggie. If you're willing to move to Chicago, I'd like to take the position."

"Okay, Frank. How about we go to Chicago next weekend and look for a new home? But tell me this: haven't you already told the senator you'd take the job?"

Frank just reached out with a grin and gave Maggie a big hug and a pinch on the rear.

THE APPOINTMENT OF FRANKLIN McKenzie as US attorney led to wild speculation in all corners of the political spectrum in Illinois. Where had this guy come from? Who knew him? How do we get to him? Can we control him? The pols were agog that the Republican senator, John McKenzie, had gone outside the state and picked a career prosecutor from Boston to be the new US attorney for the Northern District of Illinois. They thought since John and Frank shared the same last name, the senator had appointed a relative. *That* was something they could at least have understood. But they weren't related at all! What a maverick this Senator McKenzie was!

McKenzie hit the ground running, launching a relentless investigation into the Waterston accident, raising eyebrows everywhere. It became his cause célèbre.

From the Memoirs of Mars Gregory:

I LOOKED AT THIS character Franklin McKenzie, and his tactics were quite familiar to me. He was the same kind of man as my business partner, Sam. Sure, Sam was a swarthy, olive-skinned Arab, and McKenzie was a fair-haired Irishman; their backgrounds couldn't have been more different. However, each had the ability to set his sights like a laser on a single goal and go after it with an uncommon sense of purpose. Both men were experts at finding the weakness of their opponent and capitalizing on that weakness. They were unflinching and unconcerned with what others thought. Neither of them had political ties that would dissuade them from their quest.

The only difference I could see was that Sam would do anything, legal or illegal, to reach his ultimate objective. McKenzie would not. However, he was not afraid to use tactics that were only *technically* legal as bludgeoning instruments with which to beat his victim to death—figuratively speaking, of course. If you look hard enough, everyone has secrets. He would find those secrets and then use them against the person in his sights. Nothing was out-of-bounds.

Sam and Frank McKenzie were opposite sides of the same coin.

Sam knew where an investigation run by a guy like McKenzie would lead. This investigation, if it stayed on the course it was headed, could catch up to and eventually bring down the governor. The smartest political operators were beginning to hedge their bets, to adjust their plans. They always had to stay one move ahead in order to maintain the status quo. My partner was in search of a horse to back in a race where all of the traditional rules were about to change.

Chapter 10

IN THE FALL OF 2001, it was getting to be time for anyone who was going to run in 2002 to toss their hat into the ring.

Mishka "Please call me Mike" Kovach was not an impressive man upon first meeting. He was brought to Sammar's office by his father-in-law, Walter Roche, a very powerful alderman and the singular, absolute boss of one of the most important wards in the city of Chicago. Mike stood behind his father-in-law like a boy being introduced to the headmaster of his future boarding school, nervous, almost cowering. He was much like Little Lord Fauntleroy, all dressed up in his Sunday best, clearly out of his depth. And what a head of hair!

Mike was being presented to Sam and Mars as the future candidate for the governor's office. Hard to believe, but this crazy investigation by the new US attorney was making anything seem possible.

"Mike graduated from Northwestern Law School," Walter was saying, as he walked into Sam's office. "After passing the bar, he worked at the state's attorney's office, making his bones in a courtroom. He was elected four years ago as a congressman, which showed his abilities on the campaign trail. I think he's ready now for the big move to the governor's mansion."

Mars smirked visibly. He couldn't help himself. It seemed so incredibly farfetched, looking at this nonentity of a person sitting there in Sam's office.

Roche proceeded to give a remarkably cogent political analysis, even if it seemed a little over the top. "If this investigation by the Feds leads where I think it will lead, Ed Parker's through. The Republicans will then run Thomas Parker, the state attorney general, because they have nobody else to run. If that scenario plays itself out, the Democrats will regain the governor's seat. Nobody is going to vote for another candidate named Parker. Most of the voters won't know the difference, or they'll think he's related. A Democrat, frankly any Democrat, will be able to waltz right into the governor's office."

Roche looked at his son-in-law tentatively. That was not exactly a ringing endorsement, but good old Mishka ("Please call me Mike") didn't seem to mind or be in any way offended by the backhanded compliment. Roche continued, summing up his very unusual pitch. "So, the real election will be the primary, to get the Democratic nomination. We would like your support."

The political insiders, of course, had figured out that Sam had played a key role in getting Molly Brannigan nominated in the previous governor's race. Sam had established himself as a man who could raise money for political campaigns, a man who could raise *a lot* of money for said campaigns, so it was no surprise that Walter had brought Mike by to meet Sam. He was looking for a commitment from Sam to help out his candidate.

Sam stroked his chin thoughtfully. "Very compelling, Walter, very compelling. Have you thought about who's going to run the campaign?"

Roche did not hesitate. "We've already signed up Johnny Jarzik."

This brought a smile to Sam's face. "We know him well."

There was a reason Walter Roche had accumulated a great deal of power.

He did his research. He knew and understood exactly who he was speaking to. Sam's reaction was priceless. When Roche said the magic words, "I can promise you this: you would have a friend in the governor's office who knows how to repay a favor," Mars knew he was looking at Sam's newest candidate for governor. There would most certainly be others. Of course there would be others who would run, but this young man was going to be the candidate who would be supported by Sam Alsheriti.

But before he would commit, Sam had some business to do.

"Mike, you have very impressive credentials," Sam said, with that smooth, oily tone of his. "I absolutely believe you are the man to be the next governor."

Mike beamed from ear to ear.

"But, Walter," Sam said softly, almost so softly you couldn't hear him, "there are a couple of things we need some help with." He had subtly turned the dialogue from Roche's empty-suit son-in-law to the real power broker at the table.

Roche was very experienced at this game. He kept his face totally impassive, waiting for Sam to make the ask.

Sam tilted his head skyward, as if he was studying the ceiling tiles. It was one of his idiosyncrasies, almost as if he didn't like making eye contact when floating a political proposition.

"Well, Walter, as you know, we've been working quite hard to buy the South Loop 64 acres."

Roche nodded. "Yeah, the old railroad yard, right?"

Sam and Mars both nodded.

"We're about to go before the City Council Zoning Committee for the development plan approval. We really need that to pass."

Roche nodded. "No problem," he said in a matter-of-fact tone. "Ray DeRossa has already signed on to help us in the campaign."

Sam and Mars exchanged a quick, knowing glance. DeRossa was the all-powerful chairman of the Zoning Committee, and DeRossa was already in Mike's camp, so it would be child's play for Roche to get him to back the zoning plan.

"That's very much appreciated, Walter," Sam said, patting the powerful alderman affectionately on the arm. "You may have heard," he continued cautiously, as he figured a man like Walter Roche probably heard everything, "that our friends on the other side of the aisle are very unhappy with their current senator. In fact, I'm hearing that they're so unhappy with John McKenzie that they've told him they won't support him if he runs again."

Roche nodded his head. "Yeah, but you're talking about 2004—that's three years from now. We're talking about next year, the governor's race."

Sam held his face impassive. Mars knew that look meant something big was coming. "Our dear friend Malik Alawi is looking at that US Senate race for John McKenzie's seat."

Roche merely nodded. "Who the hell does this kid think he is, with limited experience in the state senate and he's already thinking about running for US Senate? He doesn't have any name recognition."

This was a rather ironic statement, considering that no one had ever heard of Mike Kovach, either. But Roche was an astute politician, always looking for political intelligence.

Roche said with a snort, "What the hell does Malik Alawi have going for him?"

Sam looked at him with eyes that were focused like lasers. "A black guy will get one hundred percent of the black vote. That's about 38 percent of the total votes in a Democratic primary. We will engineer a three-way race. In a three-way race, the black guy wins."

Mars appeared shocked.

Roche shrugged. "Hard to deny," was all he could say. After all, that was how Harold Washington had become the city's first African-American mayor, beating both a white incumbent woman and the son of Richard J. Daley.

Sam pressed his advantage. "If we can get any white support at all, especially someone of your stature, Walter," he said, in his best ingratiating manner, "Malik will win."

Roche was quickly evaluating the pros and cons in his mind's eye. On the one hand, the senate race was off in the future—a lifetime in the world of politics. Why bother worrying about it now? On the other hand, Mike was going to need support in the black community to win the Democratic nomination in the governor's race. Suddenly, he had a flash of his own inspiration. "Suppose Mike trades endorsements with Malik?"

Sam just about jumped out of his chair. "Yes! Yes! Malik will deliver the black vote to Mike, and in three years, if you can get even a small percentage of white votes for Malik, they'll both win!"

Roche looked at Mike, who responded with a blank stare. The kid didn't get it. But then, he didn't have to. This deal had been cut.

When Sam shook Mike's hand, he looked like a shark that had just spotted floundering fish in his path. Sam loved young politicians he thought he might be able to mold and ultimately control. He'd become an expert at recognizing the type. It was his true genius, and you could see in his eyes that Sam believed he had just struck gold.

Sam had been waiting for an opportunity like this for years, since he'd first read the article in the *Tribune* about that terrible accident and begun fantasizing about the outcome of the investigation. He always had his ear to the ground, and he knew the truth about where the bribery scandal would lead. That investigation could very well shift the reins of power in the state-house. Sam knew this, and he was ready to pounce.

If Sam could help this young, naïve political newbie become governor, and make a deal that could send a United States senator to Washington, Sam would be the kingmaker of Illinois politics.

He came around from behind his desk and greeted both men with a broad smile and pats on the back.

"Let's have lunch. Are you hungry?" Sam said with relish, rubbing his hands together. "It's on me."

SAM WANTED TO IMPRESS the young future governor, so, of course, they went to Gene & Georgetti, where anyone with Sam was treated like royalty. Although he had been to G&G before, Mike was doing a good job of acting impressed as he scanned the room, discreetly pointing out a number of judicial and political heavies he recognized.

It was a long lunch, with lots of drinks, during which they talked about everything from sports to history, entertainment to politics. Sam ordered steak salad with ranch dressing, of course.

Mike had all of the standard-issue qualifications it took to become a politician in the city of Chicago. He had a modest upbringing with first-generation, ethnic, hardworking parents, who sacrificed and scrimped on behalf of their two boys. Mike grew up in apartments in the Slavic area of the city, a real rags-to-riches story. He did well in his studies all the way through law school. He was perfect for Chicago-style politics.

Kovach came out of his shell as the drinks flowed, and, as it turned out, he was really quite likable—a regular comedian, outgoing and gregarious.

"I've always been a big reader," he told us. "I read a lot of history and biographies, and I'm a big fan of Abraham Lincoln and John F. Kennedy. I also love Elvis Presley."

This got everyone laughing. What a crazy segue, from Abraham Lincoln to Elvis without a break in the timeline. It gave everybody whiplash. The kid talked a blue streak. Plus, one look at the pompadour on his head and you thought Elvis might actually be stopping by to visit his twin.

"I loved being a prosecutor, you know, enforcing the law," he went on, without skipping a beat. "I worked a year in the courtroom for the judge known as the 'hugging judge'—he used to make the baddest-ass, droopy-pants-wearing gang members or the craziest, tattooed, pierced, purple-Mohawk-sporting punk rockers hug their mothers in front of the whole courtroom, or he'd lock them up until they did. It was great."

Sam was picturing Mike standing in front of the microphone at a political rally with Sam pulling the strings in the background and Mike parroting every word of a carefully prepared script. Mike was not dumb; he was well-read and conversant, but you could see that he just wasn't savvy in any way. He was just a real *Mr. Smith Goes to Washington* kind of fresh-faced kid who would do or say anything he was told to get into the limelight. He was an excited boy on his first trip out of Palookaville.

Sam leaned far back in his chair, took a long draw on his big black cigar, and let a blue cloud drift into the air above him. Then he leaned forward and said quietly, seriously, looking at Roche, "We will get started right away, Walter. Your son-in-law will make a great candidate." He turned to Mike and kept his gaze, eye-to-eye.

"Mike, you are going to be governor. I'll see to it. We will raise enough money to ensure a victory. But, that will just be the start, my friend. You are going to have a long, successful career representing the people of this great state. Someday, you could be on your way to Washington."

This statement raised eyebrows all around. Sly smiles appeared at the corners of the mouths of each and every member of the little lunch party.

Walter Roche laughed out loud and cracked, "Yeah, but I imagine your skinny black friend might have something to say about that!"

They all laughed, except Sam.

"Don't underestimate Malik," he said quietly. "The kid has talent."

Kovach was hooked. His eyes were like saucers. You could see him joining in on Sam's grand self-styled fantasy for him. He was 110 percent on board.

Ever the politician, Sam excused himself to work the room a bit. When he reappeared, he was accompanied by a familiar face.

Orenthal Mitchell was a handsome, well-built young man in his early thirties with an engaging way about him. He was clean shaven, well over six feet tall, with medium dark skin, and he wore his hair tight to his head. His brilliant smile radiated warmth, and he spoke with confidence in a deep voice smooth as silk. He was proud to be born and bred in Chicago. Oren's parents were active in their community, and had made certain that Oren not only graduated high school, but would go on to attend a local college, which would serve him well as he pursued a career in the Chicago political scene. While Oren's size could be intimidating, he was actually a gentle soul who made friends easily, and he was always there when you needed him.

"Mike," Sam said to Kovach, "I would like you to meet Orenthal Mitchell. He is a guy to keep your eye on, a real go-getter, a good guy to have on your side." He turned to Orenthal and locked his gaze on him. "Oren," he said, "meet Mike Kovach, our next governor! You should get to know each other. You are both part of the future of this city and this state."

Both men beamed. Mike stood and warmly shook hands with Orenthal. Then he invited him to sit down and join the group. Oren begged off, saying he was with another party. However, he immediately whipped out his card and gave it to Mike. "Another time," he said. "Let's get together real soon. I'd like to help you in any way I can."

Just then, a very comely, sexy waitress leaned over to put plates on the next table. As she did, her rather short skirt rode up and very nearly exposed her perfect ass to the world. A flash of pink undies was visible for a split second—enough to cause every eye at the table to wander and every man to momentarily lose his train of thought.

There were snickers and quiet laughter, the universal language of men worldwide. The girl seemed to be oblivious. Mike stood again, chuckling, and shook Orenthal's hand with a warm smile and a hearty pat on the back. "We'll get together very soon, Oren, I promise. I'll call you . . . we'll have lunch . . . nice to meet you, my friend."

THOSE TWO YOUNG MEN would never forget that meeting. Mike would always remember having been introduced as "our next governor," and Oren would always remember how he was included in a group he perceived as a bunch of political heavyweights.

It wasn't long before Mike kept his promise and called Orenthal. Following a long lunch together, and a lot of laughs, Oren became an ardent supporter of the campaign to elect Mike Kovach governor of the State of Illinois, and the young men became fast friends.

Sam had been certain that would happen. He just had a knack. He also knew that both men would see him, Sam Alsheriti, as the guy who brought them together, the one that started it all.

It was the beginning of a wild ride.

Chapter 11

JOSHUA BAKER WAS THE chief investigator assigned to the office of US Attorney Franklin McKenzie. Josh and the staff had spent years doing tedious, patient, gumshoe work. Now McKenzie was kick-starting a whole new intensive approach to the investigation, holding weekly briefing and strategy sessions, assigning extra investigators and federal agents, and pressing for results. The investigation was finally working its way up through the Ed Parker political organization. Baker, his partner N. J. Novak, and their team started with the bag men at the Joliet DMV, relentlessly pressuring layer after layer of political intermediaries and fixers to roll over and rat out the link above them in the chain of command.

Baker was just a little smug about how he had perfected the technique of pressuring these cogs in the machine to break. He would have Novak and at least two tall and sinister-looking federal agents in razor-sharp blue suits and aviator sunglasses show up at the target's home at six a.m. They would bang loudly on the front door, wake up the entire household, and demand to talk to the target.

Usually, it was the wife who answered the door, hair askew, half asleep in her bathrobe, shocked when one of the agents shoved his gold badge into her face. Often the wife was so disoriented and frightened, she actually invited the agents inside to wait while she fetched her husband. The agents absolutely loved that, because now it would be harder, if not impossible, for their target to get them out.

Then the husband would stumble down the stairs, rubbing sleep from his eyes, still in his pajamas or sweatpants, totally panicked. In some cases, the guy would break down right then and there and spill the beans, pleading through tears to the agents that he had only been following the orders of his supervisor. Crying and pointing he had a wife and kids upstairs, he would do anything, just cut him a break.

As they made their way ever higher in the Parker machine, the going got tougher. By now, the politicians in question knew what was coming and had lawyered up. When the agents made their raids at the crack of dawn, they were politely given a lawyer's business card and told, "I'm happy to cooperate with you. Please contact my lawyer to arrange a meeting."

Unless they had a warrant, there was nothing the agents could do but turn tail and lumber back down the front walk to their cars, holding the lawyer's card in their hands.

When this happened, Baker would unleash a blizzard of subpoenas, targeting the guy's income tax returns, his email, his credit card records, his telephone records, his expense account reports, everything. They would pore over each and every entry. Every bill and statement and record would be scrutinized. Novak was tenacious, and with his background in forensic accounting, it usually didn't take long to find some indiscretion or transgression. All it took was a failure to report some item of taxable income, some reimbursement of a phony expense claim, or, best of all, the discovery of an illicit affair. Most of these men were married. Once they had stockpiled evidence against him, they would meet with the guy and his lawyer.

Baker and Novak loved these confrontations. They would hold the interviews at their federal offices, which were incredibly intimidating to begin with. The visitors had to be signed in and buzzed through several security doors by stone-faced personnel before ending up in a sparse interviewing room. The gray cinder-block walls were intended to evoke the idea of already being in prison. Baker would make the poor sap, his target for the day, sit with his nervous lawyer, waiting in that bleak room, intentionally letting the possibility of incarceration sink in.

Eventually, Baker would make a grand entrance, always accompanied by a few agents in their standard-issue blue suits, looking very somber. The politician would sit there silently. His lawyer was obviously going to do all the talking. The lawyer would come in figuring that his client had been fingered by some flunky subordinate, and the case was going to be a "his word against mine" kind of thing, almost always misjudging and underestimating the government's case.

Baker would then lay the evidence before the lawyer and his client.

"Allow me to show you this series of expense reports," Baker would say. "Do you see these claims for mileage and meals on such and such date?"

The lawyer was trained to remain impassive, but the pol would start squirming.

"Yeah, so what?" the lawyer would ask.

"Well, if you'll kindly look here at these sign-in sheets from the security desk at your client's office building, you will see that for each of the days that your guy is claiming he was traveling, as set forth on those mileage sheets, your guy was actually in the office all day. Do you see his signature there? It's his, we checked it out."

Baker would then put down on the table each of the sign-in sheets, next to the respective expense reports. The lawyer would scan them, sometimes running his finger from page to page, looking diligently, making sure the dates linked up.

After a few minutes, the lawyer would feign outrage. "This is penny-ante stuff. This is no federal offense."

Baker would hand the lawyer a sheet of paper.

"That's the text of United States Code, Title 18, Section 1341. I'm sure you've read it before," he would say coldly. "It's the federal mail fraud statute. These reimbursement claims were mailed to Springfield, and the checks were mailed to your guy. That's two counts of mail fraud for each and every one of those phony vouchers. The penalty for each offense is up to twenty years in prison. We have your guy on sixteen counts. That means technically we can seek up to 320 years."

This is when the client would turn white.

"But relax," Baker would continue, coming in for the kill. "The judge doesn't always sentence the max and usually lets the sentence on each count run concurrently. Your guy will probably be out in five or ten years."

This is when the lawyer would turn white.

"I would like to meet privately with my client," the lawyer would invariably stutter.

After a short intermission, Baker and his team would be called back into the room, and the lawyer would proceed to ask what kind of deal the Feds were offering.

This scenario never failed. It had been played out time after time, so often it had become entertaining to McKenzie, Baker, and their team. They would sometimes place bets on how long it would take for a guy to crack. There were office pools.

Baker would always have what he needed to start the cycle again on the next guy in the chain. And it had taken them nearly all the way to the top. Underling after underling had folded as they slowly worked their way up the chain of command. Now they had the key witness who could give them the ultimate prize. They had the governor's chief of staff himself, a fellow from a famously prominent Republican family, squarely in their sights.

They were only one step away from adding that final trophy to their wall: Governor Edward G. Parker.

BAKER AND NOVAK PLANNED their typical meeting with Skylar Stillwell and his attorney. But this time, things did not go exactly as expected. Within one step of the governor himself, Baker's process stalled.

This time Baker was up against a highly experienced attorney, one of the best money could buy. Stillwell had hired Charles Davies, a former top assistant to Dan Gallagher himself, the former US attorney whose position Frank McKenzie had filled.

In the parlance of the trade, Davies, after retiring from public service, had "gone over to the dark side." He was now in a lucrative private practice representing wealthy people accused of white-collar crimes. Davies knew all too well how the game was played from the other side, and he had thoroughly prepared his client. When Baker and his team confronted Stillwell with the sworn affidavits of three subordinates, all of whom were prepared to testify that Skylar had orchestrated a cover-up attempting to keep the heat of the commercial driver's license scandal off the governor, Davies patiently explained that Skylar would not, under any circumstances, roll over on his political patron. He was determined to stay loyal to the governor, and he would take the fall himself if need be. Davies said he was prepared to confront at trial each and every one of the witnesses who had given the affidavits. He was quite ready to take them apart on cross-examination as petty criminals who'd lied to save their own skins.

Baker knew Davies well. He and Novak had worked with him on numerous cases back when Gallagher was their boss. It would be one helluva tough trial.

Josh Baker wrote a memo to his boss, Frank McKenzie, detailing the dilemma. A few days later, McKenzie summoned Baker to a meeting in McKenzie's spacious office on the fifth floor of the Dirksen Federal Building on Dearborn Street.

As Baker walked in and settled himself into a red leather chair in front of McKenzie's expansive desk, he could see McKenzie, surrounded by stacks of paper, reading his memo.

McKenzie looked over the top of the document, his eyes blazing at Baker like hot coals. He was not the type for friendly formalities.

"So this prick Skylar Stillwell is still stonewalling us?"

Baker replied, "Boss, we put the full court press on this little shit. We hit him with everything we had. He's not budging. He told us Parker was good to him, and he wasn't going to roll over on the governor."

McKenzie sneered. "Let's put him in a cell with Bubba. That'll change his tune."

Baker shook his head. "I don't think we can play it that way, boss. Charles Davies is not going to let that happen."

McKenzie's eyes narrowed to thin slits. "Fuckin' Davies. I hate people who turn traitor." He shook his head. "I made a promise to clean up this town and this state. That's what I'm gonna do. Let the chips fall where they may."

"Boss, what do you want to do about Stillwell?"

McKenzie picked up the memo and turned to a page where he'd made a big checkmark in the margin next to one of the paragraphs. "You mention here Stillwell was carrying on an affair with a gal who was working for a state agency."

Baker nodded. "Yeah, but he was in the midst of getting a divorce, so we couldn't get any leverage on him there. In fact, he's still seeing the woman. Some people think they may be getting engaged."

McKenzie thought for a second. "I may have a way to get to this guy. Did our friend Skylar get her the job with the state?"

"No," Baker sighed. "We checked that out. She was hired by the state two years before she even met Stillwell. They met when she was working at an event where the governor gave a speech."

McKenzie sat back, deep in thought, pressing the tips of his fingers together, almost as if he were praying.

"Send Novak and the agents to roust her out of bed. Let's see what she says."

Baker was surprised. "Boss, really, she has nothing to do with this. She has two kids from a prior marriage, two little girls. Stillwell was getting a divorce, he asked her out, they did the wild thing, and now they're playing house. Where is this going to take us?"

"Maybe we'll get lucky," McKenzie said, with a sneer. "Maybe she'll lie to us."

Baker rubbed his forehead with his hand. "I don't know, boss. Really, this seems out of bounds to me. We have no reason to think she did anything wrong."

"Out of bounds?" McKenzie jumped to his feet. He began to pace his office. "You gotta be kidding me. We're up against the most corrupt, immoral, greedy political organization in the country. Six kids died in that fucking accident . . . six little innocent kids! Nothing is out of bounds!"

Baker held his ground. "Come on, boss. You know as well as I do the media doesn't like it when we go after innocent family members. This could hurt our image—your image."

McKenzie shot an icy cold glare at his colleague. "Fuck my image and fuck the goddamn media! We're gonna turn Stillwell, whatever it takes!"

Baker was genuinely shocked now. He had worked for five different US attorneys in his career. He'd never seen anything like this. He took a deep breath. He only needed a few more years to qualify for his pension. He didn't want to spend it collecting tax liens. "Okay, boss. I'll set it up."

———————————

TWO WEEKS LATER, AT six on a rainy Monday morning, Frank McKenzie got what he wanted.

Lisa Gronkiewicz was sleeping soundly in her bed in her comfortable suburban home, wearing only a faded, oversized College of DuPage T-shirt. She was abruptly awakened by a persistent, loud pounding on her front door.

She scurried downstairs, hoping to stop the noise before it woke her two children. When she opened the door, her heart leaped into her mouth. There were four men standing on her front stoop; three of them were tall and trim, dressed in matching blue suits and aviator sunglasses, and standing at parade rest behind the fourth man. The fourth man was holding a gold badge in a leather case and was dressed in a wrinkled tweed sport jacket and loosened brown tie. The guy with the badge did the talking.

"Ms. Gronkiewicz, my name is Joshua Baker. This is my partner, N.J. Novak, and agents Kelly and Reed. We work for the federal government. May we come in, ma'am? We would like to ask you some questions regarding a Mr. Skylar Stillwell."

Lisa didn't know that she could have just said no; most people don't. So she stepped aside while two of the men, Baker and Novak, entered her home. The two other agents went back down the walk and stood by a black Ford Crown Victoria while they whispered into the cuffs of their shirts.

Her two young daughters huddled at the top of the stairs, crying.

Lisa ran upstairs, grabbed a robe, threw it on, and tried to comfort her terrified children. She brought them downstairs to the kitchen and began to make them breakfast.

She was so stunned by the early-morning intrusion and the pointed and embarrassing questions that were being asked about her relationship with Sky, right in front of her little girls, that Lisa blurted out, through intermittent tears, that although she knew Skylar Stillwell, they were just friends. There was no relationship other than professional between them. After all, Skylar was a married man. She proceeded to tell lie after lie, denying that she had ever been in an intimate relationship with him, insisting they met through work channels, and that was the extent of the relationship. She just wanted the questions to stop.

Within an hour, Baker had what he needed.

No one ever told Lisa Gronkiewicz it's a federal crime to lie to a federal agent about anything, even if what you're lying about is not a crime. No one ever thought to tell her because, although her boyfriend was a target of an investigation, and had a very good lawyer, no one, least of all Skylar Stillwell, ever dreamed that Lisa could become a target in any way. He'd taken great pains to ensure she was insulated. He'd kept her away from anything that could become a problem. Lisa had done absolutely nothing wrong.

The last thing Baker told her before they left was that she should not say anything to Skylar Stillwell about this interview. "If you tell him about this, you're interfering with a federal investigation," Baker said.

This was bullshit, but she was so petrified, she believed it.

A federal indictment of Lisa Gronkiewicz was prepared and filed. Frank McKenzie ordered it held under seal, until they were ready to use it at their next meeting with Skylar Stillwell.

Chapter 12

AT NINE O'CLOCK ON a beautiful Friday morning, Mars was rushing out the front door of the Whitehall Hotel on East Delaware Street, having spent the previous evening in town entertaining a few bankers into the early morning hours. As he often did, he'd chosen to sleep an extra forty-five minutes rather than take the time for breakfast. Prior to flagging a cab, he ducked into Starbucks and grabbed a venti latte. He needed to clear the cobwebs before his ten-o'clock meeting. He reprimanded himself for having too much scotch and ordering that third bottle of wine.

As Mars waited in line to place his order, he noticed a familiar face at a nearby table. It was Claudia Wodecki, a secretary from his old law firm, sitting with a very attractive friend. Mars hadn't seen Claudia in years.

Claudia had been the best looking woman at the firm, by far. All the men, single and married, had admired her beautiful face and impeccable style. Mars had had a crush on Claudia, but never let anyone know. Claudia's only possible flaws, in his mind, were her relatively flat chest, and maybe her size eight was a little larger than he preferred. Mars had always been attracted to slender women. A size four or smaller, with a tight skinny ass, was his type. However, with Claudia's beautiful skin, brilliant smile, and great sense of humor, Mars could have easily overlooked any of these perceived imperfections.

Mars recalled Claudia had been studying to be a paralegal when she'd met Stephen Kaye, a tall, handsome, and successful client of the firm. Stephen was a commodity trader at the Chicago Board of Trade, and was making a fortune trading on his own account. Claudia and Stephen had met one day at the firm, and it was love at first sight. They married within a few short months, and soon thereafter Claudia had quit her job. Though the men in the firm were envious, most realized Stephen had all the goods to win her over.

After adding artificial sweetener and nutmeg to his latte, Mars walked to Claudia's table to say hello. He noticed her smile as she recognized him.

"Claudia, so good to see you. How have you been?" Mars said, as he bent down to kiss Claudia on the cheek. "How's Stephen?"

"Hi, Mars. I'm good," she responded enthusiastically. "I want you to meet my friend Alana. She and I started a new business venture last year."

"No kidding? That's great, Claudia," Mars said, extending his hand to Alana. He could not help but notice Alana's good looks and beautiful smile. Mars also couldn't help noticing that Claudia looked better than ever, and was the beneficiary of what appeared to be an outstanding boob job. *Holy cow*, as Harry Carey would say.

"I've got to run to a meeting, but let's get together for lunch and catch up," he offered.

Claudia reached into her jacket and handed Mars her card. She said, "Give me a call next week. It would be great to reconnect."

"Absolutely. Let's shoot for Wednesday or Thursday. I'll call you Monday."

Mars kissed Claudia once again on the cheek, and smiled at Alana before rushing out to hail a taxi.

On Monday morning, Mars took out Claudia's card. He had glanced at the company name when she handed it to him on Friday, but the type of business she was in wasn't clear. The card read, *Claudia W. Kovaleski, Co-Manager, Trade Show Staffing, LLC.* Kovaleski? Mars thought her last name was Kaye. He'd ask her at lunch. Mars was anxious to meet with Claudia, and he couldn't help but think about the added attraction—her new rack.

Mars was anxious to confirm the lunch meeting. He looked at his watch. It was 10:20. He thought calling Claudia now wouldn't seem too aggressive. Mars saw two numbers on her card, one ending in 5000, the other a more random sequence. He decided to call the random number, which turned out to be Claudia's cell phone.

She answered. "Hello, this is Claudia."

Mars responded, "Hi, Claudia, it's Mars. It was great seeing you Friday."

"Hi, Mars. It was good seeing you as well."

"Are we still on for lunch, say, Wednesday?" he asked.

"Wednesday is good for me," Claudia replied.

"Great. How about noon at Joe's on the corner of Rush and Grand?" Mars suggested.

"It's a date, Mars. I'm looking forward to it."

"Great. See you Wednesday, Claudia."

As Mars hung up the phone, he felt jazzed. It had been quite some time since he felt this enthusiastic. Maybe he was attending too many business meetings. Maybe he was bored with too much entertaining for people he didn't actually like; picking up the tabs, making small talk, and just plain saying and doing what he had to. Mars wanted to feel alive, and although Claudia was married, he just enjoyed being around a beautiful, classy woman with a terrific sense of humor. Wednesday could not come soon enough.

THAT WEDNESDAY MORNING BEFORE Mars left home for downtown, he checked himself in the mirror one last time. Most days Mars would dress casually, but he always kept suits and ties in his office armoire for those occasional last minute business meetings. However, this morning he dressed in his favorite suit, shirt, and tie. He groomed himself as if he were going out on a first date. He adjusted his cufflinks and headed downstairs for a quick glass of orange juice and coffee. Rochelle couldn't help but notice Mars's unusual behavior. She questioned him as if she were the prosecutor in a courtroom.

"Mars, what's the special occasion?"

"I have a meeting today," he replied—somewhat defensively, Rochelle thought.

Rochelle wasn't going to stop at that response. "Who's the meeting with, Mars?"

"A potential investor for the new South Loop project." Mars didn't make eye contact with Rochelle, and she knew something was up. Rochelle could read Mars like an open hand in a poker game.

"Are you coming home tonight, Mars, or is this another night downtown?"

Mars responded with a slightly raised voice, "Rochelle, I don't have time for this now. I'll see you tonight around eight o'clock." With that, Mars rushed out of the house.

As he neatly folded his suit coat on the back seat of his black Lexus LS, Mars settled into the driver's seat, took a deep breath, and sped out of the driveway. Mars thought, *Why should I feel guilty about having lunch with an old friend? Fuckin' Rochelle. She can kiss my ass.*

Around eleven o'clock, Sam stuck his head in Mars's office.

"How's it going, Mars? Anything new?" Sam asked.

"Good morning, Sam. Nothing out of the ordinary, just a lunch appointment," Mars replied.

"Who is she, Mars? I see that look in your face. This is not just a business lunch."

Mars answered, "I'll fill you in later." Sam gave Mars a sly smile, and went back across the office.

Mars thought, *Shit! Am I that easy to read? First Rochelle and now Sam. I don't like this at all.*

———————

Mars looked at his watch: 11:25. He planned to arrive at Joe's early, and be waiting for Claudia. He might grab a scotch at the bar. Why was he so anxious? Hell, Mars had closed tens of millions of dollars in transactions, and met many beautiful women, but for some reason he just couldn't relax. He cabbed it over to Joe's and took a stool at the bar.

At twelve o'clock sharp, Claudia entered the revolving door that opened directly into the bar area. Mars jumped up from the bar stool and walked over to greet her. She looked outstanding, Mars thought, as he gave her a hug and a quick kiss on the cheek. They both smiled. Mars took Claudia's arm and they walked toward the host, who greeted Mars with an outstretched hand, and said, "Mr. Gregory, so good to have you join us today."

Mars replied, "Georgio, it's good to see you. This is an old friend of mine, Claudia Kaye."

Georgio took Claudia's hand and kissed the top gently. Claudia smiled as Georgio said, "Ms. Kaye, it is my great pleasure to meet you." He then led Mars and Claudia to a corner booth away from most of the crowd, where he knew Mr. Gregory would be able to enjoy time with his friend.

Mars brought his cocktail with him. As they settled in the booth, he asked Claudia, "What may I order for you?" Claudia responded with a request for a glass of white wine, but instructed Mars she'd have only one. She had another appointment at three o'clock.

"That's great, plenty of time to spend together," Mars said. Actually, Mars had cleared his entire afternoon.

Mars was anxious to learn everything about his beautiful friend. "Claudia, tell me about your new company. And, by the way, who is Kovaleski?"

Claudia gave a little laugh, and said, "Let's see, where shall I start?"

During the next two hours, Mars found out that Stephen Kaye was the name her husband used in business; however, his last name was actually Kovaleski. Mars threw his head back and laughed.

"What?" Claudia asked.

"I'm sorry," Mars replied. "Claudia Wodecki Kovaleski just struck my funny bone."

Even more interesting to Mars, Stephen and Claudia had been separated for months, and their divorce would be final within weeks. Stephen's good fortune had turned sour during the last two years, and he'd lost everything. It turned out, Mr. Total Package had a very bad gambling problem. His risk-taking had led to his acquired wealth, but his lack of control had caused him to squander away every penny and then some. Claudia told Mars that for the most part their marriage had been a blast. They'd traveled first class and spent like a couple of drunken sailors. It turned out neither Claudia nor Stephen wanted children, so they just lived it up until the money ran out. Claudia admitted that she did not have any regrets. She and Stephen had lived a fairy-tale lifestyle, but it just wasn't sustainable. She was happy to have been a part of his life, and, Mars could tell, she still had feelings for him.

Mars filled Claudia in on Sammar's business, and was not the least bit modest. Claudia told Mars that she was not at all surprised by his success. She said she knew when they'd met at the law firm that he was destined for the big time.

"What about your paralegal studies? Did you ever get your degree?" Mars inquired.

"I'm proud to say, yes, I did," Claudia replied. "It was a long haul, but I knew at the end I'd always be able to find a job."

"You've got that right," Mars said, as he raised his glass her way. "Take it from me, a good paralegal is more valuable than most lawyers."

Claudia told Mars about the company she'd started with Alana. They provided hostesses and models for trade shows in Chicago. Alana was a former model and a high school friend of Claudia's. Together they saw a niche that offered an opportunity to use Alana's contacts in the industry with Claudia's strong business talents.

Their company represented over thirty ladies, with ages ranging from their mid-twenties to early forties. Claudia told Mars that they were making money through booking commissions, and an override on the ladies' hourly rates, which Mars learned was $40 to $50 per hour.

Mars thought this was a pretty good business concept. However, Claudia explained that the trade shows were seasonal. Some months there might be three shows, and other months, only one. The profits from the business alone did not provide Claudia with enough income to live. She told Mars she was planning to interview for a paralegal position beginning next month.

At this point, Mars's wheels were spinning. He had a few immediate thoughts, but decided not to offer them at this, their first meeting.

The lunch crowd had thinned out, and as Mars sipped the last of his coffee, he glanced at his watch. It was 2:30. Mars knew Claudia would need to leave for another appointment soon.

"You know, Claudia, I just might have a few ideas for you," he offered. "Would you be willing to meet again next week at my office?"

"Of course, Mars. I'd appreciate hearing your thoughts," she answered.

As Mars walked Claudia out to the valet stand to retrieve her car, he assured Claudia that he would call her on Friday to schedule a time to meet the next week. When they arrived at the valet stand, Mars slipped the attendant a $20 bill to pay for Claudia's parking, as well as a nice tip.

Claudia's immaculately detailed white Lexus pulled up to the curb, the same model as Mars's, which caused him to smile. As they hugged, Mars said, "Claudia, this was one of the most enjoyable lunches I've had in a long time. I have a few things to sort out and next week we can bounce around an idea or two."

"Mars, this was fun. I look forward to meeting next week."

As Claudia drove off, Mars decided to walk back to his office. It was a beautiful afternoon, and he wanted to think about a few options as he enjoyed the sights and sounds of Chicago.

MARS CALLED CLAUDIA ON Friday, and they agreed to meet at Mars's office at four o'clock the following Tuesday. Mars was considering extending Claudia an offer to work at Sammar. With Claudia's paralegal background, she could provide a major contribution to lightening Mars's workload. He had two administrative assistants who did their best, but to have a paralegal would be a luxury. Additionally, Mars could not stop thinking about those thirty gals who worked for Claudia's company. He was certain that most of them, if not all, were extremely attractive. After all, who was going to pay $50 an hour for anything less for their trade show hostess?

Claudia arrived at exactly the scheduled time. Mars loved this discipline; it showed respect for his time. Mars paraded Claudia around his somewhat understated offices, introducing her to everyone as a friend from his former law firm. Mars found Sam in his office, and stuck his head in the door.

"Sam, you have a second? I want you to meet someone."

"Of course, Mars, come in," Sam replied.

"Sam, this is Claudia Kovaleski. We worked together at my old law firm."

Sam rose from his oversized desk and came around to greet Claudia. "Claudia, it is my pleasure. Any friend of Mars's is a friend of mine." Sam, with a big smile, used both his hands to shake Claudia's.

Sam was smart enough to know that Mars was up to something. Now he understood what had put Mars in such a good mood these past couple weeks. Sam was also smart enough to keep his mouth shut, and to not embarrass Mars regarding Claudia's obvious good looks.

"Claudia," Sam said, as he walked her and Mars out to the front of his office, "you and Mars have a nice visit." Sam suspected this wasn't the first time Mars had seen Claudia in the past two weeks. One thing Sam was not, was naïve.

Mars led Claudia back to his office, where they sat across from each other in leather chairs in front of Mars's desk. He closed the door. "Claudia, I've been thinking. As an alternative to working for a big stuffy law firm, would you consider coming to work for me?"

Claudia hesitated for a moment, and replied, "Under the right circumstances, I might."

Mars cut to the chase. Sammar, he told her was growing exponentially. Their clients and colleagues—those politicians and whore lenders—not only expected to make money for themselves, but wanted to be wined and dined, or set up with women as part of any deal. Mars was constantly arranging and paying for escorts for those demanding moochers. Everyone wanted something in return for providing a favor, or just as part of the process. They expected payoff, one way or another. Mars was hoping Claudia's girls just might be great for business.

Claudia confirmed that some of her trade show hostesses discreetly accepted agreed-upon gratuities for sexual favors. Mars loved her careful wording.

Claudia continued, "I personally haven't brokered any of these arrangements. However, these ladies know the ropes. They're propositioned all day long at these trade shows. The horny, old out-of-towners are relentless, and the trade show exhibitors are even worse. The ones that are paying the $50 an hour believe they're entitled, and the other exhibitors are all scouting out each other's hostesses. The ladies are very skilled at playing the game, and taking advantage of every situation. What's an occasional blowjob, or even an all-nighter, if the price is right? Hell, they've been giving it away for years. Sometimes for no more than dinner and drinks."

Mars was thrilled with Claudia's take on the situation. This was music to his ears. Now to just bring Claudia on board.

Claudia said to Mars, "So, you want a paralegal to be your workhorse, and you want my escorts to entertain your business associates. And I want to make a good salary, with bonuses for going above and beyond my job description. Also, I want the freedom to conduct my trade show business on the side, when duty calls. Look, I have no responsibility—no kids, no pets, no men in my life. I'm willing to work long hours. I just want generous compensation and to enjoy what I do."

Mars figured it out real quick. They had established what Claudia wanted; now it was just a matter of money. Mars decided to let Claudia throw out a number. "Okay, Claudia, tell me what you want," Mars offered. After all, Mars knew Claudia could make top dollar at a big law firm. A good paralegal is worth $80,000-plus. With her good looks, and the potential, if someone were to inquire, to offer perks to clients, this was going to be a big number.

Claudia replied, "All right, Mars. Base salary $95,000, undocumented expenses $500 per month, and bonus potential of up to 25 percent of my base salary each year. The added bonuses for social coordination will be on a case-by-case basis."

Wow, Mars thought. *She knew this was coming and she gave it some thought.* "Claudia, before I respond, there are two issues for me. One, I will need you at least until two or three o'clock most Saturdays," Mars indicated. There was silence.

Claudia said, "What's the second one?"

Mars hesitated. "This is going to be a big one." Claudia braced herself for what she thought was coming. Another period of silence. Mars continued, "I want to call you Wodecki."

Then there was total silence for about five seconds as Mars and Claudia just looked at each other. Then they both burst out laughing at the same time. They stood and gave each other a great big hug. The deal was sealed. Claudia Wodecki Kovaleski would become Mars's executive assistant/office manager, starting a week from Monday.

From the Memoirs of Mars Gregory:

THE TIMING OF FINDING Wodecki was impeccable. I had been trying to do too much, and it was wearing me down. Between our rehabilitation of thirty buildings, managing over a thousand apartments, and now the South Loop Project, I had no time for family. I was putting in eighty-hour weeks, plus all the entertaining at night and on weekends. Don't get me wrong. I'm not complaining. Things were going well. I just needed some high-caliber help.

From the get-go, things were better. Having Wodecki was like having a working partner. She jumped right in to each and every challenge, and handled it with ease. I was feeling less stress as Claudia proactively took responsibility for many of the routine business operations of my office and my personal affairs, and utilizing her paralegal skills interacting on a daily basis with Sammar's CFO, Bob Jacoby. It was a pleasure to see her in action. In fact, it was pleasing just to see her each day, period. She was the most "can-do" person I ever encountered. With that glowing smile, and style even women admired, she was able to win her way with just about everyone.

The City Council approved our zoning for the South Loop Project, but we still needed $21.6 million, the balance of the purchase price, to enable us to close. And the deadline established by the contract was looming—if we didn't close soon, we'd be in default, and the sellers would keep our $2.4 million deposit. The project was taking nearly all my time, but I was absolutely loving it. Every day we'd have meetings with different movers and shakers, all of whom were now interested in different aspects of the project.

Now I needed Wodecki and some of her hostesses to help me persuade the Bachman Brothers' team to finance our project. Bachman Brothers was a New York investment banking firm showing strong interest in offering us a mortgage to purchase the property. Two senior members of the firm, Mario Russo, a principal, and his senior vice president, Stuart Golding, had reviewed our initial master plan, and they'd made it very clear that while they were in Chicago performing their due diligence on our loan, wining, dining, and attractive women were expected.

I scheduled a meeting one afternoon with a group proposing a movie theater complex on the site, adjacent to where an IKEA might go. I went out into the reception area to greet the theater guys, and led them back to the conference room. I was surprised to find Sam camped out there with Malik Alawi, Orenthal Mitchell, and a guy I had never met. As usual, Malik was chain smoking; the ashtray in front of him was overflowing with half-smoked butts, and the room reeked. That must have been how he stayed so damn rail-thin.

I nodded a greeting to Malik, and said, trying not to sound too irritated, "Sam, I have the conference room reserved at two o'clock."

Sam gave me a sheepish grin. He never paid attention to the scheduling sheet posted outside the conference room door. "Sorry, Mars, we just need a few minutes."

I was exasperated, and embarrassed to have to ask my guests if they would mind waiting in the reception area a few moments. But I didn't leave the conference room. I figured if I hung around, Sam would feel pressured to get his meeting over with. I turned to the guy I didn't know. He was a rather ordinary-looking guy, average height, fair complexion, hair slicked back. His only distinctive feature was his round tortoiseshell glasses, which looked very fashionable.

"John Jarzik," he said, in a slightly aloof manner, as if he didn't give a damn who I was, as if he didn't care that I was a 50 percent owner of the office he was sitting in.

"Ah, John," I said knowingly. "I've heard a lot about you."

"Anything good?" he asked, which brought a laugh from the group.

I gave him my friendly business professional smile. "Nothing but good things," I said amiably.

Then it hit me. Jarzik was working with Mike Kovach's campaign. Why was he meeting with Malik and Oren? So I asked them, "What's going on, fellas?"

Sam had his conspiratorial game face on. "We're just working out a little strategy for Malik, Mars."

This was how it would go down, then, just as Sam and Walter Roche had discussed. Malik was, in fact, going to run for the US Senate, and Jarzik would coordinate the Kovach campaign to work with Malik.

"That's great," I said, trying to sound as enthusiastic as possible. To be honest, I didn't really care that much. My mind was much more focused on keeping things on track for our big project.

I turned to say hello to Oren, and noticed he had an airline ticket folder sticking out of his pocket. "Hey, Oren, good to see you," I said warmly. This was genuine. You couldn't help but love the guy. "Where are you going?"

"Hawaii," Oren said, sounding as if he wasn't too happy about it.

"Gee, that's great!" I gushed. "Second honeymoon?"

He shook his head. "Nah, business trip."

Now this was damn peculiar. Oren's official job was with some Cook County government office, but his real job was to do political work for the president of the Cook County Board. What the hell business would he be doing in Hawaii?

Sam was looking a bit uncomfortable. He didn't want to be having this conversation, I could tell. "There has been some confusion with Malik's records out there," he said, evasively. "It's nothing really. We're sending Oren out there to get it straightened out."

Questions raced through my head. And before I could give voice to any of them, Sam announced, "Okay, guys, Mars needs the room. We're outta here!"

Chapter 13

SKYLAR STILLWELL SAT IN a small room in the Dirksen Federal Building in downtown Chicago, with Charles Davies, his distinguished lawyer and a former assistant US attorney. They both thought it was odd that the government had asked to hold the meeting at this location, but as soon as they were seated, Davies snorted in disgust.

"Now I get it," he said. "This guy Frank McKenzie is a total prick. I would never have done anything like this when I was with the US attorney's office."

He pointed to the window, at the building nearby, the Metropolitan Correctional Center, known as the MCC, a monolithic, triangular, concrete building in Chicago's Loop that was the holding center for persons indicted on federal charges. The MCC was famous for its specially designed super-narrow cell windows. The architect had done extensive research and learned that no adult human head was less than six inches in diameter. So all the windows were only four inches wide; no human being could get his head through one of the windows and escape.

"This is how they try to fuck with you," Davies said, shaking his head. "Don't let it get to you."

Stillwell was awaiting another session of questioning by the federal agents who were intent on making him give up the man who had given him so much. They wanted him to drive the final nail in Parker's coffin, to link his mentor, his boss, once and for all to the scandal that had raised its ugly head to haunt him and many of his friends and colleagues. How had he wound up here?

Sitting on a hard plastic bench, counting the concrete blocks on the wall in front of him, Skylar knew the answer. He remembered it clearly, as if it was yesterday. There was Ed Parker, sitting there in that conference room: *It's the big enchilada, Sky. The governor controls everything in this state. Everything. You can be the guy who puts me there, and I won't forget. You'll be the second most powerful guy in the state before you're thirty.*

The second most powerful guy in the state government was now sitting in a holding room, with nothing to do but watch the second hand crawl around the small government-issue clock mounted on the wall.

SKY HAD A TROUBLED feeling about this meeting. Something hadn't seemed right for weeks. Even his girlfriend, Lisa, had been irritable and aloof recently. Maybe all the pressure of this ongoing drama had finally gotten to her. Maybe she wanted to break up with him.

Just then the door opened and Joshua Baker walked in. He was alone, and he carried a manila file folder. He smiled at both Sky and Charles pleasantly.

"This isn't going to take long, guys. Sorry for the short notice, Charles. I hope I didn't pull you out of anything important," he said, all very business-like.

"No problem," Davies said, waiting for the fun to start.

"Can I get you a Coke or something, Sky?" Josh said, looking at Stillwell.

"Nah . . . I'm trying to watch my weight."

"Okay, let's get started." Baker had the slightest sound of apology in his voice. It seemed that he was a bit reluctant about the activity he was about to initiate.

After a brief pause, Baker sighed, reached into his file and pulled out two items. He laid one in front of Davies and one in front of Stillwell. In front of Stillwell was a picture of his girlfriend, Lisa Gronkiewicz. In front of Davies was a ten-page indictment of Lisa Gronkiewicz.

"What the fuck is this?" Stillwell asked, somewhat baffled.

Davies was holding up the legal document, shaking his head in disgust. "They indicted her, Sky!" He then turned to Baker, pointing. "This is really low, Josh."

The blood drained from Skylar Stillwell's face. His mouth dropped open before he blurted out, "Indicted her for what? She hasn't done anything!"

"That indictment that your lawyer is holding says different." Baker was all business.

"Let's just keep our heads," Charles Davies said, raising one hand. He was busily reading the indictment. "This is shit! You guys went out and trapped her in a lie?"

"It is impossible to trap someone in a lie," Baker said, without any passion in his voice. In his heart, though, he hated what they had done to this poor gal. But business was business, and he had done what he had been told to do. "You ask someone a question; they either tell you the truth . . . or they don't. If they lie, it's a crime."

"Oh, that's bullshit and you know it! You guys went out there to scare the shit out of her, to intimidate her!" Stillwell was nearly hyperventilating.

He was seething. "She didn't have anything to do with this!" He put his head down on the table in front of him.

Baker looked at Davies with a strangely contrite yet determined look on his face. He clearly wanted Davies to hear what he was saying. He almost pleaded when he spoke. "If you let your client go down for that criminal in the governor's mansion, it will be on your conscience forever. My boss is determined to get justice for those kids. I didn't understand that until a few days ago. It was something he said. He talked about those six little children who died in that accident like they were his own kids. I've never seen a guy so single-minded, so locked on a cause. This isn't political for him."

He took a breath and continued, with his eyes locked on Davies.

"McKenzie's not working for the Democrats. He's not working for the Republicans. He's not trying to make a name for himself. He's doing this for those kids . . . and those kids alone."

At this point Stillwell raised his head. Baker stared right through him. He turned to Davies again. "Your client has information that McKenzie wants, Charles. And he is going to get it out of him. If putting his girlfriend in prison isn't enough, who knows who will be next on the list? He is not going to stop. Everybody's got secrets. He *will* find a secret about someone else Sky loves—his mother, his father . . . it won't matter." Baker folded his hands neatly on the table. "Now, you don't have to believe me at this point, but you will believe me eventually. Parker's career is dead. He's a walking corpse. He just doesn't know it yet."

Stillwell looked at the picture of his girlfriend. The room was dead quiet. After a moment, his shoulders went limp. He knew he was defeated. He had been mentally steeling himself for this for months. He knew he might have to do time to protect his boss. He was ready to take the bullet for Parker, and would have kept his mouth shut if he was the only one who would suffer. But there was no way that he was going to let Lisa go to prison for the bullshit scheme that he and his boss had cooked up. He looked back at Baker with tears of anger welling up in his eyes—anger on a level he had never felt before.

Got him, Baker thought. He was about to give his boss his star witness. But there was no sense of pride or the usual feeling of accomplishment. He was emotionless about what he had just done. However, one thing was now clearly and inescapably true. They were going to take down a governor.

From the Memoirs of Mars Gregory:

SAM AND I WENT to—where else?—Gene & Georgetti to celebrate Sam's success. Sam was ebullient. Mike Kovach had entered the primary race for governor, and Malik Alawi was waiting in the wings, ready to declare his candidacy for the US Senate in the next election. It was going to be a huge challenge, even for someone like Sam. I was ever so slightly concerned about the direction my partner was heading. I thought I might bring up my concerns.

"You know, Sam," I said, "you should think about registering as a lobbyist. Those guys make money hand over fist. And it's legal. With the political connections that you're going to have after the election, that would be a good move."

"Yes, I've thought of that. I've talked to some people about it. There is a drawback, though: the IRS becomes your partner. You don't make cash. You get paid with checks—quite a paper trail there. You know me, Mars. I like green money."

"Yeah," I said, "that is true. But, you can't think of it that way. The money is free to begin with. Who cares if the government gets their piece? It's free money. All you're doing is having dinner like we are right now. You make an introduction, and you get paid shit piles of money for it. And it's all legal!"

Sam looked at me from across the table. The waiter was pouring water and smiling. He took our wine order and left us to ourselves. Sam continued in a very sincere, thoughtful way. He had obviously thought this through.

"Mars," he said in a low tone, "have you ever heard the fable about the farmer and the snake?"

I shrugged, not sure what he was talking about. He continued.

"One winter, a farmer found a snake stiff and frozen with cold. He felt sorry for it, so he picked it up and held it close to him. The snake was quickly revived by the warmth, and resuming its natural instincts, bit the farmer. The farmer cried out, 'I just saved you, and you bit me?' And the snake looks at him and says, 'What do you expect? I'm a snake?"

We both chuckled. Then Sam asked, "What is the moral of the story?"

Again, I shrugged. He was on a roll; let him finish.

"The greatest kindness will not bind the ungrateful. Or, better put, you cannot change human nature."

"Yeah, what's your point?" I asked, still unsure what he was trying to say. He wasn't shy about making his meaning clear to me.

"In this world there are givers and there are takers. I'm a taker. You say it's free money. I say bullshit. It's my money. I earned it and I deserve it. Why should I give some of it to this fucking government? They didn't earn it! It is my money to do with as I please."

"I see your point, I guess . . ." I didn't finish my thought.

Sam continued, "You see, I tell the story a little differently, but it speaks the same time-proven truth. If you take a pile of shit and put it anywhere on this planet, be it in the middle of the desert or the top of a mountain and leave it for an hour, flies will find it. It doesn't matter if your pile is hidden from view, tucked away in a container, or left out in the noonday sun, the flies will always come. So, too, anywhere that there is a large sum of money, whether it is personally owned, in a bank, in a vault, in a mattress, in a wallet, or if it is publicly owned as in a governmental entity, it will attract a certain number of unscrupulous people hell-bent to grab their share. As sure as night follows day, this is always true."

I nodded. All I could say was, "Okay . . ."

"Money does strange things to people, both to the people who have it and to the people who want it. How many times do we have to be told that money is the root of all evil? How many fables must be repeated before we all just come to understand and accept that one immutable fact: you really cannot change human nature, especially when it comes to money.

"This was true in biblical times. It is true today. And it will be true until the end of time. Why can't we all simply face that fact?

"Conversely, why are people endlessly and always surprised when politicians or the people surrounding them become corrupted by all of that money and power? Are we surprised when the snake bites its benefactor? It's the snake's nature to bite. It has always been the snake's nature to bite and it will always be the snake's nature to bite.

"So, again I ask, why are we surprised when politicians or people near them become corrupt? When a person has control of large sums of money, isn't it human nature to want some of it? Has there ever been a time in all recorded history when mankind was free from corruption? I don't have to answer that. You know the answer.

"Since time began, priests have stolen from their own church coffers, policemen have taken bribes, women have performed sexual favors for money, bank presidents have stolen from their banks, and politicians have stolen from the people. So, what else is new?"

Just then the waiter returned with a bottle of CARM Douro Reserva, cradled on a crisp white napkin hanging from his arm. He smiled and went through the elaborate ritual we all go through before drinking a damn glass of wine.

After the wine was finally poured, the conversation took a turn, and before we knew it we were talking about real estate, as usual. The entire previous conversation appeared to have been tabled.

But I never forgot that conversation. It was an insight into the personality of the man I called my partner. I decided on my drive home that I would keep my distance from the politics of our business and concentrate more on the real estate development. And it was that decision that made me the last man standing.

Chapter 14

VINCE WAS PACING. THERE was a board meeting of the Teachers' Pension Fund the next day, and he was in a meeting with Marvin Rosenthal to discuss the agenda. He could see the writing on the wall. It was becoming more and more apparent to him that over thirty uninterrupted years of Republican rule was about to come to an end. The control over the governor's office and the various commissions and boards that Vince and his cronies had painstakingly and meticulously cultivated in order to keep a death grip on power in the State of Illinois might very well be slipping through their fingers.

The accident that had killed six young children was the kind of tragic human interest story that would just not go away. Vince was beginning to realize he might have made a mistake concerning his handling of John McKenzie. In his zeal to get rid of the senator, he'd brought about the appointment of this Boston prosecutor who was clearly a man possessed, willing to stop at nothing to achieve his goals. For a while, Vince had been able to keep the investigation under control. But with the appointment of Franklin McKenzie everything had changed. This guy was methodically and relentlessly creeping up a very well-oiled chain of command, and it was beginning to look like he might be successful at making it all the way to the top.

"I think they've gotten to Skylar Stillwell. I hear that prick, McKenzie, indicted Stillwell's girlfriend and is threatening prison time for her. Stillwell won't let that happen, if he can help it. He'll fold like an accordion if they offer him a deal for her. And he knows everything. If they get him to talk, it's all over for Parker.

"Maybe we should have given that damn Boy Scout John McKenzie a little more respect," he continued. "That piece of shit really screwed us," Vince said as he slapped down that day's copy of the *Chicago Tribune*, which had plastered yet another article about the investigation of corruption in the office of the secretary of state all over page one, featuring US Attorney Franklin McKenzie. The article compared McKenzie to Elliot Ness. "He must be feeling pretty proud of himself right now. It looks like he might just have the last laugh in this deal."

"What are we gonna do, Vince?" Rosenthal, loyal stooge that he was, never had any ideas of his own.

"I'm working on that, Marvin. I'm working on it . . ."

ED PARKER'S LAWYER, JEREMIAH C. Marsh, was working on it too. Before the appointment of Franklin McKenzie to the US attorney's office, it was Marsh who'd been thought of as the state's toughest former prosecutor. Like McKenzie, Marsh had been bipartisan in his prosecution of corruption among the political elite, and fearless in his relentless attempts to eradicate gang violence from the mean streets of the city. He'd gone after other corrupt politicians, including a sitting governor (Illinois had no shortage of governors who'd left office early and traded in their high-priced business suits for orange jumpsuits). Marsh's career as a no-nonsense crusader against crimes of all kinds had won him the Republican nomination for governor back in the 1980s and swept him into that office in a landslide election. After he left office, they named a bridge after him. He was a bit of a legend, even though substantial portions of the Combine were actually assembled during his tenure as governor.

Marsh was tough, but he was considered sedate when compared to this new US attorney—although no one would say that to his face. But this new guy McKenzie was ruthless in a way no one had seen before.

Marsh walked into Franklin McKenzie's office and was given the proper amount of respect due a man with his reputation and credentials. McKenzie talked about how he'd followed Marsh's career from the very beginning. He complimented him on all his past efforts, and told him he only hoped he could do a job that would stand up over time to the legacy of this great man.

However, if Marsh thought he was going to intimidate or somehow try to schmooze the new holder of his former office, he was sadly mistaken.

"Frank, my client has made some mistakes," Marsh began. "But the sum total of Ed Parker's life should not be disgraced. He's been a public servant for over thirty years. His service has not been marred by any previous complaints or accusations of malfeasance. What is he now? He is a kindly old gentleman in the autumn of his life. He has a wife of forty-three years, two kids and six beautiful grandkids, and he has done a lot of good for this state."

McKenzie sat behind his huge mahogany desk with a quiet half-smile. He folded his hands together, fingertips touching, as he often did. Inside he was fuming. He didn't blame former Governor Marsh. It was expected that he would do his best to represent his client as a stand-up guy. However, every time someone tried to minimize the involvement Parker had in this tragic fiasco, McKenzie's blood boiled. It really didn't matter who it was—an investigator, a member of the press, or this nationally famous former-prosecutor-turned-mouthpiece-for-scoundrels sitting in front of him.

McKenzie stayed calm. He spoke quietly, in measured tones. "Jerry, your client is the lowest form of scum that exists. He is the lowest of the low. He has blood on his hands, and if I thought I could charge him with murder and make it stick, I would do it."

Frank specifically called him Jerry, forgoing titles. After all, Marsh had called him Frank. They were equals in here. There was palpable tension growing in the room, but McKenzie was relentless. He continued.

"What would you suggest we do with a guy who is personally responsible for the deaths of six children? Are we supposed to overlook all of that in favor of his long and valued public service?"

Jeremiah Marsh was a veteran of this process and was unfazed by Frank McKenzie's seething passion. In Frank, he could even see himself from earlier days when he'd sat behind that desk. But he was going to try to calm the waters, to make this easier on them both.

"Frank, I admire your passion. I do. Don't think for a moment that I'm put off by it. I would expect nothing less. I know Parker is through. Hell, Parker knows he's through. When you guys got Stillwell, it made your case. I would just suggest we forgo a long and very public trial. Let's take care of this, more or less, internally. Let him resign or something—maybe even an impeachment—a public flogging in the papers. Then let him fade away. Obscurity and shame are the worst punishment for a public figure. With an ego like his, it'll kill him. A prison term would just be piling it on. He's on old man. Any prison term would be a life sentence."

These two men didn't hate each other. They respected each other.

"I'm afraid I can't consider anything short of an indictment, Jerry. You understand."

Marsh sighed heavily. His first gambit had failed: McKenzie wasn't biting. "Yeah, I do. I'd do the same thing, you know. I'm going to fight you tooth and nail though, call you names in the press, all of it. You know that, right?"

"I wouldn't have it any other way. I look forward to it."

Marsh paused as if to reflect, and then moved on to Plan B. "Okay, then. I am going to ask for one favor."

"Ask away."

"If Parker announces tomorrow that he will not seek another term, you hold off on the indictment until he's out of office. It's not long. You can use the time to build your case."

McKenzie had been expecting this. "I already have a case. However, when I see the press conference on TV, I'll hold off on the indictment."

The two men shook hands.

The following day, Edward G. Parker held a press conference and announced that he would not be seeking a second term as governor.

A COUPLE WEEKS LATER, Vince made up his mind. It had been an unusually warm few weeks, creating an opportunity for him to summon Marvin to Springfield for a round of golf. Vince gritted his teeth when Marvin walked out of the locker room wearing an incredibly loud pair of golf pants, a checkerboard pattern of yellow and green.

He put his hand on Marvin's shoulder. "Marvin, you know about all these so-called hedge funds getting money from the Teachers?"

Marvin nodded. "Sure," he said. "It's pretty amazing. They have these fancy trading strategies. They simultaneously buy puts and calls, so no matter which way the market moves, up or down, they make money."

"Right," Vince said as they drove up to the first tee. "We're going to be a hedge fund. We're going to hedge the next election for governor."

Marvin gave Vince a puzzled look. "What do you mean?"

Vince took off his sunglasses and methodically cleaned a thumbprint off the left lens. "Well, it's pretty clear: with Ed Parker out of the race our Republican candidate is going to be the state attorney general."

Marvin wrinkled up his nose. "You mean *Tom* Parker?"

Vince sadly nodded his head. "Yes. It's really bad luck for us. They aren't even related, but they have the same damn name. Half the fucking voters won't even realize it's not the same guy. The worst aspects of the news concerning this commercial driver's license scandal will hit the headlines right during the campaign. The name Parker will be all over the papers and will be connected to this very ugly mess. I think we're going to lose in November."

Marvin saw his own personal gravy train grinding to a halt. When Vince Perino, the ultimate insider, Mr. Republican of Illinois, chairman of the Combine, told you that someone was going to lose, you could kiss that someone good-bye. He suddenly wanted to puke. Marvin moaned. "What are we going to do?"

Vince gave him the coldest stare Marvin had ever felt. "I just told you, we're going to hedge this election."

Marvin was lost. "I don't follow."

Vince took off his golf cap, ran his hand through his hair, and managed to smile again at Marvin. "I'm going to have to introduce you to a guy named Sam Alsheriti."

———

VINCE PERINO HAD BEEN making deals his entire political life. He was not an ideologue. He was a politician, and a slippery one at that. He had money to make for himself and his friends, and he absolutely had no intention of letting party affiliation or some silly ideological belief stand in his way. Let the blind little sheep out there in the electorate worry about their party, their principles, and their ideology. Sure, he was a Republican, but it was clear the Republicans were going to lose the governor's office, so it was time to make some other calculations, some other arrangements.

Vince leaned back in his deep leather chair and stared at the ceiling of his plush Springfield office. This one was a big pill to swallow. He had dissed Sam, blown him off, kept him out of the Parker campaign fund. There was a significant risk this guy hated his guts. He agonized for several long minutes. But in the end, he decided to go with his gut, and his gut told him this guy had no scruples. Vince pressed the button on his intercom and spoke to his secretary.

"Angie, I would like you to get Sam Alsheriti on the line."

He nearly choked to say it, but there was no avoiding the facts. Sam Alsheriti was providing most of the money for, and therefore had control of, the man who would likely be the next governor of the State of Illinois: Mike Kovach.

"I'm sorry, did you just say Sam Alsheriti?" The sound of her voice coming through the speaker was both incredulous and playful. Angie had been Vince's secretary for twenty years. There was a time during the early years of their relationship when the two of them played grab-ass, but, like in a marriage, those days had passed. Now, she was just an indispensable part of Vince's staff and a dear and valued part of his life.

She knew what her boss was doing and she was having a little fun with him.

"Don't be cute, Angie, just get the fucking Arab son of a bitch on the line before I change my mind."

From the Memoirs of Mars Gregory:

SAM WAS BEAMING. HE poked his head into my office with an ear-to-ear grin on his face. He was looking dapper in his yellow silk tie and custom-tailored suit.

"Let's have lunch. I'm buying," he said. "I have good news."

At G&G, Sam got right to it. "Vince Perino wants to meet with me," he said, in a manner that was completely out of character for my partner. The normally reserved and somewhat dour man whom I had come to know seemed uncharacteristically enthusiastic. "Do you know what this means?"

"Well, I have an idea, but why don't you tell me?"

"He wants to make a deal."

"He told you this?" I didn't know Vince Perino, but I couldn't imagine a savvy man of his stature saying anything of the sort over the telephone.

A waiter approached the table. "Mr. Alsheriti, so good to see you. Will you be having the usual?"

Sam shook hands with the waiter. This was one of his likeable quirks. No matter how powerful he might have become, Sam always went out of his way to be respectful to the "little people," as he called them.

"Yes, Armando, gotta watch my weight," he said, patting his waistline. "Steak salad, with ranch dressing."

I rolled my eyes. "You know, Sam, that's not exactly low-cal, despite what you think. Plus, all that bread and butter . . ."

Sam shrugged. "Nothing you can say can make me frown today, Mars. Why else would he ask to meet with me if he didn't want to make a deal?"

To Sam, it was too obvious to even question.

It was my turn to order. "Grilled salmon." Unlike Sam, I really was watching my intake. My waist was the same trim thirty-four inches it had been on my wedding day, and I worked hard to keep it that way. "Okay, let's assume he does . . ."

"This country has a two-party system. It is the keystone of democracy. The Democrats are supposed to be the liberals and the Republicans are supposed to be the conservatives. The two parties argue among themselves. Each has its own supporters. It is the American way, right?" Sam could hardly contain himself.

The waiter was back with our drinks. No alcohol at lunch today. We both were sipping iced tea.

"Yes . . . it is . . . so what?"

"Imagine what would happen if the two-party system were just a front, a subterfuge, a sham. What do you think would happen? It would allow a very select group of people to completely control the country, and the entire wealth of the country. We see that in many places outside the United States. For example, Saudi Arabia has that system. Qatar has it. Many of the Middle Eastern countries have it. Mars, my country, Syria, is run by a ruling class!" Sam was raising his voice and emphasizing his statements with his arms.

"Keep your fucking voice down. People don't like that kind of talk around here," I hissed. "What are you trying to say?" I looked around to see if we were drawing attention. We weren't. I was probably overreacting. After all, this was a place where everyone minded his own business.

"Americans are funny. You can compare the president of the United States to Hitler on your signs and in your protest marches, hang him in effigy if you want to, burn his picture on TV. Democrats can call Republicans fascists, and Republicans can call Democrats socialists. You claim to have free speech, but you cannot say a complimentary word about another country's form of government. No, no. That would be treason."

"Funny . . ." I looked him in the eye. "You ran away from your country, left it for good. You came here, didn't you? And, you've done pretty damn well for yourself in this country, haven't you?"

"We are getting off the subject, Mars. Listen to me. Little Mishka Kovach can be the next governor. In fact, he will be. I will see to that. Parker is disgraced. He will be indicted for his part in that horrible accident, the bribery scheme, among other things. The voters will not elect another Republican. Especially not another Republican named Parker!"

Sam was smirking, shaking his head. I knew he was right.

"So," Sam continued, "this is our time! This is our opportunity! When Mike Kovach is elected governor, he will give me the power to appoint all of the committee chairmen and board members who control the purse strings of this state. Up until now, that's been Vince Perino's job. That is how he has become so fucking rich. That is why he has so much power in this state. He controls the Combine. He controls the money. He is the head fly on the big pile of shit."

Sam spoke the truth, no question about it. I realized a few things. Not only was Sam planning to take over Vince Perino's place in the general scheme of things concerning money, he wanted control of the State of Illinois—and he could get it. It was just a matter of time. Also, although he didn't know it,

Franklin McKenzie was making Sam the new power behind the throne. By taking down Parker, McKenzie was opening the door for Sam to accomplish his goals.

"That is why Vince Perino wants to meet with me. He wants to make a deal."

Sam was still talking. I almost lost my place in the conversation. My mind was racing. It was a little overwhelming to realize I was speaking to the man who would soon be in charge of our state. It was a fait accompli. Everything Sam was saying was absolutely true. That was the reason Perino had called. This was all going to actually happen. It was that simple.

"So, are you going to meet with Perino?" I asked, squirting lemon juice on the salmon.

"Not yet," Sam said without hesitation. "He snubbed me four years ago. I'm going to wait until after the primary. Mike is going to win, and Perino is going to be even more anxious to get with the winner after the primary."

————————————

MIKE KOVACH HAD A primary challenge to contend with. His group was not the only politically active group in the state that could read the political tea leaves and see that the time was right for Democrats to move on the governor's office. However, there was no doubt that under the guiding light of Walter Roche and with financial help from Sam Alsheriti, Mike's campaign was the one with the most clout. Sam had clearly accomplished what he'd told me he was going to do from the start. He put together a coalition of investors from whom he could bundle huge sums of campaign funds. Now, there was this talk of tacit, unacknowledged support from high-placed, influential persons who normally supported Republican candidates. If that were true, Kovach couldn't lose.

But Sam wasn't stopping there. He was also coordinating Malik's campaign for re-election to the Illinois State Senate. Malik had no opponent in the primary, and the November election was a foregone conclusion. But Sam and the other insiders knew what was coming in the 2004 US Senate race, and they were busy building an organization for it. And Malik was visibly supporting Kovach in the primary for governor. The black votes he was going to deliver would be crucial in determining the outcome.

The primary was held in early March. The weather was cold and wet and a harsh wind howled across the state. This was seen as a good sign. Bad weather favors the candidates with the best organization, because they get their voters to the precincts. As the primary results were reported, Sam was ecstatic. His ship came in. Mike Kovach won the Democratic nomination for governor, thanks to nearly monolithic support in a number of wards in the city of Chicago. As expected, with the help of a surprisingly strong showing in the African-American community, Walter Roche delivered enough votes to put his son-in-law over the top in the primary race.

Mars watched Kovach's victory party on television. As he expected, Sam was nowhere to be seen on TV. But up on the platform, standing right behind Kovach as he made his victory statement, and smiling like a Cheshire cat, was Malik Alawi. It had all been arranged.

Looking at the fall election, the most astute watchers of Illinois politics were convinced that Mike Kovach would be elected governor of the State of Illinois. The Republicans had committed electoral suicide by nominating another guy named Parker.

Chapter 15

THE SIGNATURE FLIGHT SUPPORT Services terminal at Chicago's O'Hare International Airport is located far away from the hustle and the bustle of the crowds and the hassle of the long security lines, the crying babies, and the inexperienced travelers in the other four terminals at one of America's busiest airports. Out on the tarmac, there are usually three or four sleek, white private jets making preparations to depart. There are no scheduled flights, no cancellations, no late arrivals, no surprises. Your flight leaves when you're ready to go.

A week after the Illinois primary, Sam Alsheriti, feeling on top of the world, arrived in a black Lincoln Town Car and strode into the posh private terminal.

"Mr. Alsheriti, right this way." An attractive brunette in a crisp blue suit led Sam to the boarding area for his private flight to Springfield. The boarding area had a huge glass picture window so the waiting passengers could view their planes. Sam saw a small, twin-engine Aero Commander waiting outside. The registration number "VP 1" was painted on the tail. Sam smiled. Vince Perino had gotten himself a very good registration number. Minutes later, Sam was winging his way south.

Upon arrival in Illinois's capital city, Sam was met by a uniformed driver and whisked off to his meeting with Vince Perino at Tarantino's.

Until now, these two men had been political rivals. To Vince, Sam was an upstart, a new arrival on the political scene in Illinois. Vince had been at this for over three decades, and he was the master. Sam knew this, and respected Vince's ability to hold power, virtually anonymously, without grabbing the limelight. That's why he'd agreed to the meeting in Springfield, on Perino's turf. "Muhammad will come to the mountain," he joked when setting up the appointment with Vince's secretary.

There was much Sam could learn from Vince. However, Vince could not deny Sam's incredible success. Sam had come a long way in a relatively short period of time. There was no getting around it; Vince was meeting with the man who would soon control the power positions in the State of Illinois, and Vince wanted to hold on to a piece of that pie.

They were cut from the same cloth. Or, as Sam liked to put it, "We have mutual interests."

THE KOVACH CAMPAIGN WAS steaming along, slowly closing in on the general election. Their win in the primary had energized everyone involved. Mike Kovach himself had proved to be everything Sam had predicted. From their very first meeting, Sam knew if you let Mike loose in a room, he would be able to charm the masses. Just tell him what to say and give him a platform from which to say it, and Mike would shine.

Although Governor Parker had not yet been indicted for any crime, it was no secret why he'd decided not to seek reelection. The papers were filled with Franklin McKenzie's relentless investigation of the infamous accident in Waterston, and the license-for-bribes scandal. The investigation revealed other forms of corruption as well. State workers, lobbyists, and others on the periphery of Illinois politics—persons and companies doing business with the state—had been swept up in the ongoing investigation. Over eighty indictments had been issued.

It didn't take a brain surgeon to come up with a campaign slogan and a primary platform on which to run. If Mike Kovach saw a microphone, no matter where it was, he would jump in front of it and begin to tell anyone who would listen that he was the reform candidate. He was the candidate who was going to clean corruption from every corner and crevice of their wonderful state. In the years to come, the irony of this campaign pledge would become apparent to all.

Kovach by now had the support of all the regular Democrats. His father-in-law was a powerful alderman, plus, they too saw Mike's candidacy as an obvious opportunity to gain the governor's mansion.

However, the real reason for the Democrats' enthusiasm was the Republican candidate. Political insiders joked that Parker's campaign slogan should be *Tom Parker—Not Related to Ed!* But aside from that unfortunate coincidence, Tom Parker was a seriously flawed candidate with an Achilles' heel of his own.

———————

PRIOR TO BEING ELECTED attorney general of the State of Illinois, Thomas Parker had been the elected state's attorney of DuPage County. While holding that office, he personally prosecuted a case with very high visibility.

Four-year-old Jimmy Dwyer was abducted, raped, and murdered in one of the fastest-growing cities in all of DuPage County. The city of Naperville was the jewel of the western suburbs. It was a model city, with its own nightlife, great restaurants, museums, parks, and some of the best schools in the nation. It was a very appealing alternative to the crowds and the craziness of downtown Chicago. Above all, Naperville was considered safe, and it was this perception that had helped to spur its growth. In the wake of this horrific crime, local leaders scrambled to quell any doubts about the happy little hamlet's safety. This crime, this *anomaly*, had to be solved and prosecuted so the residents and visitors could resume normal life.

In the days after little Jimmy's initial disappearance, it became less and less likely that he would be found alive. It was at this point that the story took on a life of its own. *60 Minutes* picked up the mantle on behalf of the frantic parents as the story went nationwide.

Thomas Parker, ever the crusading prosecutor, appeared on national television, flanked by the devastated parents and high-ranking members of his trusted police force, and all but promised results. This was a risky political move on his part, but a successful investigation, capture, and prosecution of a culprit such as this would catapult Parker to national fame and paint him as America's prosecutor. His advisors determined that the risk was worth the reward.

As in too many cases like this, a body was eventually found in a wooded area not far from the Dwyer home. Forensics told the sad and dreadful tale of the crime: the sexual assault, the brutal murder. The search for the monster who'd committed this horrendous act was immediately accelerated. A substantial reward was offered.

The promise of the reward proved irresistible to Emil Rodriguez, a twenty-three-year-old punk with alleged gang connections. In a drunken stupor, he contacted the DuPage County authorities, claiming he knew who had killed little Jimmy.

With no other leads to follow, the DuPage authorities quickly made him a suspect.

As the days went by and the police drew no closer to cracking the case, media pressure continued to build, and Tom Parker was under the gun. Following demands from Parker's office, the police began "stretching" the evidence to build a case against the only suspect they had, Rodriguez. There were footprints in the mud near Jimmy's body; the cops hired a highly questionable "shoe expert," who concluded that Rodriguez's shoes matched the prints found at the scene of the crime.

Rather than press for the truth, Parker jumped on this travesty of investigative work and charged Rodriguez with murder in a massively covered press conference. "We will seek the death penalty for this heinous crime," Parker thundered, hamming it up for the cameras.

Emil Rodriguez became the focal point of all the anger surrounding this crime. The parents of Jimmy Dwyer appeared on national television and spat hatred toward the suspect. The members of the investigative team were commended, with pats on the back all around. Everyone involved in the case took their seemingly well-deserved bows.

The problem was the case against Rodriguez stank. As scrutiny of the shoe expert mounted, the police became more desperate, and several officers fabricated even more evidence. The suspect, obviously sober now, vehemently denied his guilt—but wasn't that par for the course? They all deny their crimes.

Parker took the lead chair on the prosecution team. He argued with heartfelt conviction that the good men and women of the police had caught the right guy. The parents of the slain little boy were more vocal than most in their support for the prosecution. And of course, Rodriguez had no money and was feebly represented by a public defender, with no funds for an investigator or any forensic work of his own. Even given all this, the case was so shaky that the jury spent two weeks deliberating before finally coming in with a guilty verdict.

Parker's political future seemed assured.

While the Court was engaged in the sentencing process, deliberating whether Emil Rodriguez should be put to death for this nightmarish crime, a small voice came from within the DuPage County Jail. A man being held on an unrelated residential burglary charge, a common criminal and local huckster, one Dexter Dunlevy, spoke up. Dexter Dunlevy sat in his cell and proclaimed that he was the guy who'd killed young Jimmy Dwyer. Even worse, in his confession, he gave the police specific details about the crime scene that had not been released to the media.

The cops who interviewed Dunlevy dutifully reported the incident to their superiors, who dutifully informed Tom Parker's office.

Which did absolutely nothing. The defense attorneys for Rodriguez were not notified, no post-trial motion was filed, nothing. A week later, Emil Rodriguez was sentenced to the death penalty, and was hauled away to death row. Justice had been done. The weeping parents of little Jimmy Dwyer stood on the steps of the courthouse and praised Tom Parker for all his diligent efforts to put this monster away.

Within a year, Tom Parker was running for the office of attorney general of the State of Illinois, which was widely seen as a stepping stone to the governor's office. His campaign ads ran that scene on the courthouse steps over and over on television. He was elected easily.

And then, as they say in the trade, the excrement hit the ventilation system.

The Rodriguez conviction was taken up by a diligent group of law students working on an anti–death penalty project sponsored by Northwestern University. They subpoenaed every record associated with the case, obtained an independent forensic analysis of the critical shoe evidence that showed it to be totally bogus, and systematically went about interviewing everyone who'd had any involvement with the investigation. And lo and behold, they discovered the police report on the Dunlevy confession.

The news of the Dunlevy confession set off a media firestorm. Parker's wobbly explanation that the confession wasn't proven, and had been disputed by the same police who had so badly tried to trump up the case against Rodriguez, was unconvincing. The state's attorney's failure to inform the defense of the confession was particularly appalling, even to the most jaded conservatives. Emil Rodriguez was kept in solitary confinement on death row for years until his conviction was duly overturned on appeal. After still more years of subsequent investigations by special prosecutors, the two cops who'd done the shabby police work were themselves indicted for malfeasance. In the heart of law-and-order DuPage County, however, the cops were eventually acquitted at their own trial.

Although Tom Parker was already the elected Illinois attorney general and steadfastly insisted he personally had done nothing wrong, the fact that he'd been so visibly involved during the prosecution haunted him. Under the shrewd coaching of Johnny Jarzik, Mike Kovach was using this history to bludgeon his opponent relentlessly. He hung the failed and flawed prosecution around Parker's neck like an anvil, running those clips from the steps of the DuPage County Courthouse again and again in campaign paraphernalia and TV ads, but with a very different effect this time around. The more the media crawled over the Rodriguez case, the farther Tom Parker was falling behind Kovach in the polls.

SAM ALSHERITI WAS LED to Vince Perino's table. The darkened restaurant was well appointed, with crisp linens over rich oak tables. Vince's table was quiet and secluded. He'd arrived first to ensure that everything was just so. After all, this was to be a critical business meeting.

The two men shook hands like old army buddies, all smiles and warmth.

They had met only a couple of times over the years, and Sam was always amazed by the contrast between Vince's enormous political stature and his slight, delicate frame.

"Sam, I'm so glad you could come."

"Good to be here, Vince, good to be here."

"How was your flight?" Vince was well schooled in the art of small talk.

"Great! Your people couldn't have treated me better. Nice plane you have there, by the way."

"Yeah, she's a beauty. I bought that plane years ago because I was so tired of that damn drive up I-55 to Chicago. Nothing but cornfields as far as the eye can see."

The waiter arrived with the wine list as the new best friends exchanged further small talk, feeling each other out.

"I hear your grandson is pitching in his little league playoffs," Sam said, with feigned interest. Sam was no slouch either when it came to pleasant, unnecessary banter.

Vince thought, *This guy is good. He's done his homework.* He then flashed his best and brightest smile and said, with honest pride, "Oh, yeah, my wife and I attend every game. If they win this upcoming series they go on to Champaign for the state championship, then it's on to the nationals, we hope. We're all quite excited for the boys. They deserve it. They've battled strongly all season. It's been fun for all of us."

"You must be very proud, Vince. The kids—they are why we do it all.

That's why we work our fingers to the bone, am I right?"

The benign sports and family chitchat continued until the menus arrived. Both men were being particularly cordial, neither resorting to their oft-played one-upmanship cards. Both brought plenty to the table. Vince had been doing for years what Sam wanted to do in this state. Sam recognized that. Vince was the unchallenged leader. He had forged the trail. However, there was no denying that this upstart from a foreign land, with his thick accent and his charming ways, showed promise. Sam had become a major player in the game. Vince recognized it. This meeting was a symphony of alternating volleys of deferential treatment. These were politicians, after all; small talk was their stock-in-trade.

"What do you recommend, Vince?" Sam asked, as he perused the menu.

"Any of the pasta dishes are superb. However, if you're in the mood for a nice thick juicy steak, they have an aged filet that will melt in your mouth."

Sam brightened at that. "How about if they slice that filet, and put it on a salad for me. I'm watching my weight, you know." He gave his trademark tummy tap. "With ranch dressing?"

"Absolutely," Vince shrugged. It was his home turf. The kitchen would prepare anything he wanted.

And so it went. The only subject that was not discussed was politics. Not until they were having coffee did that topic come up.

Vince had given it a lot of thought, and had decided to open the business discussion with a big dose of humility. "Sam," he said, with all the sincerity he could muster, "I understand that you wanted to be involved with Ed Parker four years ago, and somehow the campaign bungled that. People may have been rude to you. I'm not going to make excuses. I'm not going to try to sugarcoat it. We screwed up, period. I accept responsibility for what happened, and I apologize."

This was a brilliant ploy. Sam was unaccustomed to such direct talk in politics. He had been expecting Vince to ignore the whole episode, or try to blame someone else. Instead, Vince took the bull by the horns and apologized. There was no point harboring resentment after this. In an instant, the entire episode was expunged from Sam's memory.

"That's all in the past," Sam said, extending his hand. "We must look to our future together."

Vince reached across the table and shook Sam's hand for the second time that evening. "You're a gentleman, Sam."

"So, I imagine you are following the governor's race with interest," Sam started off.

"Yeah, you know, poor Tom Parker. Who would guess that his name alone could be such a detriment? Plus, this case with the little murdered kid . . . that's turned into a real fiasco. He has an uphill battle, to be sure. It's a shame, really. Tom is a good man, a good family man." Vince sipped his coffee, eying Sam.

Sam nodded, "I read about that murder case, that little boy. They had the wrong guy, yes?"

"It would seem so." Vince left that line of discussion hanging. He got down to business. "I'll tell you, Sam, I am impressed with this Kovach. He's saying a number of things that I agree with—for a damn Democrat!" Both men laughed. Anyone listening to this polite banter would have no idea of the gravity of the conversation. It was just two friends idly discussing politics, as far as anyone would guess.

"Well, if you mean what you say about agreeing with him on some issues, I am planning a small get-together, a bit of a fund raiser, at my home later this month." Sam was putting out a feeler.

"The press would have a field day if I attended a fund raiser for a Democrat!" Vince chuckled. "However, I know a great many people who might be quite interested."

"By all means, tell your friends. Feel free to invite all of your friends. They would be most welcome. May we count on that? Can I count on your quiet support?" Sam was looking at Vince straight in the eyes, holding his gaze.

Vince stirred his coffee. "I would like to do more than just help you with a fund raiser," he said cautiously.

Sam's eyes narrowed. This was the big step, the plunge he'd been waiting for. "What might that involve, Vince?"

"Do you know a guy named Marvin Rosenthal?" Vince asked, avoiding eye contact, his gaze fixed on the swirling coffee in his fine china cup.

Of course Sam knew who Marvin Rosenthal was. He held the unique position of serving on two separate boards, which just happened to be the two most important patronage operations in the state government. But Sam didn't understand the full scope of the setup—yet.

"Marvin Rosenthal was the campaign finance chairman for Ed Parker," Vince continued. "Suppose a guy of his stature publicly announced he was supporting Mike Kovach? Suppose he hosted his own fundraising event for Mike? I think we could probably raise at least a couple million dollars at such an event. Wouldn't that knock the hell out of Tom Parker's campaign?"

Sam was dazzled. This was the big league. Millions of dollars at a single event? And Vince was acting like it would be child's play. But he reminded himself, this was the Combine, and they didn't give anything without getting something in return. "So what, exactly . . . what part does Marvin play in this whole thing?"

Vince paused. This was the critical moment. There was risk that Sam, once he knew the inner workings of the scheme, would just take over and run it with his own people. But Vince also knew he had no other options. He knew he had to let Sam in on how the whole "finder's fee" system worked, if they were going to have any chance of continuing it under a Kovach administration.

So in a few brief sentences, he explained the whole scheme. But Vince held back a few details, most notably how the money was actually being split up. The amount he indicated would be available to Sam was actually less than Sam might have demanded. Vince had played the same game with Marvin . . . but he was expecting Sam to bargain for more, and he was leaving himself room to sweeten the deal if need be.

It was an unnecessary precaution.

Sam's head was reeling. So much money! So much power! And it was all right there in the palm of his hand, ripe for the taking.

"This is going to be a very productive partnership," Sam said, extending his hand for a third time.

Vince happily exchanged yet another handshake, feeling a flood of relief. The game would go on.

IN THE LIMO ON the way back to Springfield's small Abraham Lincoln Capital Airport, Sam sighed. He was overwhelmed with the implications of this meeting. He was going to be the most powerful man in the State of Illinois, controlling both a governor and a US senator. And he was going to be rich— rich and powerful beyond his wildest dreams. All his wishes were coming true.

A COUPLE OF WEEKS later, Marvin Rosenthal and Sam Alsheriti co-hosted the largest and most productive fund raising event ever held for a gubernatorial candidate in Illinois. Movers and shakers filled the grand ballroom at Navy Pier, a fabulous venue on Lake Michigan, with the stunning Chicago skyline in all its glory shimmering in the background.

The lavish affair was attended by hundreds of downstate Republicans. Some of the largest construction companies in the state were represented. The men responsible for building many of the existing roads in the state were there, socializing with the candidate, being regaled with stories about Elvis, Lincoln, and JFK.

One Republican who was not present was Vince Perino. But he had pulled out all the stops, cranked up the Combine, and oiled the gears. He didn't actually need to be there. Everyone knew who was the mastermind behind this show.

Instead, Vince sat in the bleachers at a minor league baseball stadium in Peoria, under the lights, watching his grandson pitch a one-hitter in game two of the all-important series for the state little league championship. He was fully convinced that the future was bright. Not only was it likely his grandson's team would be traveling to the state championship game in Champaign-Urbana, it would also seem he had averted what could have been a catastrophe for himself and his cronies. He heaved a satisfied sigh of relief. Business as usual would proceed unabated in the State of Illinois.

Across the field, cheering his own son in the bleachers for the opposing team, was Frank McKenzie, the US attorney. Vince caught his gaze at one point. There really didn't seem to be a hint of recognition. However, Vince had to wonder . . . is that the guy who will bring it all down? Vince shrugged it off, and just enjoyed the moment as his grandson struck out another batter.

Things were going as planned. The Kovach campaign was on autopilot to a victory in November . . . as long as nothing went wrong.

Chapter 16

MARS WAS IN CONSTANT communication with a number of potential investors for the South Loop Project. However, it was becoming more apparent to him that the most likely lender was Bachman Brothers, one of the larger investment banking firms on Wall Street. Their principal partner, Mario Russo, was aggressively pursuing the documentation for the financing. To Mars, this indicated their strong commitment to the project.

Mars was not naïve when it came to New York investment firms selling themselves as the best choice. After all, the fees generated for their companies, as well as their personal bonuses, would encourage them to say anything to get the deal on their books.

During their first trip to Chicago, Mario and his associate, Stuart Golding, had been wined and dined by Mars and a few escorts Mars had hired for the evening. Since that trip, Bachman Brothers seemed to be on a fast track to obtain more detailed information on the project. Mars was feeling quite confident that Mario and Stuart would deliver the financing.

Late one Thursday afternoon, Mario called.

"Mario, good to hear from you. What's going on with our deal?"

"We're moving along better than expected. Stuart and I would like to come to Chicago next Friday and spend the day with you." Russo continued, "We'd like to have dinner Friday evening and we both plan to stay the weekend, returning to New York on Sunday afternoon."

Mars got the message loud and clear. He knew what Mario was expecting, and responded with an enthusiastic, "I look forward to planning your visit. Is there a specific agenda relating to our business issues for Friday?"

"I'll email it to you on Monday. I look forward to our meeting, and I trust you to plan our social calendar."

Mars answered, "You bet. I'm on it. See you next Friday."

Usually after a call like this one, Mars needed to assess if he was being used. However, something about Mario and Bachman Brothers gave Mars comfort.

He leaned back in his high-backed leather chair, with his feet up on his desk, and asked Wodecki to come in. Mars knew the two evenings needed to exceed Mario's expectations, and Wodecki's hostesses would be the highlight. They'd spend most of their time in the Viagra Triangle, a nightlife district labeled for the abundance of mostly affluent older men who frequented the bars and restaurants. The bar stools there were always fully stocked with anxious females seeking a generous guy with a bloated financial statement.

"Okay, Wodecki, I need you big time," Mars explained. Of course, Wodecki already knew the importance of Bachman Brothers. Mars had been talking about this next meeting as the dealmaker.

Mars continued, "The Bachman boys are flying in early Friday morning, and we'll be meeting in the conference room most of the day, so make sure Sam and his cronies stay out. Let's arrange to have a full breakfast spread brought in for when they arrive around eight o'clock."

Wodecki was taking notes. Mars was on a roll.

"For lunch, call Georgio at Joe's and let him know I'll want my favorite table. I want you to be dressed to the nines. You'll be part of our entire time together. Mario has asked me more than once, 'What is the story with Claudia?' I told him you're off limits, but not to worry, he won't be disappointed meeting your girlfriends. There's no doubt in my mind you'll know how to play him."

Wodecki responded, "I have you covered. I get it."

Now Mars was really pumped. "On Friday night, the Viagra Triangle is a must. Arrange for a small private room at Gibson's. Let's have you, me, Mario, Stuart, and the four best hostesses you have. You know the drill: not only great looking, but the maturity and class to play these two guys like a Stradivarius. With four ladies, the guys can pick their playmates. Make sure the girls are promised whatever you think is reasonable. Whatever the number, you know what to do."

"I'll handle it all," Wodecki continued. "I'll book the room from six thirty for the entire evening. Also, I want Jennifer to be our captain. She's not only great looking and detail oriented, but she plays to the men better than anyone I've seen in Chicago."

"Perfect," Mars replied. "Now, Mario and Stuart are staying Saturday as well, so make sure each of the four ladies can also be available Saturday should we need them again. By the way, they're staying at the Four Seasons, which is a short walk from Gibson's, so that will at least cut down on their transportation needs. Once again, you make whatever financial deal you have to with the ladies."

"No problem," Wodecki responded.

"One last thing," Mars continued. "I obviously need you to be my date Friday night, and depending upon what the guys want for Saturday, can you be available Saturday night as well?"

"Sure, Mars. This is why you pay me the big bonuses," Wodecki said, with her usual million-dollar smile.

Mars figured this would be a $15-20,000 weekend at a minimum, plus Wodecki. But that was small change relative to the value of insuring that Mario would champion the South Loop loan approval.

CLAUDIA RECALLED MARS SAYING that Mario was tall, over six feet, extremely thin, with a dark full head of hair. He was in his late forties, and although he spoke with a mild New York accent, which she knew well from their many calls and his not so subtle flirtation, he was very pleasant. With his good looks and style, Claudia was sure the ladies would be pleasantly surprised.

Stuart, on the other hand, was of average height, at least twenty pounds overweight, with thin and graying hair. He was in his mid-fifties, and although he was not unattractive, he was less appealing. Stuart would be more of a challenge, as he most likely saw himself as more attractive than most women would perceive him. On the positive side, Stuart would be more appreciative of any attractive woman who would play him as a john for an evening or two. Claudia's girls were pros, and she would make certain they were well prepared for what the weekend had in store.

One piece of information Mars had decided not to mention to her was the feedback he'd received from the escort service he used before Wodecki came on board. The last time Mario was in town, his escort, Allie, had complained to her boss about Mario. It seemed that Mario was a marathon man in the bedroom. Mars had arranged for a six-hour evening for Mario, but Mario had other plans. Mario had Allie stay until morning, and kept drilling her as if he was operating with a box of Duracell batteries up his ass. Allie hung in there with Mario till early morning, and then asked that Mars pay an additional fee, to which he agreed. Additionally, Allie told her boss not to reschedule her with Mario again should he ever be in town, even with the extra fee. Mars figured that if this Super Mario problem came up again, he would just deal with it after the fact.

Wodecki had her assignment, and Mars was totally confident in her ability to organize the two-day entertainment for the biggest deal of his career.

Chapter 17

Late Monday morning Mars received an email from Mario outlining their agenda for Friday's meeting. Attached to the agenda was a detailed document production listing with the heading "Committee Documentation for South Loop Loan Closing." As stated in the email, Bachman Brothers was prepared to approve the loan request from Sammar, subject to all accepted conditions attached. The main purpose of the Friday meeting was to review the status of the requirements and create a timeline for a realistic closing date.

Mars immediately called Claudia into his office to review Bachman's agenda. "Wodecki, this is great news. Our loan will be approved once we meet these requirements," Mars announced. He handed her the document request and asked if they had any items outstanding.

Claudia reviewed the list. "We're in great shape. I have everything on this list, other than the final appraisal. The appraiser promised us a draft a week from tomorrow."

Mars thought for a second, and said, "We may be able to have this loan approved within a couple of weeks. This is fantastic."

Mars gave Sam the good news, and asked if he wanted to join them on Friday, but Sam passed, and Mars thought that was just as well. He liked that Sam trusted him to handle Sammar's real estate affairs. He was certainly up to the job, and he knew Friday evening was a critical component to the loan approval process. Mars and Claudia were going to pull out all the stops.

———————————

THROUGH THE WEEK, CLAUDIA and Mars compared notes and reviewed details for Friday's meeting—and, of course, the evening's entertainment. Claudia confirmed four women for dinner at Gibson's, plus whatever was needed after dinner. One of the women, Charlotte, was Claudia's favorite. She was a tall, five foot eight, classically beautiful woman with long dark hair, in her early forties, with radiant, flawless skin. She could charm the pants off any man. Claudia was certain Mario would go nuts for her.

Char, as her friends called her, was married to a wealthy jewelry wholesaler for seven years. She had been awarded a three-bedroom, three-bath condominium in a premier Gold Coast building in her divorce settlement five years earlier. The condo was close to Gibson's, so she and Claudia arranged for all four escorts to meet at Char's condo to prepare for their evening. Additionally, if the evening ended early for any of them, they could spend the night at Char's.

The other women were also beautiful and charming, and Claudia was confident Mario and Stuart would think they had died and gone to heaven. Mars had no idea how well Claudia had planned the social calendar for their guests. He also had no idea how much Claudia was offering these ladies for their services. But he trusted her judgment, and knew that whatever he paid, it was money well spent.

———————————

LATE THURSDAY AFTERNOON, MARS received an overview of Claudia's plans, plus five binders of documents for the Bachman Brothers meeting. The binders included every item on their list, as well as a letter to Bachman Brothers from the appraiser stating the appraised value would meet or exceed the loan amount requirement, and confirming that the final appraisal would be completed by the end of the following week. Mars was feeling confident about the Friday meeting and what would follow.

Claudia left no detail overlooked. She reserved a town car and Pano, her favorite driver, for the entire weekend. Pano would pick up Mario and Stuart from O'Hare and bring them directly to the Sammar offices, then take their luggage to the hotel, where Claudia had arranged to have them preregistered.

Mario and Stuart arrived at eight sharp Friday morning. Claudia was the first to greet them. "Good morning, gentlemen. We're delighted to have you with us, and look forward to hosting your weekend." With her great smile and looking picture-perfect, she offered her hand to Mario, and as he held it gently, he pulled her toward him in an embrace. Claudia allowed him to achieve his intended free feel of her upper body, as she suspected he was setting the tone for what he expected the weekend to offer. She pulled away slowly and greeted Stuart, who was all business. Claudia directed Mario and Stuart to the conference room, where Mars was waiting to greet his guests.

The entire day went as planned. Mario and Stuart reviewed the binder documents, and by lunchtime most of their agenda items were satisfied. Pano took them to Joe's for a two-hour lunch.

After lunch, the meeting continued in the conference room until three thirty, at which time the business issues were concluded. Claudia asked Mario if he and Stuart would like to head to the Four Seasons and relax before dinner. Mario said they would. Claudia rode along. She asked if Pano could pick them up at six thirty for dinner; however, Mario suggested they would just walk over to Gibson's and meet them in the bar. He wanted to arrive early, as the happy hour bar scene was filled with eye candy.

Claudia just smiled and said, "Mars and I and a few of my friends will meet you at six thirty for cocktails." As Mario and Stuart entered the hotel, Mario glanced back for one more lasting look at Claudia, who was standing next to Pano. She was well aware Mario was not finished hitting on her.

At five o'clock, Mars told Claudia he was heading over to the Whitehall Hotel, located directly across the street from the Four Seasons. He'd reserved his usual junior suite for the weekend. Over the years, Mars had used the Whitehall whenever he stayed in town; his corporate rate was so reasonable, he'd never bothered to lease an apartment. Additionally, the staff all knew him well and usually upgraded Mars to an executive suite whenever one was available. He wanted to take a shower and change into a different suit for the evening. Claudia instructed him to wear an open shirt rather than a tie.

Meanwhile, Claudia, ever the perfectionist, felt the need to double check on the evening's details. After calling Jennifer at Gibson's, she stopped by her apartment, just five short blocks from the restaurant, and performed her miraculous makeover, which in her case wasn't really necessary. But a shower, fresh makeup, and a spectacular cocktail dress with a short matching jacket was her plan. She checked herself one last time in the full length mirror, and was ready for the festivities to begin.

Just before six, Pano was waiting as Claudia exited her building. He dropped her at Gibson's and proceeded to Charlotte's to await the four ladies. Pano, an aging, southern European immigrant, had been in the car service business in Chicago for fifteen years. He was charming, and a consummate professional, but he pretty much kept to himself. Over the years, he'd observed many beautiful women painting the town, but even he was blown away by the talent that was about to grace this private party at Gibson's.

Claudia peeked into the crowded lounge, and as expected saw Mario and Stuart standing behind two young women having a cocktail. She laughed and thought, *How predictable.* When the four stunning women arrived, Claudia ushered them upstairs to the private dining room.

The large private room could accommodate a party of up to fifteen, but with just the eight diners, it seemed perfect. The ambience was elegant, but cozy. Sinatra and Bennett flowed softly from hidden speakers. Four ice buckets chilled bottles of Dom Perignon and Bâtard Montrachet.

Earlier in the week, Claudia had a lengthy conversation with Mario's executive assistant, Olivia. She learned several valuable bits of information. Mario's favorite wine was Chateau de Pommard, a French Burgundy. Jennifer, Claudia, and the restaurant's wine steward secured three bottles of a rare vintage, which Claudia justified as the cost of doing business. The Pommard would be served at dinner.

A side table was staged with an impressive array of hors d'oeuvres, specially prepared for their party. The display would be rolled into the room after the initial meet and greet.

Claudia went down to the bar to escort the men upstairs. Mars was having a cocktail with Mario and Stuart and the two young ladies. Claudia announced their room was ready and the men ordered another round for the ladies as they were saying their good-byes.

Mario was the first to enter the room, and the look on his face said it all. He looked like a young boy walking into FAO Schwartz for the first time. Stuart and Mars were equally blown away. Claudia introduced the men to Charlotte (Char); Catharina Smitts (Smitti), a gorgeous woman from Holland; Maria, a beauty from South America; and Denise, a southern blond bombshell. Adding to this bevy of beauties was Jennifer, their dinner captain for the evening, herself a real head-turner.

Claudia was amused as she watched Stuart; she suspected he was generally the recipient of his boss's castoffs. You know how it goes, when there are two women being sized up by two men, and one woman is more attractive than the other, the dominant male usually says, "I've got mine," leaving the shlub to be relegated to the least attractive. Well, tonight Stuart's ship had come in. Whomever Mario didn't choose for the evening would most likely exceed any woman in Stuart's life thus far. Mars, while astounded by the beauty of Claudia's friends, still continued to believe Claudia was the belle of the ball.

As Jennifer and her team refilled the champagne glasses, Mars suggested everyone be seated. Mario was in the middle of the table, within a comfortable distance for conversation with everyone. A beautifully printed card was placed at each setting. On the front were the date, and a welcome from Sammar to Mario Russo and Stuart Golding of Bachman Brothers. Inside was a list of the hors d'oeuvres selection, followed by the entrée choices, and lastly, the description of the delectable desserts and aperitifs that would complete the meal.

The day had exceeded Mars's expectations. He stood up to make a toast. As he raised his glass, he announced the evening was to exclude any business other than to say that he and Sammar looked forward to a long and successful relationship with Mario, Stuart, and Bachman Brothers. Mario raised his glass and enthusiastically responded, "I agree!"

Right on cue, the hors d'oeuvres were rolled in. As thin as he was, Mario loved his food and, casting his eyes over the incredible display—which, of course, included a beautifully prepared carpaccio, Mario's favorite—he again raised his glass and with gusto uttered a single word that said it all: "*Abbondanza!*"

The appetizer course completed, the waiter approached the ladies first regarding their entrée choices. As selections were made, Jennifer poured

Mario a sample of the Pommard she had selected for his approval. Mario played the wine scene with the smell and swirl before taking a sip, and with a big smile told Jennifer, "The wine is superb . . ."—rolling his eyes up and down her body—"only second to you." *What a cock hound*, Claudia thought. *This guy is relentless.*

As the evening progressed, Mario continued to entertain the group. He seemed to have an endless repertoire of stories, jokes, and anecdotes. Mars understood Mario's success in business; he was a true charmer. Stuart just sat and laughed at Mario, drinking his Dewar's and soda. It was clear he was having a good time.

Even the ladies seemed to be genuinely entertained by Mario. Mars leaned over to Claudia and said, "I think any one of your friends would be pleased to spend the night with Mario. They really seem to like him."

Claudia responded, "He is good-looking and fun to be around, so I don't imagine anyone would complain." Of course, Claudia had arranged it so that whether they were invited for further festivities or went back to Char's for a pajama party, all of these beautiful women were being rewarded generously.

Denise was showing interest in Stuart. It appeared she was perfectly content backing away from being another Mario conquest. *God love her,* Mars thought. Stuart was having a ball.

Shortly after the entrees were cleared, Claudia excused herself. She seemed to be away for quite some time, and Mars became concerned. Just as he was planning to look for her, Claudia made a grand entrance with a new group of people. Mars was stunned. What was she up to?

Everyone turned to watch Claudia and the newcomers enter the room. There was an older gentleman accompanied by several attractive young people. The room became silent as everyone recognized the man. Claudia smiled and introduced the one and only Tony Bennett.

As luck would have it, Tony was appearing Saturday night at Ravinia, an outdoor music venue in one of the North Shore suburbs. Claudia had been out recently with her friend Wesley Stone, head of security at Ravinia, and happened to mention her plans for the private dinner at Gibson's. Wesley told Claudia that coincidentally he would be accompanying Mr. Bennett to an event at Gibson's that same evening. The two had arranged for Tony to make a surprise appearance at the Sammar dinner.

Mario's assistant had told Claudia that Tony Bennett was one of Mario's favorite entertainers, and that Mario's mother was a huge fan. She said Mario had taken his mother to see Tony at Madison Square Garden years ago. This encounter was just too good to be true.

Tony couldn't help but notice the room full of beauties and joked that he would rather be at this party than the one he was attending. He sat down for a while and conversed with everyone. Claudia had one last surprise for the group; she pulled out a folder with a dozen photos of Tony. She had even prearranged Tony's willingness to sign autographs, and he graciously accommodated her request to write personal messages on each photo. Mario asked for a very personalized message to his mother. Tony wrote:

> *Dear Carmela,*
> *I enjoyed a wonderful evening with your son. We shared a glass of wine and made a toast to your good health. I hope to meet you in person someday.*
> *Best Wishes,*
> *Your friend, Tony Bennett*

Jennifer brought out a camera, also part of the plan. Tony and Mario stood in front of the Gibson's banner on the wall, and with his arm around Tony's shoulder, Mario gave a great big smile. Mario then asked Mars and Stuart to join them. The four men smiled broadly with arms around one another. Claudia suggested a ladies-only picture with Tony. Mario grabbed the camera and asked Jennifer to join the ladies. She seemed reluctant, but Tony insisted. Mario snapped two poses as he said, "Excellent," with a big smile.

Before Tony returned to his party, he handed Mario an envelope and said, "I hope you can attend." He then went to each of the ladies, embraced them warmly, and gave them a kiss on the cheek. *What a wonderful, humble man,* Mars thought.

At the doorway, Tony turned, smiled, and broke into, *"Chicago is my . . . kind of town."* He held the last note and raised his arms, as if he had just completed the finale to a sold-out concert. Everyone applauded and smiled as Tony blew kisses to his new friends and bowed out the door.

Inside the envelope were four front-row tickets to Tony's Saturday evening performance at Ravinia.

As everyone was returning to their seats, the dessert cart was presented. In the middle was Gibson's famous seven-inch-high chocolate cream pie. It looked outrageous. Enough pie to feed twenty guests. Claudia was once again armed with the knowledge of Mario's love for that exact dessert. Surrounding the pie were cookies and various tarts, three kinds of port, a bottle of Remy Martin XO Cognac—Mario's favorite—a variety of liqueurs, and carafes of coffee. Amazingly, no one appeared to be feeling the effects of all the alcohol, and seemed open to dessert, even after such a large dinner. The ladies passed on the desserts, but Mario and Stuart accepted large slices of pie, and were raving.

It was almost eleven, but Mario didn't want the evening to end. He insisted everyone reconvene at their suite to continue the party. Mars was starting to drag, but Claudia wouldn't have any whining. Mario asked Jennifer if he could take two bottles of Dom back to the suite. Of course, she didn't hesitate to bag up the two bottles, and included a corkscrew. Everyone thanked Jennifer for her excellent service. Jennifer told her guests, "This was the best group and the most fun I've had in years."

As expected, Mario was the last to say goodnight to Jennifer, giving her a big hug and kiss. He whispered something in her ear, and she laughed. Claudia doubled back to sign the check and hand Jennifer a few extra hundred-dollar bills, an additional gratuity on top of the eighteen percent added to the bill. Jennifer was worth every penny, and then some. Claudia couldn't help herself. She asked Jennifer, "What did Mario whisper?"

Jennifer laughed again. "'I would like to pour XO in your navel and lick it up.' What a player!" Both women rolled their eyes as Claudia hugged Jennifer.

PANO WAS WAITING OUTSIDE, and the ladies, all in high heels, decided to have him drive them to the Four Seasons. It was still unclear who was staying the night with Mario. Denise would be with Stuart, unquestionably. Mario, Mars, and Stuart walked the few blocks as it was a warm night and the walk was much needed after all the eating and drinking. The ladies were waiting in the lobby as the men arrived.

Mario directed everyone to a waiting elevator. The suite was perfect for entertaining. There was a large living area with a breathtaking view of the city skyline, comfortable sofas and chairs, as well as a fully equipped wet bar. A dining table and six chairs were off to one side, and two bedrooms flanked the center main living room, at opposite sides of the suite.

The ladies took off their heels and settled in for another glass of champagne. There was a knock at the door. It was Bobby from Gibson's. Jennifer had boxed up the chocolate cream pie and the other desserts, and included the remainder of the Remy Martin XO. Bobby opened the box on the dining room table, and Mars knew immediately: Claudia's fingerprints were all over this idea. Mars handed Bobby a couple of twenties as he thanked him at the door.

Mars and Claudia looked at each other as they realized Mario was not going to dismiss any of the ladies. He seemed to have big plans for the remainder of the evening, involving the chocolate cream pie and the XO. Char removed a gold cigarette case from her clutch. In it were three perfectly rolled joints. The ladies enthusiastically encouraged Char to light up, and the party was about to ascend to the next level.

Mars decided it was time to say good night. He and Claudia shook hands with Mario and Stuart as they backed toward the door. Mario grabbed Claudia in his arms and kissed her cheek. He couldn't resist; he had to tell her she was going to miss a very good after party, and invited her to stay. She respectfully declined, and she and Mars headed toward the elevator.

ON THE WAY DOWN, Mars asked Claudia to join him for a nightcap. They went to the hotel lounge where they settled in for a debriefing, so to speak.

Mars started, "I don't want to know what this night cost me. You can tell me on Monday, but whatever you spent is fine with me. You planned an amazing evening. When we close this loan, you'll be handsomely rewarded."

"Thank you," Claudia said. "This is all part of my job, and I know I'm good at it, but honestly, Mars, I love what I do."

Though it was well after midnight, the lounge was still crowded. "Since you usually stay across the street at the Whitehall, do you hang out at this lounge often?" Claudia inquired.

"Not really. I've been here possibly once or twice."

The cocktail waitress approached the table and said, "Hi, Mars, I haven't seen you in weeks."

Mars sheepishly replied, "Hi, Cindy. Say hello to Claudia."

Cindy smiled and said, "Claudia, nice to meet you. And Mars, you look like you're doing very well for yourself." Mars smiled and ordered two coffees with Bailey's and cream.

Claudia looked at Mars and laughed, "So, you don't come here often?" Mars just smiled. As Cindy was on her way with their drinks, two couples were leaving the lounge, and both women looked over and said, "Hi, Mars, good to see you again." Mars was not only embarrassed, he was busted. This actually was one of his favorite bars in town.

Taking a sip of his coffee, Mars decided to become a little personal. "It's hard to believe you weren't attracted to Mario. He seems to have a way with women."

Claudia answered, "Let me tell you, the years I was with my husband, I met Mario's type more than you can imagine. All those commodity traders thought they were God's gift. They're a total turn off to me."

Mars continued, "Don't you want to get back into the dating scene?"

"In time, I will. I have a male friend or two, but nothing serious."

Mars felt he might be stepping out of bounds with this conversation, so he went back to talking shop. After about an hour, Mars walked Claudia to the hotel entrance where Pano was waiting. He kissed her and said, "I thank you again, Wodecki, for a great evening. I know Stuart thanks you, and Mario with his three companions will certainly thank you tomorrow. And, by the way, Tony Bennett? Just aces. Amazing. Let's meet at the office at, say, noon tomorrow? We can check in with the guys, and I suspect we'll need Pano to take them to Ravinia." Mars added, "Just for fun, who do you think Mario will ask to go with him?"

Claudia didn't hesitate. "Char. He's really hot for her."

Mars added, "It seemed like he was hot for every one of them."

They both laughed and said good night. Exhausted, Mars walked across the street to his hotel, up to his room, and crashed.

———————

AFTER A LIGHT BREAKFAST at the hotel, Mars cabbed it to the office. It was a little before noon, and Claudia was standing in her office on the phone. Mars immediately noticed she was wearing tight jeans. He had never seen her in jeans before, and he couldn't believe how fabulous her ass looked. She was also wearing a tight, white, body-hugging top with a zipper in the front, lowered just enough to show slight cleavage. In all this time working with Claudia, Mars had never made a move on her. He was afraid it would become awkward, and he didn't want to jeopardize their excellent relationship or show a lack of respect. But now, it was all he could do to restrain himself.

Her phone call completed, Claudia came in to report to Mars on the after party. "Char and Denise are going with Mario and Stuart to Ravinia tonight, and with Pano handling the transportation, we're off the hook."

"Great!"

"Between the XO and the cream pie, the four of them had one hell of a time. No surprise, but Stuart only lasted less than thirty minutes after we left. Denise stayed the night and went back to Char's in the early morning. Mr. Mario, on the other hand, partied until about five. According to the three girls, it seems he has quite an insatiable sexual appetite."

"Really?" Mars laughed. "Who knew?"

Claudia and Mars continued to shuffle some papers and discuss mundane issues, but Mars was feeling something this Saturday morning. The two of them were the only ones in the office, and Mars decided to take a chance.

"Wodecki, at the risk of pissing you off, I have to tell you about a dream I had last night," he began. "In my dream, you and I were alone in the office, and I came up behind you, wrapped my arms around you, pushed my pelvis into your butt, and grabbed your boobs with both hands. Then I kissed you on the back of the neck. I hope you don't mind my telling you this, but I just couldn't keep it to myself."

Claudia fought back a smile. "And then what?"

"I was totally turned on, but unfortunately, I woke up and it was over," Mars said, with a laugh.

She remained in the chair across from Mars for a few seconds, then excused herself. *Jesus, now I've really blown it,* he thought. Within a minute or two, Claudia called to Mars from across the workstations. She was in the storage room, and directed Mars to come in. He was dumbfounded. As Mars entered the room, she locked the door from the inside. She said to Mars, "Okay, this is a one-time thing. I want you to come toward me just as you did in your dream."

Mars got hard just thinking about what was happening. He came up behind her, rubbed his crotch into her tight ass, and reached around to cup her perfectly shaped big tits in his hands. He was harder than he'd been as a teenager. Claudia smelled great. He kissed the back of her neck.

After about a minute of grinding into each other, Claudia pulled away and said, "Mars, we need to stop. Just like in your dream, you have to wake up. It's a very bad idea for this to go any further."

Mars reluctantly knew she was right.

Claudia turned around and kissed him gently on the lips. She had never offered her lips to him before. She turned to open the storage room door and said, "Sometimes the things that *don't* happen turn out to be the most memorable. You're a great boss and friend." She went back to her office.

The rest of the afternoon was spent doing paperwork and sending emails. When he saw Claudia again later, they both just smiled.

––––––––––––

ON MONDAY MORNING, WODECKI buzzed, "It's Mario, line one."

Mars picked up. "Mario, good to hear from you."

"Mars," Mario said, "I want to thank you and Claudia for our weekend. I can't remember a better time. Claudia's friends are incredible. And, Tony Bennett . . . just an unbelievable time. We can't thank you enough."

Mars replied, "Sure you can. Send us the final approval for the South Loop loan."

"It's in legal as we speak. Subject to the appraisal amount, the loan is approved. Of course, the lawyers will now take over, so hopefully we can have this funded within a couple of weeks. You know the devil is always in the details. Now, you understand we must have your personal guaranties on the loan."

"No problem," Mars replied. He thought to himself, *What's one more loan guaranty? We've already personally guaranteed dozens.*

"One last thing, Mars. You can't tell me you're not hitting Claudia. I just don't believe it."

Mars laughed and said, "Only in my dreams, Mario . . . only in my wildest dreams."

Chapter 18

ALL CANDIDATES WHO RUN for public office need the nod from their party's leadership. They also need support from big-ticket donors. Usually, these are men and women with a clear agenda, but that's a necessary evil; without their funding, there would be no campaign. However, when all is said and done, no matter how much support a candidate has in high places, the candidate also needs a huge volunteer contingent—the people who actually do the cheering and the phone calling and the mailing and all of the other grassroots, boots-on-the-ground, get-out-the-vote, grunt work that no campaign can be won without.

To build a volunteer base, the candidate has to inspire voters to get out and support him. And although these on-the-ground forces can be manufactured—Democrats use the unions or patronage workers, and Republicans use the Chamber of Commerce or the NRA or the evangelicals—it is preferable to have that one guy, that truly populist candidate, whom everyone genuinely loves and is truly inspired by. That guy can generate a genuine outpouring of popular support.

Despite his intellectual limitations, Mike Kovach was very good at capturing voter support. He was completely comfortable in the spotlight. It was his favorite place to be. If he hadn't gotten into politics, he probably would have been a stand-up comic. With his incredible way with words and the innate ability to entertain a crowd, it was clear to everyone that all they needed to do was let him loose in front of a microphone, and the masses would follow.

———————————

MANY, IF NOT MOST, campaign volunteers are young and enthusiastic kids who believe completely in their candidate. They are often totally committed and unflappable, willing to do almost anything in support of their favorite guy or gal. These are the idealists. They're ready to do whatever it takes to get their candidate elected.

Sometimes, these young supporters can be a bit overzealous. Enter Tony Kinahan, the son of a successful entrepreneur and businessman from the suburban North Shore. His father was a big contributor to the Kovach campaign and recommended his son for the unpaid position that would be Tony's introduction to the politics of big business in the city and state.

His father offered one important piece of advice. "Tony, if you should run into any problems—anything you feel you shouldn't try to handle on your own—you need to talk to my friend, Johnny Jarzik. He's helped me through some difficult situations. If you ever find yourself in trouble, Johnny should *always* be your first call."

Tony's father gave him Jarzik's personal cell phone number, adding, "Johnny always answers the phone. And, I mean it, son—he's your *first* call."

———————————

ONE BLUSTERY OCTOBER NIGHT, shortly before Halloween, and a few weeks before the election, Tony and a bunch of like-minded compatriots—six guys, two girls, most of whom had been encouraged by their parents to get active in the Kovach campaign—set out to prove their undying commitment to Mike Kovach.

It was almost midnight. All the other campaign workers headed home, but for a small nucleus of the truly faithful. Eight twenty-somethings remained in the darkened campaign office.

"Are you sure this is okay, Tony?" asked Diane, a pretty blonde with beautiful green eyes.

"Stop stressing, Diane," Tony chuckled. "This is nothing. Our little plan is penny-ante compared to the crazy things that go on in most campaigns. You wouldn't believe the dirty tricks perpetrated every day all across this nation during an election season. Haven't you ever read *All The President's Men?*" Tony laughed.

"Yeah, Diane, stop fussing," a big redheaded kid named Patrick offered. "This is more of a prank than anything else, especially when you compare it to the kind of crap other fucking campaigns pull. Even if we're caught, which we won't be, the cops would just laugh this off. So, don't worry your pretty little head. This is going to be fun, that's all."

It was a simple plan. They were going to change some political signs.

They piled into a van, rented by the campaign, which was loaded with red-white-and-blue signs touting Mike Kovach for Governor. Each wore dark clothes in anticipation of their clandestine little stunt.

Once in the van, Tony and Patrick passed out black ski caps and black gloves, and they all enthusiastically pulled on the knit paraphernalia. They looked like an honest-to-goodness second-story gang.

Tony pulled away from the curb into the sparse middle-of-the-night traffic heading toward a posh suburban neighborhood that was a well-known Republican enclave. Tony had scouted the neighborhood the night before and found the lawns covered with green-and-white placards and signs supporting Kovach's opponent, Thomas Parker.

There were very few, if any, admitted Democrats in the nicer northwest suburban areas, where financially well-off conservative bankers and corporate types lived side by side. This was Fox News country.

Everyone suspected that there were Democrats hidden in the homes without signs out on their front lawns, but very few were brave enough to boldly and publicly admit to it by putting up this year's red-white-and-blue signage of the Democratic candidate. After all, they wanted their kids to have friends.

"Okay, guys, we're almost there. Keep it down!" Tony had to yell out over the music and the excited laughter as he drove. Everyone was pumped up and having a good time. Any nervousness and concern had been completely replaced by a sort of team spirit. These kids had no true malicious intent. They were just out on an adventure.

As the van slowed to a stop, Tony clicked off the headlights, and the laughter died down. Tony spoke in a loud whisper, "Okay, it's show time!"

It was dark on this section of the block, with only a crescent moon to highlight the manicured lawns. The kids, in their dark clothes and stocking caps, blended into the bushes and shrubs as they stealthily scurried across the suburban landscape.

They whispered to each other and giggled as they changed one sign after another. It was easy: pull up a sign, throw it on the ground, stick a new sign right in the hole from the first one. The mission was going as planned. By morning, this neighborhood would be temporarily Democratic.

Diane and Patrick, acting as a team, tiptoed across a lawn near the end of the block, passing a pickup truck parked in the driveway. On that truck was a green-and-white Parker bumper sticker, and next to that was another sticker that read in bold red letters: *I SUPPORT THE NRA*. Under that, in smaller print, it stated clearly: *You can have my gun when you pry it from my cold dead hands*.

"This is the last one," Patrick whispered, as they crept across the dew-soaked lawn toward a large Parker sign next to a big oak tree. "I'm out of signs. Plus, I'm getting cold."

"Okay, pussy, we can head back if your widdle fingers are getting cold," Diane chided good-naturedly. Actually, she was shivering and was glad to be heading back to the van herself.

Inside the darkened house, Wilfred Stodemeyer stirred next to Claire, his wife of thirty-three years, who continued to snore quietly. He hated getting old, just hated it. Since he had passed the age of fifty-nine, he'd rarely slept through the night. He always had to get up to pee at least once, sometimes twice.

Suddenly, Wilfred heard a sound from outside in front of the house. He slowly rolled out of bed and lumbered over toward the window. His back creaked and strained. He shook his head. He expected to see the paperboy on his bike, or maybe the garbage men. He was groggy from sleep and had no idea what time it was, or even what day. He glanced at the bedroom clock:1:22.

"That's odd," he grumbled to himself, as he hobbled sleepily. "It's too damn early for the paperboy."

When he got to the window and peeked through the blinds, he straightened and was immediately wide awake. He shook his head again and snapped himself into full consciousness. He split the blinds with his fingertips and peered out of the window once again. What he saw was clear to him. In the shadows of the bushes and the large oak tree in his front yard were two dark figures creeping across his front lawn. One was carrying something over his shoulder. He couldn't make it out. The figures sneaked from shadow to shadow slightly crouched, obviously trying to avoid detection.

"Claire!" He whispered hoarsely, his gravelly voice coming to life. "Claire, wake up!"

"What, dear? What's wrong?" she asked, half-asleep.

"Wake up, now! We're being robbed!"

"What? We're what?"

"Robbed," he said. "There are robbers on our front lawn!"

Wilfred hustled back toward the bed, dropped to his knees, and reached underneath it. He pulled out a Remington Model 1100 Classic Field auto-loader shotgun and checked to see if it was still loaded with shells. It was.

"Stay here," he hissed to his wife. "Get on the floor."

"Wilfred . . ."

"Don't come downstairs," he whispered, as he left the room and headed for the stairs. "Call 911," he barked over his shoulder.

When he stepped into the front room of their home, Wilfred went straight to the curtains framing the picture window. He stopped and peeked around the curtain, all but his eyes hidden behind it. He wasn't wrong and he wasn't imagining things. There were two figures boldly snaking their way across his lawn, from bush to bush.

Adrenaline pumped through his veins as he snapped up straight, his back to the curtains, shotgun at present-arms, tightly against his chest.

He peeked around the curtain again. They were coming closer to the house. The one carrying something over his shoulder was leading the way. Wilfred couldn't make out what it was in the darkness, but he had absolutely no intention of waiting to find out. His wife was upstairs. He had gone over in his mind a thousand times what he would do in this situation.

Wilfred bolted to the front door and looked through the tiny round window at eye level. They were coming closer. He snapped on the outside light and flung open the door in one continuous action. He stood in the doorway, filling it. Two people were caught in the glare of the porch light like deer in headlights, eyes bulging.

Wilfred raised his shotgun, aimed, and fired.

The explosion echoed throughout the quiet neighborhood. The two intruders turned and started to run.

"Big mistake, motherfuckers!" he bellowed. He squeezed the trigger again. The big gun discharged once more, sending out reverberating echoes.

Diane shrieked, spun around, and fell to the ground.

———

When Tony Kinahan heard the deafening blast from Wilfred Stodemeyer's shotgun, he was no more than thirty yards away. He was running toward the sound of the first gunshot when he heard the second shot ring out. He watched in horror as his beautiful friend collapsed.

He was at Diane's side in seconds. She was pale and had a look of fear and befuddlement on her face, but she was surprisingly calm. She looked up at him. "What happened?" she asked softly.

"Where are you hit? Can you tell?" He carefully brushed strands of blond hair from Diane's eyes. Tony felt wetness around Diane's right shoulder and then he noticed two separate small spots on her neck where blood was oozing a couple of inches apart. Buckshot, Tony thought.

Already Tony's mind was racing. He knew they couldn't stay there; they could not be caught there, and he was sure the police were on their way. He wasn't concerned what would happen to them; he was just calculating how this incident would reflect upon his boss, the candidate, Mike Kovach.

Tony looked up and could see that the lunatic on the porch was reloading. "We gotta get outta here!" He reached into his pocket and pulled out keys to the van.

"Patrick," he almost whispered, "get the van and get everybody in it. Get them all to calm the fuck down. I'll bring Diane. I'll help her. We gotta go, man."

Patrick grabbed the keys and nodded.

The sound of sirens in the distance filled the air as Tony gingerly picked up Diane and carried her to the street. He wobbled briefly under her weight, but got her to the curb just as Patrick screeched to a stop in front of them and the side door of the van slid open. Everyone carefully helped Diane into the van and gently laid her down on the floor, as they all huddled around her, offering support.

Only a few minutes had elapsed since the first shotgun blast interrupted the quiet night. Patrick drove within the speed limit and away from the sound of the sirens. A squad roared past them, lights blazing. Tony noticed it was a Cook County Sheriff's car, not from a local suburban police department. That was odd.

Tony heard his father's words echoing in his mind as he took out his cell phone. He drew a deep breath and scrolled to Johnny Jarzik's number.

———

JOHNNY JARZIK HAD BEEN in politics all of his life. He'd become adept at getting his candidate's name in the papers when it would help him get elected. That was an important part of his job. He could also be relied upon when it was absolutely imperative to keep his candidate's name *out* of the papers. He was accustomed to phone calls in the wee hours of the night.

"Hello?" he said, still groggy with sleep.

"Johnny, it's Tony Kinahan. We've got a problem. I need your help."

"Tony, Jesus, it's two a.m. What the hell is going on?"

Tony went on to briefly explain the situation. Part of Johnny Jarzik's genius was that he didn't get mad when he got bad news—he just went to work. After hearing Tony out, Jarzik sprang into action.

"How badly is she hurt? Is she conscious?" he asked quickly.

"Yeah, she's conscious, alert, calm, but she's bleeding from the area around her shoulder and I can see where buckshot entered her neck."

Johnny thought for a split second. "Where did this happen?"

"I thought we were in Mt. Prospect," Tony said, "but the police cars were from the Cook County Sheriff."

Jarzik pondered this for a minute. The Cook County Sheriff was responding to a 911 call? They must not have been in the Mount Prospect city limits, they must have been out in unincorporated Cook County where the Cook County officials have jurisdiction. That was a *huge* break.

"Do you have a pencil or pen?" he said suddenly, and waited for Tony to acknowledge that he did. "Okay, write this down. Dr. Kenneth Jensen, 5858 West Austin. Get on 90 to the Kennedy. Get off at the Austin/Foster exit. At this time of night you'll be there within fifteen minutes. The doctor will be waiting for you."

Tony yelled to Patrick, "Get on the Kennedy and head toward the city!"

Johnny continued in Tony's ear. "It'll be okay, kid. Just get to the doc. Step on it!"

Johnny Jarzik then made another call. It rang and rang, and he began to wonder if it was too late to try to pull this off.

"Hello?" came a thick voice on the other end.

"Oren?"

"Yeah. Who the hell is this?"

"It's Jarzik."

Jarzik waited a few moments for this to penetrate Orenthal's half-conscious brain.

"Johnny, what the hell?"

"Oren, I'm sorry to bother you at this hour, but we've got a crisis."

"A crisis? What the hell? At two a.m.?" Oren was awake now, but still befuddled.

"We had an incident near Mt. Prospect. Kids were changing lawn signs and a girl got shot by some pain-in-the-ass homeowner. She seems to be okay. They're on the way to Dr. Jensen's. But, we need someone to go to the scene and contain it. Now."

"Goddamn it, Johnny, it's the middle of the night. Why me?" Oren demanded. He was awake enough to realize the implications of getting involved in a mess like this, and he was having doubts.

"The Cook County Sheriff responded to the call. With all your friends in the county, I'm thinking you're the guy to get out there and manage the situation."

Oren felt reassured. "Oh, okay. Cook County Sheriff. Right. We have lots of friends over there. Let me call somebody."

Relief surged through Jarzik. "Find out what we need to do, who saw what. You know the drill. Get the coppers to help contain this—you know, just kids playing pranks, Halloween kind of bullshit, no big deal. And talk to the asshole with the itchy fucking trigger finger. Get going before they take this too far to contain it."

Oren hung up. Jarzik made another call. He would never call this guy in the middle of the night if it wasn't an emergency. But he was going to need cash to deal with this situation, and the man with the cash was Sam Alsheriti.

THE VAN LURCHED TO a stop in front of a brick bungalow that looked exactly like all the other bungalows on the street, except for the porch light burning brightly. The group got out and Patrick and Tony reached in and gently helped Diane out of the van. With their help, she could stand and walk, which was a good sign.

A kind-looking older gentleman came out onto the porch and watched the slow-moving group of kids heading toward him, assisting a pretty young girl across the front yard to the well-kept home. He was balding, and it was clear he had hastily thrown on baggy trousers and a button-down shirt. The hair that was left on his head was askew.

"Let me see," he said, delicately pulling back Diane's sweater to examine the wound. "Oh, this isn't too bad. I'll have you fixed up in no time."

THE NORMALLY QUIET TREE-LINED street where the Stodemeyers had lived for twenty-five years was abuzz with commotion. Lights were on in several of the homes on the block, and a couple of neighbors were on their front stoops gawking. Two Cook County Sheriff's squad cars and an ambulance were parked on the street, blue and red lights flashing in front of the darkened house. Only Mr. Stodemeyer stood out in front of his house speaking with a uniformed police officer. His wife was mortified over the scene her husband had created. How would she explain all this to the girls over coffee in the morning?

A black Ford Crown Victoria pulled up to the scene without fanfare. It had the antennas, spotlights, and the absence of hubcaps that were always the dead giveaways of an unmarked police car. The passengers were in plain clothes.

Orenthal Mitchell got out at the curb. The driver was the night watch commander from the Cook County Sheriff's Office. They immediately began to question the uniformed officers on the scene, and then spoke with Mr. Stodemeyer.

Oren called Johnny Jarzik.

"Nobody saw a thing. A couple of shots were fired from a shotgun. The guy who had the gun swears that he saw people creeping across his lawn dressed in dark clothes, but the officers on the scene are skeptical. They're putting this down as a teenage prank. It looks like we got off easy with this one."

He hung up.

Jarzik called Dr. Jensen and confirmed that the girl was okay. And he assured the doctor that someone would drop off a nice little package in the morning.

Then he called Sam to confirm that the problem was totally contained, but they would need the cash in the morning for the doc.

"No problem," Sam said simply. "Send Oren to my office to pick it up."

His night's work done, Johnny went back to bed and laid his head on the cool pillow. *We literally dodged a bullet on this one,* he thought, just before he fell asleep.

Chapter 19

November 5, 2002. Election Day.

It was a banner day for Sam Alsheriti.

Sam spent the evening at the Chicago Hilton, where Mike Kovach was holding his election night event. The candidate was ensconced in a suite, watching the returns roll in. He was flanked by his father-in-law on one side and Sam Alsherti on the other.

Midway through the evening, Sam went down to the ballroom to press the flesh. He was *the Man*. Everyone came up and shook his hand. They all knew he was the guy who'd provided the funds—the funds that bought the advertising, leased the campaign offices, and greased the outstretched palms. They also knew he would be the guy to get things done.

Mars was with him that night, watching Sam revel in the glory.

This time, Sam did climb onto the platform to stand with Mike during his victory speech, and to his right stood Malik Alawi, flashing that now standard grin, having just been reelected to another term in the Illinois senate. And people in the know knew that Malik was being slated to run for the US

Senate. Sam seemed to be radiating power as he moved about the room.

Mars couldn't help but remind Sam that in ancient Rome, when a victorious general was granted a triumphal parade by the grateful senate, he was accompanied in his chariot throughout the parade route by a loyal follower whose duty it was to keep repeating to the general, as he basked in the adulation of the masses, "All fame is fleeting."

Sam looked at Mars as if he was crazy.

THE ELECTION OF MIKE Kovach as governor changed the course of Illinois politics in several ways—some foreseeable, some not.

The candidate received a great deal of support from the downstate areas that were traditionally Republican strongholds. This was directly attributable to the alliance between Vince Perino and Sam Alsheriti. Perino was flexing his muscles. He wanted to show off. He sent out his minions in full force, and the result was an amazing Republican turnout in favor of a Democratic candidate, normally unheard of in that part of the state.

Suddenly, whether you were a Republican or a Democrat mattered much less than it had in the past. It was significantly more important to be a part of the "in crowd" if you wanted to make piles of cash by providing goods or services to the State of Illinois. The death grip on power that the Republicans had enjoyed for well over a generation had been diluted; that was true. However, certain Republicans could live with that so long as the bucks continued to flow uninterrupted in their direction.

MIKE SET UP HIS "kitchen cabinet"—a close-knit group of his most trusted friends and advisors who would always have his ear and his back. There were meetings in Sammar's office at least twice a week with Mike and this group. Sam Alsheriti was his primary fund raiser and fixer. Terry Monahan had been Mike's best friend in law school and had stuck with him throughout his previous campaigns. Mike considered Terry his closest friend, the guy he could talk to about anything. Chuck "Chip" Faldo was an accountant, and Mike's go-to guy to handle all the financial aspects of the campaign.

This was the core group.

Others were also regular attendees at these informal meetings. Among them, of course, was Orenthal Mitchell. He and the new governor had become fast friends. Loyalty paid off with both Mike Kovach and Sam Alsheriti. If you stuck by the candidate and worked hard to get him elected, you were rewarded accordingly. Oren was one of Mike's earliest supporters, and now his turn had come. He could consider himself a true insider, a member of the inner circle, very close to the governor.

Mars admitted that at first, it was pretty heady stuff. After all, how many people do you know who host the governor of the state for private meetings twice a week? And how many people get to be on the inside, to know who's going to be appointed to what powerful positions, long before it hits the media?

What everybody didn't know—what nobody could have predicted—was the insatiable thirst for power growing within Sam Alsheriti.

He had told Mars his plan years ago. *Politicians have power, Mars, and through them . . . I can get power for myself.*

It seemed that Sam's understanding, and his predictions concerning the inner workings of the average, run-of-the-mill politician, were spot on.

The meetings in Sammar's office between the new governor, Sam, Terry, and Chip increased in frequency. Mike Kovach publicly announced that he planned to run the state from his home in Chicago rather than the governor's mansion in Springfield. This decision kept him close. Everyone in the know came to realize that the State of Illinois, or at least the executive branch, was being run out of Sammar's little office on Milwaukee Avenue, led by none other than Sam Alsheriti.

It was at one of these meetings that the subject of the shooting at the Stodemeyer home came up. Mike Kovach was absolutely flabbergasted to learn that he might have lost the election due to such an arbitrary accidental event. When he heard the specifics, he thanked Sam and Oren profusely and assured them that he would never forget what they'd done for him.

Sam never did anything by chance. He had just opened the door to discuss something that had been on his mind for a while.

"I want Johnny Jarzik to come and work for us," Sam said, rather unexpectedly.

Terry Monahan laughed. "Are you kidding? Jarzik is famously shy about connecting himself to any one candidate or politician. He's a free agent. That's his trademark. He belongs to no party and is beholden to no single elected official. You're not the first political advisor who's fantasized about having Johnny Jarzik on his team. I just don't think we could get him to commit to us exclusively."

"Who said anything about asking him to be exclusive?" Sam asked, offhandedly. It was clear Sam had something up his sleeve.

"What are you getting at?" Mike asked. His curiosity had been piqued.

"Suppose we were to offer him a free office right in the State of Illinois Building downtown. We could set him up on the same floor as your office, Mike. But, he would have his own separate phone service, his own separate prorated bills for heating and air conditioning, his own secretary and reception. Now, we would pay those bills . . . and consider those costs, together with a reasonable monthly stipend, as a retainer for his services. Yet, he remains an independent contractor, an independent entity. It would make him much more available to us, without making him an employee of the state." Sam paused and looked around at each and every one in the room. "Who would pass up an opportunity like that?"

Why would he pass it up? Mars thought, what the hell, he'd throw in his two cents. "What's the benefit to the state? Other than the access, why do it?"

"Oh, I'm sure we will think of a viable reason to justify the expense. The expense would be nominal, right? We have other political consultants on retainer," Sam questioned. "Why don't we look into it? It is just something to consider . . . something I was kicking around. After all, Johnny really saved our collective asses following that ridiculous shooting. Maybe we should show our gratitude."

"He would be a good guy to have around, you know. He's a magician when it comes to unpredictable situations," Chip added. Chip was the one who would look into the logistics. "I'll check into it. I'll approach Jarzik and float the balloon." Chip made a note on his Blackberry, and that was the end of that.

From the Memoirs of Mars Gregory:

IT WAS A LONG day, an incredibly important day for Sammar. At four o'clock on Thursday afternoon, the closing of our purchase of the land for the South Loop project, with a mortgage loan provided by the Bachman Brothers, was completed. We secured an appraisal showing the value of the 64 acres at $40 million, even though we were only paying $24 million for the property. The appraisers agreed that our work to rezone the property for development had caused a significant increase in the value. On paper, we had already made a cool $16 million. Even better, this higher valuation enabled us to get a loan that not only included funding for the land acquisition, but provided funds for our initial development costs, saving Sammar from having to advance those costs ourselves. True, Sam and I had been required personally to sign a guarantee of repayment: if the shit hit the fan, and the project went down the drain, Bachman Brothers could come after Sam and me for everything we had—our houses, cars, personal bank accounts, everything. But what the hell—things were going so well, this wasn't much of a worry for us. Thanks to the hard work of Wodecki and our staff, the initial funds were in our account. I was on cloud nine.

Sam, however, was preoccupied as usual. On the biggest day of our real estate company, I could not allow Sam to forgo, at the very least, a cocktail celebration. I invited him to meet me in our office courtyard, and greeted him with a bottle of Macallan 25 single malt scotch, a rare and expensive gift given to me by one of our contractors years ago. I had been saving it for a special occasion.

I poured us each a couple of ounces in cocktail glasses containing one ice cube, and we toasted the South Loop closing.

Sam looked at me and smiled. "Mars, you did one hell of a job putting this project together. And hiring Claudia was a brilliant move. Just be careful, though—she could be a home wrecker."

I responded, "Sam, that would only happen in my wildest dreams."

"Whatever you say, Mars," Sam answered, with a shrug of his shoulders.

That comment implied he was certain I was having an affair with her; however, I realized he wouldn't believe anything I might say regarding Wodecki, so I said nothing. We raised our glasses one more time and enjoyed the moment. For a second or two, I thought about sharing with Sam the value Wodecki had brought to this transaction, and the fact I had rewarded her with a $25,000 bonus, which she felt was very generous. I thought otherwise. Sam seemed as though he couldn't care less about our South Loop milestone.

Within minutes the subject changed. Sam was moving on to his favorite topic, politics. "Mars, I told you that politicians would help me," Sam was saying, in a moment of pure candor.

I nodded my head. "Yes, you did, Sam. Yes, you certainly did. And it sure looks like you were right."

"Mike has given me authority to make all the board appointments," Sam said offhandedly.

"What do you mean?"

"Mike Kovach, our governor, believes that it is his job to attend to the 'big-picture' concerns. He likes to delegate the day-to-day activities and responsibilities to others. That is his management style. I wonder where that came from?" Sam was smiling that sly smile of his. Sam was telling me that it is the province of the governor to make the appointments to all the boards and commissions in the state, but that Sam had convinced his friend and protégé, Governor Kovach, to allow him to make those appointments. Sam now had that power.

All I could respond was, "That's fantastic, Sam. He must really trust you."

My partner smiled. "Who better to make these appointments?" he asked, totally serious. "I know who our friends are, who our contributors are, don't I? I will be able to reward the people who will continue to help fund our campaigns, who will always be willing to show their gratitude."

If what Sam was saying was true, he had, in fact, become one of the most powerful men in the state. He would appoint people who would control billions and billions of state funds, state contracts, and state expenditures. People appointed to these positions would be indebted to him for life. He was never elected to any office, but he had all the power of someone who had been.

"It is a lot of power, Mars, a lot of power. My boyhood wishes are being fulfilled."

Just then a short and rotund figure appeared. He had the worst comb-over I had ever seen.

"Ah," Sam said, rising to greet the newcomer. "Marvin! How are you?"

"Hello, gentlemen. Am I interrupting anything important?"

"No, no," Sam assured him. "Marvin, you remember my business partner, Mars Gregory."

I shook hands with the little weasel. "Oh, yes," I said, "we met at your joint fund raiser for Mike."

"Yes, sure, of course," Marvin said, trying to sound sincere. But I could tell he didn't give a damn about me; he was here to see Sam.

"Marvin, go on to the conference room. I'll be there in just a minute," Sam said.

I waited until Marvin was out of earshot.

"For chrissakes, Sam, that guy is the front man for the Combine! What the hell are you doing with him?"

Sam paused, putting his hands together and touching his lips. "Rosenthal is working with us now."

You could have knocked me over with a toothpick. "Be careful, Sam. Be careful," was all I could say.

Sam nodded as he headed off to see Marvin. "You worry too much, Mars. You always have."

I watched him walk away. This game was getting pretty risky.

————————————

ON THE DRIVE HOME, I realized for the first time that Mike Kovach was no more than a pawn to Sam, a means to an end. Now Sam had power that only a governor could give him, and it was a great deal of power. And yet, Sam wasn't content. No sooner had he attained that degree of clout than he was looking for a way to get more.

And then it hit me.

Malik Alawi was the key. He had what Mike Kovach didn't have. Alawi could actually be president. It all seemed so clear. It wasn't Kovach. It was Malik Alawi all along. And the next step was going to be getting him elected to the US Senate.

Chapter 20

IN EARLY 2003, SHORTLY after the swearing-in of Mike Kovach, former Governor Edward G. Parker was named along with others in a twenty-two count federal indictment that included charges of bribery, racketeering, extortion, money laundering, and tax fraud. The investigation, under the leadership of US Prosecutor Franklin McKenzie, had ballooned into a sweep of over a hundred state workers and ancillary government operators and providers. Amazingly, it had all begun with that horrible traffic accident in Waterston, Illinois.

Inside the Dirksen Federal Court Building, the spectacle du jour played itself out in the packed, standing-room-only courtroom. The circus atmosphere outside the building was what everyone saw on the TV news. Trucks with colorful logos identifying their news organizations, with huge white satellite dishes on top, were parked in every available legal and illegal space surrounding the building. Talking-head men and women were connected by miles of thick cable to the trucks that would immediately beam their reports to waiting newsrooms all over the country.

Once again, an Illinois governor was on trial.

Gone were the familiar cigar and the confident swagger that usually epitomized this seasoned politician. The always-present plastic smile and the glad-handing ways were replaced by the sagging shoulders, trudging gait, and tired appearance of a beaten, seventy-year-old man. Parker appeared in court as a gray-haired, aging shell of his former self, relying only on his wife of forty-two years for support and comfort.

The trial proceeded day after long, laborious day as one nervous, frightened witness after another walked to the stand, sat, then turned and pointed an accusing finger at their former boss.

Skylar Stillwell was the key witness against Parker, and delivered the final blow.

Edward G. Parker was found guilty on all counts.

The defense argued that any significant prison term would be tantamount to a life sentence, which, although true, failed to sway the presiding judge. Parker was sentenced to six and a half years in federal prison. The gossipmongers said that due to his failing health and advanced age, it was unlikely Ed Parker would ever again take a breath of air as a free man.

That suited Franklin McKenzie just fine. Asked his opinion on the matter, if he thought the sentence was too harsh, Frank would simply remind the person that six innocent little kids ceased to breathe any air at all the day that Juan Espinoza crashed into the side of their family's red van.

"People seem to think that the misuse of tax dollars, graft, bribery, and political corruption are victimless crimes. They're not. Just ask the parents of the Winters kids," he would routinely say. "They are the direct victims of Ed Parker's acts."

Frank McKenzie slept well following the trial of Ed Parker. He never once second-guessed himself.

From the Memoirs of Mars Gregory:

"Don't you think it's time to register as a lobbyist?" I asked Sam again. I was concerned for my partner, and somewhat concerned for myself and our business. Sam was passing out board appointments like candy—many of them being awarded as a direct result of campaign contributions previously made or soon to be made—and I worried that it could come back to haunt us. We were making a lot of money, and I was fine with that. But I didn't want to see a bunch of Feds streaming into my office and upsetting the applecart.

"You worry too much," was all Sam would say when the subject came up.

My involvement in politics was becoming more and more limited. Politics was all Sam seemed to care about, though, and that was just fine with me. I was busy running the day-to-day operations of our very successful real estate development firm. Thank God I'd hired Wodecki, or all this would have killed me. Sammar, LLC now employed over seventy-five people, and we were working on a dozen projects at any given time. The office was a hub of excitement and activity. The South Loop Project was moving forward and was, by far, the most ambitious development project in the city.

———————

ONE DAY, SAM POKED his head into my office.

"Mars, I have hired some help for you." Sam was ushering a very familiar face into my office. "Now, you won't be pulling your hair out quite so much."

Annie Kovach was the first lady of the State of Illinois and the daughter of Alderman Walter Roche.

When I saw Annie's smiling face, my first fleeting thought was whether or not there might be a perceived conflict of interest if we hired the daughter of a ward boss and the wife of the governor. After all, our firm did hundreds of millions of dollars' worth of business with the city and the state. It was Sam's idea to hire Annie. The governor and the alderman had surely vetted this decision, right? They had skin in this as well.

I came around my desk with an extended hand and a big welcoming smile.

"Mrs. Kovach—" I began, but was cut off.

"My name is Annie. No formalities here. We're going to be working together. You're my boss! Hell, call me 'Hey You' if you want to," she laughed, as she strode toward me and opened her arms. Politics makes huggers out of everyone.

"I thought Annie could help us scout properties. What do you think, Mars? She knows a lot of people in this city. She can keep her ear to the ground, right?" Sam was always figuring the angles. What an operator.

"I just hope I can help out," Annie said, quite sincerely. She seemed enthusiastic, which was good, but I didn't see myself firing the governor's wife, so it really wouldn't matter much if she helped out or not. It was a done deal.

———

EARLY ONE EVENING, I was finishing up some paperwork. Everyone in the office had gone for the day, and I thought I was the only one left. I enjoyed this quiet uninterrupted time. As I filled my briefcase with a few reports to review at home, I heard voices coming from the conference room. I looked up to see Sam and Malik entering the hallway wearing big smiles, Sam with his arm around Malik's shoulder. Neither one looked back, and I don't believe they knew anyone was still in the office.

Sam walked Malik to the door, and I watched as they held their hand-shake. Malik pulled Sam toward him, as if to give a little gentlemanly hug. I heard Malik say, "I don't know how to thank you, Sam."

"Malik, I'm happy I could help you out," Sam replied.

Malik left and Sam went back to his office. Before I headed out to my car, I stuck my head in the doorway. He looked up with an expression on his face I knew well.

He said, "Mars, this was an *exceptional* day," sounding very pleased with himself. "Wait just a second, and I'll walk you out to your car."

After turning out the lights and locking up, I said, "It appears you had a good meeting with Malik."

We were now in the parking lot, and Sam turned to me and said, "Mars, Malik owes me big time—I mean, big time."

I could tell he didn't want me to ask any details, so I just looked him in the eye and stated, "I don't doubt that for a minute, Sam. Have a good evening. I'll see you in the morning."

I got into my car, tossed my briefcase on the passenger seat, and never gave Sam's comment another thought.

Chapter 21

FRANK MCKENZIE FELT SAD as he scanned the *Tribune* article reporting that his great patron, Senator John McKenzie, had announced he would not run for reelection to the Senate. The paper was full of speculation that Senator McKenzie had been bluntly told to expect a tough primary challenge from a candidate to be strongly backed by the Republican establishment, and the senator had decided the odds were too long against him.

He felt anger rising as Josh Baker came in to give him a regular status report on the ongoing probe of corruption in Illinois politics.

The bulldog prosecutor got up and paced the length of his large office in the Dirksen Federal Building. "What the hell is wrong with these assholes?" he asked no one in particular, though Josh Baker was sitting across the desk from him. He was pissed about rumors that the newly elected governor and those around him were not proving to be any better than the last one.

"Well, for example," Josh began, "there's this guy, Saidah Alsheriti—he's known as Sam. This guy is an immigrant from Syria . . . naturalized citizen . . . made a bunch of money in restaurants. It looks like he's gotten very close to our new governor. He held a bunch of fund raisers for him. Raised a lot of money. So now he and the governor are pals, right? Okay . . . that's okay, I guess. Why shouldn't they be buddies? The guy almost singlehandedly got Kovach elected, for chrissakes. But then we hear that the governor's *wife* is now working at his real estate development firm."

Frank looked at the ceiling and groaned. Jeeezzzus! Josh, I want you and Novak to sniff around and see what you can find."

"Will do, boss," Baker replied.

Within a week, Josh was back in Frank's office.

"So, we started checking into things. You might want to sit. This could take a while."

"I don't have a while, Josh. Just give me the CliffsNotes."

"You know that Kovach is married to Walter Roche's daughter, right?"

"Of course I do."

"Well, I hear that Kovach, while a pleasant and likable guy, who happens to have that son-of-immigrants-grew-up-in-apartments-nose-to-the-grindstone perfect political story . . . is, for lack of a better word, a bit of a dolt. You know, not that bright. So he's easily swayed by a slick operator. Now, others see this and are crowding around him looking for their piece of the pie. He just goes where he's told, says what he's supposed to say. You know, kind of oblivious to it all. Well, it's becoming clear that Alsheriti is the slick operator who has his ear right now." Josh paused for effect.

"And? And? Come on, Josh, don't fuck with me!"

"Well, let me give you one example—one of several. Keep in mind, we don't have the evidence on this shit yet, but we suspect it's true. You've heard about our efforts over the years to nail the mayor of Rosemont, who's very cozy with the mob? Well, our mole in the city government tells us there's a new effort to pass a gambling bill, and guess what? Sam Alsheriti has a deal cooking to buy the land next to where the mayor is going to build the casino. He's going to put a fucking parking garage on it!" Josh could see that his boss was interested, so he decided to set the hook. "And here's the kicker: Sam Alsheriti is also the chief fundraiser for Malik Alawi."

This had the desired effect. McKenzie remembered who'd appointed him. And he had heard, of course, that Malik Alawi was going to run for John McKenzie's seat. He considered Alawi a weak replacement for John McKenzie, a man Frank knew to have real integrity.

"Okay, let's put a couple guys on this to nose around and see what else turns up."

"Will do, boss." Josh was pleased. Very pleased.

From the Memoirs of Mars Gregory:

I WAS SITTING AT my desk going over some paperwork when I noticed a tax bill for property in the city of Rosemont. We'd started investing in a few suburban-area developments, but I didn't remember any projects in this particular suburb. Since Rosemont is one of the 'burbs that borders O'Hare, there are several large, high-end hotels and restaurants there that cater to travelers in and out of one of the world's busiest airports. In fact, there are far more transient persons traveling through Rosemont at any given time than there are permanent residents of the city.

"Sam, what property is this?" I asked, as I walked into his office. He looked at the tax bill.

"Ah . . . this is a property that will be worth a lot more when the gambling bill is passed," he said, scribbling *PAY THIS* on the bill and handing it back to me.

"Gambling bill? What gambling bill?"

Sam sighed and put down his pen. "You know, Mars, the mayor of Rosemont has what amounts to a fiefdom out there. He's like a feudal lord. Did you know the only people who live in Rosemont work for the Village of Rosemont, and the mayor controls every single job in that town—from the chief of police to the cab drivers? It's true! He is a king who allows his subjects to call him Mr. Mayor."

I rolled my eyes, unable to believe what I was hearing. "That's very interesting. Actually, I heard he's pretty mobbed up. He may run the town, but I'm pretty sure the Chicago Mafia runs him."

"That's crazy talk. The mayor is his own man." Thank God he was chuckling as he said this. Everyone who read the papers knew about the alleged exploits of Joey D., the esteemed mayor of Rosemont.

"I guess it really doesn't matter. What property is it, and why did you just mark the bill to be paid?"

"Mars, sit down. Let's talk," he waited for me to take a seat. "Our new association with Vince Perino has opened up some new opportunities. Vince has control of all of the remaining gambling licenses in the state. Rosemont is submitting a bid for one of those licenses. This bid will be supported by the governor and accepted by the General Assembly. We have several of our friends working on this to ensure that Rosemont's bid is accepted. There is no place better suited for a casino. Rosemont is perfect. People fly into town. They stay near the airport while attending meetings in the city. Rosemont has the restaurants and hotels—they always have. This fits right in with the area there. It's the perfect location."

"Everybody knows they've been discussing this for years," I said, not impressed.

"Yes, they have. However, now there is a Democratic governor who will work together with the Republicans on this issue. The point is, I bought property next to where the casino is to be built, where I'm going to build a parking structure to service the casino when the bid is accepted." He picked up the tax bill off the pile on his desk and held it up. "That's what this is for. So, it must be paid, you see?"

The fact that Sam kept referring to "I" rather than "we," didn't go unnoticed. It downright pissed me off. "So, Sammar will own the parking for the casino in Rosemont?" I inquired.

"That's the plan. Pay the bill."

Chapter 22

Vince Perino needed this putt. Marvin Rosenthal had beaten him during three previous outings, and he wasn't having it this time, not on your life. This was probably going to be the last match of the season. Fall was in the air and soon winter's snow would blanket the entire course. Vince walked across the green and removed a leaf that might have interfered with this all-important shot.

He stroked it perfectly. The ball slowly rolled across the wet, dew-soaked, early morning green, breaking perfectly as it neared the cup, then it dropped, with one of the most satisfying sounds in life: the ball hitting the bottom of the cup. That hollow rattle—nothing sounded better.

"Finally, you go down," Vince crowed to Marvin, his fist clenched and shaking. "Yes!"

As the two men walked toward the clubhouse, Vince turned to his partner in crime. "This new arrangement with Alsheriti and the Dems is working out pretty well. I might even kind of like the Arab asshole, ya know? He kinda grows on you after a while."

"He's got some strange quirks. But who doesn't?"

"I think we should solidify our relationship with him. He's the guy controlling the governor now. When he says jump to that little twerp, Mikey just asks how high. Whether we like it or not, Sam is valuable to us. And he's going to need our help soon."

Marvin scraped the bottom of his golf shoes on the wire brush provided to clean spikes. "What are you getting at?"

"Well, there's an open US Senate seat, now that our dear friend John McKenzie has pulled out." Vince said, with more than a hint of self-satisfaction over having engineered that result. "And Sam's convinced that Malik has a good shot at winning that seat."

"You can't be serious," Marvin said, for once getting the drift immediately. He of course knew about the Kovach/Alawi deal and that the young black man was preparing to run for McKenzie's seat. "It was one thing to put a Democrat in the Governor's office, but a senate seat? That's huge."

Vince shrugged. "A senate seat isn't all it's cracked up to be. We know that from personal experience, don't we?"

"Yeah, but still . . . a senate seat has national implications."

Vince and Marvin had arrived at the country club lounge. It was time for a drink.

"Well, let's see how things develop," Vince said as they were waiting for their drinks. "This could be an opportunity. I may need you to raise money for Malik."

"Why am I the one who always has to do this sort of crap?" Marvin said petulantly.

"Because you are the guy I trust the most, Marvin. You da man!"

For the first time in their relationship, Marvin seemed to balk.

"What's wrong?" Vince asked.

Marvin looked doubtful. "I gotta tell ya, Vince, if it turns out we gotta help this guy Alawi, we're gonna have to find some other way than raising money. I just don't think any of our big hitters are going to go for this Alawi character. They all think he's a fuckin' Muslim!"

Vince frowned. "You may be right," he said. "Let's test the waters with a few of our best supporters."

Marvin beamed. "For once, I'm way ahead of you," he said with a snicker. "I've already talked to our five biggest, most reliable check writers. They don't want to touch this fuckin' guy."

Vince felt suddenly weary. This was going to be harder than he thought.

From the Memoirs of Mars Gregory:

I SPENT VERY LITTLE time with Sam and his new collection of pawns, the gang who were now running the entire state. I would come back to the office from meetings and see them huddled in our conference room or out in the courtyard, puffing on cigars and laughing.

If I needed help with a political problem, even if I needed the governor to show up somewhere and shake a few hands, Sam would see to it. But Sam and I just weren't connecting like we had in the past. We would talk sometimes, late at night, before heading home, but the level of communication between us was rapidly diminishing.

Don't get me wrong—our partnership was making money hand over fist, so I had no complaints. Even Annie Kovach was becoming an asset. She found a property that made us a million-dollar profit, and we didn't even have to sink so much as a shovel into the ground. We put it under contract, and then flipped the contract to another development company without even closing on the land. I always heard the politically connected people made all the money. It turns out that's true, and it's pretty sweet when you're on the receiving end of that deal, I have to say.

On the ominous side, however, we were beginning to have problems with Bachman Brothers. Shortly after we'd signed the final papers, I learned that the Bachman firm had a reputation for getting involved in big, lucrative projects and slowly, insidiously, taking over the deals, ultimately acing out the originators. That was not going to happen to me, to us. I told Sam we needed to get together for a formal meeting to discuss partnership matters.

"We may have a problem with our lender. They're being difficult about advancing additional funds to pay the bills for the project. These Bachman guys are starting to concern me," I began.

Sam smiled at me. "You worry too much, Mars."

"This is not just me worrying too much," I continued. "These guys are maneuvering to take over. They have the largest share of cash in the deal, and they're going to try to leverage that—" Again, he stopped me.

"We have the right to pay them off, correct?"

"Yes, of course, they're a lender, but finding someone to take them out would be really tough."

"Then that's what we will do."

"You can't just say that, Sam! We're talking about thirty million bucks!"

Sam was nonplussed. "We'll get it."

He stood up to leave.

"That's it? You're leaving? What the fuck?"

The meeting was over. I was steamed.

Sam's nonchalant attitude toward this potentially catastrophic situation was infuriating. He didn't seem to get it. This could kill the deal for us. If the Bachman firm was allowed to implement their plan, our participation in the project would be minimized, at best, or completely extinguished, at worst. Either way, I was looking at millions of dollars of potential profit simply floating away to nothing.

I followed Sam into his office and closed the door.

"What the fuck are you talking about, Sam? *We'll get it?* It's thirty million fucking dollars! Without it, we're screwed! These guys will waltz in and take over everything!" I was trying my best to impress the gravity of the situation upon my seemingly uninterested partner. "You have to take this seriously!"

"Mars, I understand, and I am taking it seriously. Have you ever seen a situation that involved money that I didn't take seriously? Leave everything to me."

That was it.

———————

SAM'S CELL PHONE RANG. His face lit up. "Malik, I thought your announcement yesterday was outstanding, really tremendous," he said. "You outlined a great theme for the campaign. We're all proud of you."

I listened with half an ear to this one-sided conversation, more preoccupied with our Bachman Brothers issue. Malik had declared his candidacy yesterday for the US Senate seat, but it was going to be a bitch of a primary. There was yet another multimillionaire white businessman who had declared, and this guy wasn't going to be a slouch. What was it about the US Senate that drew all these rich guys to throw millions of their own money at trying to get themselves elected? And then I heard something that left me shaking my head once again.

"Yes, yes," Sam was saying, "I've already talked to him, it's all arranged. He's going to declare he's running next week. It's going to go down just the way we planned."

When Sam hung up the phone, I gave him a sideways look. "Who's going to declare next week?" I asked.

Sam shrugged. "Do you know the State Treasurer, Wes Neary?"

I had heard the name, never met the guy. He was a Democrat, holding the low-profile office of the Illinois State Treasurer. The office did nothing but cut the checks for spending approved by the legislature. "He's going to run for the Senate? Are you kidding?"

Sam smiled. "We need to get a third candidate into the race. This guy is a friend of ours, he'll bleed away white votes from the other guy.

"Yeah, but what's in it for Neary? Won't he just embarrass himself?"

Sam gave me a knowing look. "In the 2006 election for governor, the current lieutenant governor won't be running. Mike has agreed that if Neary makes this race for the US Senate, and loses, he'll put Neary on the 2006 ticket with him for lieutenant governor."

I left Sam's office, still laughing. These guys were unbelievable.

Chapter 23

EVEN WITH ALL SAM'S maneuvering on Malik's behalf, the 2004 Democratic primary battle was a dogfight. The rich white guy was saturating the airwaves with flashy ads, and Sam was hard-pressed to raise enough money for Malik to stay in the game.

And then fortune smiled once again on the ambitious young state senator.

At a campaign event for the rich white guy, only two weeks before the primary, with the cameras rolling, a young lady climbed on a chair and started screaming. "You fired my father, and he killed himself. His blood is on your hands! You killed my father! You killed him!"

The campaign staff quickly hustled the young lady away, but the damage had been done.

The media of course checked into the story. The rich white guy had bought a run-down steel company that was losing money and about to go out of business. He'd turned the company around, mainly by laying off all the older, higher-paid workers, and replacing them with younger, lower-paid workers. He had made a fortune for himself. However, one of the laid-off workers, despondent over the loss of his job, had committed suicide.

The backwash from this incident was immediate, and pronounced. The rich white guy dropped six percent in the polls—which was exactly the margin by which Malik won the primary two weeks later.

The night of the victory celebration, Sam took Johnny Jarzik aside.

"Great work," he said, slapping his favorite political operative on the back. "How the hell did you ever find that girl?"

Jarzik just grinned. "That's what I do, Sam. It's why I get the big bucks."

EVEN WITH A BIG primary win behind him, Malik Alawi was in a fight for his political life. He was polling very well in Chicago, which was to be expected, but this was a US Senate seat, and the Republicans brought their A game, nominating Brad O'Neil, an extremely charismatic young businessman, who, after having made millions of dollars as a bond trader, had stepped away from the business world and taken a job teaching math at a Chicago public high school. Most people saw this as the cynical political move that it was, but the guy looked good on television and was articulate. Just like Malik. O'Neil did have one little problem, however. He'd gone through a nasty divorce. Surely that wouldn't be much of factor . . . would it? Not only was this guy popular with the Republicans downstate, he was actually showing better than anticipated in and around Chicago in the polls. This election was going to come down to the wire.

Malik had been a distinguished member of the Illinois State Senate and had made a name for himself working with the poor on the South Side of Chicago. However, Brad O'Neil was a tall, dark, and handsome man in his early forties, who had given up a lucrative career to go teach in the Chicago public schools. He resembled John F. Kennedy, Jr., with a gift for saying what the voters wanted to hear.

Both Malik and Brad appeared to be ideal candidates. But only one was going to win the seat. It was totally up for grabs. Sam redoubled his efforts. This election could put a US senator in his pocket, together with a governor, and he was going to make certain the outcome was within his control, come hell or high water.

After a particularly bleak meeting on the status of the campaign fund-raising, Sam decided to bite the bullet. He called Vince Perino.

"Sam, my friend," Vince said cautiously, always careful on the telephone. "What's up?

Sam, who was equally cautious in such conversations, said simply, "We have a little problem with our friend Marvin's reappointment to the Teachers Pension Board." Sam had picked this topic with care: Marvin's term was expiring, and it would be up to Mike Kovach to fill the position.

Vince was surprised. "Marvin? You're kidding. What's wrong?"

Sam was opaque, by intention. "There are a number of people urging Mike to appoint someone else. We need to get together and discuss it."

The gears inside Perino's head were already spinning. He had a hunch this was just a ploy—and he suspected he knew what was behind it.

"No problem," Vince said amiably. "My wife and I are going to be in Chicago next week. Let's do lunch."

Given the circumstances of who had asked for the meeting, it was agreed that Vince and Sam would meet on Sam's turf, in a private room at—where else?—Gene & Georgetti.

"Sam, my friend, what is this all about?" Vince asked, as the waiters placed the dishes before them.

Sam took a minute as the waiters cleared the room, and pushed the ranch dressing around on his steak salad, avoiding eye contact as he said, "We've been very pleased with how things have been working out with the Teachers' Pension Fund. But I've been getting a lot of heat over Marvin's upcoming reappointment."

Vince, highly skilled in these situations, asked in a completely noncommittal tone, "Why is that?"

Sam started slicing a strip of the prime filet atop the iceberg lettuce he loved. "Well, Marvin has been helping Brad O'Neil with fund raising, and this is causing a lot of criticism from the national party," he said quietly. "They want Mike to pick someone else."

Vince sighed. He'd anticipated this subject would come up. He liked Brad O'Neil, Malik's opponent, he really did. Vince also knew O'Neil had an excellent chance of beating Malik. But this was serious business, and if he had to sacrifice a US Senate seat to keep his hammerlock on the money flow to the Combine, it was a price that must be paid.

"For complicated reasons," Vince said, "it's almost impossible for me to lie down on the fund raising. The national party would notice, the president would notice, and it would upset too many other arrangements."

Sam kept chewing his steak. He knew there had to be something more. Vince would not just walk away from the goose that was laying the golden egg without offering something.

Vince pulled an envelope out of his suit coat pocket and placed it on the table.

For a moment Sam thought it was money, but he immediately realized Vince was far too sophisticated for something as crass as simply handing over cash. It was a document of some kind.

"You've heard about Brad's problems with his divorce, I'm sure," Vince said simply.

Sam nodded. "Well, yes, we keep hearing that it was really nasty, but the court papers have been sealed. No one can get their hands on them. It's very frustrating."

Vince tapped the envelope. "Sam, I am a man who believes in showing friendship. I always try to do something for someone before I ask them to do something for me. Let this be the demonstration of my desire to be your good friend."

He picked up the envelope and handed it over to Sam. It took all his emotional energy to maintain the cool, calm, almost indifferent demeanor he displayed. "This envelope is nitroglycerine. It's so explosive, it will guarantee that Malik Alawi is the next United States senator from Illinois."

Sam could barely believe his ears. He opened the envelope and withdrew the document. It was a copy of a court filing, from the divorce case between O'Neil and his wife. Sam scanned it quickly. His hands began to tremble, his breath coming in short gasps.

If anything, what Vince said about the document being explosive was an understatement. It was a fucking nuclear bomb.

"This is incredible," Sam said. "You're giving up a Senate seat?"

Vince looked at Sam sympathetically, as if he were mentoring a young protégé.

"Senate seats aren't what you think they are, Sam. These assholes get elected to the Senate, they spend all their time out in Washington, hobnobbing with big money lobbyists and the national media, they posture to get on the Sunday morning talk shows, their egos get bigger and bigger, and they become impossible to manage."

Sam nodded thoughtfully, but said, "I think Malik will remember where he came from. And anyway, the senate seat is just one more step on the path to the real objective."

It took a lot to shock a grizzled political veteran like Vince Perino, but this statement nearly knocked him out of his chair. In a flash, he realized what Sam was after—the senate seat was just a way to position Malik Alawi to run for president of the United States. He nearly laughed out loud at the mere thought of it—this skinny black kid, who half the voters thought was a Muslim, was going to run for president? It was insane! Vince let none of those thoughts show on his face.

"We shall see," Vince said, sounding fatalistic. "Maybe you'll have better luck with your guy than I had with mine. But what you're holding is going to put him in the Senate, no doubt about that."

"You are a true friend," was all Sam could manage. "Vince, I believe we are going to do a lot of business together."

"What about Marvin?" Vince asked pointedly.

Sam folded the paper carefully and put it into his own suit pocket. "I think I'll be able to persuade Mike that Marvin has done such a good job, he deserves another term."

And with that, they both laughed.

WITH SIX WEEKS TO go until the election, Sam scheduled a private meeting in Sammar's conference room with his two key confidants, Oren Mitchell and Johnny Jarzik. Until this meeting, Sam had told absolutely no one about the envelope he'd received from Vince Perino at their lunch.

Mars appeared unaware of Sam's meeting as he opened the conference room door, thinking the room was his to use. Sam looked annoyed at the interruption. Oren and Johnny were reading a document, looking like they'd seen a ghost.

Sam said, "Mars, I only need the room for a few more minutes."

Then as if to justify why he seemed so preoccupied, Sam told Oren, "Mars is a lawyer himself. Give him that court document, let's see what he thinks."

Mars scanned the papers, and within seconds had to sit down. It was beyond shocking. It was downright mind-boggling. He muttered, "This is going to change everything. Where did you get this?"

Sam gave Mars a sly smile. "Oh, it's from a reliable source. I'm about to guarantee that Malik Alawi will be our next United States senator. The Republicans won't have enough time to mount a campaign for a new candidate."

Mars looked over at Oren. Oren was tightly connected in Cook County, and it seemed likely that he had received this document from one of his cronies in the office of the circuit clerk, where the records were kept. But if that were the case, why had Oren appeared shocked? Mars tried to work out what was going on, but did it really matter how this explosive device made its way into Sam's hands? Did Mars really want to know? The release of a court-sealed document was pretty dicey stuff.

Sam took the document back. "Go back to whatever you were doing, Mars. You can have the conference room in five minutes. Oren and Johnny have an appointment with the *Chicago Tribune*."

———

THOMAS GAZDIK WAS A staff reporter for the *Trib*. He had dreams of someday writing for the *New York Times*, which he regarded as the bible of all newspapers. Tom was trying to build a resume. Like every other young

journalist, he hoped for that one big story that would break him out of the
farm team and into the big leagues. Understandably, he was intrigued when
Johnny Jarzik called him and said he and Orenthal Mitchell had something
big, really big, to see him about.

They met at the Billy Goat Tavern, a pit of a place located near the
Tribune offices on a subterranean level below the Michigan Avenue shops.
Historically, the Billy Goat was the hangout for some of the most infamous
journalists in Chicago. It was a dive that John Belushi made famous with
his "Cheeseborger, cheeseborger, cheeseborger, no Coke, Pepsi" rants on
Saturday Night Live.

Johnny hunched conspiratorially over a beer, eyeing the eager young
reporter.

"This absolutely cannot be linked to either one of us," he said. "You have
to swear to protect your source."

Gazdik was overwhelmed with curiosity. What the hell could be so sensitive? "Absolutely. I'll go to jail before I give you up."

Oren hesitated for a moment. He was clearly weighing whether to trust
this young kid. Tom was a bit of an unknown character, but he had been
helpful to Oren on a couple of occasions in the past, when he'd needed to
plant a favorable article or to blunt media criticism of Oren's boss, the Cook
County Board president.

"You guys can trust me. I swear, I'll never disclose the source. What the
hell is it?"

They decided to roll the dice. Oren handed the document to Tom.

Even a cub reporter could have grasped the significance of what he was
reading. And Gazdik was no novice. This would propel him onto the front
page of the Sunday edition.

"Incredible. Just incredible. Brad O'Neil is finished," was all he could say.

Oren nodded. "Just remember, the court record is sealed. You're going to have to say you got this from sources known to be reliable."

Gazdik nodded. He assumed that Oren had somehow gotten his hands on this bombshell material through all his contacts in the county government.

Which is exactly why Sam had sent Oren as the delivery boy and Johnny to spin the story.

———————

MARS WAS ENJOYING A rare weekend at home. Taking off on a Saturday was like a mini vacation for him. Rochelle was used to Mars arriving home late Saturday afternoon, too exhausted to socialize. Oh, Mars would make small talk and interact with the kids, but he was usually preoccupied with work. The marriage was somewhat strained, as was the case with most of Rochelle's friends who were married to highly successful professional men. The wives were happy as long as they had one another to constantly bitch to about their respective situations, and had unlimited access to the credit cards.

On Sunday mornings Mars liked to sleep late. In the earlier years of their marriage Rochelle liked to wake Mars up by giving him a frenzied ride, but those days were long gone. This early October Sunday morning, Mars was surprised to see Rochelle standing by the bed. She threw the *Tribune* on his chest and said, "I see your partner is up to his scheming tricks again." She stomped off, angry as usual.

Mars turned the paper right-side-up and broke into a big grin looking at the headline.

O'NEIL IN SEX SCANDAL
Republican Senate Candidate Forced Wife to Participate
In Wild Vegas Sex Parties
by Thomas Gazdik, Staff Reporter

Even though Mars had known it was coming, it was still rich to read it in print.

Brad O'Neil's ex-wife, April, a famous Hollywood actress, alleged in her divorce filing that her husband had repeatedly asked her to join him in sex orgies at a nightclub in Las Vegas known as Caligula. She acknowledged accompanying him once to the club, where Brad watched and pleasured himself while a woman lay across a table, allowing a progression of men to use her body. April maintained she never participated and found the whole scene appalling. It actually made her sick, she claimed.

———————

THE MEDIA FIRESTORM THAT followed Gazdik's exposé about O'Neil's adventures at Caligula was overwhelming. The TV stations had a field day, sending reporters to broadcast live outside the Vegas sex club. Other newspapers picked up the ball and ran with it. The *Tribune* went into court to demand that O'Neil's divorce papers, which had been previously sealed by court order, be released to the press. Supporters of Malik Alawi sprang into action. The results were predictable. The story broke worldwide.

Suddenly, across the world O'Neil was known as the man who took his wife—actually now his ex-wife—to sex clubs in an attempt to feed his wildest fantasies in public.

April O'Neil was beautiful, with an incredible body. Most men could only dream of being seen with a woman of her looks and fame, but this weirdo of a man risked his marriage and entire career on his fetishes? What a fucking loser. It didn't matter that no crimes were committed, or that this was arguably consensual behavior between a husband and wife.

Under tremendous pressure from the Republican establishment, O'Neil withdrew from the race. Never before in political history had a candidate for US office disappeared from the public eye so quickly and so completely.

People called Malik Alawi one of the luckiest politicians who ever lived. His chance of winning this race before the O'Neil story broke had been even money, at best. Now, it was thought he couldn't lose.

The Illinois Republicans scrambled to put up a candidate to run against Alawi, but it was a futile effort. Thanks to behind-the-scenes maneuvering by Vince Perino—working in concert with Sam, of course—the Republican ticket now boasted a perennial candidate, a man who'd run for office on several occasions, mostly in situations where he had absolutely no chance of winning. They actually moved him into the state from his retirement home in Arizona in order to meet the residency requirements. It was a fiasco and an embarrassment to the Republican side of the race.

Sam Alsheriti's favorite son, his protégé Malik Alawi, was on his way to Washington, DC. He was going to win in a landslide.

Chapter 24

SAM WAS SO CAUGHT up in his political game that Mars was starting to wonder if he'd forgotten about Sammar's problem with Bachman Brothers. Finally one Wednesday morning, Sam poked his head into Mars's office. He smiled and said, "I am setting up a meeting with a man who will make all of your concerns about a hostile takeover of our South Loop deal go away."

ABDUL-MATAAL ABAZA BELONGED TO a very small, very exclusive club. By most accounts, he was one of the world's 100 wealthiest men. Different reports had him at different places on that list. Some said he was #72, others pegged him at #84. It was rumored he'd once worked for Saddam Hussein, possibly as Saddam's personal accountant, the guy who oversaw and invested the vast sums controlled by the despot. Others speculated he was much more than just a money man, involved in more of the darker aspects of the regime. Whatever the truth was, it was a well-kept secret. Abaza's murky and mysterious past generated controversy wherever he traveled.

Sam was now traveling in some high Arab circles where it seemed everyone knew everyone, as they say. Sam had met Abaza through another Arab friend, the Emir of the State of Qatar, Hamad bin Khalifa Al Thani. Just to make the connection even more clandestine and opaque, it seems that Sam solidified his connection to Mr. Abaza through another old pal, an Arab businessman he'd run into at a casino in Las Vegas.

Whatever the complicated and convoluted path, Sam had engineered a meeting with Mr. Abaza to discuss investments in Illinois, including the South Loop Project. Sam was planning a number of receptions for the mogul, where he would meet several dignitaries from the state.

This was quintessential Sam. He was running around with the governor of the State of Illinois, touting the opportunities that were going to be afforded to scores of people in the state as a result of this visit, drumming up interest on the part of many high-level persons, when all he really cared about was saving Sammar's South Loop deal.

Mars was relieved Sam had been taking his concerns seriously. He should have known: when it came to making money, Sam always listened.

———————————

DUE TO COMPLICATIONS IN Mr. Abaza's schedule, the visit couldn't be scheduled until after Malik had been sworn in as the new junior senator from Illinois. Sam attended the event, as Malik's personal guest of honor.

And now the plans for the grand reception for Abdul-Mataal Abaza were in full swing.

He was flying in on his private jet. Upon arrival, Mr. Abaza would be whisked off in a stretch limousine from Midway Airport to the Ritz-Carlton, where he would be provided a sprawling suite from which to conduct business and receive various dignitaries, many of whom were salivating at the opportunity to pitch the billionaire on one project or another. The primary reason for his visit, however, the preeminent and overriding purpose for his time in Chicago, was to review the specifics for Sammar's South Loop Project.

The following evening, another reception was planned at Sam Alsheriti's home on the North Shore. This would be a much more intimate affair, with the guest list cut down significantly to include only Sam's closest allies. Sam and Mars would have uninterrupted face time with Mr. Abaza.

They had the architectural scale model of the completed project professionally moved and reassembled at Sam's house. An electrician was brought in to install the appropriate lighting above the model to enhance its effect. No expense was spared, no detail overlooked.

The day of Mr. Abaza's arrival, Mars waited in the limo with Sam, Governor Kovach, a couple of security guys, and Terry Monahan, the governor's best friend and advisor. As the limo drove into the private terminal off Central Avenue at Midway, word arrived that Mr. Abaza's personal jet had been cleared to land.

While waiting for the plane, an unusual procession of black SUVs with flashing red and blue lights, together with two black Ford Crown Vics, also with red and blue flashers blinking in their grills, suddenly appeared. They slowly drove along the side of the inner airfield along the fence, coming from some unknown, undisclosed place, and pulled up to the edge of the runway near where the limousines were parked. They stopped. They waited.

Everyone in the limos just looked at one another and shrugged.

When Mr. Abaza's private plane landed and was taxiing, the procession of black cars sprang into action. Like dancers in a well-choreographed routine, they surrounded the plane as soon as it rolled to a stop.

The governor was completely befuddled. He sent one of his security men to check out the situation. When Kovach's security officer came back to his car, what he said would have been funny if it hadn't been so sad and infuriating.

The guys in the black SUVs were federal agents. It seemed that Mr. Abaza had been placed on the no-fly list, and that extended to private planes. Who knew? So the honored guest, the man for whom reception after reception had been planned, the man who was going to save Sammar's collective ass with regard to the South Loop Project, the one who everyone in the group was assembled to see . . . was not going to be allowed to step on US soil.

Sam looked like he was going to have a conniption fit. His face got red and the veins in his neck popped out so far it looked like they would burst. He immediately got on the phone and started making calls. He screamed at the security detail, telling them to stop the federal agents from doing anything embarrassing. He first called his friend and protégé, Malik, the new US senator. He called the White House. He called every person in his contacts list who he thought might have any ability to help.

Sam walked off on his own, away from the car, pacing back and forth with his phone to his ear, the sleek private jet as a backdrop, one hundred feet away and surrounded by black vehicles and armed men wearing sunglasses. On that jet was a man who had done things that had pissed off the leaders of the US so badly that they were not going to let him step off his own private plane.

However, as impossible as it was to believe . . . it seemed that Sam Alsheriti was truly a force of nature. His demeanor became visibly more calm, his pacing less and less forced, more like a stroll. After twenty minutes, he walked back toward the cars. He was smiling.

"They're going to give him a three-day visa," he said, with a broad smile. "The word will reach these men shortly and we will be able to continue on our way."

And that is exactly what happened.

Within fifteen minutes, the men in suits and sunglasses began to touch their fingertips to their hidden earpieces, nod, and look around. Soon they were back in their vehicles driving away. It was that simple.

Then, a striking Arab man dressed in flowing white robes trimmed in gold with matching headgear appeared at the top of the stairs that were lowered from the doorway of the small jet. He walked down the stairs followed by aides and his many yes-men. Sam and the governor scurried to meet him at the bottom of the steps and introductions were begun. There were uncomfortable half bows and bobs, hugs, and handshakes. It looked like the first tee at a Japanese country club.

Mr. Abaza was ushered into Sam's limo, and soon the caravan was headed for the Ritz-Carlton as if nothing at all happened. The strange and surreal course of events that had just occurred didn't seem to bother Mr. Abaza one bit. It seemed he was used to it.

THAT EVENING, THE FIRST reception was held in honor of the man in the robes with the big bucks. Politicians and dignitaries lined up to figuratively kiss his ring. The line included, of course, Illinois's governor and newly installed senator.

The intimate gathering at Sam's home took place the next evening as planned. Sam had outdone himself with the rented furniture—the place looked spectacular. There, people could really put on the full-court press on behalf of their particular special cause. Senator Alawi was also in attendance at this function, and it was here that he helped the Sammar pet project.

After a forty-five-minute private meeting with Mr. Abaza, Malik walked up to Sam and Mars and said, "Now you guys finally owe *me* for something."

Sam looked up at Malik with his usual grin, and said, "Oh, really, Mr. Senator? Do you actually believe that?"

Throwing his head back in laughter, Malik squeezed Sam's shoulder, reaching out to shake his hand, and said, "C'mon, Sam, you know I'm just joking. I'll *always* owe *you* big time."

As the crowd began to wane and the party was wrapping up for the night, Mars turned to Sam, and whispered, "I think Malik helped us with Mr. Abaza."

"Malik will help us in many ways over the coming years, Mars," he said discreetly, with a confident smile. "That guy is going all the way, you mark my words."

Chapter 25

FRANK MCKENZIE WAS LIVID. "You mean to tell me that we indicted the last son of a bitch to hold that office, and by doing so we paved the way for this new little twerp to become the governor, and now he's fucking it up too?"

Nobody wanted to confirm his observation for fear McKenzie would shoot the messenger. It fell to Josh Baker to be the brave soul.

"He's not just fucking it up, boss. He's worse than the last guy. He makes Parker look like a Boy Scout. I sent you a memo about Vince Perino. Did you see it?"

To lighten the mood, McKenzie said with a smile, "I read every word of every memo you send me, Josh, right before they go into the shit can. Why don't you refresh my recollection?"

"Thanks, boss. That's a comforting thought."

"You know I'm kidding. Perino is the one who deep-sixed the guy who appointed me, Senator John McKenzie. He also runs the Republican Combine."

Josh was proud and pleased. His boss actually was reading his memos.

"Yeah, you got him pegged. Perino has had control of the Republican machine in the State of Illinois for too long."

"Okay, why are we talking about him?" McKenzie was genuinely interested.

"Well, what we're hearing is that Perino has made a deal through Sam Alsheriti to join forces with the Combine. Imagine that fucking Alsheriti with all the downstate and suburban Republican crooks, the governor's office, the Cook County and Chicago Democratic crooks . . . These bastards have been raping this state, and they will continue to rape this state, boss. The only thing we had going for us was the fact that the Republicans hated the Democrats, and vice versa. If they start working together, well, that's a fucking disaster."

McKenzie leaned forward. "Okay, I'm authorizing you to look into this. Make it a high priority. Spend what you have to, but don't go nuts. Let's put our best on it, and let me know what you find out as soon as you can."

McKenzie had no intention of letting this situation blossom into something he would not be able to control.

SOMETIMES LIFE IS HARD. Then sometimes cherries fall right into your pocket as you walk by the tree. Three weeks after Josh Baker assembled his team and began the investigation of the Combine—Vince Perino, the Sam Alsheriti connection, and their specific link to the new governor—cherries fell into Baker's pocket.

"Josh." An excited paralegal stopped Baker in the reception area as he was returning from lunch. "There's a woman on the line, Elizabeth Schmitter, says she's the chief administrator and CEO at Naperville Sachs Hospital in DuPage County. She wants to report a high-level corruption. She says a guy on the Illinois Health Facilities Planning Board, a guy named Marvin Rosenthal, tried to shake her down."

"What?" Josh could not believe his ears. He knew Rosenthal's name well. He was one of Vince Perino's prime stooges.

"She says that this guy on the Board tried to strong-arm her into enlisting the services of a certain builder, circumventing any standard bidding practices." The paralegal decided to cut through the formalities and speak in plain language. "They're building a wing on their hospital and Rosenthal basically tried to tell her she had to use a certain builder in order to get Board approval!"

This had Vince's fingerprints all over it.

"Put her through to my—no, never mind." Josh lunged at the phone on the reception desk. "Which line?"

The receptionist handed him the phone and punched a button. Josh started snapping his fingers and pointing at a legal pad that was out of his reach.

"This is Joshua Baker," Josh said as pleasantly as if he had been sitting at his desk waiting for the call. "Yes, ma'am, I am the chief investigator . . ."

Josh stood at the reception desk, furiously scribbling on that legal pad for over twenty minutes. When he was finished, he hung up the phone and said, "I want everybody in the conference room in fifteen minutes! Anybody who isn't here, find them and get them here ASAP!"

He walked into his office and immediately sat down at his computer to check out the information he'd just received from Elizabeth Schmitter.

NEVER IN A MILLION years could Elizabeth have imagined that she would ever be a part of something like this.

She was seated on top of a plain folding table in a small room in the bowels of the Chicago office of the United States Attorney, wearing nothing but her pantyhose and bra. Two earnest-looking female federal agents were trying to figure out how best to locate a tiny microphone, and the thin wire connecting it to a small transmitter with a built-in battery, to her body.

"Mrs. Schmitter, unfortunately, you have a very petite bosom," the younger of the agents said. "Usually, with women, we put the microphone in the cleavage. You don't seem to have any."

Elizabeth blushed and smiled apologetically. "I'm sorry; it's what God gave me. I've had to work harder my whole life because I couldn't get promoted as a direct result of my boobs. It wasn't easy to become head of a hospital with nothing to flash in the face of the chief of surgery."

The female agents smiled knowingly.

"Well," the agent said, intently feeling along the line of Elizabeth's underwire bra, "I think we can connect it here. I'm just worried that the outline will show under your blouse."

She clipped the small black device to the satin-covered underwire, just beneath the left nipple. She adjusted it and stood back to look at her handiwork.

"I don't know . . . Don't do a lot of jumping around," she said skeptically.

The other agent, older and more hard-bitten, shook her head. "I think it'll be okay. She's got a nice suit, and the jacket should cover it. Mrs. Schmitter, just be aware of it, and try to keep it covered to the extent you can." She uncoiled the wire, attached it to the microphone, and let it dangle in front of Elizabeth's trim tummy. "The transmitter can make a little bulge, so we like to put it just above the pubic area. Can you just pull down the top of your pantyhose for me?"

Elizabeth flushed scarlet with embarrassment. "Do you have to put it there?"

"It's the ideal place," the crusty agent said. "The primary concern here is that it not be discovered, you know?"

Elizabeth looked away and bit her lip. "Oh, yes, of course . . . sorry."

The agent shrugged. "Ma'am, we've secured this to your body in such a way you won't be compromised." She looked at her watch as if to communicate they were running short on time, and Elizabeth rearranged her blouse. After all, the critical appointment was to start in less than an hour.

————————————

THE TWO FEMALE AGENTS drove Mrs. Schmitter to her dinner meeting in a nondescript government-issue black Chevrolet. Elizabeth was in the passenger seat with the agent driving the car, the older agent in the back seat, accompanied by a gruff man in a rumpled suit and loosened tie. He had a small identification badge clipped to his suit coat, but Elizabeth couldn't read the name.

"Mrs. Schmitter, my name is Joshua Baker; we spoke on the phone the other day. I'm the chief investigator working on this case. Now let's go over this one last time. Tell me the story again."

Elizabeth now realized that all the press about the intensity of McKenzie's investigation had not been understated. She grimaced as she looked out her passenger-side window. She was tired of having gone through this, over and over, but she was keyed up with nervous energy, and very aware of the surgical tape holding the transmitter in place under her pantyhose.

"Okay, I was sitting in my office in Naperville at Sachs Hospital, running the day-to-day hospital business as always, when I received a call from one of my board members. He told me he's friends with this guy named Marvin Rosenthal, who used to be in the health insurance business, and Marvin is now on the Illinois Health Facilities Planning Board. He said he asked Marvin how our application to add the new cardio clinic to the hospital was coming with the board."

Baker was following along, looking at his notes in a manila folder. "And your board member's name was?"

Elizabeth rolled her eyes. "Bart Reiner. But Bart's not involved in this. He just passed along the call."

The investigator made a note. "Right, right, we're not going to bother Mr. Reiner, unless we have to."

Elizabeth sighed. "So, anyway, Bart told me that Rosenthal said our application was getting a lot of opposition from the staff at the planning board. They don't think Naperville needs a new cardio clinic. Well, that's just a bunch of bullshit. We desperately need that new wing."

"Right," the investigator nodded, noting her displeasure. "But then what happened?"

"So . . . Bart says he can set up a meeting for me with Rosenthal so I can lay out the facts regarding our application. I said that would be great."

"Okay," Baker said, scribbling another note, "So it was Reiner who actually suggested the meeting, right? Not you?" He gave a knowing look to the agent who was driving, and she returned it with a smarmy shrug.

"That's right," Elizabeth said, "but you have to get off this Reiner connection to Rosenthal. It's a casual friendship, I'm sure of it."

"We understand, Mrs. Schmitter. Just keep going."

"So a few days later—you have all the exact dates from the phone records—I received a call from Mr. Rosenthal. He said Bart had suggested he call me to talk about our application for the cardio clinic. I thanked him for the call, and said I'd be happy to discuss it with him. He said he could meet me for dinner at the Standard Club downtown. Where we're headed now."

"Yes, but tell me again about the contractor," the agent said, looking at his notes.

"Well, he said he was 'recommending' his friend Don Knollwood. He told me that Knollwood owns a construction company that's very experienced building medical facilities, and suggested we consider using him for our project."

Baker looked straight at her. "Did he specifically say that you had to use Knollwood?"

"Not specifically, no," Elizabeth said, clenching her jaw. "He was slicker than that. He said, 'Of course, you're under no obligation, but I can tell you, our board has a lot of respect for Mr. Knollwood, and if he's your contractor, it might help demonstrate the ability of your hospital to get this built on time and within budget. That's very important to the board.' As soon as he said, 'You're under no obligation,' I realized this was a shakedown, and that's why I called you."

The agent driving the car frowned. "Why do you say that, Mrs. Schmitter?"

Elizabeth gave her a laser-beam glare, and the driver had a flash of appreciation for the toughness that had earned this lady the top position at a major hospital. "Because in my world when someone powerful tells you 'You're under no obligation,' what he or she is really saying is 'You better do this, or your project is dead.'"

ELIZABETH SCHMITTER WALKED INTO the dining room and approached the maître d'. Under her crisp blue business suit and silk blouse, she was wired for sound. She was determined to accomplish her task. As far as she was concerned, this was the one and only time she was ever going to allow herself to be put in this position. She'd adopted a hairdo in the style of Margaret Thatcher because of her admiration for the Iron Lady, and today she was going to show that she, too, was tough as nails. After this meeting, she fully expected to hear or read in the papers that Marvin Rosenthal had been arrested by federal authorities. That was her single-minded goal.

"I'm meeting someone . . . a Marvin—"

The professional greeter, dressed in a black tux and white bow tie, immediately interrupted her with a huge grin and a great flourish. "Ms. Schmitter, Mr. Rosenthal is already here. He is waiting for you at your table. Right this way, ma'am."

Rosenthal stood, holding a drink in his hand. The maître d' pulled out Elizabeth's chair and she sat down. The dining room was quietly elegant, with a high vaulted ceiling. It was one of the great venues in the city.

"I'm so glad you could come, Ms. Schmitter. I hope this means you are considering my suggestion." Rosenthal wasn't wasting any time getting to the point.

"Well, Mr. Rosenthal, I'm here, aren't I?" Elizabeth was smiling, gracious. "Call me Liz," she added for effect, though she had always hated the nickname.

The two of them continued to banter as they ordered. The conversation turned to their kids, their schools, their sports teams, dance lessons, and other subjects common between them. Elizabeth played along, feigning interest, as she slowly worked the conversation back to the topic of the new hospital wing. After the food arrived, they were back to talking shop.

"Are you simply recommending your contractor, Mr. Rosenthal?" she asked when the subject returned. "Or is it a condition of the approval, and by extension, the entire deal?"

"Ms. Schmitter . . . Liz . . . I cannot force you to enlist the services of a particular contractor, you know that. And, I assure you, I would never try. However, as you know, I have the ability to persuade the board to support or reject a project. I would consider it a personal favor to me if you would consider our recommendation for the general contractor. And I am a guy who knows how to return a favor."

"What exactly do you mean by that, Mr. Rosenthal?" Elizabeth felt her stomach churning, not because she was nervous or apprehensive—quite to the contrary, she was involved and focused; however, the man sitting in front of her was beginning to make her physically ill. Although he was wearing a two-thousand-dollar suit, he seemed sleazy. Rarely had she met a person this distasteful.

Marvin smiled like a snake oil salesman working a crowd.

"Well, your permit has to be approved by our board," he said. "You are also looking to obtain bond financing for your hospital through another state agency, the Illinois Development Finance Authority. I have friends over there. If you will do me this small favor, and award the construction project to Knollwood, I can assure you that your bond deal will skate through."

Elizabeth was stunned. She had no idea that her bond financing could be in jeopardy if she didn't play ball. "That sounds almost too good to be true . . . Mr. Rosenthal, are you telling me I can count on this . . . as long as the bids . . . you know . . . the bidding process . . . for the contactor goes, well . . . goes in your friend's direction?"

"My contractor will win the bidding contest." Rosenthal was smiling with an air of confidence as he sipped from his glass of wine. He had clearly had this conversation—or a conversation substantively the same as this one— with many others before her. He believed he was coming in for the kill, the final deal clincher.

"How can you be so sure of that?"

"Why don't you just leave that up to me, Liz? I'll take care of everything."

Just then, Marvin Rosenthal looked up at an approaching man wearing a broad smile. He looked back at Elizabeth.

"What an interesting coincidence," he said with glee as he stood to greet the surprise guest. He shook hands with the man warmly, and turned to Elizabeth.

"I know you are going to think this was somehow planned, but, I assure you it wasn't. I would like you to meet Don Knollwood. Don is a general contractor. He builds hospitals, among other things. Don is the contractor who would be working with us on your planned expansion—the very contractor that I've been telling you about. This is such a coincidence that I'm sure you think it was prearranged. I swear to you again, Liz, it was not."

Elizabeth could not believe the audacity of this man. She was offended by the mere fact that this seedy operator thought so little of her that he would attempt to pull off this silly ploy. But her tendency to feel angry was immediately supplanted by the knowledge that this conversation was being monitored and, therefore, a brand-new asshole was about to be caught in the net.

Elizabeth half stood from her chair as she shook the hand of the contractor. He too had a tailored, expensive suit, and perfectly coiffed salt-and-pepper hair. Marvin was making introductions and asked their visitor to sit.

"Liz, do you mind if Don joins—"

Just then, Knollwood interrupted. "I can't stay. Forgive me, but I'm here to meet another party. Thank you, though. However, Ms. Schmitter, I would like to say that I certainly hope we all will have the opportunity to work together." Knollwood again stuck out his hand.

"I'm sorry you have to go, Mr. Knollwood," Elizabeth lied. "This would have been an unexpected opportunity to discuss this matter in more depth. I must say, I was somewhat curious as to how we would be able to ensure that you would be able to submit the winning bid."

There was a short, uncomfortable silence. Rosenthal was first to break it with a boisterous laugh. Knollwood spoke first.

"Ms. Schmitter, I'm going to let Marvin put your mind at ease when it comes to those concerns," Knollwood said smiling. "But, here,"—he reached into his pocket and produced a business card—"feel free to call me personally if you have lingering questions. All I want is to have a smooth process that results in a successful deal and a beautiful, functional, new wing to your fantastic hospital."

He was shaking her hand and edging away, smiling.

"I'll try to clear up any questions Liz may have, Don. Thanks for your help, as always." Rosenthal, too, was smiling broadly. After Mr. Knollwood left them, Elizabeth Schmitter went in for her version of the kill. She wanted Rosenthal to go right onto the record. She wanted him to fully incriminate himself for those who were listening.

"He seems nice," Elizabeth began, adjusting the white linen napkin on her lap.

"Oh, I've known him for years. Wonderful guy . . . beautiful wife and children. You can absolutely count on anything he promises. He's a guy who always comes through for his partners."

"I'll take you at your word on that, Marvin." This was the very first time that Elizabeth had called Rosenthal by his first name. It did not go unnoticed. "But, I'm just wondering how we ensure that Don, there, submits the lowest bid. Call me crazy, but I thought that was the very purpose of having sealed bids."

Marvin Rosenthal cleared his throat. It was the first time during the meeting that he seemed at all concerned about the way things were progressing between them. A momentary flash of mistrust came across his face.

"Don't you worry your pretty little head about the details, Elizabeth, my dear. Suffice it to say, I have friends in important places. I told you that. This is not my first fox-trot around this dance floor. If you can guarantee that there will be no active objection to Knollwood Construction, Inc., I will guarantee, right here and now, three things. One, your proposed expansion will be approved by the board. Two, Don Knollwood will win the bid as general contractor. And, lastly, your bond financing will be approved by the State of Illinois. How does that sound to you?"

Elizabeth should have received an Oscar for her performance. Not only did she let the condescending, male-chauvinist statement "Don't worry your pretty little head" go by unchallenged, she simultaneously flashed her most charming smile, giggling cutely, all the while wondering if she had gotten this monumental asshole to say enough to sink him. She wasn't a lawyer, but she felt very good about how the sting was turning out.

"That's a lot of promises, Marvin. You sound quite sure that you can deliver on all of them. As a CEO, I would be more confident if I knew all the details, I suppose, but I believe that I will take some of this on faith. I believe that you can deliver what you say. You do impress me that way. So, how does this work? Where do I sign, so to speak?"

After a quiet chuckle, Rosenthal continued. "Oh, as you might expect, there is nothing to sign. This type of arrangement does not end up in a written document. There is a level of trust that must exist. Plus, of course, the mutual benefit that will result to each of us—that always helps to serve as sufficient incentive for the parties to keep to the spirit of the agreement."

This cold, pointed concluding statement sent a chill up Elizabeth's spine. It was delivered with an icy stare and a sure attitude. She thought of the thin wire snaking up her midsection to the microphone pinned to her bra. She felt that was as close as she was going to come to an out-and-out admission with this slippery character.

The microphone and transmitter were working flawlessly. Marvin Rosenthal clearly had no idea they were being taped by the Feds sitting in the car outside the Standard Club.

"Isn't this view wonderful?" she said, changing the subject and ending their discussion of their business deal. The rest of their time together was judiciously dedicated to any other subject. She did not want to screw up what she considered a successful mission.

WHEN ELIZABETH REACHED THE car in the downtown parking lot, she finally was able to relax. She heaved a long sigh. She was glad it was over. The men and women in the car congratulated her and praised her bravery and fortitude. When they arrived at the office back at the Federal Building, she immediately removed the wire from her person. She felt like she needed a shower.

"Did you get enough to put that bastard away?" she asked, with unadulterated disgust for the man with whom she had endured a long dinner. "I cannot believe that he had the balls to have that other son of a bitch show up at the restaurant."

All of the agents standing in front of her were nodding and smiling.

"That was actually a lucky break," Josh interjected. "We knew he normally used Knollwood Construction. At least, we knew he used them in the past, but that little meeting cinches it. We can focus now on both of them. We cannot thank you enough, Ms. Schmitter. Your country thanks you as well."

As Elizabeth drove home, she couldn't wait for a long, hot shower and a tall glass of wine. She felt proud of herself for having done the right thing. She thought about her meeting with Rosenthal and about how easy it would have been to be corrupted. They had the ability to let her pet project slide right through the process, or die on the vine.

She shook her head. She felt she had done her duty as an American citizen. She felt a realistic and well-deserved sense of pride. It was a better feeling than she'd expected. She smiled as she drove home to her family.

A WEEK LATER, JOSH Baker appeared as a witness before a specially desig-
nated federal judge in a closed proceeding. He laid out the government's
investigation into a possible extortion scheme underway at the Illinois
Health Facilities Planning Board. He presented a transcript of the meeting
between Rosenthal and Ms. Schmitter. The court authorized the attachment
of wiretap devices to the office, residential, and personal cell phones of
Marvin Rosenthal and Donald Knollwood.

—

From the Memoirs of Mars Gregory:

OUR OFFICE WAS STILL being used by the governor, his people, and my partner as a satellite office from which to run the state—and, some would say, milk it dry. Secretive meetings and clandestine activities were becoming the rule rather than the exception. Everybody seemed to be looking over their shoulder. I would open the morning paper and see my partner's name mentioned, often in headline bold print, in connection with one person or another under investigation and being questioned by the US attorney's office. This did not sit well with me.

I was guzzling Pepto Bismol morning, noon, and night. I would see strange cars parked near our office at all hours. I became anxious on a level that was unhealthy.

Despite all this, the United States attorney's office and the possibility of indictments, although quite disconcerting, wasn't my biggest worry. My main concern, what kept me awake at night, was much more nerve-racking.

When a development the size and scope of our South Loop Project is contemplated, there is the need for significant government involvement. This project would require the building of roads, sidewalks, the creation of a sewer system, water, streetlights—all of the systems and infrastructure that a multi-level hunk of urban landscape requires to function as a neighborhood. This, after all, was going to be a significant new portion of the South Side cityscape of the third largest city and market in the country. The cooperation of both the City and State were absolutely necessary for such a development to proceed. The cooperation of the State was a no-brainer, of course; the governor damned near lived in our office. However, the cooperation of the City of Chicago was a whole different matter, as it was not only approval by the City that was needed. That would be easy to get. No one would deny the benefit of such an undertaking. It was the financing that was going to be tricky.

We'd applied with the City of Chicago for Tax Increment Financing, or TIF, which is a common way to procure the huge sums of cash required to build the large-scale public systems, services, and facilities required for this type of massive project. Basically, the city pledges the future property tax increases that result when land is developed, to pay off bonds, which are issued to pay the development costs. When a city plans to build a football stadium or multi-use sports arena and complex, or an airport expansion, for example, a TIF is often used.

Our TIF had been preliminarily approved, which was a huge load off my mind. I was in discussions with the mayor's office, and everyone, including the mayor himself, was reported to be very excited about this welcome development and rehabilitation of a huge area of unused land in the heart of the city. Only the details had to be addressed, and this whole project would be a go, as they say.

Ah, but the devil is always in the details.

Word began to seep out that my partner was under investigation by the Feds. Suddenly, we were getting bad vibes from personnel in various city offices. Phone calls were not being returned. Letters and email communications were left unanswered. Things did not seem to be moving along as smoothly as they had in the past.

And to make matters even worse, we were burning through the development money that Bachman Brothers had provided at a prodigious rate. There were so many expenses: the City wanted traffic studies, environmental studies, engineering studies, on and on. If the City didn't come through with the TIF financing soon, we would be out of money, and the Bachman Brothers would be in a position to place us in default and take over the project. Oh, and there was the minor matter of that personal guaranty.

A knot the size of a watermelon affixed itself to the pit of my stomach, and it wouldn't go away.

I requested and was able to schedule a meeting with the mayor of the great city of Chicago. It was a fifty-million-dollar meeting.

———————————

THE FIFTH FLOOR OF the old City Hall building in Chicago is devoted to the office of the mayor. The worn marble floor echoes and reverberates with each step as you get off the elevator and walk through the high-ceilinged, cavernous, open area that leads to the rich oak doors of the outer offices. You cannot help but feel a sense of history.

The office used to be occupied by the current mayor's father. I wondered, *Did John F. Kennedy walk here? Maybe grab the handle on this door? How about his father Joe or his brother Bobby? What about Dr. Martin Luther King?*

My visit to the fifth floor was historic as well. This great city has always been famous for its neighborhoods and my own company was about to add one more. It was exciting. I was on time for the meeting. My critics would tell you that it was the first and only time in my life that I arrived on time to a meeting.

I gave a great deal of thought to what I should wear to this critical meeting. I didn't want to wear a super-expensive designer suit—the mayor was known to be a meat-and-potatoes kind of guy, and he might think a guy wearing a $1,500 suit doesn't need any money from the city. So I selected a very staid Hart Schaffner Marx blue pinstripe suit. Taking a page from my partner's code book of attire, I added a yellow tie. He always said yellow was a power color.

I walked confidently up to the receptionist and gave her my name. That is when the wind went out of my sails.

Instead of the mayor, I was greeted by the mayor's personal secretary, a very prim and proper looking older woman with her hair up in a beehive. I wondered if she had originally worked for the mayor's father.

"Mr. Gregory, I'm Marge, the mayor's secretary. I'm so sorry. The mayor regrets he has been called away and will not be able to attend this meeting. However, you are to meet with Janet Andersen, Director of Planning & Development. I believe you know Janet? At least she said that the two of you know each other. Is that correct?"

A bit flustered and disappointed, I tried to recover. "Yes . . . yes . . . of course . . . of course I know Janet. We're old friends."

"Well, Ms. Andersen is waiting for you in her office. Will you come with me, please?"

Feeling dejected, but trying to put on my best business face, I was led back through the doors of the office of the mayor, past the elevators, and across the hall. As we walked, I felt my heart sink. I knew this was a problem . . . a big problem. As I trudged behind the mayor's secretary, I imagined a little bird carrying a bag filled with $50 million flying away, never to be seen again.

We arrived at Janet's office, and she jumped up and came around her desk to greet us. The years had been kind to her. Janet was as energetic and vivacious as ever. And she still looked great in a tight sweater.

"Mars, it's so good to see you. How have you been?" she said, as she approached. Janet shook my hand and hugged me, smiling warmly. She thanked Marge as she turned and left. "Have a seat. The mayor sends his regrets. But, he has allowed me to deliver what I consider to be good news. Very good news!"

I started breathing again, as we made ourselves comfortable on the leather couch alongside her desk, which was buried in paper.

"The mayor is genuinely excited about this project," she said, taking off her fancy Gucci eyewear with the golden logo on the side. She made eye contact and held it. She had luxurious brown eyes, the color of milk chocolate, the kind of eyes that could draw you in and keep you captivated. "This is a fabulous idea. That land has just been sitting there waiting for someone with vision to see its potential. During all my years at the Department of Planning and Development, I wondered if someone would ever come up with a viable proposal for that parcel of land. Never would I have guessed that it would be you, my old friend Mars, who would offer the perfect vision for this property. Everybody's very excited about it, including the mayor."

I smiled. "Well, all we need is $50 million of TIF financing, and the mayor can preside over the biggest ribbon cutting of his entire time in office."

Janet gave me a sad look. "We want to help, we really do. But, I have to tell you, Mars, there is a fly in the ointment."

I was on a rollercoaster, one minute relieved, the next petrified. My heart was racing.

"What problem could there possibly be? I thought we had covered all the contingencies. The plan is very well formulated."

Janet suddenly was studying a spot on her glasses, breaking eye contact. "You and your people have been wonderful. The planning for this site is detailed and comprehensive. You have dotted every single i and crossed every single t. The mayor supports a TIF for your project. He wants this project to proceed. He has every intention of backing you on this, fighting for you, pushing it through the city council. I think he may even be more excited about this damn project than you are. He told me to tell you that 'this is a fantastic effort and it will be a great addition to our great city.' Those were his exact words."

"Then what is the problem? What is the fly in the ointment?" I tried to sound genuinely puzzled. As if I didn't know.

"Your partner, Sam Alsheriti. Your partner is the problem."

"In what way is he a problem?" I asked, though I knew perfectly well. I wasn't fooling her either. She leveled me with a simple, knowing look.

"Mars, come on now. Don't insult my intelligence or the mayor's or belittle your own powers of perception. Who are we trying to kid here?"

I took one more shot. "He hasn't even been accused of anything, Janet! I would think the mayor, of all people, would be sympathetic to how unfair the media can be."

She laughed at that. "The mayor and I both have had our problems with the media. But we haven't had the Feds in here."

I broke eye contact, and knew she recognized my capitulation.

Janet continued. "Your buddy Sam has gotten his fingers into a lot of pies. We cannot approve a TIF for a project that is being run, at least in part, by a guy whose name is starting to become synonymous with *federal investigation*. Forget about the political ramifications for the administration and for the mayor personally, which are damn near infinite, by the way. Forget about that for now. The other problem is that it's not even possible. The statutes preclude it. It would be against the law, plain and simple.

"I'm going to make this very clear for you. We cannot and will not allow the City of Chicago to provide funds through a TIF for a project that is being run by a reported crook. Now, Mars, that isn't meant to cast aspersions on you. We've checked you out. We know that you have kept your head above water on this thing. But, as long as this project has Sam's name attached to it in any way, there will be no public financing, period. As much as I want this project for this city, as much as the mayor wants this project, we will kill it dead as a doornail if we smell Sam anywhere near it. Do I make myself clear? Sam has to be out."

"Jeeezzz, Janet, why don't you just say what you really mean?" I was trying to add a tiny bit of levity to a tense situation. Both she and I had to chuckle a bit. "I fail to see how you could be any more clear. I would say the mayor picked the right person to deliver the news. I'll deal with this problem." I started to rise out of my chair. "I'll get back to you. Should I contact you directly? Are you taking point on this?"

"Call me directly. I am supporting you. It really is a worthwhile project. It has all the makings of a plan for a great new neighborhood for our city. I want this project to proceed. I like everything about it, except that one aspect. I will work with you on any other glitches that may pop up, but not on this one," she said, with a firm grip on my hand as she began to walk me toward the door. She smiled and gave me a look that inspired confidence. I knew what I had to do.

Obviously, Sam would not be happy about the news from City Hall, to put it mildly, so, before I approached him, I did my homework. I figured out several different ways to extricate him from our deal structure, while ensuring that he would receive his full share, so he wouldn't be out one single dime. Even if his name was removed from every nook and cranny of this project, he would receive his full portion of the proceeds.

I wasted my time.

Sam was furious. He cursed our fair mayor and his decision. Then he took a very simple and intractable position.

"I will not remove my name from this project. Fuck the mayor! Oh . . . and fuck Janet Andersen while you're at it!"

"Janet didn't make this decision. You can't blame her. Plus, you can't even blame the mayor. His hands are tied here. This is not an option. We need the TIF to complete the project. The whole project is dead in the water without it."

"I will get the financing," Sam said with a snarl. "I will get it on my own!"

"From where? How can you—" I began, but he cut me off.

"I will talk to Malik. He told me Janet Andersen would like to work with him in Washington. They are close."

This time I interrupted. "Janet Andersen does not have the power to change anything! You know that. You're sounding crazy. Wake up, Sam. The mayor couldn't change this, even if he wanted to. You've got too much heat on you, with the Feds, the newspapers . . ."

"I will get my own financing!"

"That is absurd, and you know it. Even if you could find someone that would dump that kind of money into the project, you could never find anyone to do it without diluting our interest. If we don't use the TIF to finance the infrastructure improvements, we'll make far less money, significantly less. Now, I've figured out how to protect your interest even with your name out of it."

"I will not do it, Mars. That is it! That is final. I will not give up my participation." He stalked out of the office.

Chapter 26

WHEN THE UNITED STATES attorney's office had bugged everything Marvin Rosenthal touched, they had been expecting to overhear and record a run-of-the-mill extortion and kickback scheme between Rosenthal and Knollwood. But not even the most cynical, worldly federal agents could have imagined what the Rosenthal tap would expose on only the third day of the eavesdropping program:

> *Transcript of Conversation dated June 24, 2006, 2:30 p.m., from incoming phone no. 312-555-7654, registered to Randy Timmerman*
>
> *[Phone Ringing]*
>
> *Rosenthal:*   *Hello?*
>
> *Timmerman:*   *It's me.*
>
> *Rosenthal:*   *Randy, baby, are you naked for me?*
>
> *Timmerman:*   *Always ready for your sweet ass, Marvin.*
>
> *Rosenthal:*   *Are we all set for tonight?*

Timmerman: Yeah, all five of us will be there. But we have a special treat for you tonight, darlin'.

Rosenthal: Oh, how so?

Timmerman: Our usual friends will be there, but we have a new recruit. You're gonna love him.

Rosenthal: Tell me more, baby.

Timmerman: Black as night. Got the biggest dick I've ever seen. I'm talking, like, Secretariat-quality. He's going to ride you into next week.

Rosenthal: I can't wait. Do you have some good stuff for us tonight?

Timmerman: World class. We got the usual merchandise, but tonight I got some special meth.

Rosenthal: Special?

Timmerman: Yeah, I found a new supplier. He's got connections to a group out of Pittsburgh. They cook the meth in a lab. You're gonna love it.

Rosenthal: That sounds exciting.

Timmerman: Looking forward to tonight, baby. It's all cool.

Rosenthal: Ok, great. Wow. I can't wait. Black guy, huh?

Timmerman: I'm telling you, Marvin, you're gonna love him.

Rosenthal: I'm so ready.

Timmerman: Wear that cobalt blue dress tonight, it contrasts with the color of the hotel so nicely.

Rosenthal: [Laughing] I was gonna wear the red dress, with the red thong panties. I thought you liked it best.

Timmerman: Not tonight, Marvin. I want you in the cobalt blue dress. And bring the white frou-frou puffy slippers. They really show off your legs.

Rosenthal:	*Anything for you, Big Boy. Which wig do you want?*
Timmerman:	*Go redhead, baby. It'll compliment the dress nicely.*
	Gotta go, baby. See you later, same time, same place.

[End of Call]

THAT NIGHT A SURVEILLANCE team followed Marvin Rosenthal to an oddly famous little hotel on the north side of the city. The first thing they noticed about it could be seen long before the agents pulled into the parking lot adjoining the ten-story tower. The entire hotel and all of its several connected buildings were painted a deep periwinkle blue. It stood out as an ugly blue monolith disrupting the surrounding landscape. The hotel was universally known as the Periwinkle Hotel.

The agents took photos of Marvin entering the building, and photos of half a dozen other trim, handsome young men who arrived shortly thereafter, all carrying overnight bags.

When the last of the group departed, the agents visited the night desk clerk, flashed their badges, and quickly learned that Marvin had rented the executive suite on the top floor of the hotel the last Saturday of every month for several years, and that a group of young men showed up each time.

The next morning, Josh Baker urgently requested to see his boss, Frank McKenzie.

McKenzie was busy, and he seemed annoyed at the interruption. "This better be good, Baker."

"Boss, you're aware of the Rosenthal operation, right?"

McKenzie sat up in his chair, suddenly very interested. "Yes, of course. We think he can lead us to the Ringmaster himself." Ringmaster was the government's code name for Vince Perino. "What do you have for me?"

Baker gave his boss a huge grin. "Boss, you are *not* going to believe what we've uncovered."

"I want that fuckin' Rosenthal. I want them all! I want cameras and bugs and wiretaps! If they open their mouths to talk, I want to hear every fucking word they say. I don't care if they're talking on the phone, on a walkie-talkie, or into a cardboard cup. I want it recorded. If they talk in their cars, I want to hear what they say. If they whisper something to their lover in bed, I want to know about it. Hell, I want to know what color their shit is when they leave the toilet! I don't want to leave anything to chance. Am I making myself clear on this?""

Frank was pacing as he barked out orders to Baker and Novak. They sat in front of Frank's desk, taking notes.

Baker looked up from his notepad and smiled. "These guys think they're untouchable. They won't expect a thing. They aren't like the Mob. They do this shit right out there in plain sight in front of everyone. We'll be able to get them on tape fairly easily."

McKenzie stopped pacing and leaned over his desk. "Well, boys, let's get it done. Let's get all of this evidence in front of a judge and get warrants."

Considering the information they'd gathered to date, it wasn't hard to convince Judge Clifford Ashworth to issue a warrant to bug and wiretap the Periwinkle Hotel, the homes of all of the perpetrators, their offices, and their cars. The judge peered through reading glasses perched on the tip of his nose at all the evidence presented, shook his head in disgust, and quickly scribbled his signature on orders authorizing every request. The government now had the tools they needed to conduct a full-scale investigation.

The electronically recorded sights and sounds of the activities taking place at the Periwinkle Hotel would make a porn filmmaker blush. There were always six or seven men, some dressed as women. It would often be the same men, but sometimes newcomers would show up, all of them cavorting for hours at a time, fueled by enough drugs to put the crowd at a Grateful Dead concert to shame. These men would arrive at the hotel dressed like businessmen, in expensive suits and silk ties. They could just as easily be going to a high-level meeting of the board of directors of a Fortune 500 company, and in some cases, that's exactly where they had been earlier in the day. Once in the room, out of their overnight bags would come some of the most elaborate costumes—chiffon dresses in shocking pink and baby blue; makeup to beat the band, haphazardly smeared on beard-stubbled faces; and cheap wigs.

The men would speak freely and carelessly between snorts of long lines of white powder off mirrors and long pulls from various bottles of expensive Champagnes and aged whiskeys.

Rosenthal was a treasure trove of information. He was often high on one drug or another and would ramble on endlessly about his various scams and illegal ventures as if he was proud and trying to impress his guests, oblivious to the hole he was digging for himself. After the Periwinkle taps and surveillance footage was presented to the judge, it became a cakewalk for McKenzie's office to obtain warrants for Rosenthal's personal and office phones. All the agents had to do was turn on the recorder and listen. Rosenthal did the rest.

The investigators quickly learned that aside from running scams as a member of the Illinois Health Facilities Planning Board, Marvin Rosenthal had also deeply corrupted the Illinois Teachers' Pension Fund Board. There were thousands of teachers in the state of Illinois, and the board controlled *billions* in retirement funds on behalf of all those teachers.

It wasn't long before they learned the basic framework of the order of things. Rosenthal was Perino's lackey. The pieces were coming together. It was nearing the time to make an arrest and seriously squeeze Rosenthal for the whole story.

"WHAT DO WE HAVE so far?" Frank McKenzie asked impatiently. In his office were Baker, Novak, and two of Baker's men.

"Well, Rosenthal has his fingers into a lot of things. From his position on the Health Facilities Board, he steers contracts to his crony builders, who pad the bills, and he takes kickbacks from them under a phony consulting contract. We're not quite sure how Perino gets his piece, but we will find out. From his position on the Teachers' Pension Board, they're funneling millions to favored investment firms. There are finder's fees involved in those deals. They can actually take some of those fees on the books."

"Can we arrest him yet?" McKenzie was tapping a yellow pencil on the desk, which Josh knew was a sign of impatience.

But Josh was a methodical investigator. "At present, we have enough with the tapes from Ms. Schmitter to arrest him on the activities regarding the Health Facilities Board. We have him on tape pushing her to hire his builder. I think if we bring him in, though, his secret life and his secret parties at the Periwinkle will get everything we need. This guy has a wife and kids. He's been an invited guest at the White House, for chrissakes. He's on arts boards and zoo boards and many high-profile committees. He pretends to be a stand-up citizen, a regular guy. He hobnobs with Chicago's elite, goes to fancy parties at the Art Institute. He isn't going to want the crazy shit he does at that hotel to get out."

McKenzie was seething. "Here's the problem, Josh," he said, thinking in practical terms. "This guy Rosenthal and his boss Vince Perino are Republicans. Kovach and his crowd will claim this is all holdover from the corrupt Republican Combine. We have to tie this to the governor—and then to his top benefactor, Alsheriti."

Josh picked up a file. "Here's what we know. Perino and Rosenthal have been at this for years. They control the boards and committees that invest literally billions of dollars of state funds. They've created ways, some of them almost legal, to skim millions off the top of that huge pile of money. It's a very sophisticated scheme involving illegal kickbacks, legal finder's fees, which are then divided up illegally, and steering contracts to favored contractors, which also results in illegal kickbacks. These guys have this state wired, boss. It's really kind of amazing how it all works."

McKenzie shot an impatient look at his top lieutenant. "Kovach. The governor. That's who we want. How do we get to him?"

Josh pulled a sheet of paper from the folder and handed it to McKenzie. "That's a copy of a letter from Mike Kovach, governor of the State of Illinois, reappointing Marvin Rosenthal to the Board of the Illinois Teachers' Pension Fund."

McKenzie finally grinned. "So Vince and Marvin have gotten Kovach to let them keep the game going! But how does Alsheriti figure into this?"

Josh withdrew another document, this one several typewritten sheets stapled together. He handed it to McKenzie.

It was the transcript of a telephone wire tap.

[Text]

Ringing phone registered to Sammar, LLC.

Voice:	*Hello?*
Rosenthal:	*Hey, Sam, how are you?*
Voice:	*Marvin, how are you?*
Rosenthal:	*Good, Sam, good. It was really great to see you last week at Mike's fundraiser.*
Voice:	*Yes, very nice. Thanks for your all your help. It will be recognized.*
Rosenthal:	*Well, now that you mention it, I just wanted to check. I got my reappointment to the Teacher's Pension Board, but now my term on the Health Facilities Board is about to expire. How's my reappointment letter coming along?*
Voice:	*No problem, Marvin. The letter is in process. I've already gotten Mike's approval. It's done.*
Rosenthal:	*Fantastic. That's very much appreciated.*
Voice:	*Just keep doing what you've been doing, Marvin. We will all participate.*
Rosenthal:	*Ok, great, Sam, great. I'll let you go.*
Voice:	*Ok, thanks, talk soon.*

[End of Call]

McKenzie cast a cold look at Josh. "How do we know this 'Sam' that Marvin was talking to is Sam Alsheriti? The transcript says the phone is registered to something called 'Sammar, LLC.' What the hell is that?"

Josh handed McKenzie yet another sheet of paper. It was an official-looking document from the Illinois secretary of state.

"What is this?" McKenzie asked, looking it over.

"It's from the corporate records of the secretary of state," Josh replied. "Sammar, LLC is Sam Alsheriti and some guy named Marston Gregory."

"This is good," McKenzie nodded. "This will prove that Rosenthal talked to Alsheriti, they specifically agreed to 'participate' in what's been going on, and Kovach is going to reappoint Rosenthal so they can keep the game going."

Josh nodded. "With this, we can get wiretaps on Alsheriti's phone."

McKenzie broke into a big grin. "Now *that* ought to turn up a treasure trove of good stuff!"

They both laughed.

McKenzie studied the paper for another moment. "What about this Marston Gregory character? If he's Sam's partner in this business, he's got to be dirty too, right?"

Josh rubbed his jaw. "We've never come across him in anything, boss. Maybe he just runs the legitimate side of the business."

McKenzie rolled his eyes. "I doubt that. He and Sam are probably cut from the same mold. Check him out thoroughly. Maybe he can help us squeeze Sam."

Josh had long since given up trying to restrain his boss from going after people who simply were near the people he wanted to get. It was McKenzie's favorite tactic. "I'm going to need a bigger team."

"I don't care what it costs," McKenzie said, gesturing with his fist. "I want you to put every available man and woman on this case. If you need more help, pull people off some of the other ongoing investigations. I want cases built against each and every one of these shysters."

"But, boss . . . the other investigations—"

"What part of 'I don't care what it takes' did you not understand, Josh?" McKenzie's tone was ice cold. It sent shivers down Josh's spine. "I'll say it again . . . I don't care what it takes. When we finish this investigation, they're gonna rename this town 'The *Very* Windy City!'"

From the Memoirs of Mars Gregory:

DESPITE ALL THE SUSPICION and rumors of corruption bubbling just below the surface, Mike easily won reelection to the governor's office in November. But things were not getting better; my partner was in the papers more often than ever before, and none of the articles were the least bit complimentary, not by a long shot. But, frankly, that was the least of my worries. There was always a nondescript, unmarked van parked somewhere on the street outside of our offices. There were unmarked squads making passes by the building or in our rearview mirrors wherever we drove.

These guys were not being even a little subtle about it. They made their presence known. Guys in wrinkled suits and coffee-stained shirts would exit the van in plain view and wander off to the closest fast food restaurant, bringing back bags of food and gallons of coffee to their vehicle. If this wasn't strange enough, like a bad cop movie, occasionally these smart-asses would smile and nod at me if they caught my eye while I was heading to my car at the end of the day.

So, the articles in the papers, to which I had become somewhat accustomed, were not that worrisome. The fact that every person who came to our office seemed to be the subject of attention for these government types was much more of a concern. After all, I was obviously one of those people.

I wasn't the only one observing the surveillance activity outside our offices or reading the articles in the paper. Everybody who worked for us could plainly see what was going on as well. An air of nervous confusion settled among our staff. On the one hand, there were men who were considered dignitaries, including the damned governor, stopping by at all hours. This activity normally would have instilled confidence in those working for us. *Boy, our bosses must be really important. We must be involved in big government-backed deals.* However, in this case, most of the men and some of the women who were turning up at our office, spending time in our courtyard, and having late night meetings, were also the same men and women who were showing up in articles under headlines that almost always included the words *suspected of corruption.*

Under normal circumstances, this probably would have given rise to office meetings where calming words would be spoken to the staff, together with promises and guarantees that "everything is fine" and "you have nothing to be concerned about." Instead, we were giving briefings on what to do if the Feds showed up at their houses at six a.m.

The only good that came from this new level of scrutiny was that the governor's wife stopped coming to the office. Without any fanfare or formality, she just resigned. I guess someone close to the governor decided it was best for her to steer clear of us for the time being. That suited me just fine.

———————

WODECKI CAME IN MY office, looking like she'd seen a ghost. She was carrying a certified letter. The return address on the envelope showed it was from Bachman Brothers.

I have to admit, my hands were shaking as I opened the envelope. My heart skipped several beats as I scanned through it.

My worst fears were realized. Bachman Brothers were declaring us in default. They were demanding full and immediate payment of their $30 million loan, and they were threatening to sue Sam and me personally on our guaranties.

I went to the washroom and puked.

The default notice was the icing on the cake. Under the various documents, we'd been given 120 days to "cure" the alleged default, by coming up with more money to meet the ongoing cash needs of the project. By now, I was not sleeping at all. I was scrambling to find another investor who would inject some fresh money into the project, and get Bachman off our backs.

Plus, Sam and I were communicating less and less because of the intractable position he had taken regarding the South Loop Project. He wouldn't tell me what he was doing about this looming wall we were about to hit with Bachman Brothers. All he would say was "I'm working on it."

I had signed a personal guaranty to repay $30 million to Bachman Brothers. That was $30 million I didn't have! If they sued and won, I would lose everything. And I mean *everything*.

I'd thought I had control over the variables and could make the proper adjustments. In other words, I'd assumed I could fix the problem. In this instance, the problem was my partner. This should have been a very simple matter. A meeting or a long lunch should have been all that was necessary. However, it turns out that when your partner is the problem, and he's taken an absolutely unreasonable and unflinching position, it makes for a truly unsolvable situation.

As if the news couldn't become worse, Wodecki walked into my office and parked herself in one of the chairs in front of my desk. It was a Friday, very late in the afternoon. She'd waited until everyone had left for the day and then told me exactly what I didn't want to hear.

"I want you to know this isn't easy for me," she began, "but I feel the Sammar ship is sinking, and I need to resign before it's too late."

I tried my best to convince her I was doing everything in my power for the business to survive, and I needed her to help me run the day-to-day. I'll never forget her exact words.

"Mars, you're asking me to stay on to rearrange the deck chairs on the Titanic."

After hearing her take on our current situation, I realized she'd already made her final decision. I asked her if there was anything I could say or do for her to reconsider, but she was adamant. This was not about money; it was about timing, and she wanted out.

Wodecki handed me an envelope containing her written resignation and asked if she could leave effective that day. She offered to make herself available by phone should I need her from time to time for operational advice; she had, after all, been practically running the business. Although she wasn't offering me the customary week or two notice, I understood.

I came around the desk as she stood up, and gave her a long extended hug, telling her I would really miss her. She pulled back, and I saw a few tears running down her cheeks as she said, "I really am sorry, Mars. I'll miss you too, but I have to go."

I became teary-eyed as well, realizing I was losing one of my arms. Claudia Wodecki Kovaleski was great at her job, and a real trouper, but I knew I had to let her go. I left the office before her, as I couldn't stand to watch her pack up and walk out.

Chapter 27

FROM THE MOMENT HE arrived in Chicago, Franklin McKenzie was a no-nonsense, rough and tough, balls-to-the-wall prosecutor.

The Kovach investigation had now become the center of Frank's life. He was finding it hard to concentrate on anything else. It was beginning to affect his relationship with his wife.

Frank's wife, Mary Margaret, was a good Irish Catholic girl who married the guy most likely to succeed. She'd been a pretty redhead when Frank had met her and won her heart back in Boston. Everybody saw their marriage as picture-perfect. Maggie was the wonderful mom and community leader, always volunteering at the school or at church; Frank was the tough but fair dad and hard-bitten prosecutor and community leader, making headlines, always in pursuit of the bad guy.

This case, however, with this group of scoundrels he was chasing, had created cracks in the bliss of his home life. Frank would bring home the pressures of the day, causing friction with his wife. They would have a spat about some unrelated issue or another. Then he brought the stress from the tensions at home back to work, making him short-tempered and irascible toward his coworkers. It was a vicious cycle.

One night, while sitting with his wife after dinner in their family room, it all came to a head.

"Honey," Maggie was saying, "if this is getting to be too much, you can always resign. Why do you seem to believe that you and you alone are the only person suited to take down these corrupt bastards? Maybe it's someone else's turn to take up the mantle of crime fighter. You've now been doing this in Chicago for over five years! I support you. The kids support you. But maybe we have done this long enough. Maybe it's time to cash in on all of this experience and notoriety. You would be hired in a second by any big law firm out there. Would it be so bad to be able to take the kids on a nice vacation? Maybe buy yourself a nice car?"

Frank jumped out of his recliner and stared down at his wife. "I cannot believe that you would even suggest that, Maggie. I can't quit! I can't abandon my post."

Maggie looked at her husband with frustration. "Frank, there *are* other good, honest lawyers. You are not the only one."

"This is my job, Maggie, my *job*! I took it on, and I'm going to finish it."

"At what cost, Frank? Do they expect your wife and children to suffer? They certainly don't pay you enough! The government expects you to work your fingers to the bone, to solve society's problems—their problems—and then what? A watch and a plaque, and a pat on the rear? 'Thank you for your service, Mr. McKenzie'; now it's some other sucker's turn?"

Frank's eyes became saucers. "Oh, now it's about the money? That's beneath you, Mag."

"You know perfectly well that I don't care about the money, Frank. If I did, I would have been gone long ago. I care about you. I care about us. I care about our kids. I don't want to see you doing this to yourself. Remember back in Boston, when we used to say that soon it would all be over? Then we would take a cushy job in a big firm and enjoy the rest of our lives? Do you remember that, Frank?"

Frank was softening. He looked at his wife. "Of course I remember."

"The kids and I are with you all the way, Frank. We always have been. The question is, are you with us? We've stood by you while you saved the world, both in Boston and now Chicago. Isn't it time you stand by us?"

Frank took his wife's hand. She was right. He knew it. He made a promise. "When this case is over, I'll resign this post. No more stress, no more saving the world, I promise. Can you live with that?"

His wife looked at him. "I can live with that," she answered.

Frank walked around the table and gave her a hug. "You're still the best."

The phone rang.

Frank said, "I have to take that, honey. We have a big raid going down tomorrow. Very big."

Maggie sighed as Frank headed for the den.

From the Memoirs of Mars Gregory:

EVEN AS HE TEETERED on the edge of the abyss, Sam's power and influence were growing almost exponentially. His fingerprints were on nearly every major campaign in Chicago and its environs. He had reached a point where he thought he was untouchable.

And then I discovered something that absolutely knocked me on my butt.

I passed by our reception area one day, and noticed that Johnny Jarzik and Oren Mitchell were sitting there.

"Hey guys, how are you?"

Oren got up to shake hands. Jarzik acted like he couldn't be bothered.

"Mars, how you doin', man?" Oren said, gregarious as usual, and talking like we were old pals from the 'hood.

"Great, Oren, great," I said, even though nothing could be further from the truth. "If you're waiting for Sam, he's not back from lunch."

"No problem, no problem," Oren said, laughing. "He'll be here when he gets here!"

I noticed that Oren was carrying a folder. There was a bumper sticker affixed to the front. I almost burst out laughing when I read it: *Alawi for President.*

"Is that a gag gift for Sam?" I asked. They couldn't be serious. "He's a junior senator who hasn't even served one term, and he's already thinking of running for president? Is he nuts?"

"No, no," Oren said. "Malik is forming an exploratory committee. He's *looking* at running for president."

I couldn't believe it. "You've got to be kidding."

Oren looked offended. "Why do you say that? He's got as good a chance as anybody."

I looked at Jarzik, figuring he might be a voice of reason. He merely shrugged. I realized this is a guy who gets paid to organize campaigns. For a big enough fee, he'd sign on to promote Satan.

"So, Johnny, you're going to be working on this exploratory committee?" I asked.

Jarzik nodded. "It could be historic. Think of it: the first African-American president."

I didn't believe this guy for a New York minute. It was all about dollars and cents with him. "So, you'll be taking a leave from your consulting job with the governor?"

"Nah," Jarzik said evasively.

Oren could see my bewilderment, and he said to me, "Johnny doesn't actually have to show up there. He just maintains an office and provides them with cell phones."

Jarzik shot a death ray at Oren. *Jarzik was making cell phones available to the governor's team?* This had to be a ruse to avoid wiretaps. Almost in a daze, I begged off from further conversation and headed for the men's room.

As I thought about it, the idea of Malik running for president began to take on a logic of its own. He'd given an amazing keynote speech at the 2004 Democratic National Convention, when he was running for the Senate, and ever since then, there had been people mentioning Malik's name as a potential contender for president. Hell, Sam was one of the people who mentioned it the most. So, when Sam later confirmed to me that they were forming an exploratory committee to evaluate whether Malik should make a run for the White House, I could see how Sam, with his ever-increasing master-of-the-universe mind-set, could believe that he might actually pull it off before Malik had even served a single term in the Senate.

During that brief conversation, Sam's phone rang. He pulled out his cell phone and I noticed it was a Motorola model; I knew that all the Sammar-issued phones were made by Nokia. Maybe Sam was using one of Jarzik's cell phones.

I stuck my head back in the sand. I didn't want to know what the hell he was doing.

Sam would be spending most of his time on politics, and even less on our South Loop problems. This was the last straw. It was time we met for a full-blown sit-down, to discuss all aspects of our business.

I CORRALLED HIM IN his office later that night, when he was without his customary entourage.

"Sam, we haven't talked in a while. Perhaps it's time we do."

As he looked up from the papers on his desk, he smiled. "Sure, sure. Come in and sit down. It has been a while. What's on your mind, Mars?"

"Well, frankly, I was hoping we could have one final discussion about the South Loop deal. You know, if we can just get the TIF approved, then the Bachman Brothers financing will be reinstated, and we can get back to business as usual. But, as long as your name is on it, the mayor—"

He interrupted me without malice or any sign he was perturbed about revisiting the issue. He had a pleasant smile, almost condescending, like I was the problem that had to be handled. This was unsettling. Usually when he took on this tone, it was because he knew something I didn't know. "Mars, we have reached a new place. The mayor will come around. He will have to. We have the governor's office behind us. Let me remind you, our friend Mike Kovach has given me complete discretion as it pertains to the appointments to the top committees and boards that control all commerce in this state. We have systematically placed people who are sympathetic to us in all of those key slots. These are people who helped us during both campaigns. We have a great deal of leverage, you know."

I couldn't believe the gall of this guy. "You may be underestimating the power and influence of the mayor, Sam."

Sam nodded. "The mayor is a powerful force. He's been in office a long time. He has gained a great deal of respect. Plus, we cannot deny the influence that comes from being the son of a true legend. He was born to be the mayor of Chicago, and he is a good mayor. However, a mayor is not a governor. We control the whole State of Illinois. The mayor needs help with lots of issues in Springfield. And, when he comes to us for that help, we will be able to bargain with him, I promise you. If I didn't believe we have a strong position in this matter, I wouldn't take such a hard line on this."

"But, Sam, the deal is hanging by a thread. Literally, hanging by a thread. We could lose *everything*!"

Sam looked me up and down. "Mars, have you lost your stomach for risk?"

This really pissed me off. "I have my name—my personal name—on a bunch of pending deals that we're working on. My name! Not your name. Not the partnership's name. My own personal guaranty is on the line on way too many projects for me to just continue to sit by and watch this all come crashing down. We need that project. We need the money that it'll bring into this firm. We cannot lose this deal!"

Sam suddenly looked like a hunter who'd just sighted a big buck. He said, in that oily tone that I'd come to know so well, "Mars, if the pressure is too great for you, perhaps I should buy you out of the 64 acres?"

I couldn't even respond, I was so shocked. Finally, I managed to mutter, "Buy *me* out of the project?"

Sam sat back in his chair and pulled a cigar out of his pocket. It was in one of those fancy metal cases that announces *expensive cigar*. He took a gold-plated cigar cutter out of his pocket and chopped off one end, then lit the cigar. I caught a whiff of the smoke, which I hated. Sam bore a striking resemblance to a sketch on a Monopoly card—the one with the bald-headed guy sitting behind a desk, puffing away.

"Mars," he said evenly, "I have been telling you for ages, you worry too much. As your friend, I would say if the stress of this business is too much, you should get away from it. Let me buy you out of the 64 acres."

I was stunned. How in the hell could he possibly have the money? Sam looked at me from across his desk in a way I had never seen before. Pompous, aloof, and condescending. In all our years—nearly twenty of them—in business together, I'd never felt as if he thought of me as anything less than his equal. He needed me and I needed him. That was always the basis of our very successful partnership. It made us both millionaires many times over, at least on paper. Liquid cash was another thing. Now, Sam was giving off a vibe I didn't like. He seemed to imply that my contribution was somehow less than his. I was furious, but I didn't show it. I didn't want to give him the satisfaction.

"Right now," he continued, "we owe Bachman Brothers the $30 million, and we don't have the TIF. Bachman Brothers is threatening to foreclose and take over the deal, leaving you penniless. So right now, the value of the project is totally speculative, and you yourself are telling me it's falling apart. I would say the value of the project right now isn't very much, wouldn't you agree?"

I was silent. He took my silence as a tacit acknowledgement that he was right.

"Suppose I offer you a million dollars to step out of the deal, and take you off the personal guaranty. You'd be liberated."

I couldn't believe the nerve of the guy. Here we were, on the brink of catastrophe, and he's offering me a million dollars to walk away? Marshaling all my energy, I managed to hold my temper.

"Let me think about it," was all I could say.

I got up and left.

In retrospect, it was this conversation that ultimately saved my ass.

ON THE DRIVE HOME, I had time to reflect. I'm not going to lie: I liked being rich. I liked being a good provider. I liked being able to do whatever I wanted when I wanted. I liked all of it.

I did not like being thought of as some sort of subordinate. During my whole career, I'd always been my own man. The promise I'd made to myself years before—never to take a partner—began to reverberate in my psyche.

I decided to call Phil Angelino.

Phil had been a dear friend for years. He and his firm had often provided legal work for us in the past, including the initial purchase of the South Loop property. He'd been to the office on many occasions. He knew the situation inside and out. He'd observed the politicians and the political hangers-on come and go. He knew Sam and how Sam operated. He was close enough to the problem to fully understand my concerns, yet far enough removed to be able to give me an unbiased opinion. Plus, I trusted him. I felt his counsel might be beneficial.

"I don't know if you would call this a coincidence, or what," Phil said to me as soon as he heard my voice. "I was planning to call you."

"Well, I just left a very disconcerting meeting with Sam, and I need some legal advice. What did you want to talk to me about?"

"I've been hearing some rumors—rumors that may greatly affect your relationship with your partner. Sam is under investigation. Under *serious* investigation."

"What have you heard? Should I be worried?"

"Well, you know, I haven't been concerned in the past. There are always endless rumors and whispers. They often don't amount to much. The legal profession has its soap opera aspect. Plus, you know the newspaper business. They're always in stiff competition with one another for readership, and they over-dramatize everything. But this is different."

"Phil, get to the point, please."

"Okay. You should distance yourself from Sam. You should get as far away from that son of a bitch as you possibly can. Begin unraveling your business relationship with him immediately, even if it costs you big money. Even if it means losing money on some of the projects that you have with him. You need to be disconnected from him, and you have to do it as quickly as possible."

Considering the reason I'd called Phil, which I hadn't yet even mentioned, I was reeling. I'd called to ask about Sam's offer to buy me out of the 64 acres, but before I even said a word about it, Phil had told me in no uncertain terms that I should not only end my business relationship with Sam, but distance myself from him completely. I realize now, it was the hand of God that had made me pick up the phone to make that call.

"Why are you telling me this now? What exactly is going on?"

There was a short pause on the other end of the line.

"Look, you know the drill here. You used to practice law. There's only so much I can say. I have confidentiality concerns. Suffice it to say, I am telling you this as a friend and as a lawyer: run, don't walk, away from your present business partner."

This took a few seconds to sink in. He was clearly not fucking around.

"I'm personally on the hook for many of our pending projects. If I walk away, I stand to lose millions. I'll also be personally sued on several of the loans. Everything I have could be at risk! I'm not sure you know what you're telling me to do here."

After another pause, Phil got cryptic. "You can only buy so many candy bars and cigarettes, Mars."

I didn't know what he was trying to say. I actually pulled the car over to the side of the road. I wanted to be sure I wasn't distracted. "What are you talking about? Candy bars? Cigarettes?"

"In prison it doesn't really matter how much money you have. You can't just buy anything you want. All you can use money for is candy bars and cigarettes from the commissary."

My heart was pounding like a rabbit's. I had known Phil for over twenty years. He would not be saying these things as some kind of sick joke. He was trying to help me without compromising his own situation. He was probably telling me more than he should. Phil was treading lightly through a minefield at some personal risk to himself and to his family. The gravity of the situation was beginning to sink in.

"Phil, I'm going to end this conversation at this point. I want you to know how much I appreciate your advice and counsel. I'll never forget this. You've been a great help. Thank you."

I hung up, checked my rear view mirror, and slowly pulled away from the curb. I drove off in a fog, running on autopilot. I don't even remember what route I took from that spot to my house. It was all one big blur.

My head was spinning. I knew my partner was involved in some shady political dealings, although I didn't know many details. I certainly hadn't been involved in anything illegal. They couldn't get *me* for anything.

Then I started thinking about what the Feds did to Skylar Stillwell to bring down Ed Parker. How they go after people close to the guy they really want, and think nothing of ruining the lives of sometimes-innocent people in order to get the dirt on their target. I knew perfectly well what was going on in our offices. The meetings . . . the whispering . . . the dirty deals. If it was subjected to serious scrutiny, some of it was surely illegal. Some of it was in that gray area between actual illegality and just plain sleaze.

I was partners with a man who played without rules, a man who convinced and corrupted others into believing rules were made for other people. He persuaded me and others around him to think that we were the ones who made the rules. And worse, this was the natural order of things, this was all okay, just as long as we continued to fly high above the fray.

I guess I was having some sort of half-assed epiphany.

I made up my mind.

I punched the speed dial number for Sam's cell phone.

After a couple of rings, he answered.

"Mars, what's up?" he asked, sounding a little irritated. "I have asked you before, be careful what you say on the phone."

Sam was operating now on the assumption that his phone was being tapped.

"No problem," I said cheerfully. "I just want to confirm, are you still a buyer for my interest in the project?"

"Yes, of course."

I took a deep breath. "Well, if you're a buyer, then I'm a seller."

Chapter 28

Frank McKenzie received the call he'd been waiting for from Josh Baker, seeking the final go-ahead to roust Marvin Rosenthal. McKenzie didn't hesitate. The raid was approved.

True to form, Baker and his team arrived outside of Rosenthal's North Shore home at six o'clock sharp the very next morning. There was an ornate gate in front of a long winding driveway, meandering through immaculately manicured grounds. However, the yard was not fully fenced. That actually pissed Baker off. The gate was not for security, something he would have fully understood. It was simply a pretentious requirement to gain access to the property by car. You had to ring to be admitted, thereby creating the illusion of great wealth, but if you were on foot, you could simply pass through an open gate and stroll up to the front door without a problem. The mailman, or anybody else for that matter, had no impediment to access the property.

One man stayed on the street with the cars as the rest of the team went up the winding walk and pounded on the front door of the grand residence until Rosenthal himself appeared, sleepy-eyed and shocked, wearing purple silk gym shorts and a T-shirt, rubbing his eyes in bewilderment like a kid.

"What the fuck is this?"

"Marvin Rosenthal, we are federal agents. I'm Joshua Baker, and this is my partner, N.J. Novak. We would like you to come with us, sir," Josh commanded. "We would like to ask you some questions regarding your activities and your meeting with one Elizabeth Schmitter."

"Am—am I—I un-un-under arrest?" Rosenthal was now petrified and stuttering.

"Do you want to be?" Josh snapped at him.

They could have arrested him based on the information they had already gathered from the recordings. However, the Feds had made the decision to handle this in a slightly different manner. Josh stepped closer to Rosenthal and put his nose within inches of Marvin's face, eyes boring into him. He spoke a little like a drill instructor.

"You are coming with us, Mr. Rosenthal. Now, you can come voluntarily, in which case we will give you a minute or two to change your clothes, kiss your wife and kids, and leave here with a modicum of dignity. Or, we can arrest you, cuff you, and cart you off from this very spot like a common criminal, dressed exactly like you are. Now, which would you prefer?"

Marvin was so terrified, he completely forgot all the coaching he'd received about what to do if the Feds showed up on his doorstep. He should have said, *My lawyer is so-and-so, let me call him, and if you want to arrest me, you'd better read me my rights.* Instead, he pleaded, "Please, please, don't take me away like this. Let me go up and change my clothes."

Josh had been doing this for a long time. He knew a few things. It was easier to get a guy to talk if he felt he was being treated with respect. Further, if the subject comes voluntarily, which technically Rosenthal was about to do, as Josh could see in his eyes, this was not officially an arrest. It was simply a person of interest coming down to the station to answer questions of his own volition. No lawsuit could ever result from that.

Rosenthal turned slowly and looked back into his home. He turned back to Josh.

"Give me fifteen minutes?"

"You've got ten, Mr. Rosenthal. Don't do anything stupid."

"I'll be right out." The level of resignation in Rosenthal's voice was telling. It was almost as if he knew that the wild ride he'd been on had an inevitable ending, and that ending was some variation of this very event. He was so petrified, he didn't even think to call his lawyer.

Eleven minutes later, Marvin Rosenthal walked out the front door of his mansion dressed in black linen slacks, a starched white cotton button-down shirt, no tie, and a beautifully tailored herringbone sport jacket. His thinning hair was combed over his bald dome and there was a hint of expensive cologne in the air behind him. He looked like he could have been going out to a business meeting. He sauntered down his red brick walk toward the waiting cars outside the gate at the end of his driveway. He got into the rear seat of the car in which Josh Baker would ride shotgun.

It's hard to imagine what was going through his mind. But one thing was certain: his life had changed forever.

What qualifies someone as a big-time criminal? Is it the number of people he or she has hurt or killed? The amount of money they have stolen as a result of their illegal activities? Whatever the criteria, Marvin Rosenthal fit the bill. He'd made a significant amount of money from his nefarious deeds.

Because Marvin had corrupted the decision-making process, every naïve bidder and applicant who never got fair consideration had suffered.

But no self-respecting big-time criminal would have turned into such a sniveling little crying pussy of a man the very minute he was brought into the Federal Building and confronted with the recording of his telephone calls setting up the trysts at the Periwinkle Hotel.

He visibly shivered when he saw the cold, stark, cinderblock cubicle and the large pane of one-way glass along the wall of the interrogation room where he was brought for questioning. Josh hit the playback button, and Marvin soon heard himself babbling on to his friends at the Periwinkle Hotel about gay sex and drug orgies. He listened to all of the promises he'd made to Elizabeth Schmitter on the recording she'd bravely secured by wearing a wire. And when Josh and his agents laid out plainly in front of Marvin the case and the information they had regarding his private life, his sexual perversions, and the hard evidence they'd collected, Marvin Rosenthal rolled over on his back like a whipped dog and proceeded to piss all over himself.

This was the cave-in of the century. Marvin proved to be an enormous source of information—almost too good to be true. Through tears and snot and abject fear, Rosenthal started talking, and once he got going, he never shut up.

"I can't go to jail. I can't go to jail. Please! I'll tell you anything you want to know. But, please, I can't go to jail," he began, burying his head in his hands and sobbing.

"Oh, you're going to jail, Mr. Rosenthal. The question only remains, how long and under what circumstances?" Josh Baker was speaking directly and confidently. "If you don't want to go away for virtually the rest of your life, you'll cooperate fully with us. Then we can talk about what kind of deal we might be able to cut."

Marvin straightened and suddenly showed a flash of spine. "If you're going to insist on jail time, I'm going to call my lawyer."

Josh was highly experienced at this gambit. He'd gotten to this point many times, and he knew exactly what to say. "You are entitled to a lawyer. The Constitution guarantees you that absolute right. If you want a lawyer, we will stop this session and you can get yourself a lawyer. Do you want to do that? Do you want us to stop this session?"

Josh was being cagey. He was taking a risk. In fact, Rosenthal had not yet been charged with a crime. If Josh could get him to waive his right to a lawyer, he knew he would get a lot more valuable information. Josh was playing it by the book. He offered his subject the right to retain counsel.

He banged his fist on the table across from Marvin. He stood up abruptly, acting disgusted. He came around the table and got up close to the broken lump of a man sitting in front of him. He leaned into him and spoke into his ear. Rosenthal could feel Josh's breath on the side of his neck. He could smell this morning's coffee.

"You should know, Marvin," Josh spoke softly at first, "that if you piss me off, all deals will be withdrawn. If you piss me off, no lawyer on this planet is going to be able to save your perverted, fat ass." As he spoke his voice got louder, more threatening. "If you piss me off, I will take personal pleasure in telling your wife and kids just what kind of depraved individual you really are. Don't forget, we have tapes. You listened to those tapes. Your wife is going to hear every single word. I will go to your house personally and pick her up as a person of interest, a person who has benefitted greatly from your illegal activities. I will drive her down here and I will put her in this room and I will tell her everything I know about your little escapades at the Periwinkle Hotel." Josh's voice and demeanor were icy cold. "I will play her those recordings and I will add my own commentary. I will tell her that she is subject to arrest because she has benefited directly from a continuing pattern of illegal activities that has been ongoing. By the time I'm done with her . . ."

That was enough. Marvin was broken.

"Stop! Stop! I'll talk to you! I'll tell you anything you want to know! Don't involve my wife! Please . . . my kids!" Rosenthal again buried his face in his hands, moaning. "Please stop. I'll tell you everything!"

That was it. That was all Josh needed to hear. He reached down and slid a piece of paper across the table. "Read this," he said, very matter-of-fact. As Rosenthal looked at it, Josh continued. "This document says that you are willing to speak to us without requiring the presence of a lawyer. Do you understand what you are signing?"

"Yes. Yes, I do."

"Do you feel that I have coerced you in any way to sign this document?"

"No."

"So, you are signing this document of you own free will, is that correct?"

"Yes."

Marvin signed.

The Combine was about to be dismantled, bolt by well-oiled bolt.

———————

BY THE TIME JOSH Baker and Marvin Rosenthal walked out of that small interrogation room almost six hours later, the lives of some of Illinois's most powerful men had been destroyed.

Josh walked into Frank McKenzie's office feeling very proud of himself. He found his boss with his feet on his desk, fingers interlaced behind his head, leaning way back in his chair and staring at the ceiling. When Josh entered, Frank sat up straight in his chair. He was suddenly all business. But, there was that moment when Josh saw a level of self-satisfaction on the face of the United States attorney for the Northern District of Illinois that was quite telling.

Frank had been watching a movie play out in his mind of the next several years of his life. He knew the plot of the film, and he knew the ending. He saw one conviction after another of each and every one of the sons of bitches who'd brought down the good senator who'd offered Frank this job, a job he loved, a job he was born to do. Frank was going to be the guy to put things right.

McKenzie began with a surprising question.

"That little twit in there was talking about a shooting, said some young girl was shot during Kovach's campaign? What the hell was that all about?" As far as Frank knew, there had been absolutely no report of any kind filed regarding this incident. This was a bit shocking. He didn't like to hear that kids were being shot on his watch without any information surfacing about the whole thing.

"Oh, yeah. He said a guy by the name of Orenthal Mitchell handled that. Evidently, a bunch of kids were out swapping campaign signs. You know, the young campaign workers go running around a neighborhood taking down the opponent's campaign signs and replacing them with a sign for their own candidate. It's all done in good fun."

"Who the hell is Orenthal Mitchell? He's not an elected official, right?"

"No, he's a Cook County guy, works for the president of the Cook County Board. Does a lot of political operative work."

McKenzie shook his head. There was no end to the parade of political hacks turning up in this investigation. "Okay," he said. "Bring him in too."

Baker was surprised. "He's small potatoes, boss. Not worth the effort."

McKenzie suppressed his annoyance. "Call it instinct, Baker. Roust that guy. He'll be useful. I can feel it in my bones."

"Boss, our next target was going to be Mars Gregory, Alsheriti's partner. We have them on tape from the bug on the Sammar phones the other night, talking about some kind of buyout deal. We think it has potential."

McKenzie shook his head. "Do it my way, Josh. Get this Orenthal character first, and let's see what it gives us. Mars Gregory isn't going anywhere. He'll get his day in the barrel soon enough."

From the Memoirs of Mars Gregory:

MUCH TO MY CHAGRIN, Sam became partners with his newest best buddy, the super-rich Arab mystery man, Abdul-Mataal Abaza. The new partnership was going to buy the 64 acres. Sam had persuaded Mr. Abaza to agree to a price that would provide enough cash to pay off Bachman Brothers, and pay back our original investors with a modest ten percent annual return. What about the million dollars I was supposed to get?

"Mr. Abaza won't advance that money, Mars. I'll have to give you a promissory note. I'll pay you a fair interest rate."

Alarm bells went off in my head. No cash? A note from Sam? The same Sam who had Feds lurking around every corner? Was he nuts?

"Uh . . . let me think about that." There was no way in hell I was going to go for it.

An hour later, over lunch at our favorite steakhouse, Phil Angelino convinced me to change my mind. "Take the note. You can't get away from Sam fast enough," he said. "Maybe we should order Sam's favorite salad in his honor," Phil added, trying to insert a bit of levity.

"Are you crazy? I'll never see a dime of that money!" I was beside myself.

Phil grabbed my wrist with a viselike grip. He tilted his head toward mine and said in a low whisper that not even a concealed wire could have picked up, "I hear that the Feds are about to get to Orenthal Mitchell. If they get Oren, Sam is a goner."

Suddenly, my appetite was gone. Orenthal Mitchell? Holy shit! Oren and the house deal. Oren and the shooting. Oren with the sealed court documents? I ran a panic-driven scan through my mind's recorder, trying frantically to think of anything that Oren could say about *me*.

Amazingly, Phil seemed to read my mind. "Stay calm, Mars. You're a bit player in this drama. But they're definitely on Sam's tail, and they're going to get him. Have you lawyered up yet?"

I had, in fact. I'd hired an old law school classmate, himself a veteran of the US attorney's office, so I'd be prepared in case anything happened. I'd already given him a $50,000 retainer, so if the Feds played dirty and tried to freeze my assets, I'd at least have a lawyer to defend me. "Ed Swinson," was all I said.

Phil nodded in agreement. "I know Ed. He's a good man. He's told you what to do if they show up on your doorstep at six a.m.?"

"Yes, yes, of course," I replied sadly. "Everyone in our office has been drilled on what to do in that instance."

"Take the note, Mars. It's time to get out of Dodge."

I was miserable, but knew he was right. I trudged back to my office, thinking things couldn't get any worse.

I was wrong.

Chapter 29

A COUPLE FEDERAL AGENTS paid Orenthal a visit. One of the lower-level persons of interest already interviewed had mentioned his name in conjunction with some sort of shady hospital deal. It was revealed that Oren had a financial interest in a data-management firm that had secured a contract from the Cook County Hospital. The same Cook County Hospital controlled by the president of the Cook County Board. The same president of the Cook County Board for whom Oren worked.

When the standard-issue black SUV appeared at Oren's house at six a.m., rousting him and his family from bed, Oren took it much more to heart than any of the others who had been through the drill. He went with them quietly, head held down, ashamed and embarrassed. A few neighbors were walking their dogs or out for an early morning run. Oren's wife Martine was visibly shaken and trying to comfort their crying children as he was escorted to the vehicle. This was his lifelong nightmare. He'd spent countless sleepless nights worrying about this very moment. And here he was, living it in real time.

When Oren later returned home, he discovered his wife and kids had gone to her mother's. Oren shook his head and hung it low. He made a few phone calls during which, through tears, he quietly explained he'd kept his mouth shut. He said the Feds had promised an indictment as soon as the US attorney's office brought the case in front of a grand jury. Oren made it clear he had always been afraid that this day would come.

Oren walked into the tastefully decorated family room of his beautiful home, a home purchased through ill-gotten gains. The walls were rich wood, lined with shelves filled with books. It was right out of the pages of Architectural Digest. As he walked past the antique pool table to the wall of floor-to-ceiling windows overlooking the sloping lawn and the wooded area behind his house, he rolled the cue ball slowly toward the corner pocket. It dropped with the familiar sound of balls clicking against one another, the only sound in the expansive south suburban home.

Oren went to the bar and pulled a bottle of Jack Daniel's off the shelf. He grabbed a rocks glass and splashed four fingers of straight Kentucky bourbon. He raised the glass to his lips, and with a backward wrench of his head, he drained it. He let out a deep sigh as he wiped his chin with his sleeve, looked at the bottle with a mournful smile, and repeated the same process twice. Now, with about nine or ten ounces of courage coursing through his veins, he grabbed a notepad off the bar and scribbled hastily. He took the bottle, left the glass, and walked slowly, a bit unsteadily, through the room and out to the kitchen. Momentarily, he thought about going up to his room and falling on the bed. Instead, he grabbed his jacket and went out to his shiny red Cadillac in the garage.

He started the car, pulled out of his driveway, and drove slowly away from his house. He had a destination in mind, if he made it that far.

Four hours later, Oren was on the other side of Lake Michigan. He'd all but killed the bottle of Jack Daniel's. Only a couple ounces remained. During the drive, he'd thought of many things: his marriage to his beautiful wife, the births of their two kids, birthday parties. He remembered the day they bought their home. The look of joy on Martine's face made it all worthwhile at the time. They'd enjoyed many loving and wonderful years in that house.

But soon Oren's thoughts locked on his many mistakes. Tears streaked his face as he relived all the decisions he'd made to bring him to this moment. He recalled every one. They were seared into his memory.

The Michigan side of the long, great lake was dark and wooded. No streetlights or strip malls. Occasionally, a deer would freeze on the side of the road, surprised by Oren's bright headlights, then bound away into the darkness as he passed. He knew the way even in the dark. He'd been taking this route since he was a boy, to the cabin his grandmother had once owned.

He drove slowly through the thick growth down the winding, gravel lane, almost a path, that led down to the lake where the cabin stood. The only sound, once he'd killed the V-6 engine of the Caddy, was the sound of nature. Not a honking horn or a siren, nor a speeding truck in the distance, just crickets and the gentle cadence of the lake lapping the shore.

Oren sat on the old wooden boat dock and looked out over the endless blackness of the water. The night sky was brilliant with stars, their reflection in the dark lake making it difficult to tell where the water ended and the heavens began.

His house was nearly a straight shot, due west, on the other side of the lake. He was only maybe fifty miles, as the crow flies, from his home. As he sat quietly for a few moments, a peaceful calm came over him. It was beautiful there.

Then he silently raised the .44 Magnum he had taken from his glove box, placed the barrel in his mouth, and pulled the trigger.

From the Memoirs of Mars Gregory:

I KNEW SOMETHING WAS seriously wrong the minute I walked into our reception area. Carla, our receptionist, and my secretary, Lori, were holding each other in their arms, weeping.

"What's happened?" I asked, gravely concerned.

Carla fought through her tears. "It's Mr. Mitchell, Orenthal Mitchell," she managed to get out, before being overcome with grief.

"What about Oren?" I pressed. "What's happened to him?"

Lori gathered herself. "Mr. Mitchell disappeared from his home last night. They found him today over in Michigan, at his beach house. He shot himself in the head."

———————

NO MATTER HOW MANY times you experience the death of someone you know well, it's always a shock. If nothing else, it forces you to confront your own mortality. I'm normally not a fan of the Reverend Jesse Jackson, but I once heard him say something that really resonated with me: "We live our lives as if life is certain, and death is uncertain. It's the other way around."

This one really sucked all the strength out of me.

Sure, I knew that Oren had been a longtime political bagman, doing all kinds of skulduggery for the president of the Cook County Board and for Sam and Malik and others. But he was a charming guy, a loving father, and a lot of fun to be around. He would always entertain you with a joke about some prominent person, or some inside tidbit of political news. We attended ball games, we traveled to Vegas on business trips together, assuring each other that "What happens in Vegas . . ." Sam was godfather to Oren's youngest son. I was there for the kid's first communion party. That's how deeply we were connected. You couldn't help but love the guy. And now he was gone?

It was totally inexplicable. How could he take his own life?

The answer quickly became apparent. Over the next couple days, the newspapers provided various details. It was known that the Feds had interviewed Oren extensively in connection with the Kovach investigation. There were rumors they went through all of his financial records, his tax returns, his investment partnerships, etc. They apparently came up with some shady deal involving a Chicago firm in which Oren had invested, and the firm was awarded a lucrative contract from the Cook County Hospital, which is controlled by the president of the Cook County Board. According to the papers, the Feds were getting ready to indict Oren in connection with that deal. Of course, they didn't give a damn about any hospital contract. They wanted Oren to roll over on Sam.

OREN'S WAKE WAS LIKE a Who's Who of Chicago and Illinois politics. Virtually everybody who was anybody showed up to pay their respects. Mike Kovach put in an appearance, the president of the Cook County Board, the mayor of Chicago; they were all there to offer their condolences to the shattered widow and family.

With one exception.

Malik Alawi was nowhere to be seen. He was fighting for the Democratic nomination for president, and the all-critical Iowa caucuses were looming. He was neck and neck in the polls with another Democratic senator who was also trying to make history by becoming the first woman to be elected president. It was great theater and riveting history, but I have to say, it pissed me off. Oren had been a loyal trouper for Malik. The guy had risen like a meteor, from state senator to U.S. senator to a candidate for president, and now he wanted to be nowhere near the family of a guy who was "tainted" in the media.

At the funeral, Sam was at the side of Orenthal's widow throughout. He was seen comforting Oren's children. He had been stoic in front of our staff and others, showing very little emotion, trying to be a pillar of strength. But inside, I knew he had to be churning. Oren had been his henchman, his bagman, his gofer, his utility infielder, his arms and legs. He'd spent hundreds upon hundreds of hours with Oren. They were practically inseparable.

As we were leaving the gravesite, heading toward the waiting cars nearby, Sam took me aside. "We have the money lined up to close on the 64 acres. We can do it next week."

Behind me, I could hear the hum of the machinery lowering Oren's casket into the ground. The horrible thought of being in a metal box and buried forever was overwhelming to me, and here was Sam, talking business. It hit me. Sam didn't care about anybody on a personal level. Oren was a pawn, the pawn was off the chessboard, and Sam was looking at the pieces still in play.

"Okay, Sam," was all I could muster. "Fine."

Chapter 30

WITHIN THE US ATTORNEY'S Office, the reaction to Orenthal Mitchell's suicide was not shock, but anger.

"We invested a lot of work into setting up that prick for prosecution," Frank McKenzie said in disgust. "Didn't he understand the game? Didn't he know we didn't give a shit about him? Mitchell could have negotiated for a suspended sentence, for chrissakes, and he goes and offs himself? Unbelievable."

Josh Baker considered himself a hardened investigator, but even he was surprised by this development. He tried to keep the focus on the case, not the personal tragedy.

"Let's be analytical about this," McKenzie said. "We have Rosenthal cold. He's implicated Vince Perino in this scheme involving the Teachers' Pension Fund. We were able to trace the movement of money from the Teachers' to the investment advisors who took the finder's fees, and from them to a company that Vince Perino is involved with. So we have the Ringmaster, too. Rosenthal was reappointed by Kovach on Sam's recommendation, so they could continue the payoff scheme, but we busted him before they were actually able to complete any deals to kick money back to Alsheriti. So we can prove a conspiracy, but we have no hard evidence against Alsheriti. We have to get him, and through him, get Kovach. What did Mitchell give us on Alsheriti?"

"Not a damn thing," Josh said wearily. "We gave him the full treatment, threw the book at him. He insisted on bringing in a lawyer, and when the lawyer showed up, he said that his client wasn't going to cooperate, and we had to let him go home."

"And that night, he blew his brains out," Frank said, in a matter-of-fact tone of voice.

If this had been any other prosecutor, Josh would have been dismayed at the utter lack of empathy. After all, they had driven a human being—no matter how flawed and corrupt the guy was—to take his own life, leaving behind a wife and kids. But this was Frank McKenzie. *He's a heartless bastard,* Josh thought.

"Okay, we have to play the cards we've been dealt. Who's next?" McKenzie asked.

Baker did not hesitate. He slid a file toward his boss. "Mars Gregory," he said simply. "Sam's business partner."

McKenzie rubbed his temples. "Is he going to cooperate? What do we have on him?"

Josh smiled. "There's always something. Gregory is no choirboy."

From the Memoirs of Mars Gregory:

THE DEATH OF ORENTHAL Mitchell shook the Illinois political community to its core. Suddenly, people realized, this shit was for real. Everybody
had been going along, oblivious to the pitfalls of skimming off the taxpayers'
money like it was their own. All of a sudden, reality set in.

Oren wasn't even a big player, in the general scheme of things. He was
small-time, if anyone wanted to take an accounting. However, a funeral has a
way of putting things into perspective.

I was hanging on, trying to get by, day by day. The closing of my sale to
Sam was only a couple of days away. I was beginning to see light at the end
of tunnel.

––––––––––––––––

I HAD BEEN SLEEPING restlessly for months, but that morning for some
reason I was sound asleep, lying next to my wife. First, the doorbell rang.
Then, the loudest pounding I ever heard in my life shook our entire house.

I jumped out of bed and looked out the window. In the circular drive was a black SUV, and next to it a black Ford Crown Vic.

It was my turn.

_____

THE AGENT FLASHED A badge and introduced himself as Federal Agent Joshua Baker. With a nod, he indicated his partner, N.J. Novak. He said they would like to ask me some questions about my business partner, Saidah "Sam" Alsheriti. I vividly remember him saying that. The rest is a bit of a blur.

I told them my lawyer was Ed Swinson, and gave them his card, which I remembered to grab off my dresser on the way downstairs. They said fine, they would call him and he could come down and meet us at the Federal Building.

I thought for a minute about playing lawyer. After all, I had been to law school, and practiced law for several years. I could have demanded, "Am I under arrest? If not, go away and leave me alone. Call my lawyer."

But I also remembered what Ed had told me. If you pull that kind of crap with them, you just piss them off, and they dig even harder and longer to find some unpaid traffic ticket to charge you with. So I went along with them.

They allowed me tell Rochelle where I was going. She wasn't frightened. She was just angry—about what I would have expected from her. They also gave me a minute to change my clothes. I wasn't in handcuffs. This was considered a voluntary act. Let's just say they had a broad definition of the word *voluntary*.

I don't remember the ride downtown. Then, I was suddenly in a cinder-block room with a large glass mirror on one wall. I remember thinking it all seemed like a scene from a movie.

Since I demanded to have my lawyer present, they left me alone in that room for a couple of hours. Ed was a prince. He managed to arrive by nine thirty. All that time, however, I was sitting there, alone, without a cell phone, nothing to read, nothing to do, but try to control my fear. It's amazing how slowly time passes when you're isolated like that. It struck me: *This is what being in jail is like.*

When Ed arrived, we talked for a few minutes. Though Ed's features were mild—medium height, with a trim build and a full head of dark hair—he had a bit of a bulldog demeanor. That's what I wanted in a defense attorney. We had previously agreed that we would be cooperative. I was certain I had done nothing wrong, and there was no point putting myself on the Feds' shit list.

After a while, I began to realize that I was more surprised by their questions than I probably should have been. This was more of a revelation to me than it was to my interrogators. As the morning progressed, it became more and more evident that I didn't know anything. At least, I didn't know anything they thought I would know.

It was Josh Baker who asked the questions.

"Mr. Gregory, you have consented to this interview and to having this interview recorded electronically, both audio and video, is that correct, sir?"

I looked at him for a long moment before answering. "It is . . ." I was momentarily tempted to further discuss the concept of *consent*, but in the end I let it go.

"This interview is your free and voluntary act, is it not?"

"Yes, it is."

"And, Mr. Gregory, you realize that you're not under arrest, that you are free to end this conversation at any time, is that correct?"

"That's correct."

"In fact, you are yourself an attorney, are you not, and you understand fully your constitutional rights regarding this, ah, conversation? Is that a correct statement of the facts, sir?"

"It is."

"Mr. Gregory, I am not going to spend a lot of time on the basics. As I am sure you are aware, we have been conducting an investigation of a number of individuals, including your business partner, Saidah "Sam" Alsheriti, among others. Were you, in fact, aware of that, sir?"

"You guys haven't been making a secret of it. I read the papers."

"Is that a 'yes,' sir?"

I realized then and there that this was a no-nonsense interview. The look on Baker's face spoke volumes.

"Yes, it is," I finally said.

"During the course of our investigation, sir, certain individuals have been observed frequenting your offices on Milwaukee Avenue. Can you name any of the individuals who have been regular visitors to your offices?"

I gave Baker a puzzled look. "I guess this is where you would like me to tell you that the governor has been a regular visitor to our offices?"

"Has the governor been a regular visitor at your offices, sir?"

"Yes, he has."

"And, by your answer you mean to identify the sitting governor of the State of Illinois, Mishka 'Mike' Kovach, is that correct, sir?"

"Yes, that's the governor."

"Sir, for what purpose does the sitting governor frequent your office?"

"He attends meetings there. He has meetings with my partner, Sam Alsheriti, and others."

"And, Mr. Gregory, have you also attended these meetings?"

It was at that moment that I knew. At that very moment, I realized I wasn't going to be joining my business partner and his friends at the defense table at some future trial. I don't know why it hadn't dawned on me before.

They say that a person who represents himself has a fool for a client. When you're too close to the action—when *you're* the subject of an investigation—all impartiality flies out the window. You're acting and responding on pure emotion. Your brain stops working and your heart and gut take charge. I almost forgot everything I ever learned in law school or as a practicing attorney.

Fortunately, Ed Swinson reminded me that I had never sat in on a single meeting involving the governor. Although I thought I knew what had been taking place in our offices, I was never personally privy to a single conversation behind closed doors. I attended a few of the parties and the fundraisers. I saw the meetings take place. But I never participated.

For the rest of the day, we danced. They asked questions, and I gave them honest, straightforward answers. There wasn't a single thing I said that couldn't be backed up by the testimony of over seventy employees or by the records found in any file drawer in the office. As it turned out, I was much too busy running the real estate side of the business to involve myself in the other goings-on in that office. All of it was absolutely true. The more they dug, the more questions they asked, the more my innocence became apparent.

Oh, I suppose they learned a little from me. I confirmed much of what they already knew. I told them who came and went, as if they hadn't been watching. After all, a van had been parked outside our offices for months. They had photos of everybody. They knew their names. The photos were of some of the most famous faces in the state of Illinois.

They were frustrated. They must have thought I would be the key to their entire investigation.

Ed Swinson was looking pretty pleased. We'd been through nearly five hours of questioning, and they hadn't gotten shit out of me. Absolutely nothing.

"Are we about finished?" Ed asked politely, hinting to them that this was going nowhere.

Josh Baker ignored Ed's question. He pulled out another file.

"Mr. Gregory, I'd like to ask you some questions about how you arranged the financing for the closing of your purchase of the 64 acres known as the South Loop Project," he began, looking at me carefully.

I was confused. What the hell did that have to do with Sam or the governor?

He proceeded to ask me several questions about the composition of the original group of investors in the 64 acres, name by name, amount by amount, and how we found them. Within minutes, he had honed in on the fact that back when the sellers were demanding a $2.4 million deposit to hold the property under contract, we only had $2 million raised.

"So, Mr. Gregory, you were $400,000 short, isn't that right?"

"Yes, we needed an additional $400,000."

"And were you able to obtain that money to keep the contract alive?"

The game had turned deadly. I was being extremely cautious now. They clearly were aware of what had occurred. But I'd done nothing wrong! Ed Swinson was sitting there, clueless. We had never discussed this.

"Yes."

Baker did not look up. He kept his gaze fixed on an accounting spreadsheet that showed the makeup of the investor group. How the hell had they gotten that?

"And where did those funds come from?" Baker asked.

"I invested $400,000 myself."

Swinson was shifting in his chair. He could sense that something was going very, very wrong.

"And were these your own personal funds?"

I did not hesitate. "I would like to consult with my attorney about this."

Baker was unfazed by this request. He did not react visibly. He just got up, and showed us to a small room down the hall from the interrogation room. This room was for attorney-client consultations and supposedly was not bugged.

Once the door closed behind us, Swinson was all over me. "What the hell is this all about, Mars? You never told me there was anything shady about the 64 acres!"

I was genuinely stumped. "I don't get it," I said. "I borrowed $400,000 from my mother, and put it into the deal. We had a promissory note, and I paid her back with interest. What the fuck does the federal government care about that?"

Swinson was no simpleton. "You borrowed it from your mother? You went over to see her, and asked her for the money?"

"Not exactly," I said, a little evasively. "My mom was in the nursing home, with severe Alzheimer's. She didn't know what day of the week it was, or even who I was."

"So how did you get the money?" Swinson pressed.

"Well, I was the trustee of her trust. I loaned myself the money."

"Christ!" was all Swinson could say.

"What the fuck? I signed a note, with market-rate interest, and we paid it all back shortly after the closing. Nothing illegal about it!"

Swinson pondered for a moment. "Let's play this out and see where they're going with it."

We found out soon enough. Baker had obtained a copy of the trust document itself. There was a provision that said any loan by the trust to a related party required the consent of all beneficiaries.

"You, as trustee, were clearly a related party, isn't that right?" he demanded.

"Well, yes, I suppose, but—"

"And there are two beneficiaries of this trust after your mother dies, you and your brother, isn't that right?"

"Yes, that's right, but—"

Baker moved in for the kill. "And did you get your brother's consent prior to making the loan?"

"Well, no, but—"

Baker cut me off again. "Mr. Swinson, could we have a minute with you privately?"

What the hell was going on? Why did they want to talk to Ed alone?

I sat there, alone again, watching the second hand sweep inexorably toward my fate. I felt like I was on death row.

A few minutes later, Swinson motioned me out into the corridor and led me back down to the consultation room. He was beet red and sweating.

"They're going to indict you for defrauding your mother's trust. They've already been to the grand jury. They can file the indictment any time they want."

It hit me like a ton of bricks. I couldn't believe my ears.

"Indict me? Are you serious? How the hell did they get all this information?"

Swinson had a defeated look on his face. "They've been interviewing people on your own staff for months. You weren't aware, because they were threatened with obstruction of justice charges if they told anybody."

"Was it Bob Jacoby? Bob is the most straight-laced guy you've ever seen. I know Bob had some trouble in his past. Could they have him on some kind of charges, and he rolled over on me?"

"Actually, no, it wasn't Bob," Swinson began. "The Feds put the heat on Claudia, and she chose to save her own ass."

"Claudia?" Mars felt like he had just been punched in the gut. "I never would have thought she'd turn on me."

After a long pause, Mars realized Claudia had had real legal exposure and no options with the Feds breathing down her neck.

"They're ready to indict you today if you don't cooperate," Swinson advised.

"For defrauding my mother's trust? What the hell? She got paid back every penny, plus interest! That's outrageous! No harm, no foul!"

Swinson shook his head. "I agree, Mars. It's outrageous. It's totally out of bounds. But they don't seem to care. They believe they actually can win a conviction. They probably figure they'll ruin you with publicity and the cost of the defense, and you never know, juries sometimes get confused in cases like this. They figure they might get lucky."

I was gasping. "But what do they want? I've answered every one of their questions, and truthfully, I don't know anything! I never sat in any of the fucking meetings!"

Swinson was at a loss. "They think you're holding back. They figure you have to know something. Anything. Think, Mars, think! Is there *anything* you could give them to get the hounds off your trail?"

I racked my brain. I was terrified. I could see myself on the ten o'clock news being led away in handcuffs. A couple of hours in that interrogation room were enough for me. I couldn't begin to imagine a couple of years like that.

"Ed, really, I'm baffled. Honestly, I can't think of anything . . ."

And then it hit me. I thought about it for a few seconds. I knew I had it. It was perfect. The Feds were going to love it.

"Let's go back in there. I can make all of this go away."

My lawyer's somber face lit up. "What, Mars? What can you give them?"

I couldn't help but smile. "I'm going to tell them about a guy named Johnny Jarzik."

TWO DAYS LATER, WE closed on the sale of the 64 acres to the newly created partnership of Sam Alsheriti and the Iraqi billionaire. They paid off Bachman Brothers. I walked away with two pieces of paper. One was my personal guaranty of the Bachman Brothers loan, marked "canceled." The other was a promissory note for one million dollars, signed by Sam Alsheriti.

I moved all my personal belongings out of my office at Sammar, LLC. I was done with Sam.

As instructed by the Feds, I didn't say a word about my interview. I already had an indictment for misusing my mother's trust hanging over my head. I didn't need a charge of obstruction of justice on top of it.

Chapter 31

Johnny Jarzik had been up all night, watching the returns from the Iowa caucuses. He was ecstatic. Malik Alawi had pulled off a stunning victory, and capped it off with an amazing motivational victory speech. As hard as it was to believe, Malik was on his way. He unquestionably had a real chance to be the next president of the United States.

The following morning, Johnny was on the way out to his car for his usual trip to the gym, a ritual he'd consistently maintained to preserve his physically powerful image. He looked at least ten years younger than his fifty-four years. When he reached for the door on the driver's side of his Mercedes SL500, a black Ford SUV pulled up alongside him. The smoked glass passenger window emitted a quiet, high-pitched whine as it descended, exposing the smiling face of Josh Baker.

"Good morning, Mr. Jarzik. We would like you to come with us."

Jarzik's reaction was quite predictable. "Who the fuck are you?" he asked indignantly.

Baker realized he had forgotten to flash his badge, a mistake he quickly corrected. "My name is Josh Baker, Mr. Jarzik, and I am a federal agent assigned to the United States attorney's office here in Chicago. We have some questions for you. It won't take long. We will have you back here in plenty of time for you to work out this morning."

The rear passenger-side door magically opened. A third man, wearing aviator sunglasses and a black suit, was sitting in the rear seat.

"Get in, sir." Baker continued. "Don't make this difficult, please. Let's keep this friendly."

Johnny didn't want to piss off the Feds. The last thing he needed was a concerted investigation of all his past activities. If he cooperated, it would make them happy and lessen the chances they would crawl up his ass with a microscope. He had zero allegiances to anyone. Therefore, he had no one to protect except himself. Who the hell cared what they asked? He'd tell them anything they wanted to hear. What difference did it make to him?

He got into the SUV without a fuss.

———————

WHEN JOSH WALKED INTO the interview room with Johnny Jarzik, he used a very different approach.

The first thing he did was offer Johnny something to drink.

"So, Johnny, you want coffee, or a Coke maybe?"

Jarzik said he'd have coffee with cream and sugar. He sat opposite Josh Baker, quite relaxed. He smiled and explained that he was willing to discuss anything they wanted to discuss. He had nothing whatsoever to hide.

As they were sipping their coffee, Josh began.

"We are conducting an investigation regarding several members of the Kovach administration, and your name came up. How are you involved with the governor? Or, perhaps I should first ask, are you involved with the Kovach administration in any way?"

"I am a self-employed political consultant. I have been in business for fifteen years, give or take. I do not work for Kovach, or any other politician, exclusively. However, I presently have an office in the State of Illinois Building on Randolph Street, which the governor's people insisted I take. I thought it was ridiculous. I never go there. Well, I shouldn't say that. I rarely go there. It's on the same floor as the governor's office. But, I don't have my name on the door, and I am not on the governor's payroll. I'm paid as an independent contractor, from the governor's campaign fund. I am not a state employee."

"I see," Baker said, still a bit confused. "Then, what would you say your job entails? What do you actually do?"

"I offer political advice. I help with potentially damaging political problems."

"And, what does that mean, exactly?"

Jarzik let out a long sigh and took a sip of coffee. "Let's say a candidate says something stupid on the campaign trail that pisses off the unions. He says something that makes him sound like he's anti-union. No candidate can afford to sound anti-union, right? I smooth it over. Maybe I get him a meeting with some of the union leadership. Maybe I set up a photo-op that makes him look pro-union. Maybe I do both. I fix the problem. I make the problem go away. I fix the optics."

"The optics? What does that mean?" Josh was scribbling notes.

"The optics. You know, how a given situation appears to the public. I change the perception of how a candidate, or a sitting office holder, is viewed by the people. My clients make foolish mistakes, mistakes that make them look stupid. I fix those mistakes."

Josh looked up from his notepad. "So, let me get this straight. You don't really care what a politician actually believes. You're only concerned with what it *looks* like he believes. You don't care if he is, in fact, anti-union. You just make sure he doesn't *look* like he's anti-union."

"Very well put. You described my job perfectly. I make sure a politician looks good to his constituency. That's my job. Very good, Mr. Baker. Most people don't get it."

The conversation was going well, in Josh's estimation. Jarzik was laughing a little. He was talking about himself. He seemed comfortable. Josh figured it was time to get down to the nitty-gritty. He felt it was time to drop a bomb.

"Well, Johnny, what is this shit we hear about you hiding a shooting? What was that all about?"

Jarzik was absolutely cool. He took the question in stride. He seemed no more affected by this question than by any other.

"Oh, that? One of the young workers for Kovach's campaign got winged by a trigger-happy NRA type, a gun lover. They called me to clean up the mess."

Josh was a bit surprised that Jarzik was so nonchalant.

"You don't consider that a problem?"

"What problem?"

"Didn't you conceal a shooting from the police?"

"Not at all. The Cook County Sheriff's Office responded to the incident. They decided it was an accident. I just concealed it from the public. It would have been devastating for the campaign."

"Have you ever heard of obstruction of justice?"

At this point, Jarzik smiled. He wasn't worried. He tilted back in his chair so far that the front legs of the chair came off the ground. He offered a puzzled look at his interrogator.

"It was an accident. Nothing more. Do you have any idea how many accidental shootings go unreported in America each and every year? Hunting accidents . . . gun cleaning accidents? In fact, if I'm not mistaken, I believe that our vice-president—you know, the vice-president of the United States of America—just had something very similar happen to him not too long ago. You heard about that, didn't you? It was in all the papers."

"Maybe we don't see it the same way. Maybe we see it as concealing a crime." Josh was using his most serious, intimidating voice.

"Look, this incident was fully reported to the Cook County Sheriff. They didn't see a crime to prosecute. I never spoke to them. I didn't do anything to obstruct their investigation. They quit on their own. There was no crime to conceal."

"What about the aftermath? What about the kids?"

Jarzik laughed this off. "What? You're gonna arrest me for giving some kids the address of a good doctor? I wasn't even there, for chrissakes! I was home in bed. You're going to arrest me for seeing to it that a young girl got immediate medical care? Good luck with that!"

He sat forward abruptly, causing the front legs of his chair to bang loudly on the tile floor and echo throughout the small room. He then reached both his arms across the table as if he were offering his wrists to be put in handcuffs. "Good fucking luck with that, Josh," he said, looking at Baker dead in the eyes, challenging him, smiling confidently.

Josh made his next move. "Okay, let's move on. Let's go back to that office you have in the State of Illinois building."

Jarzik nodded. This was what he had been expecting all along.

"What else can you tell us about the arrangement?"

"We can continue to play this game," Johnny said. "Or, you guys," Johnny motioned his head toward the large mirror on one wall, intending to include by reference all those who were listening, "can completely forget my name in return for some information."

"What information?" Josh asked.

Johnny now had the attention of Josh Baker and all the agents listening in, including Frank McKenzie.

"I read in the paper the other day that Kovach challenged you to tap his phones. He said something about how he never says anything that's not true, that he always tells the truth. Some shit like that. Did you read that article?"

Josh simply nodded.

"Well, if you have tapped his phones, or if you plan to tap his phones, he's not going to say anything to incriminate himself. He is not going to say anything on those phones that will help you in any way. He expects you to be listening. I mean, let's face it, Kovach is dumb, but he's not that dumb. Neither is Sam Alsheriti."

Josh looked surprised. "We haven't asked you anything about Sam Alsheriti."

Jarzik laughed. "Sure, not yet, but who's kidding who here? You guys want Sam and you want the governor. Let's cut to the chase with this thing. I can help you, but I have to walk away from all this completely clean. No charges, no indictment, no nothing, because I'll never work again if I get tagged by the Feds."

Josh could play tough too. He said, "You're dreaming."

"Oh yeah? You're such great investigators. You don't have Mike Kovach on tape saying anything, do you? He never talks on the phones you've tapped, does he? Suppose I could tell you why you don't have him talking on those phones?"

It was Josh's turn to be a smartass. "You mean you want to tell us about how you've been supplying Sam and the governor with cell phones that are registered to someone else?"

For the first time in the interview, Jarzik sobered up. In a flash, he realized that someone had already told them. Somehow, they knew about the cell phones. His mind raced as he quickly ticked off the people who were privy to this arrangement. He knew the Feds had been interviewing everybody. Who could it have been? Maybe Oren? Maybe that's why he killed himself?

Jarzik continued to think hard. This was life and death, and he couldn't blow it. *So . . . they know about the cell phones . . . but they clearly don't know which phones. If they knew that, they would have already tapped them. They wouldn't need me.*

Josh let Jarzik engage in this mental calculus. Josh knew what Jarzik was trying to work out, but he was betting that Jarzik would never guess the leak came from Mars Gregory. Even though Mars had told them that Jarzik was supplying cell phones to the governor, Sam, and others, the Feds were stuck, because despite all their best efforts to identify the phone numbers of the cell phones Jarzik had supplied, they had come up empty. The phones weren't registered to Jarzik or anybody that Jarzik had ever called. Baker was good, no doubt about it. He played cat-and-mouse with Jarzik, not telling him what the Feds knew and didn't know. He was hoping Jarzik would bargain.

A moment later, his hunch was confirmed. "Suppose I could tell you the phone he *is* talking on?" Jarzik asked. "Suppose, just suppose, I could give you a cell number that Kovach considers completely and totally secure, one on which he believes he can speak freely, without worry of being heard by others?"

"Go ahead, we're listening," Josh answered.

"Well, I want something in writing, something where you agree I'm not going to be prosecuted. Period. Don't try to bullshit me with all your technical legal games about the different types of immunity you could give me. I don't get charged with anything, about anything I've ever done, period."

This was a steep demand, because the Feds hadn't done a thorough investigation on Jarzik. Who knew what might turn up? Josh needed to talk this over with the brass.

He said, "I'll be back," and left Jarzik sitting in the room alone. Frank McKenzie, of course, was behind the one-way glass listening to every word.

"We don't have to cut a deal with this scumbag," Josh said. "We can put more agents on him. We'll figure out how he's supplying the cell phones to the Kovach circle."

Frank was tired of how long this investigation was taking. It would take weeks, maybe months, for them to do a deep colonic on this guy Jarzik. They would get something eventually, but it would slow the whole thing down, and he wanted action. Now. And he didn't give a damn about this prick.

"Make the deal," he said.

Josh stared blankly at his boss for a few seconds, then shrugged and returned to the interrogation room, shaking his head. "Okay, Jarzik, you got it. You get a total immunity bath. No charges about anything you've ever done, through today's date. Period. So what's the situation with the phones?"

"I'll tell you right now," Johnny started, "if you take out your pen, put in your own handwriting what you just offered, and sign it with today's date. Then I'll hand over the numbers."

"Done," Josh confirmed, starting to write. He handed Johnny his signed Get-Out-of-Jail-Free deal and waited.

Jarzik pulled out his wallet and removed a small, folded slip of paper. Written on the slip, in hand lettering, were six telephone numbers. He handed it over to Josh.

"Very helpful, Mr. Jarzik," Josh said, trying to conceal his excitement. He realized he was holding the keys to the kingdom. *Once we tap these phones, we'll have everything on tape. There will be no need to prove a complicated case with documents or other people's testimony. We'll have the perps themselves talking about their schemes.* "Do me a favor, will you? Don't make us go through the rigmarole of tracking this down with the phone companies. Who's the registered customer for these phones?"

Jarzik broke into another grin. "They're registered to my second cousin. A nice girl. You would have never figured it out. And by the way, if you think you're going to go nab her to get back at me, forget it. She's fourteen years old."

Josh had to laugh, he couldn't help himself. This guy was smart, no doubt about it.

Even Frank McKenzie was laughing behind the glass.

From the Memoirs of Mars Gregory:

THE GOVERNMENT'S INVESTIGATION OF Sam and Kovach had suddenly gone radio silent. Weeks went by, and I didn't hear from the Feds. As the season turned from winter to spring, Malik Alawi was closing in on the Democratic nomination. It was still hard to believe. The kid I had interviewed for an entry-level job had bullshitted his way to the top of the Democratic heap of presidential contenders. It looked like he was going to sew it up—at least if there were no embarrassing indictments to upset the rhythm of the campaign.

The highlight of the primary season for me was when the crackpots on the right wing realized that Malik was going to win the nomination, and he was leading the Republican candidate by a wide margin in the polls. In their desperation to come up with anything they could do to slow down Malik's momentum, they began circulating stories that Malik was not born in the United States, and therefore was ineligible under the US Constitution to be elected president.

———————————

MEANWHILE, I HAD PROBLEMS of my own. Rochelle was all over my case. She wanted me out of the house, but for now I was ignoring her request. It seemed very clear to me she was planning to protect whatever might be left of her claim to our assets. At the very least, I suspected she was preparing to file for divorce and go after the equity in our house. It was a full time job juggling all these problems coming at me at once. But I refused to cave, and became even more determined to be a survivor.

I WAS FORCED TO face the reality of my situation. Sam hadn't kept his promise to pay off Sammar's creditors, and the lawsuits were piling up. I kept telling the plaintiffs I had been bought out and they now needed to seek payment from Sam, but they were like locusts, intent on devouring anyone and anything in their path.

Sam clearly had other problems on his mind. I heard from my former office staff that he was increasingly absent from the office, apparently spending more and more time in the Middle East. His priority was courting relationships with the emirs, sheiks, and mullahs who were running the show—and who, of course, controlled billions of dollars of oil money.

Since the buyout of my interest, I hadn't spoken with Sam. But the office staff confirmed that Sam was intimately involved with the Alawi presidential campaign. He was doing everything he could to help Malik secure the nomination. People in the office were joking, "Maybe Sam figures that if he gets indicted, Malik will give him a pardon." The more I thought about it, the more I began to wonder: maybe it wasn't a joke, but his ultimate exit strategy.

Chapter 32

THE IMPENDING PRESIDENTIAL ELECTION was in fact having an impact on the investigation in Chicago, but not in the way the cynics would expect.

Franklin McKenzie was summoned to Washington for a private meeting with the attorney general of the United States, his ultimate boss. Technically, Frank reported to the head of the Criminal Division of the Justice Department, but the directive was to meet with the attorney general himself. They wouldn't tell him what the meeting was about, just that he was wanted in Washington.

With a great deal of apprehension, McKenzie boarded a special government jet for an early-morning flight to Washington. This had to be big. The plane landed at Andrews Air Force Base, rather than DC National. No nosy media were allowed at Andrews.

The ceremonial office of the attorney general looked like a movie set. It was large and ornate, with dark wood paneling framing walls full of thick law books. The finely patterned parquet floor, heavy furniture, and crystal chandelier were reminiscent of an eighteenth-century barrister's chambers.

Frank was led to the real working office of the attorney general, which was a smaller, more utilitarian room behind the main office.

"Frank, good to see you. Thanks for coming out to see me," the attorney general said, rising to shake hands with his star prosecutor. Enrique Cisneros had been in the job for eighteen months, replacing the previous attorney general after he resigned due to illness. Cisneros's primary qualification for this prestigious position was that he had been counsel to the governor of Texas, then appointed to the office of general counsel to the president when the governor of Texas was elected president. The attorney general appointment followed a couple of years later. Nobody ever accused Enrique Cisneros of possessing a keen legal mind. His principal quality was loyalty. He was one of the good ol' boys. And the lame-duck Republican president of the United States put a very high value on loyalty.

McKenzie had met Cisneros before, and was always amused by how short he was. He topped out at maybe five foot six, so he was always prone to what McKenzie liked to call "Little Man's Syndrome," more commonly known as a Napoleonic Complex.

Enrique escorted Frank to a conference table and motioned for him to be seated. The attorney general was not wearing his suit coat, and his sleeves were rolled up. This was to be a working session, for sure.

"Frank, we are proud as hell of you," Enrique began softly. "The president has specifically asked me to tell you how pleased he is with all the work you've done to clean up the mess in the State of Illinois."

McKenzie was wary. This was buttering-up talk. They hadn't brought him all the way to DC to listen to praise.

"Well, sir, I owe it all to the tremendous efforts of our investigators and assistant prosecutors," Frank said. "They've been outstanding, working day and night to make these charges stick."

"Excellent, Frank, excellent. And how are you getting along? Family good? How's Maggie?" Enrique was trying to make McKenzie relax, which only served to heighten his apprehension. *What the hell was going on?*

"Ah, she's fine, sir. So are the kids. We've come to like Chicago very much."

"That's great, really great," Enrique said, smiling. This offered the segue he was looking for, to get to the real purpose of the meeting. "So, you think you want to stay in Chicago permanently?"

Warning sirens went off in Frank's head. What were they thinking? They were going to replace him with less than a year left in the outgoing president's term? "Well, we really haven't made any plans, sir. I was recruited to clean up the political situation in the state, and it turns out we've got more work to do."

Cisneros laughed. "I'd say you've already done plenty! But I've read your reports to the deputy attorney general heading the Criminal Division, and you're right, there's still more work to do. That's why I wanted to see you privately."

McKenzie shifted in his seat.

"Your memos pointed out that your office is targeting various people who've been involved with Malik Alawi in the past," Enrique stated. He picked up a typewritten sheaf of papers on his desk. As he flipped the pages, McKenzie could see it was a copy of his own status memo written to the head of the Criminal Division. McKenzie began to stiffen. He was expecting Cisneros to tell him it would be very helpful to the Republican campaign to smear Malik Alawi with stories about the prosecution of his friends. McKenzie was determined not to be made a political pawn of the Republican campaign apparatus.

So he was stunned when what he was told was exactly the opposite.

"Frank, this is a very sensitive subject. It's why I wanted to see you privately, face-to-face," Cisneros said, putting the document back on his desk.

"I'm going to give it to you straight. We're very concerned that your efforts to prosecute people associated with Malik Alawi, no matter how justified, will bring a great deal of criticism from the media. They'll spin that we're trying to influence the outcome of the election. That's very bad for the president. He fully understands the historic significance of this election, if the Democratic nominee turns out to be an African-American."

McKenzie couldn't believe what he was hearing. He was expecting the AG to pressure him to hurry up and indict Alsheriti and the rest of Malik's pals. "You mean you want me to lay off these guys? Really?"

Cisneros eyed his prosecutor carefully. He knew McKenzie could be a bull in a china shop. Most of the people he'd already brought down were Republicans, and that had caused the president a lot of grief, but the president had played it straight. He never meddled one iota in McKenzie's prosecutorial decisions. This was different, though. The national Republican strategists had reviewed this situation thoroughly. They'd run focus groups and conducted discreet polling.

"If you start hammering Malik Alawi's supporters this close to the election, the media is going to have a field day. They're going to say we're harassing him. They'll claim the prosecutions are politically motivated, even though you and I both know nothing could be further from the truth."

McKenzie shook his head. "So you want *me* to be politically motivated, and *not* prosecute these guys? Respectfully sir, that's unacceptable to me."

The attorney general smiled. This was precisely what the deputy attorney general had told him to expect. "No, no, we absolutely wouldn't tell you to back off. You can keep the dogs at them, full bore. We're not giving anyone a pass, no way. We just don't want you to actually *charge* anybody connected to Malik Alawi between now and the election. No indictments until after the last vote is counted."

McKenzie paused to reflect on this instruction. He realized this was a very subtle game being played here in Washington. It was like chess, where you can only win by looking four or five moves ahead. The whole thing made him angry, but he fought to control his temper.

"Respectfully, sir, I don't know. It's hard for me to just sit and do nothing for the next few months."

Cisneros played his last card. "Who said anything about doing nothing? You can indict any Republicans you want!"

McKenzie felt like Alice, lost in the Wonderland of the Justice Department. Nothing was as it seemed. It was like trying to sew a button on a shirt by looking in a mirror. You had to get right by going left.

He considered this further. There was, in fact, more work to be done before bagging Alsheriti and Kovach. The wiretaps on the Jarzik phones had just been placed, after some wrangling before the judge over obtaining the warrants. For some reason, the judge was wary about tapping the cell phone of a fourteen-year-old girl. But in the end, he signed off. It was going to be a treasure trove of information, but it was going to take some time to get it all in place.

"So, you don't object if we move ahead with the Perino and Rosenthal indictments?"

The attorney general took his glasses out of his pocket and put them on. He picked up the status memo again. "It says here, 'Permission is hereby requested to file indictments against Perino and Rosenthal.' Is that right?"

McKenzie nodded. It was Justice Department policy to require approval from Washington before issuing any indictments of any state or local government officials or their accomplices. Rosenthal, who was still a member of two major state boards, was covered by this rule, as was Perino, as a "co-conspirator." Even though Perino was, in fact, the Ringleader.

Cisneros took out his fancy pen, a Montblanc. He removed the cap.

McKenzie noticed it was embossed with the seal of the Office of President of the United States. The pen had probably been a gift to Cisneros from the big guy himself. "So, Frank, are we in agreement about holding off on indictments of any Alawi supporters until after the election?"

Frank took a long, deep breath, and let it out slowly. "As you wish, sir."

Cisneros turned to the last page of the status memo, where there was a signature block for approval to be evidenced. He scratched his name onto the document, and waited a few seconds for the dark blue ink to dry. "Here you go, Frank. Give 'em hell."

From the Memoirs of Mars Gregory:

THINGS HIT BOTTOM ONE evening when I arrived home and found Rochelle standing in the foyer, looking like the Wild Woman of Borneo. Before I could even get my coat off, she threw a bunch of papers at me.

"I hope you're happy!" she screamed. "It's not enough that federal agents come here in the middle of the night and terrorize us! Now the sheriff shows up here to serve a summons on you at your home! I opened the damn door, so he served the papers on me!"

I was dumbstruck. I tried to gather up the documents to see exactly why the summons was issued. But she kept ranting.

"At your home! You always told me this shit was just business, that they'd never be able to get to you personally!"

"Dammit, give me a break. Let me see what this is."

"You can wipe your ass with it, for all I care!"

Later that evening, I tried to reassure her. "Rochelle, this is all bullshit, trust me."

"Trust you? Are you out of your mind? You, who picks one shady partner after another, each one a bigger scumbag than the one before? They're going to get your friend Sam, and you're going to be caught in the net!"

I was already caught in the net, but I hadn't told her about the indictment. I was hoping, in my poor deluded brain, that somehow I would dodge the charges, and she'd never know.

"Calm down. Everything's going to be fine."

"You're blind, Mars. And you think everyone around you is blind too!"

I was starting to boil. I could only take so much of her shit. "Look, dammit, I have given you a fabulous home, a fancy car, everything you could ever want. Cut me some goddamn slack and let me work this all out!"

"Oh, I'm going to cut you some slack, all right," she snarled, turning her back. That sounded ominous.

THE NEXT MORNING, I dressed for the day and started down the stairs. There was Rochelle standing in the foyer again. She was holding something, only this time it was a newspaper, not a summons. I didn't like the look on her face.

"Your friends are in the news! I hope you're happy now," she screamed, throwing the paper at me. The headline blared:

ALAWI NOMINATED FOR PRESIDENT

There was a huge picture of Malik, grinning that trademark toothy smile of his. Why would this set her off? It was completely expected, after all. And I then I saw it. Right there, just below the fold, was the reason she'd thrown the paper at me:

Perino, Rosenthal Indicted

Top GOP Fundraisers Accused in Pay-to-Play Scandal

Needless to say, this was quite a shock. The article indicated that Rosenthal had already negotiated a plea deal. He'd agreed to accept a five-year sentence and was "cooperating fully with federal investigators" by testifying against Perino and "others said to be targets of the ongoing investigation."

Five years! Holy shit.

Chapter 33

As HE SAT THERE in the processing area of the US attorney's offices, waiting to be booked as an accused criminal, Vince Perino was thinking about the past. Why hadn't he gotten out of the game just a few years earlier? Before the demise of Ed Parker over that crazy business of the accident in Waterston, he could have moved to Florida, or Belize for that matter. Maybe Hawaii would have been a good fit; anywhere warm and on the water. He could have enjoyed a life centered entirely around the game of golf, with maybe a day or two deep sea fishing thrown in for good measure once or twice a month.

He had more money than he'd ever dreamed of having as a young man. Money had ceased to be his motivation years before. So, what was it? As he met with his lawyers and bankers to prepare for the upcoming legal ordeal, he wondered. He'd known his turn was coming; it was just a matter of time. Once Rosenthal was brought in for questioning, Vince began moving assets around, converting as much as he could to cash. Whether it was in a month or a year, he knew the shoe would drop eventually. He knew he would need money, *lots* of money, for bail and legal fees.

Marvin fucking Rosenthal had helped to make him a shitpile of cash. But Marvin fucking Rosenthal was not able to stand up under the harsh lights and the hammering questions thrown at him in the cold, dark interview rooms deep in the bowels of the Federal Building. No way. Not that little wuss.

Perino recalled that he had thought long and hard about using Rosenthal in the first place. The advantage was that Marvin would do anything he was told, exactly as he was told to do it, without so much as a whimper or a complaint. But, when the shit hit the fan, Vince had somehow known the little twerp would fold. There were too many skeletons in Marvin's closet. Way, way, too many.

So, why the hell didn't Vince get out?

Actually, that question is only asked by someone who has never been there; who has never walked tall with a couple lackeys following close behind, carrying your bags, as you stride up the steps of a private jet, which is waiting for you because you and you alone have all the answers. That question is only asked by someone who has never commanded a room full of very important men. Everyone hangs on your every word, your every syllable. That question is only asked by someone who has never known what it feels like to have a beautiful woman, with a body that won't quit, interested in you even though you're a skinny, frail old man with liver spots.

He often wondered how Meyer Lansky had done it—the famed mobster of days gone by. How do you wield all that power and never really take advantage of any of it? That guy died quietly, a kindly old grandfather, at eighty years of age, without ever having spent a day in jail.

So, yeah, Vince knew the reason why he hadn't gotten out of the game. They say heroin is addicting. They say crack cocaine or homemade meth will control your life. Nothing—nothing in this world—is as addicting as power. That he knew. And, now he was finally going to pay the piper. After all these years . . .

From the Memoirs of Mars Gregory:

EVEN THOUGH I OFTEN thought he was full of crap, I, like so many Americans, watched Malik's election night party in Grant Park with tears in my eyes.

It was truly historic. His rhetoric that night was soaring. Anything seemed possible. This skinny black kid, who'd sat in our offices lighting one cigarette after another with the burning ash of the previous cigarette, was standing on a platform, in front of hundreds of TV cameras broadcasting all over the world, claiming victory.

The most powerful man in the world.

The thought occurred to me: it all could be traced back to that damn traffic accident. That accident had irrevocably set in motion a mind-boggling series of events. It pissed off a sitting Republican senator, who retaliated by appointing Frank McKenzie US attorney. McKenzie brought down a sitting governor, opening up the path for a fool like Mike Kovach to get elected, paving the way for Malik to be elected to fill that Senate seat, and position himself, in less than one Senate term, to be elected president of the United States. The first African-American president.

It was astonishing.

You would think, on this night of triumph, Sam Alsheriti would be somewhere on that stage with all of Malik's top supporters. As the camera panned over them, I saw many people I knew. I especially noted the presence of Janet Andersen. I remembered that day in her office at City Hall, when she told me Sam had to be out if the city was going to provide any financing for the 64 acres. Then I realized why I couldn't see Sam anywhere in the crowd on the stage: Janet must have gotten Sam banished from the public reception for the president-elect.

My curiosity got the better of me. I picked up my phone and dialed the number of my old secretary, Lori, who somehow had held on to her job at Sammar.

After exchanging some pleasantries and talking about how extraordinary it was that the kid who used to hang out in our offices had just been elected president of the United States, I noted that I hadn't seen Sam on the dais with Malik and his family.

"Oh, he's overseas again," she said. "Isn't it odd? You'd think he would want to be here tonight, of all nights."

He must really be desperate for money, was my guess.

Chapter 34

TWO DAYS AFTER MALIK'S election, Josh Baker burst into Frank McKenzie's office, unable to contain his excitement. He was waving a small portable tape recorder.

Frank looked up curiously. "What the hell?"

"Boss, boss, you aren't gonna believe it!" Baker was like a little kid, breathless.

"What, Josh, what?"

"The wiretaps on Kovach's cell phone! He's talking with Alsheriti! We have them, boss. We have them ice cold, on tape! You're not going to believe it!" Josh was fumbling to set up the tape player so McKenzie could hear it for himself.

"For chrissakes, get control of yourself. What the hell have they done now?"

Baker took a deep breath. "It's the Senate seat. Malik's Senate seat!"

Frank gave Josh a puzzled look. "What about it?"

"Under Illinois law, when a Senate seat becomes vacant, which is going to happen when Malik is sworn in as president, the governor gets to appoint the replacement. They're trying to sell it. They're trying to sell Malik's seat in the US Senate!"

Not even Frank McKenzie could believe what he was hearing.

[Phone Ringing]

Alsheriti:	*Hello, Mike. What's up?*
Kovach:	*Sam, where the hell are you today?*
Alsheriti:	*Qatar. You'd like it here. The women wear regular dresses. [Laughs.]*
Kovach:	*What the hell time is it over there?*
Alsheriti:	*We're nine hours ahead of Chicago. It's 10 o'clock at night.*
Kovach:	*Oh, sorry, I hope I'm not waking you up?*
Alsheriti:	*No problem, no problem. How are the discussions going?*
Kovach:	*We're having problems. Malik's people are saying they won't make any definite commitments to me if I appoint Janet Andersen to the Senate.*
Alsheriti:	*What do you mean?*
Kovach:	*I mean, I talked to that arrogant little prick congressman who's going to be Malik's chief of staff, Eli Steiner? He told me that they would "appreciate it" if I would consider appointing her. So I said, "Appreciation doesn't mean shit, Eli. What is Malik going to do for me?"*
Alsheriti:	*And what did he say?*
Kovach:	*He said, "We can't do any quid pro quo stuff, Governor. You know that." So I said, "Like hell. You tell that boss of yours that if he's going to run the country like this, it's gonna be a long four years." [Laughter]*
Alsheriti:	*Let me call Malik's office, Mike. I'll talk sense into him.*
Kovach:	*Sam, I gotta get something for this. This thing is fucking golden!*

Alsheriti:	*What about the others?*
Kovach:	*I'm trying to get Ed Herrington to get the House to pass my Child Medical Care bill if I appoint his daughter to the seat. She's already the fucking attorney general, for chrissakes.*
Alsheriti:	*Fuck that.*
Kovach:	*Right. I also got a crazy group of Indian businessmen offering me a million-dollar campaign contribution if I appoint Calvin Washington. That has good cover, Sam, because I could say I'm replacing one black senator with another.*
Alsheriti:	*Right, right. But a million isn't enough. Not for a seat in the US Senate!*
Kovach:	*Damn straight.*
Alsheriti:	*You keep pushing Washington's people. I'll try to work Malik's staff.*
Kovach:	*Okay. Get some rest. Thanks, Sam.*
[End of Call]	

McKenzie and Baker sat there looking at each other.

"What the hell are we going to do?" Baker asked. "We can't just let him sell an appointment to the United States Senate. Jesus Christ!"

McKenzie picked up the intercom. "Get me Attorney General Cisneros. Tell them it's absolutely critical."

Josh's eyes widened. "What're you going to do?"

"We're going to bust him. Right now. We're going to arrest him before he can do anything."

"You're going to arrest a sitting governor?"

"Go assemble your team, Josh. The election is over."

UNFORTUNATELY, NOT EVEN FRANK McKenzie could just run out and bust a sitting governor. There were details to coordinate, and the attorney general wanted to hear the tapes himself before authorizing such a drastic step.

Then before they could make their move, another serious problem erupted.

THOMAS GAZDIK HAD BEEN swiftly promoted to senior reporter by the *Chicago Tribune* shortly after his earth-shattering, career-changing article exposing the lurid sex scandal of former senatorial candidate Brad O'Neil. Although the promotion was his dream come true, Thomas quickly discovered the harsh reality of the number-one rule in the media business: *What have you done for me lately?* No more high-profile scoops had come his way. He'd been languishing at a dinky little desk in the bowels of the *Tribune* Building, trying desperately to keep his sea legs in an ocean of competitive reporters who were just as good and just as ambitious. It seemed that one big story, even if it was a blockbuster that altered the course of a senatorial election and helped to elect the future president to the US Senate, could carry a guy only so far. The readers expected him to keep up that level of reporting. They wanted more big stories. They wanted more spilled blood. Gazdik was beginning to question his future in the newspaper business.

Fate was about to knock once more.

JOHNNY JARZIK HAD AN uncanny ability to manipulate his network of contacts and sources. One of his friends was a woman who worked in the US attorney's office. She was aware of the wiretaps on the cell phone numbers

Johnny had provided Josh Baker. Johnny received a call from her revealing to him that the Feds now had their smoking gun. There was no doubt: the recorded conversations between the governor of Illinois and Sam Alsheriti would lead to the imminent federal indictment of the governor.

With the ink barely dry on his Get-Out-of-Jail-Free card, Johnny hopped in a cab and said two words to the driver: "*Tribune* Tower."

Crossing the Michigan Avenue Bridge over the Chicago River, with the *Tribune* Tower just ahead filling his field of vision, Johnny knew what he was about to reveal would guarantee him certain mileage in the future. This reporter was about to get the tip of his lifetime. It could elevate him to national journalist status. Gazdik was going to owe Johnny big-time. And it never hurts to have a nationally recognized reporter in your back pocket. Johnny navigated the bustling, expansive city desk room of the paper until he spotted his prey. Seated at his desk, busily typing some unimportant assignment piece about the theft of a sports trophy from a local high school, was Thomas Gazdik, completely oblivious and unaware that his ship was about to come in . . . again.

He looked up and saw Johnny Jarzik standing in front of him. "Johnny, what the hell brings you here?"

Jarzik gave him his best conspiratorial smile. "Do you have a private room? I've got a bombshell story for you."

JUST AS THEY WERE finalizing the details for their planned early-morning raid to arrest the governor at his home on the north side of the city, Frank McKenzie got wind that the *Tribune* was going to print a story, under Tom Gazdik's byline, that the government had discovered Mike Kovach and his top cronies were using secret cell phones for their illicit dealings, and the Feds had taped the governor's conversations. The paper was planning to run the story the next morning.

McKenzie went ballistic, raging at whoever was in his path, swearing he would find out who leaked the wiretap operation to the press. The seasoned hands around the office knew better. Reporters were covered by "shield laws" that enabled them to protect their sources. Gazdik wouldn't talk. They'd never be able to prove who had blown the story to the media.

Finally, McKenzie's media advisors were able to prevail upon him personally to call the editor-in-chief of the *Tribune*. He would tell the editor that publishing this story tomorrow could seriously compromise a major US government prosecution effort, involving officials "at the highest levels" of the state government.

McKenzie held his nose and made the call. The editor-in-chief was reluctant. There was a tremendous resistance among journalists regarding what was known as "prior restraint"—otherwise known as "censorship." McKenzie, however, was able to convince the *Trib* to hold the story for a few days, but only after promising to give them an exclusive interview once the bust went down, detailing the whole sordid story.

McKenzie hated playing this game, but he was desperate. Against all his principles, he agreed to compromise his convictions.

From the Memoirs of Mars Gregory:

I WAS SLEEPING ALONE. Outside, the winter wind was howling. Christmas was only a week away, but I don't give a shit about Christmas.

When I refused to move out of the house, Rochelle said she couldn't take it anymore. She rented a house near her parents.

Shortly thereafter, I learned that I had underestimated my wife's resourcefulness. I'd been so preoccupied with my own business, I hadn't thought twice about her excessive cash requirements. I was so happy to keep her off my back, I'd stopped paying attention. I just opened my wallet or wrote a check.

Between the spa treatments, lunches with her friends, trips with her friends to get away—mostly from me—cash for staff for our property, and all the other overhead, Rochelle had been redirecting funds and hoarding the cash for years. Somehow, she had managed to accumulate hundreds of thousands of dollars. I was astounded.

But to be perfectly honest, with all my troubles, I was glad to be alone. So when the phone rang at seven thirty a.m., jarring me from whatever non-REM sleep I was getting, I was not too thrilled to hear Rochelle's voice.

"Mars, it's me." I was immediately alarmed; she sounded shaken.

"Rochelle, what's wrong?"

"Turn on the TV. Right now."

I was still groggy. "What? Do what?"

"They've arrested the governor. You have to turn on the TV."

I groped for the remote, and fumbled to turn it on.

The talking heads on the local news were all agog. Federal agents had arrested the governor at his home that morning. He'd been taken to the Dirksen Federal Building for processing. The TV station cut over to a press conference in progress. The US attorney, Frank McKenzie, appeared before the cameras to announce the governor's arrest and outline a program of stunning illegal activity culminating in the attempted sale of Malik Alawi's Senate seat to the highest bidder.

"This is a crime spree on steroids," McKenzie told the media, sounding as if he had rehearsed that sound bite. "Illinois is the land of Lincoln, and Abraham Lincoln is rolling in his grave this morning over the revelation of this criminal activity." McKenzie went on to say the information for this prosecution had been obtained by court-authorized wiretaps on cell phones being used by the governor and his top aides, all of which were registered to another individual.

I smirked at that. I knew how they had gotten that precious tidbit of information!

And then McKenzie said something that made my heart stop.

"We have also indicted Saidah 'Sam' Alsheriti, the governor's top fund raiser, as a co-conspirator in this scheme. We have him on tape as well."

I literally collapsed onto the floor. It had all come crashing down at last. Sam was going to go jail. And I had made it all possible, giving Jarzik to the government. No matter how angry I was at Sam, no matter how bitter

I was over the loss of the 64 acres, the human side of this tragedy was still overpowering.

And then something else suddenly occurred to me: Sam wasn't going to be able to pay off the million dollars he owed me if he was sitting in jail.

IN THE DAYS THAT followed, we all watched, transfixed, by the little comedy being played out by Sam Alsheriti.

He was in Qatar when the indictments were handed down by the grand jury. The US government was peeved to realize they had no extradition treaty with Qatar. Sam could stay there as long as his pal, the emir, would allow him to stay.

A few days went by, and then a week. Sam wasn't budging.

Part of me was hoping he wouldn't come back.

The government was frantically trying to figure out an angle to return Sam to the United States. They scrambled to try to find something with which they could charge his wife or kids. That's how desperate they were.

Josh Baker directed one of his agents to contact me to see if I knew anything incriminating.

I told them the truth, of course. I had no knowledge of any wrongdoing by any member of Sam's family. They didn't seem particularly disappointed; they were just checking off another name on the list of people they had to interview.

But I couldn't help asking, "Why don't you guys put pressure on the emir to send Sam back? We basically defend that country from Iraq and Iran. They'd be invaded if we weren't propping them up."

"State trumps everybody," the agent replied simply.

I was lost. "I beg your pardon?"

"The US government is set up with a pecking order," the agent explained. "The State Department takes precedence over everybody. If they don't want us to push something, we drop it."

"And the State Department has other business with Qatar that they don't want interfered with because of Sam Alsheriti?" I stated the obvious.

"Bingo," the guy said. "But you didn't hear that from me."

So the Mexican—or perhaps I should say, Qatari—standoff continued. Frankly, I was relieved. I figured if Sam stayed in the Middle East, they'd never bring him to trial, and all the possible repercussions, including a lengthy stay as the guest of the taxpayers, would be avoided.

Then the newspapers reported that Sam had left Qatar and traveled to his country of origin, Syria. After only three weeks in Syria, Sam announced he was returning to the US.

He had to be fucking nuts!

Speculation was rampant. Why was he coming back? Had he cut a deal with the newly installed Alawi administration for a pardon? Was he going to turn state's evidence against the governor? Why had he gone to Syria?

My theory was he'd gone to Syria to make sure his money was stashed safely away, and then he would come back for one reason, and one reason only: Sam still thought he was bulletproof. He thought they would never bring him down.

He was wrong. Seriously wrong.

The Feds were waiting for him at the airport when his plane landed. Sam didn't even get to deplane as a free man. The agents boarded the 747, put him in cuffs right there on the plane, and took him away.

It was the last time he saw daylight for months.

Chapter 35

HAVING INDICTED SAM ALSHERITI, known to be the political godfather of the new president, Frank McKenzie suddenly had the greatest job security of any federal employee. Malik Alawi would not go anywhere near him. If Malik attempted to remove McKenzie, the media would scream loud and clear that he was doing so in an attempt to thwart the investigation, and prevent Sam from rolling over on him.

Which is exactly what Malik's critics hoped would happen. These people were desperate to find something—anything—to discredit the president. They kept insisting that Malik was not a born American, despite what his birth certificate said. For the most part, the "birthers" were a small, but incredibly vocal minority, who kept themselves in the public eye.

However, as the months passed, and McKenzie systematically went about obtaining conviction after conviction, nothing tied Malik to any wrongdoing.

For reasons known only to the US attorney's office, they'd made a plea bargain with Marvin. He would testify against everyone else in exchange for an agreed five-year sentence, to be served at one of the country club prison camps. Then they moved against Mike Kovach, after winning a critical ruling by the judge, himself a former prosecutor. None of the explosive evidence about Marvin Rosenthal's sex and drug parties would be allowed into evidence to impeach the testimony of the corrupt financier. It wasn't relevant, the judge ruled.

Kovach, of course, had already been impeached by the Illinois legislature; while he wasn't the first Illinois governor to be arrested, he was the first to be removed from active office. Not even that den of thieves could minimize the public outcry of a sitting governor under indictment. They voted unanimously to give him the boot, but graciously deferred the effective time of removal by six hours, to enable Kovach to fly back to Chicago on the State's airplane.

In a spectacular trial that stretched over a six-week period and featured testimony by Marvin Rosenthal and hours upon hours of taped conversations, Kovach was convicted.

The government hoped by convicting Kovach first, the others would give up and negotiate plea bargains.

No chance.

First Vince Perino went before a jury of his peers. Guilty on all counts.

Sam Alsheriti was next. Somehow, the guy caught a small break. The jury actually acquitted Sam on four charges—not that it mattered much. The convictions on sixteen other counts would be enough to keep him locked up for a very long time.

They have a maxim for defendants in the federal courts: If you're accused of a crime and insist on going to trial, you had better win, because if you make the judge sit through a trial and you lose, the judge will make you sit in jail . . . for years.

Kovach was given twelve years. Sam received ten and a half. Not surprisingly, after moving pleas about his advanced age, Vince Perino skated with only a year. For him, it would be like going to camp. Camp Fed, as they called the minimum security facility in Wisconsin. After all, Vince had been responsible for most of the sitting federal judges in the Northern District of Illinois getting appointed to the bench!

McKenzie wasn't finished, however. He was holding out for the possibility that they might turn Sam Alsheriti, and convince him to implicate the president himself in one or more crimes. It was the ultimate big-game hunt, and McKenzie was salivating.

But Sam Alsheriti wouldn't crack. They tried every trick in the book. They held him in solitary for days on end, they moved him from jail to jail just to fuck with him, and they even put him in a death row cell. He was made of iron. They couldn't break him.

Chapter 36

McKENZIE CALLED BAKER INTO his office. He had his suit jacket off and tie loosened. It was the first time in a long time that Baker had seen his boss looking so relaxed. McKenzie put his hands behind his head and leaned back in his chair. "Josh, you've done one helluva job. I want to just take this time to acknowledge your hard work, and tell you how important you've been to the success of this office."

"Thanks, boss, I appreciate that. I've just been doing the job the best I can." Baker continued, "You know, I worked for a number of your predecessors, and you're the toughest, but the most effective, I've ever run across. I respect the hell out of you."

In the back of his mind, Josh was thinking, *Damned straight, McKenzie was the toughest. And there were times he went out of bounds, totally off the grid. But damn if he didn't get the job done.*

"I just want you to be the first to know, now that this investigation is virtually complete, I intend to hang up my shield. I've put in the years needed for my full retirement, and I'll be stepping down at the end of the year."

"I don't blame you, Baker," McKenzie replied. "You've been a top-notch agent, and you deserve time to enjoy your pension."

Baker paused, and added, "You know, boss, Novak deserves to be considered for promotion to chief investigator when I leave. He's loyal, highly skilled both in forensic accounting and the law, has terrific common sense, and he's tough as nails."

McKenzie replied, "I will certainly consider your recommendation. By the way, Baker, what is N.J.'s first name? I never thought to ask."

"The *N* stands for Novak," Baker replied.

McKenzie, always deadly serious, cracked up. "That's just plain fucked up! What mother in her right mind would name her son 'Novak Novak'?"

Baker explained, "Well, it really isn't as fucked up as it might seem. N.J.'s father came to this country from Poland. When he got off the boat at Ellis Island, he was told to fill out forms for immigration. His given name was Novak Grzegorewski. So when he filled out the forms, he wrote, Gregory Novak. When N.J. was born, his mother wanted him to have his father's given first name, so that's how he became Novak Novak."

McKenzie snickered again. "That explains why he uses his initials. I still think it's fucked up, but I'll make sure they use the initials on his new name plate."

Josh left McKenzie's office feeling relieved. It was the first time in all the years they'd worked together that they'd enjoyed a lighthearted, personal conversation.

Chapter 37

JANET ANDERSEN, THE NEW attorney general of the United States, was called in to see the president.

President Alawi sat down with her on the lovely pale yellow couches in the Oval Office. Yellow: the color of power.

"So, what are we doing about the situation in Chicago?" the president asked.

The attorney general was cautious. "Well, all the big trials are over. Kovach, Perino, and Sam. The next move is up to McKenzie."

The president stroked his chin, deep in thought. "He's nabbed everyone he said he was after. Wouldn't you think it's time for him to move on?"

Janet Andersen knew this conversation was potentially explosive. "Perhaps. Yes. But I just don't think we can take the political heat over removing him."

The president focused on a bronze bust of Abraham Lincoln that was affixed to the mantel. "We have a major war on terrorism underway," he said. "We could use a man like McKenzie in that war. He'd be relentless tracking down the terrorists."

Janet Andersen smiled. "You mean, kick him *up*stairs?"

The president feigned surprise. "Madam, your cynicism is unbecoming the chief legal officer of the United States." They both laughed. "Put it in your journal: I want the best man for the job. Who better than Frank McKenzie, the scourge of public corruption?"

She was surprised. "You know about my journal?"

The president rolled his eyes. "Everybody has a journal. They all think there's a juicy book contract waiting out there."

The attorney general shrugged. "I'll try, sir, but I don't think he'll take it."

The president shook his head. "Maybe not. But tell him the president is convinced the country needs him."

———————————

IN FACT, THE PRESIDENT had nothing to worry about; Frank McKenzie found himself walking down nothing but blind alleys.

Sure, they had some minor dodgy stuff involving the president back before he was the president; that nonsense with the house in Hyde Park was probably the worst of it. But most of the threads seemed to run through Orenthal Mitchell and Sam Alsheriti. Now Mitchell was dead, and Sam was in jail, but even after being handed a stiff ten-year sentence and being fucked with in every way the Feds could muster, he wasn't talking. They'd hit a brick wall. McKenzie was forced to admit: Malik Alawi was an extremely clever operator, some might suggest slick, and he'd left virtually no trail behind him.

Frank talked it over with Maggie and made up his mind. It was time to make some real money for his family. The kids were fast approaching college age. It was time to resign and enter private law practice. Although it was common enough, Frank thought it unseemly to approach any firms while he was still in office. He would announce his resignation and wait for the phone to ring.

But before Frank could make his announcement, he received another summons to the attorney general's office in Washington. Same routine as before: private government jet to Andrews, escorted through the fancy ceremonial office, all the small talk and buttering up, etc., etc. It was like déjà vu all over again.

Janet Andersen, Malik's newly appointed attorney general, greeted Frank with a warm smile and a two-handed handshake. She invited him to take a seat on the sofa across from her commanding high-backed chair. She started with the usual small talk about his flight, but shortly directed her conversation to the business at hand. Janet praised Frank for his tremendous job cleaning up Illinois, and the resulting prosecutions and convictions beyond anyone's expectations. She told Frank that everyone in Washington was talking about his success, and how he would be an example for future US attorneys. Janet even labeled him a "modern-day Elliot Ness."

Frank pretended to be flattered, and to some degree he was, but he wanted Janet to address the real reason she'd summoned him to Washington.

"Frank," Janet said, "the president and I would like to offer you the job as head of the US government's elite anti-terrorist unit in the Department of Homeland Security here in Washington. Is that a position you might consider?"

The truth be told, Frank did think about it for a few moments. It could be exciting, chasing down terrorists, defending America from attack. But then he remembered his promise to Maggie. No, he decided, she's suffered enough.

"Thank you, ma'am," he said politely. "It's a tremendous expression of confidence by the president, and please tell him I'm grateful, but I've got kids headed to college, and after twenty years living on a government salary, we have very little savings. I have to go to the private sector, or my wife will probably divorce me," he admitted.

They both laughed at that. "I understand completely," the attorney general said. "I've got the same problem myself. My own financial exit strategy is sitting right there." She pointed to a small leather-bound volume on her desk. "I'm keeping a journal. It'll be the basis for my book, when all this over."

McKenzie cocked his head. "Well, ma'am, please record in your journal that I was extremely flattered by the offer, and while I am torn making the decision, my family considerations compel me to enter the private sector."

They laughed, shook hands, and parted ways.

JANET ANDERSEN CALLED ELI Steiner, the White House chief of staff, and asked for five minutes privately with the president. It was a request from a top cabinet officer, and was immediately granted. Eli didn't ask her the subject of the meeting; such was the closeness of her relationship with the nation's chief executive.

She hurried down the granite steps of the Justice Department building, surrounded by her security detail, and into the waiting limousine that whisked her to the White House. No matter how many times she took this trip, she just loved the views, all the grand buildings, the dome of the Capitol gleaming in the distance. She had to admit to herself, it was pretty heady stuff.

Janet found the president in good spirits, notwithstanding all the problems pressing down on him. She marveled at the range of his intellect. He could switch from dealing with Israel to negotiating with Russia to managing trade disputes with China to jawboning some congressman who wanted a new dam in his district in exchange for a vote on the health care bill, all without missing a beat.

"Madam Attorney General, how are you today?" the president asked, looking splendid in a perfectly tailored blue suit, television-blue shirt, and an electric blue tie. He rose from behind his desk to shake her hand and give her a quick kiss on the cheek.

"Very well, Mr. President. Very well indeed."

They sat in the same spots on the yellow sofas as they had a few days before.

"What can I do for you today, Janet?"

"Mr. President, I'm afraid I have bad news for you. You're going to have to find someone else to run the anti-terrorism unit."

The president held his face completely impassive. "He said no?"

She gave him a sad look. "Unfortunately, that's correct. He wants to enter the private sector, practice law. He's got kids heading off to college."

The president nodded. "It's a loss to the nation. When is he going to announce?"

"Probably next week."

"Very well, thanks for the effort. I'll notify the personnel office they have a position to fill." He rose, signifying that the meeting was over.

The president was escorting Janet to the door of the Oval Office when she paused and leaned close to him. "May I ask you a question, sir?"

"Sure, anytime."

Janet took a deep breath. "What's the real reason you wanted to offer McKenzie this position? He's made life miserable for everyone back home. He's even been trying to dig up dirt on you. But my sources out there are telling me he's found nothing on you, nothing at all."

There was twinkle in the president's eye as he reached for the door.

"Maybe," he said with that famous mile-wide grin, "I wanted him to quit looking."

Janet Andersen paused to reflect on that statement.

The president put his hand in the small of her back, giving a gentle push toward the door.

"And that," he said seriously, "doesn't go into the journal."

ON THE FLIGHT HOME, Frank McKenzie was reflecting on the attorney general's offer to head the government's elite anti-terrorist unit in the Department of Homeland Security. It was difficult for Frank to believe the president would extend an offer for such a significant and important post without a hidden agenda. After all, it was unrealistic to think the president unaware of Frank's determination to find something, *anything* improper, which could lead to him taking down the president.

Malik and everyone around him knew Frank resented Malik's meteoric rise to take the US Senate seat of Frank's biggest fan, Senator John McKenzie. Then there was Malik's connection to Sam, and the fact that that sleazy, slick con artist had wrangled so much power through his financial influence.

Why was the president now willing to offer Frank such a generous and prestigious assignment in Washington? Had he missed something in his investigations of the president? Was the president trying to buy his loyalty? Was the president attempting to deflect any additional scrutiny?

Frank mulled all of these questions over and over in his mind. Should he return to his office, take all the files home and personally start from scratch? Perhaps he'd missed a significant issue that might cause the president to be vulnerable?

The prosecutor in him wanted to reevaluate this turn of events, but Frank knew this would take weeks, maybe months, and he still might come up empty. Frank knew if he raised this issue with Maggie, she would go through the roof. After all, he'd promised he would leave public service, and think of their family first.

As Frank was filtering his thoughts, he occupied his time by perusing two days' worth of personal mail that he'd thrown in his briefcase prior to leaving for Washington. As he discarded the insignificant junk, he came across what appeared to be an invoice from the University of Pennsylvania. He opened the envelope and was faced with the reality of his son's first-semester tuition: $23,500, *plus* housing, meals, and miscellaneous expenses. Frank was looking at over $30,000—for just half the year! By the time the flight landed, Frank had made his decision.

Within days of his public resignation as United States attorney for the Northern District, the biggest and best law firms were calling. In addition, there were multiple offers for speaking engagements at prestigious law schools across the country.

Franklin McKenzie was a free agent, and he was going to sit back, relax, spend quality time with his family, and enjoy sorting through the opportunities for his future.

After all, he had earned it.

The Final Memoir of Mars Gregory:

IT'S 2015, AND I'M now sixty-two years old. I've had more than enough time to reflect upon these events that have greatly affected my life. I ended my career with Sammar, under severe duress, virtually destroying my total existence. Since that time, I've been humbled beyond description. The government ultimately insisted on filing an indictment against me, but they allowed me to enter a guilty plea in exchange for a year of probation. I filed personal bankruptcy to be rid of all the creditors and their judgments. My ex-wife received the equity in our house, as I had transferred ownership to her prior to signing the Bachman loan guaranty. At the very least, she had to admit I'd done something right. The remainder of my personal assets, which were spared from the bankruptcy, went to pay legal fees. I've been depressed, angry, and just plain frustrated. But I have no one to blame but myself.

True friends stick by you in good times and in bad. I learned the hard way that most people are only your friend during good times. When you can offer them something, you're a friend. When you need something, even just someone to talk to, they stop returning your calls and avoid you like the plague.

As Warren Buffet said, "Bad things aren't obvious when times are good." I can't think of a more appropriate quote. I was so driven by the success of our business that I was blinded by the risks and flaws of my partner, which led to our demise. The life I chose to live destroyed my marriage and my family.

I now live alone in a modest one-bedroom apartment in a working-class neighborhood on the northwest side of Chicago. I'm involved in fixing up low-income single-family homes and renting or flipping them for small profits. I've barely been able to keep my head above water, but I'm fortunate to have my freedom, which was in doubt a few years ago—a freedom most people take for granted.

I was paid a fee to tell my story—a modest fee, but a fee nonetheless, because I was the last man standing. The company that purchased the rights required total creative control and insisted this book be a fictional account of the events and the characters. I had no control or advance approval as to how this story would be told, and will read it for the first time when it's published. To that I have agreed.

I must admit, I miss the daily action, the excitement of being around the movers and shakers, being an insider, and helping to shape the face of the city of Chicago.

Malik has now been president for over six years. Isn't it ironic—for most of the years when her kids would have been young enough to enjoy it, Vicki didn't even need that side yard she'd insisted on so persistently.

I played a major role in bringing Malik to Chicago. After all is said and done, I feel a strong sense of pride that I helped my country elect the first African-American President of the United States.

Epilogue

IN 1947, THERE WAS a great deal of excitement around the country when Branch Rickey handpicked Jackie Robinson to be the first black major league baseball player. The country was plagued with segregation on every level, from bathrooms to hotels to drinking fountains. Years later, Rosa Parks led the bus boycott in Montgomery, Alabama, and Martin Luther King became the voice of the Civil Rights Movement.

In 2008, Malik Alawi was chosen when the country was finally ready to elect the first president of color. The country had come a long way, but it was obvious there was still a lot more work to be done.

If destiny occurs because the stars are in total alignment, Malik was gifted with the entire universe aligned in his favor. This young, aggressive, charismatic lawyer who came along at the right time was the beneficiary of any and all cosmic offerings. It didn't exactly hurt his chances when the dysfunctional Republican Party nominated an old war horse as their candidate. The GOP nominee chose a female running mate, who might have been one chicken bone away from becoming president of the United States, and who created more of a side show rather than adding credibility to his campaign. She ultimately gave up politics to promote her celebrity.

Malik's first term was rocky. Despite a pretty mixed set of results, he was elected to a second term, mainly because the Republicans nominated a super-rich white guy whose main platform called for the deportation of millions of illegal immigrants. Malik received eighty percent of the Hispanic vote, putting him over the top in all the swing states. A side note regarding the swing states—Malik carried the key state of Ohio by a narrow margin. Malik's campaign coordinator for that critical state was none other than Mr. "I have no political affiliation" Johnny Jarzik.

Vince Perino was given an early release from his minimum-security federal prison and retired to live out his days quietly in Florida.

Marvin Rosenthal is still serving time. His wife left him. She took most of his assets and the government took the rest in fines. Before reporting to prison, he was working as a dispatcher for a messenger service in Chicago. When he gets out, maybe he'll be lucky and they'll hire him back.

Mike Kovach wound up at a minimum-security federal prison in Utah—his sentence was too long to qualify him for Club Fed. Insiders report the hardest issue for him is the prison won't allow him to dye his hair. It's now almost totally gray.

Mike's wife and kids are okay. Despite all the indictments flying around, the Feds never laid a glove on his father-in-law, the powerful alderman Walter Roche. Walter takes very good care of his daughter and grandchildren.

Orenthal's oldest son went to law school. He got a summer job with Phil Angelino's law firm. The Feds couldn't do anything to a dead man, so Oren's savings, his pension, and his survivor's benefits were enough to support his wife and children adequately.

Ed Parker was released from prison in 2013. He served his six-and-a-half-year sentence in Club Fed. He was a broken man when he was released, having lost both his wife and his dignity.

The Iraqi billionaire apparently decided to hold on to the 64 acres indefinitely. It's still sitting there, vacant, full of weeds. A wasteland of shattered dreams. Only a billionaire can justify waiting for someone to make the right offer.

Sam was given a sentence of over ten years for his crimes. In prison, he was assigned the job of cleaning bathrooms. It's been reported he's lost all his belly fat, and actually now has a small waist. Based on everything we know about Sam, a safe bet would be he thinks he can start over again and make back everything he lost. Then again, he may still think Malik is going to pardon him at the end of his second term.

Franklin McKenzie took a job with a big New York law firm. He defends giant corporations who are accused of paying illegal foreign bribes. He is also a sought-after keynote speaker throughout the country.

As YOGI BERRA SAID, "When you come to the fork in the road, take it."

There were many forks in the road of Malik Alawi's life, and some of his choices were laden with controversy.

Sam and Oren found a controversial solution for the purchase of Malik's home.

After a number of meetings with Malik at the Sammar offices, Sam emerged one day saying to Mars, "Malik owes me big." To this day, no one knows what Sam was referring to.

Oren was directed to travel to Hawaii, and to this day only Sam knows why.

Oren committed suicide. Some speculate it wasn't suicide.

In late 2013, a small plane with nine passengers aboard made an emergency landing off the shore of one of the Hawaiian Islands. All passengers faced imminent death, but only one of the nine died. That passenger happened to be the woman who'd signed Malik's birth certificate.

The pattern of facts wavers in and out of that proverbial gray area. If you ask Franklin McKenzie, he would call it a *very* gray area. Many answers are simply just not black and white.

Love him or hate him, Malik has dodged all the bullets and arrows, and some way, somehow, he's always given the benefit of the doubt.

Maybe Malik is the luckiest guy in the world.

Or, maybe, just maybe, as he told Mars when they first met, he really was the smartest son of a bitch we knew.

CPSIA information can be obtained at www.ICGtesting.com
Printed in the USA
LVOW07*1211051015
456390LV00001BA/3/P

3703612190

Praise for *ASP.NET v. 2.0—The Beta Version*

"This ⋯⋯⋯⋯⋯ ⋯⋯⋯ to ⋯⋯⋯start your ASP.NET 2.0 experie⋯⋯⋯ ⋯⋯⋯ coverage of all of the new bits and had me tapping away at my keyboard in no time."
—Darren Neimke, Microsoft MVP–ASP.NET

"The new features in ASP.NET 2.0 will amaze and astound you, and these authors have methodically outlined the features with clear and concise examples. An absolute must for your library!"
—Ronda Pederson, consultant

"These authors take the pain out of getting up to speed on the many new features in the ASP.NET 2.0 beta."
—Ken Cox, Microsoft MVP–ASP.NET
and ASP.NET Developer

"A clear and concise, yet thorough, introduction to new and improved features that are set to take the Web development community by storm in ASP.NET 2.0. An excellent resource for any ASP.NET developer."
—Olga Londer, Microsoft MVP–IIS/CMS
and Principal Technologist, QA

"ASP.NET 2.0 is not just a minor update. It allows you to create Web applications in an entirely new way. Just reading the chapter on the new membership and security features of ASP.NET 2.0 will make this book worth your while."
—Douglas Reilly, MVP–ASP.NET
Access Microsystems Inc.

"There's a large 'wow' factor to this book, which, coupled with the well-worded text and excellent examples, makes you wish the final release wasn't just out of reach."
—Dan Maharry, *.NET Developers Journal*

Praise for *A First Look at ASP.NET v. 2.0*

"I would highly recommend *A First Look at ASP.NET v. 2.0* to existing ASP.NET developers. The topic is exciting and the authors did a great job of covering the bases in an enjoyable and easy-to-follow format."

—Scott Forsyth, Microsoft MVP–ASP/ASP.NET,
Director of IT, Orcsweb.com

"Those of us lucky enough to attend PDC or have an MSDN universal subscription can access the ASP.NET 2.0 alpha. For the rest of the world with an interest in 'Whidbey,' the next best thing to the actual bits is this book."

—Scott Cate, Senior Engineer,
myKB.com Corporation

"I couldn't wait to get my hands on this new title—not only does it open with Scott Guthrie's foreword, but it includes a chapter on caching by Rob Howard and features the exceptional writing talents of Alex Homer and Dave Sussman."

—Rob Chartier, Microsoft MVP–ASP/ASP.NET